Sarah's Way

AMBER N. PAUL

Fulton Books, Inc.
Meadville, PA

Published by Fulton Books 2021

ISBN 978-1-64952-627-4 (paperback)
ISBN 978-1-64952-901-5 (hardcover)
ISBN 978-1-64952-628-1 (digital)

Printed in the United States of America

Chapter 1

2008

Meeting Alex

Sarah found that she could not sleep the night before because of all the thoughts and memories racing through her mind, so she went ahead and got up to conquer her day. As she sat at her kitchen island drinking her morning cup of Earl Grey tea in her light-purple terrycloth robe thinking about all that she had to do that day before walking down the aisle to the man of her dreams, she could not help but stop to think about her life and all the moments that led her to this moment in time. The memories started rushing through her mind taking her from Monday, May 12, 2008, to the present:

Sarah was a student at Spring City University, where she studied to become a historian; she worked at the local coffee shop, Caffeine Blending House, as a barista to help pay the bills while she went to school, which is where she also met her first husband, Alex, when he came in and started flirting with her, causing a commotion in the coffee shop.

The little coffee shop had enough tables and chairs to allow up to sixty people to enjoy their coffee and freshly baked assorted pastries. As Alex walked in the coffee shop on that cold, rainy Monday morning, he looked up to the counter, approximately fifty yards from the front door. He was immediately drawn to this tiny little blonde bombshell standing about five feet, four inches.

She appeared to be one who knew how to treat her body like a temple; she looked as though she ate healthy and diligently worked out. Upon first glance, she appeared to be around 135 pounds. He thought she looked to be about two years younger than him, possibly nineteen but no older than twenty. He was drawn to her eyes, a beautiful blue color that lured him in and made him want to keep the connection rather than looking away from her. Alex did not have to even talk to this barista to know that there was something special about the girl standing there serving coffee to her customers.

She noticed him when he first walked in the door. He looked to be about two years older than her, with a five o'clock shadow around his square jaw. He was not quite a foot taller than she was, standing at six feet tall. His chocolate-brown hair was trimmed up high and tight; obviously he was a military man. The gray T-shirt he was wearing pulled tightly across his chest and biceps, making it very apparent that he was a man who went to the gym and worked out. She noticed his eyes as soon as he got close enough for her to look into them; they were a honey color, which matched his olive-skinned complexion. She tried to look away, but he held her gaze as he walked all the way from the front door to her counter.

As soon as Alex walked in, Sarah forced a smile onto her face and said, "Welcome to Caffeine Blending House. What can I make for you on this dreary afternoon to help you warm up?"

He jokingly replied back, "Oh, you can show me a glimpse of those legs and that tight little ass of yours."

"Um, excuse me? What did you say? Do I need to have you escorted out of here?"

"I was just joking around. I didn't mean to upset your uptight little ass. You can get me an extra-large hot white Russian coffee."

"Keep going, prince charming, and I'll have your ass escorted out of here faster than you can say White Russian again, which by the way, I don't have the stuff to make, so you will need to find a new place to frequent, pretty boy."

"Oh, so you think I'm pretty, do you?"

"I never said that! Don't go putting words in my mouth. I think you need to leave now," she said as she felt herself getting flustered and blushing.

"I'm not leaving until you make me something to warm up my day."

"Fine, what do you want?"

"I see you really are uptight and don't know how to have any fun in life, but I'm not going anywhere until you either agree to go out on a date with me or make me a hot white Russian coffee! Whichever you can do first will get me to walk back out the door."

"Why would I even consider going out with you and your loud mouth, pretty boy?"

"You'll go out with me because your tight little ass wants to have a good time, and I can guarantee that you've never experienced anything like me before. Have you even ever had a boyfriend?"

"That is none of your business! I will not go out with you, and I cannot make you that hot white Russian coffee because I do not have the vodka and Kahlúa to make it. What else can I make you? Otherwise, I'm going to have to ask you to leave immediately!"

"Fine, make me a black coffee with cream and sugar. I am not going to give up. I'll come in here every day until you to agree to go out with me. So you might as well just agree to go out with me now, unless, that is, you want me to keep coming in here every day pestering you to go out with me until you finally cave. I promise, if you just agree to go out with me that you won't be disappointed."

Alex handed her his debit card, and she briefly noticed his name on the card: Alex Clark. Sarah observed that there was a line forming behind Alex and that guests were starting to get irritated about the holdup. She angrily turned on Alex and said, "You've got to be kidding me! This is absolutely ridiculous! Why would I *ever* want to go out with you? You aren't even my type. Now, you need to leave. There are people behind you waiting to be served."

"I have to say that I don't really care about the people behind me. If you want me to leave, you will need to agree to going out with me. You won't be disappointed if you do. I'll treat you to a night out at Esposito's Italian Restaurant, where there will be a huge bouquet of flowers waiting for you on the table, followed by a night out dancing, where you will decide you want to come back to my place to spend the rest of the night with me, doing the walk of shame the next morning going back to your place in clothes you wore the day before."

"I'm not into flashy. I don't need an expensive night out to make me happy. I prefer a long hike followed up by a picnic at the top of the peak before hiking back down the mountain. After the hike, I like to enjoy a nice three- to ten-mile run, length of the run depending on how long it takes to hike, followed by a nice long hot bath, which I will do alone and you will not be invited to join. I do not like flowers, chocolates, purses, or anything else that most women enjoy. I spend my free time running or working out when I am not here or attending class. Finally, I absolutely hate dancing with a passion. So, if you're going to take me out, you're going to have to be able to keep up with me at my pace."

One of the male patrons behind Alex spoke up just then, "Hey, buddy, take the hint and just leave already. You are just pathetic. Not only that, you are starting to piss the rest of us off!"

Alex reeled around on the six-and-a-half-foot-tall body builder behind him and started yelling, "Why don't you mind your own business, buddy? I will leave when this cute little tight ass tells me to, and if you continue to interrupt us, there will be a problem."

"You will be the one with the problem, buddy, not me. Pick this up some other time when there aren't twenty people in line behind you! Get your fucking coffee and move on."

Sarah's manager, the owner of the coffee shop, Oliver Peterson, came out to the front to see what all the commotion was and asked Alex to leave so that Sarah could serve the rest of the patrons. Oliver told her to move on to the next customer while he went out behind the desk and got into Alex's face. "Young man, you need to leave right now before I reach out to the local sheriff to have you escorted off my property. Do I need to call the sheriff's office, or will you leave on your own?"

Alex looked longingly at Sarah and asked, "With all this commotion, do you not see that I will go to any length to get you to agree to go on a date with me?" He then turned back to Oliver, feeling defeated, and agreed to leave without any further commotion.

Sarah looked at a dejected Alex, felt sorry for him, and asked, "Are you saying that you can hang and keep up with me on a hike and run to follow?"

He perked right up and advised, "I'll go out for a hike and run with you on the first date if you promise to go out to Esposito's and dancing on our second date."

"Listen, I'll only promise one date, pretty boy. That is all you get. Now, I need you to get out of here before you cause any more trouble for yourself or me."

Alex stammered, "I need your address so I know where to pick you up and your number so that I can text you and set up our date."

"Good news, we can meet here Saturday morning at eight. Your pretty boy ass better get a good night's sleep before I run you through the ringer."

Before Alex walked away from the counter toward the door, he turned around to Sarah and said, "See you then, can't wait to see your tight little ass in your skintight workout gear for the hike! You'll be singing a completely different tune when we finish our hike and run to where you won't want to be alone for that hot bath. Oh, yeah, by the way, you're bringing the sandwiches."

"Get your ass out of here! If you are late on Saturday, the date is off! Make sure you are here no later than eight on the dot."

First Date

Sarah finished the week between school, work, and her workouts. Sarah stood in her tiny kitchen, which was just big enough for fridge, stove, and dishwasher, where she made a pan of angel hair pasta for dinner and made sandwiches for Saturday's hike. Once she finished eating, she cleaned up the kitchen and then went to bed.

Saturday morning, Sarah woke up around four thirty, earlier than normal. Sarah pulled out her sociology paper. She finished writing and editing the paper before submitting it to her professor. She dressed in her black hiking pants, turquoise-colored long-sleeve shirt, and hiking boots. She grabbed the sandwiches she made the night before, along with a half dozen bottles of water, and stuffed them into her hiking bag. She went down to the coffee shop, getting there about thirty minutes early. She was shocked but pleasantly surprised to find that Alex was already there waiting for her.

She immediately saw that he was not dressed appropriately for the hike but chose not to say anything. She shook her head as she looked at him; he wore a pair of short running shorts and running shoes.

"Hey there, tight ass, I beat you here. What do you have to say about that?"

"Well, pretty boy, if you truly wanted to make a positive impression on me, you would stop calling me tight ass and start calling me by my name."

"All right, are you ready to get this party started, Sarah? You think you can keep up with me?"

"Are you sure that is what you want to wear on a hike?"

"You said we're going on a run after the hike."

"That's true. However, the hike I'm taking you on requires shoes or boots with a sturdy sole. Do you have anything else you can wear?"

"Naw, I'll be fine with what I have on."

Sarah shook her head and replied, "If you say so. I don't want to hear any complaining on the way up or back down when you realize you made a mistake."

"I'll be fine. Where are we going?"

"Oh, you don't get to find that out until we get there. I'll drive, and you will just be the obnoxious passenger."

Alex followed Sarah back to her brand-new dark blue-pearl 2008 quad-cab Ford F250 parked behind the Caffeine Blending House. He opened the driver's door and watched her get in, shocked that she was able to get in by herself. He then went around to the passenger side and hopped in next to her. He noticed that the interior of the truck was immaculate, not a speck of dust to be found. She drove in silence with Alex talking her ear off the entire sixty miles to the base of the Manitou Incline. When they arrived, they both got out of the truck. Sarah grabbed her bag with their lunch and water. They set off on their adventure up the side of the mountain.

The hike took the two of them around three hours to get to the top with Alex stopping to catch his breath every twenty minutes.

When they got to the top, Alex hunched over and struggled to catch his breath, panting heavily. Sarah found a level spot to lay down the red, white, and black checked blanket she packed in the bag. She laid the blanket down and then pulled out the sandwiches, chips, carrots, celery sticks, and two water bottles. After five minutes, Alex finally came over and joined her on the blanket, his breathing back under control.

"That was exhilarating!" he exclaimed.

"What was? Stopping every twenty minutes? I can't believe how out of shape you are, Alex. For being a fit military man, you sure aren't very fit," she taunted him.

"Oh, you think that's funny? What would you have done if I had keeled over and died?"

"I would have kicked your ass over the trail and left you there. Nothing gets in the way of my workout," she teased.

"You are ruthless." He smiled.

"Damn right!"

They sat in silence for a few minutes, ate their lunch, and looked out over the valley below them. Alex spoke first, breaking the silence, "Thank you for bringing me along with you today. I will agree with you that this is definitely a better first date than going out to dinner and dancing. This is an absolutely beautiful view. I am very grateful that you brought me along with you."

"Oh, the day isn't over. We still have to get back down the mountain and then I plan to run at least six miles today."

"Are you the Energizer bunny where you keep going and going and going?"

"And what if I am?" She smiled at him.

"I've definitely got my work cut out for me," he responded.

Sarah sat staring off into the distance; she got lost in her own thoughts: *I can't believe how well this date is going, way better than I thought it would. Alex is a very attractive man. Why am I attracted to him? He isn't my type... He's full of himself, cocky, and very loud. I normally like guys who are quiet and less boisterous about their accomplishments. This guy is damn good-looking. I would have thought he would be better at hiking than he was. He took forever to hike up the mountain.*

Sarah was startled back to reality when Alex kissed her. She reached out and slapped him with an open hand on his cheek.

"What was that for?" he gasped as he put his hand to his cheek to rub it.

"Just what the fuck were you doing? Who the fuck do you think you are?" she sputtered at him, her face turning red from anger and embarrassment.

"Whoa there, tiger, it was just a kiss."

"I don't like surprises like that."

"Obviously!"

She immediately got up and packed the blanket and the remaining food back into her bag. She turned around and looked at him; he looked dejected with a frown on his face. "Listen, I am sorry that I responded that way, but I don't know you, and I refuse to let this get out of control. I know you are used to getting your way with women, but I will tell you right now—I am different than any of the other women you've been with."

"I will let this go if you just admit that you're attracted to me," he retorted.

She put her bag over her shoulders and turned back toward the path. She set off down the mountain, not looking behind her to see if he was coming or not.

Alex stood there for a couple of minutes and processed all that had just transpired: *That was a nice lunch, even if it was simple. I don't like to feel all weighed down before a run, and I feel like I can easily hike back down and then run after this. I can't believe how beautiful Sarah is—she absolutely glows in the sunlight standing over there in the distance. Why am I so attracted to this woman? She is definitely not like the other girls I've been with. She seems to be a very straight-laced girl who isn't giving in to my attractiveness. Why does this make me want her that much more? I need to land this girl. This will be a fun conquest.*

He jogged the distance between where Sarah left him at the top of the mountain and where she was on the trail leading back to their parking spot. "How did you get into hiking?" he asked her when he caught up to her.

"I don't really remember. I've been hiking since I can remember learning how to walk."

"Really? That's crazy!"

"Well, my father enjoyed hiking. He always wanted my brothers and me to be comfortable in nature so he brought us out on the trail every chance he got. What about you? You clearly aren't experienced in hiking. What kinds of things do you like to do in your free time?"

"I don't do much other than work out at the gym and play video games with my roommate."

"What made you decide to join the Air Force?"

"I know this is going to sound cliché, but I wanted to explore the world."

"Nothing cliché about that, if it's true. What do you do in the military?"

"I'm an MP, military police officer."

"How long have you been in?"

"I joined when I was seventeen, so I've been in five years now."

"How were you able to join at seventeen? Don't you have to be at least eighteen to join?"

"I graduated from high school when I was sixteen. I didn't want to have to work forever in a dead-end job making minimum wage, so I convinced my parents to sign the paperwork allowing me to enlist before I was eighteen."

They continued down the hill and got into the truck. They drove back to Spring City. Sarah pulled into the coffee shop parking lot and parked.

"I thought we were going on a run?" Alex asked, looking puzzled.

"We are, but I'm not going for a run in my hiking clothes and boots. I will be right back." She grabbed her gym bag from the back seat and then turned and walked away from the truck carrying her bag over her right shoulder.

Sarah returned about five minutes later wearing a pair of black running tights under a pair of black runner's shorts. She wore a purple long-sleeve running shirt. Her shoes matched her shirt.

"Ready? You sure you can keep up with me?" she asked him.

"Question is, can you keep up with me?"

"Let's go," she said as she took off down the sidewalk behind the coffee shop. She set a fast pace from the very beginning. She wanted to run six miles in under an hour so she set out at an eight-and-a-half minute per mile pace, which would put them just under an hour for the run.

"This ain't nothing," she heard come from behind her.

"Are you a long- or short-distance runner?"

"I prefer to run shorter distances, no more than two miles at a time. I can run my PFT in about nine and a half minutes."

"How far is your PFT run?"

"One and a half miles."

"No wonder you can do that in nine and a half minutes. I would think you were a pussy if it took longer than that."

"Ouch!"

"Most people whom I run with tend to be shorter distance runners, so I want to make sure you can keep up with me the entire run. If I set out at a faster speed now, I guarantee you won't last the entire six miles and then you'll piss me off because you'll make me slow down. I am a long-distance runner. I've trained for the last thirteen years to run longer distances at a six-mile-an-hour pace. I can run ten miles in an hour, and I've run a full marathon in just over three hours."

"Damn!"

Sarah felt Alex's pace slow down when they hit the three-mile mark. "I knew you couldn't keep up with me! Do you need to stop and wait for me to return back for you with the truck to take you back to your car?" she taunted him.

"You are ruthless!"

"I am! If you can keep up with me on the way back, I will consider going on a second date with you. If you puss out, I won't ever go out with you again."

With that, she quickened her pace back up to an eight-mile-an-hour pace. She felt Alex speed up to match her pace. She heard his labored breathing.

"You need to breathe slowly, in through your nose and exhale out of your mouth. I usually do an eight count in and an eight count out. I time the counting with my footsteps. This will help you to control your breathing and will help you not pass out when you finish. You'll want to make sure you stretch out really well when we finish and will want to get some protein in your system as soon as possible."

He was so out of breath that he could not reply back to her, although she did hear a difference in his breathing; his breathing became more regulated. She smiled to herself and kept moving.

They made it back to the parking lot in an hour and fifteen minutes—a slower pace than she originally wanted to run, but for his first long-distance run with her, she was impressed that he kept up and did not give up or quit.

He walked around the parking lot, slowing his breathing and heart rate. When he felt like he could talk again, he said, "Well, I believe you owe me a second date."

"Says who?"

"Me! I kept up with you."

"Is that what you think?"

"I do."

"You slowed me down. It took longer than it should have because you are not a long-distance runner."

"I still ran with you the whole way and I didn't stop."

"All right, you make a good point. I'll hold up my end of the deal."

"How about tomorrow night?"

"I can't go out tomorrow night. I have a paper due by Wednesday morning. I planned to take all day tomorrow to revise it."

"It won't take you all day to revise a paper. I think you need to go out with me. You won't regret it if you do. I need you to be dressed and ready to go out by six, and I'll swing by your place to take you out to dinner. We will go to Esposito's Italian Restaurant, and then who knows, maybe you'll agree to let me come back to your place to spend the rest of the night with you."

"I will agree to dinner at Esposito's. However, you will not be spending the night with me at my place. I don't roll like that. I will meet you here, dressed and ready to go by five forty-five."

"Why do you keep insisting I meet you here for our dates?"

"I don't want you to know where I live."

"Really, why?"

"I don't know you. I don't want you to know where I live or what I do or do not have in my place."

"Are you this untrusting with everyone or just me?"

"Everyone! My inner circle is very small for a reason." Sarah turned and opened her truck's door. "Goodbye, I'll see you tomorrow."

Alex got in his blue 2005 Chevy Camaro and drove over to his girlfriend Lauren Rodger's place. He pulled up into the parking lot and noticed that her lights were on. He walked up to her first-floor, one-bedroom apartment and opened the door. He walked into the main hallway, past the kitchen and laundry room on the left. The breakfast bar separated the dining room and kitchen. Lauren had a brown leather couch and love seat in the living room across from the kitchen. Beyond the living room was the sole bedroom with a queen-sized bed and an oak chest of drawers. The bathroom had two doors, one into the bedroom and one into the hallway.

Alex walked right past Lauren sitting on the couch. He looked over and saw her sitting there in the nude. Lauren weighed 150 pounds, was out of shape, and had brown hair and brown eyes. She was a foot shorter than he was.

"Where were you?" she asked him.

"I went out for a run, no big deal."

"Who did you run with?"

"I ran by myself. Now, I need to go take a shower."

She joined him in the shower. Alex turned on her: "What are you doing?"

"Why are you mad?"

"I don't want you in here," he said.

"I haven't seen you all week. I just want to spend time with you, baby. You seem so distant."

"Just shut up!"

"Baby, why don't you ever want to make love to me anymore? Are you cheating on me with another woman? I just want you to make love to me, Alex."

"I told you to shut up," he said as he pushed Lauren up against the shower wall.

"Ouch! Alex, that hurt."

"You brought this on yourself, bitch. I told you to shut up."

When he finished, he got dressed and went back to his apartment.

Second Date

Sarah got dressed in a nice pair of black slacks and a purple button-up dress shirt. She pulled her hair into a tight bun. Once she was ready, she got into her truck and headed toward the coffee shop.

She was pleasantly surprised to see Alex waiting for her in his Camaro. She got out and greeted him. "Hi there."

"Hi, Sarah. You ready to go to dinner?"

"I guess."

Alex opened the door and escorted Sarah into the car seat before shutting the door and climbing behind the steering wheel. They drove to the restaurant.

He parked the car and immediately got out to open her door. They walked side by side into the restaurant. Sarah could not believe the romantic ambiance. The place had a quiet, old-world environment that complemented the Italian dishes. Inside the restaurant, Sarah noticed the limited seating when they got to the hostess station.

"Welcome to Esposito's. How can I help you?" the petite blond-haired hostess asked when she met the two at the hostess station.

"We have a reservation for six o'clock."

"What's the name the reservation is under?"

"Clark."

"I see your name right here on the list. Please follow me." She smiled seductively at Alex before showing them to their table.

As they walked, Sarah was not 100 percent certain, but she swore that the hostess was trying to seduce Alex. She shook it off thinking she was seeing things. She followed him to the table.

She opened her menu and looked at what was offered. She immediately dropped the menu back on the table when she saw the prices. "We can't eat here. This place is too expensive."

"I picked the place, didn't I?"

"Yes, but I can't in good conscience eat here. This place is way too damned expensive." Sarah stood up from the table and started to walk back toward the door.

Alex reached out and grabbed her arm. "Sit back down. I knew the prices of this place and still I asked you to join me here. Don't make a scene! Sit back down, please."

Sarah sat back down and took the menu back in her hands. She looked for the cheapest thing on the menu. She decided to go with the spaghetti; it was the most inexpensive item on the menu, and it came with a salad.

"What are you going to get?" Alex asked her.

"Spaghetti."

"You know you can order something else if you want to. I don't want you to worry about the pricing."

"I like spaghetti, that's what I want for dinner. Do you have a problem with that? If you do, you can take me back to my truck."

"Spaghetti it is!"

They finished eating their dinner and left the restaurant. Alex opened the door and walked Sarah back to the car. He opened the door and shut it behind her. Sarah was quite impressed with how much of a gentleman Alex was.

They drove back to the coffee shop and grabbed a cup of coffee together. Sarah was not sure she was ready for the night to end, but she knew that she was not ready to bring him back to her place for the night; she learned her lesson with the last guy she dated and would never make that mistake again:

> It was a cold night as Sarah closed her history
> book and looked over at her baby-faced, blond-

haired, brown-eyed classmate Bobby sitting next to her at the table.

"How's it going over there?"

"I hate History! How can you enjoy it?"

"It's always been easy for me to remember dates and names."

"You're such a nerd! You wanna do the dirty with me?"

"No. I need to go to sleep now. I need you to leave, please."

"But this has made me horny."

"Sounds like a personal problem to me. Out!"

He left her sitting there at the table. She packed up her schoolwork and hopped in the shower. She went into her bedroom and fell asleep.

She woke up a couple of hours later to the crashing of her front door as Bobby busted into her apartment.

"What the fuck?"

"No one turns me down, Sarah."

"I did, now get the fuck out of here."

He came at her, brandishing a knife. She grabbed her Glock from the nightstand. "You need to leave now. Trust me when I say I know how to handle this."

He lunged at her, catching her a bit off guard. He caught her right arm with the knife before she rounded on him and shot him in the shoulder.

She vowed that day that she would never let another man into her home. She could not take any chances of letting a psycho back into her life.

After coffee, Sarah got in her truck and went back home. She finished revising her Civil War history paper that was due the middle of the week. Once she was happy with the paper, she logged into her class through the school's website and uploaded the paper for her professor to review.

Alex left the coffee shop and went back to his apartment. He could not stop thinking about Sarah on his way home. She made him horny and frustrated in a way that no other woman ever had. He could not believe that she was not begging him to sleep with her by the end of the first date like all the other girls; he was even more confused by the fact that he now had gone out with Sarah twice and she still was not interested in sleeping with him. Now he knew that he had to keep dating her to see how long it was before she wanted to have sex with him.

Alex got home and changed clothes then went over to Lauren's place. He walked in the door and found Lauren on the couch watching a movie. He sat down beside her and pulled off her clothes before he climbed on top of her. She tried to push him off her, but he forced himself onto her, pushing her into the couch.

"What the hell, Alex? I don't want to."

"When did I ask you what you wanted, Lauren?"

"Alex, please don't force me to do this. I'm not in the mood."

"I don't give a shit whether or not you're in the mood."

She started crying. "Shut the fuck up, bitch."

He continued to force himself on her until he ejaculated; he enjoyed watching her cry as he got off. The more she cried, the rougher he was with her.

"You forget that I didn't want to stay with you. You begged me to stay with you and promised that you would do whatever I wanted whenever I wanted to get me to stay. Well, this is what that looks like. You'll have sex with me whenever I want to, I don't care if you're in the mood or not, you understand me?" he raised his voice as he asked.

She quietly nodded, tears streaming down her face.

"I asked you a question, bitch! Now, I require an answer. Do you fucking understand me that if you want me to stay, you'll do whatever I want, whenever I want?"

"Y-yes," she stammered between sobs.

"Good, now get the fuck out of my sight."

Third Date

The week went quickly and quietly for Sarah. She attended all her classes and worked her shifts without hearing anything from Alex. She was shocked at how disappointed she was at this realization. As she finished up her morning shift at the coffee house one week after their first date, she looked up and saw Alex standing at the front of the coffee shop. She immediately felt giddy and could not believe he was actually there.

"You miss me, sexy?"

"Nope!"

"Whatever, I saw how your face lit up when you saw me standing here. Ready to go blow off some steam and go for a run?"

"I thought you hated running?"

"Well, I do, but if it's a way to spend more time with you, then I'm willing to do it."

"Really? That seems kind of silly, don't you think?"

"Not at all. I know that it's something you enjoy, and I want to spend more time with you. There's something different about you, Sarah Jackson. I'm intrigued and can't stop thinking about you."

"If you can't stop thinking about me, why did it take you six days to reach back out after our second date?"

"I was wrong to wait so long, I do apologize."

"How did you know I was here?"

"I was driving by earlier and saw your truck in the parking lot. I know that you work the early shift when you work weekends, so I figured you would be getting off about now. I ran home and grabbed my running clothes. I know you said that you always keep a spare pair of clothes and running shoes in your truck, so I figured it would be a nice surprise. What do you say? You up for a run?"

"You think you can keep up with me?"

"Well, I was hoping for a nice gingerly pace today as a way of saying thank you for thinking this would be the perfect way to end your shift."

"Not a chance! This is the time I take advantage of getting lost in the run. I do not set a speed or a distance, I just run until I no longer feel like running."

"I don't understand that process. How about we just do a three-mile run today? I nearly died on the six-mile run we did last weekend, especially after hiking. I need to build my stamina to keep up with you, Sarah. You're like the Energizer Bunny… You just keep going and going and going and going. I think it's all that coffee you must drink working in the coffee shop."

"First of all, I *do not* drink coffee—never have, *never will*. That shit is just *nasty*. Second of all, I am not pink like the Energizer Bunny, and I do have an off switch. It's called my pillow every night at nine. Third of all, if you want to keep going out with me, you're gonna have to build your stamina quickly. I'm not going to allow you to hold me back forever. I will cut you loose as a running partner if I don't see quick improvement in your running."

"Oh, snap, Sarah has spoken!" he teased her.

Sarah grabbed her spare workout bag from the backseat of her Ford F150 and walked into the coffee shop to change. She smiled at her boss, Oliver, when she walked in the door. She had never really noticed until just then how handsome Oliver was for an older man, her father's age. He had jet-black hair with silver streaks running down his temples. He had a tan complexion from being out in the sun during the summer months constantly tinkering in his yard. He took care of himself, unlike many men his age, his body was very well toned from lifting weights every day.

"You going for a run, Sarah?"

"Busted! You know me too well, don't you?" she laughed.

"I saw that loud-mouth jerk from last week in here earlier, what are you doing with the likes of him?"

"Oh, you know, Oliver, he really isn't that bad once you get to know him."

"Just be careful, Sarah. I don't want to see you get hurt! Boys like that guy are dangerous to women's hearts."

"Thanks, Dad!" she laughed.

"I'm serious, Sarah!" she heard him reply back as she walked into the coffee shop's restroom to change.

Once finished changing, Sarah went back out to the parking lot, half expecting Alex to be gone but was pleasantly surprised when he was still there. "You all stretched and ready to go?" she asked him as she started jogging in place, getting her muscles warmed up.

"As stretched as I'll ever be. Let's get this show on the road."

She set off down the sidewalk, leading back toward the Spring City University campus and downtown area. She set a pace for eight-minute miles and decided to run a mile and a half out and a mile and a half back. Alex kept her pace, practicing the breathing technique she showed him during their last run.

When they arrived back at the parking lot, Sarah turned back the way she had just come and started walking. A confused Alex asked, "What are you doing?"

"Well, you need to cool down your muscles so that your legs don't cramp up, like I'm sure they did after last week's adventures. Did you end up feeling dizzy or faint after the run?"

"How did you know?"

"Because not stretching and cooling your muscles down properly is a rookie mistake. When you stop working out without doing a cooldown, your heart rate stops abruptly, and your blood can pool in the lower body causing dizziness and fainting."

"No shit?"

"No shit!"

They finished walking a half mile out and then back again. "How are you feeling?"

"My breathing isn't labored anymore. I'm feeling pretty good, like I could take you back to your apartment and get frisky with you." He reached out to pull her in tight to kiss her, but she pulled back.

"Whoa there, tiger, don't make me beat the shit out of you."

"Are you ever going to let me kiss you?"

"Who knows! Maybe, only time will tell."

"God, Sarah, you are such a dick tease. You look so hot when you're all sweaty, your skin just glistens in the sun. I want you so badly!"

"Well, you can wish in one hand, shit in the other, and see which fills up faster. I don't sleep with any guy just because that's what he wants. If you don't like that, you can hit the road. I wasn't looking for a relationship when you walked in the coffee shop door, and I'm not sure I'm looking for one now either."

"Harsh! Your telling me off just makes me want you that much more."

"Tough! Not going to happen!" With that, she turned around and got in the truck and drove off. She drove around for a while thinking about the conversation she just had with Alex: *Sarah, what the hell were you thinking? You can't lead him on like that!*

It sure is nice to know that he wants me.

Fuck that shit, Sarah, you can't get involved right now. You're not ready for that. I don't know that you'll ever be ready for that.

He is so freaking handsome. I don't know if I can hold out forever. He makes me feel certain ways that I haven't ever felt about a guy before.

Part of me wants to just give in and say fuck it. I don't know if I can continue to decline his advances.

What the fuck, Sarah, snap out of it! You don't need a man to be whole.

Alex stood there watching in disbelief as she drove away. He could not believe that he now had spent time with her on three different occasions and she was not begging him to sleep with her.

How is that possible? I've never had a woman turn me down after just talking to her. Is there something wrong with me? This woman drives me fucking crazy. Why won't she just let me fuck her already?

He got in his Camaro and drove home. He continued thinking about Sarah through his shower and could not shake his thoughts.

Thinking about her body as she stood there in the sun glistening from the sweat made him horny; he needed to blow off some steam.

When he got dressed from his shower, he walked out into the living room of his three-bedroom condo just off base that he shared with two other Airmen from his unit. He saw his roommate, Michael, a tall, lanky kid about a year younger than him. He stopped short of the couch and asked, "Hey, Michael, you wanna go to the bar and let off a little steam? See how many chicks we can hook up with tonight?"

"Sure! I'm game," Michael responded back.

They went down the road to the Springs Tavern, the only night club for miles from the base. They went to the bar and grabbed a couple of beers and shots before finding a table near the dance floor. One of the cocktail waitresses, dressed in a black micromini skirt and a black lacy halter-top bra, saw the two standing at the table and approached.

"What brings you two fellas in here on a night like tonight?" she asked, licking her lips, playing with the curls in her hair and twirling her hips slightly in a seductive manner.

"Oh, you know, just looking to get laid," Alex responded. "You willing to let me take you in the bathroom and bend you over the sink to get in that tight ass of yours right now?" he asked as he grabbed her by the butt and pulled her in close to his body.

"Oh, aren't you just forward," she replied back as she grabbed his crotch. "You boys into a threesome?"

They looked at each other then looked back at her. She was all of 130 pounds with a size D cup bust with blond curly hair.

"I'm game if you are," Alex said as he looked at the waitress and Michael.

"Meh, I think I'll wait here for my own piece of action," Michael replied. "You two go ahead and have fun without me."

With that, the waitress grabbed Alex by the crotch and led him to the door in the back corner of the club. "I know a quiet place we can go where no one will bother us," she said as she led him into the office.

As soon as the door closed and the waitress locked it, Alex picked her up and ripped off her mini skirt and her halter-top brazier, exposing her naked body. She reached down and unbuckled his blue jeans and exposed his erect penis. She bent down and pulled him into her mouth.

"Oh, yeah, suck that good!" he moaned as she licked his shaft and played with his balls. "Take that all in," he said as he started pushing and pulling her head faster and faster in rhythm with his orgasm. He came in her mouth and watched as she swallowed.

She then turned around and bent over the couch. "Okay, big boy, I made you cum, now it's my turn! Get over here and get that tongue into action."

He gladly obliged her request, finding it easy to satisfy her request. When she orgasmed, she turned over on the couch and pulled him on top of her. He quickly indulged her by sliding himself right into her and pushed, harder and harder until he came again, this time inside her.

"Oh, sweet Jesus," he said as he finished and pulled out. "I needed that tonight, thanks." He bent her back over the couch and smacked her hard in the ass.

"Ouch! That hurt."

"Good! But it turned you on, didn't it?"

They got dressed and left the room. Alex walked back out into the bar and found Michael chatting with another girl at their table. He went back to the bar to grab another drink before leaving for the night.

Meeting Sarah's Parents

The next few months went by quickly. Alex got into the routine of swinging by the coffee shop to run with Sarah after her shifts during the week. Every Sunday they went for a hike together and then finished out the day by grabbing dinner. Sarah finished out her spring and summer semesters with a 4.0 GPA and made the dean's list.

After dating for about three months, Sarah finally felt secure enough to invite Alex to meet her parents. She made reservations for the four of them to eat dinner at Zippy's Italian Restaurant, her favorite place to eat in town.

Sarah got dressed in a nice pair of low-rise boot-cut jeans with a white tank top she wore under a navy blue-and-white plaid button-up shirt; she left the top three buttons undone and tied a knot at the bottom. She wore a pair of black suede ankle boots. She pulled her hair back in a French braid.

Once she finished dressing for the occasion, she got in the truck and drove over to the coffee shop to meet Alex. Alex pulled in about five minutes after her. He got out of his car and walked over to her truck. She lowered the window and whistled at him. He wore a pair of relaxed fit jeans with a blue button-up shirt. He had a fresh haircut from earlier that morning.

"You clean up real good," she teased him.

"Oh, I do, don't I?"

"Yep, now hop in. I don't want to be late getting there."

They drove the twenty minutes from the coffee shop to the restaurant in complete silence. Sarah was so lost in her the thoughts racing through her mind that she jumped when Alex opened her door and finally spoke, "Earth to Sarah!"

"Oh, Mylanta, you nearly scared the shit right out of me."

"Sorry, I wanted to know if you're ready to go inside."

"How about you go? I'll stay right here in the truck," she replied, smiling.

"I'll give you a couple of options: you either get your tiny little ass out of the truck and accompany me inside the restaurant to have dinner with your parents or you take me back to your place for the first time and let me screw your brains out."

"Well, I guess we should head inside then." Sarah took Alex's hand and carefully jumped down onto the ground. Alex took her right hand in his left, and they walked inside the restaurant together. Once inside the big arched doorway leading into the restaurant, Alex and Sarah were greeted by the hostess.

"Welcome to Zippy's. What is the name on the reservation, please?" she asked, never taking her eyes off Alex.

"The reservation should be under Jackson for four adults," Sarah replied.

"Are the other two members of your party here, or would you like me to go ahead and seat you?"

Sarah looked at Alex hesitantly. He gave her hand a gentle reassuring squeeze. "Do you mind seating us and then showing the other two to the table?"

"It would be my pleasure. Please follow me to your table."

As they walked through the restaurant, Sarah saw the bar off to her left, just inside the door. It was stocked full of many different types of top and bottom shelf liquors. Off to the right, about three hundred feet, was the open-air kitchen. She was greeted by the smell of freshly baked bread.

The tables were all set up in rows, making the walkways for the servers easier to maneuver. The restaurant had some tables for two people, four people, and as many as ten people. Along the far wall, they also had six or seven booths.

"Would you prefer a booth or a table?" the hostess asked.

"Can you put us in the corner booth?" Alex asked.

"Anything for you," the hostess replied.

They sat down with their backs facing the wall, giving them the best viewpoint to see her parents when they arrived. As soon as the hostess was out of earshot, Sarah turned to Alex, "I can't believe she had the nerve to flirt with you with me standing right there."

"I don't know what you're talking about," he replied.

She shook her head and then looked over Alex's shoulder and saw her parents walking toward them. "Oh my god, is it too late to leave?"

"It sure is. Sorry, Charlie, but you're stuck here until dinner is over at this point."

"I know we've talked about this before, but please don't get offended if my mother makes it clear she doesn't approve of you. She doesn't usually like new people."

A minute later, Sarah and Alex crawled out of the booth to say hello to her parents. Sarah introduced Alex to her parents, "Alex, this is my mother, Violet, and this is my father, Matthew. Dad, Mom, this is Alex." The three of them shook hands, and Sarah gave both of her parents a quick hug.

Sarah was pleasantly surprised by how smoothly dinner went; Alex seemed to get along very well with her parents. Her parents immediately took to Alex. They asked questions to get to know him better; Alex gladly shared his childhood stories.

Matthew asked, "What made you want to join the Air Force?"

"Well, sir, my grandfather served and so did my father. I felt like that was the right thing to do, following in the footsteps of two amazing men."

"Good for you, I followed in my father's footsteps as well. I tried to get Sarah's older brothers to join, but neither one of them wanted want to join the Corps."

After dessert, Sarah and Alex got ready to leave for the night. They hugged her parents and walked out to the truck.

"Your parents are cool, I don't know why you were so worried, Sarah."

"Well, my parents have always been protective of me. However, my mom seemed to be smitten with you."

"Well, I seem to have that effect on everyone but you, Sarah."

"What is that supposed to mean?" She looked at him, a little hurt by the comment because she was totally smitten with him, more than she ever imagined she would be with a man.

He helped her up into the truck and jumped in on the passenger side before replying, "Well, Sarah, you are the first woman who has ever withdrawn from my sexual advances for this long. I am not going to lie, I'm used to having girls throw themselves at me. I'm tall, olive-skinned, and very fit, which is what most girls are obsessed with. The only thing that would make me a better package is if I had blond hair and blue eyes. You, Sarah, you baffle me because you have not thrown yourself at me. In fact you do quite the opposite. Every time I try to suggest sleeping with me, you change the topic. Do I repulse you?"

Sarah sat there with the truck running, listening to what he had to say before responding, "Oh my god, how could you possibly think that?"

"Well, because you seem completely disinterested in having sex with me."

"Just because I am not ready to give you my body doesn't mean that I am repulsed by you. In fact, it's quite the opposite. You intrigue me and drive me crazy because I don't want to feel the way I do about you. I wanted to be a crazy old spinster for the rest of my life, but you have wormed your way in, making me wonder what it would be like to be with someone the rest of my life."

"Well, Sarah, if you truly feel the way you say you do, you need to let me in. Be honest with me. Why do you reject having sex with me?"

Sarah started turned away from him and started softly crying. Alex reached over and gently turned her face so that she was looking at him. He reached up with his left index finger and wiped away her tears from her right eye.

"Sarah, what is it? Let me in," he begged her.

"I-I'm not ready yet." She turned back around and faced front. She reached up and put the truck into reverse and pulled out of her parking spot. They drove back to the coffee shop hand in hand but in complete silence, noiseless tears still falling from her eyes. Sarah stayed stoic, not sniffling, because she did not want to scare him off. She wrestled with the notion of telling him why she did not want to have sex with him or not telling him and risk losing him. She knew a man like Alex would not stick with her forever, especially if he did not understand why she was scared.

They pulled up to the coffee shop parking lot. After she placed the truck in park, she looked over at Alex, who was sitting there staring at her. She squeezed his hand and asked, "Would you like to join me for a cup of coffee before we call it a night?"

"I'm not ready for the night to end, Sarah."

He helped her out of the truck, and they walked into the coffee shop. Oliver stood behind the counter and welcomed them in. He took their orders and handed them their drinks before walking back to the office.

Sarah led Alex to a secluded corner booth where she crawled in opposite of him. She held on to her hot chocolate cup for dear life, afraid of the fallout she anticipated happening after she let him into her dark place.

"What is it? Sarah, I can see something is eating you up inside. Now out with it so I can help you."

"You're going to hate me once you know the truth. I won't blame you for hating me and walking out of my life." Tears flowed down her cheeks again.

He reached over and softly pulled her face forward into his hands. As he rubbed the tears away, he replied, "Sarah, I could never hate you."

"Promise?"

"I promise."

She looked deeply into his eyes before deciding it was safe to tell him. "When I was fifteen and a freshman in high school, I was very developed for my age. I liked to go to the high school gym and work out, don't ask me why, but I've always enjoyed working out. Anyways, I was in the gym working out, not really paying attention to the fact that I was in the weight room with the entire varsity football team. It had never been a problem before, so I didn't expect that day to be any different. I-I'm not sure I can go on," she said, trying to pull back from Alex, tears surfacing again.

"Sarah, it is okay for you to tell your story."

"O-okay," she sobbed as she recollected herself. "I was so immersed in my routine that I didn't see everyone on the team, but the starting senior quarterback left the weight room. I didn't think anything of it at that point because I had been in the weight room before with the guys and nothing had ever happened. That day was different: I went to the women's locker room to grab my bag with my books and my school uniform. I was unaware that the quarterback followed me into the locker room. He grabbed me from behind and shoved me down onto the bench. He covered my mouth with his hand and proceeded to rape me, right there in an area that should have been safe for me to be in. The more I cried, the louder he laughed. When he finished, he let me up. I immediately ran to the nearest garbage can and puked. He laughed, he thought my reaction was funny."

"Did you tell anyone?"

"Who was going to believe me? He was the starting quarterback for the football team. He took us to state that year. No one was going to believe me over him."

"Sarah, did you tell your parents?"

"I was too embarrassed. I hid from my parents and my brothers until I could pretend everything was okay. I knew if I told my brothers that they would try to beat the shit out of the guy and then I would be blamed for ruining the school's shot at going to the state championship game. I was also attacked in my own apartment by a classmate after he broke into my apartment and cut me."

"Sarah, have you talked about this with anyone?"

"Nope, you're the first person and will be the only person I ever tell. Now do you understand why I have been so reluctant to sleep with you?"

Meeting Alex's Parents

The week passed too quickly for Sarah's liking. Sarah only heard from Alex once the week after she told him what happened to her and explained why she was scared to be intimate with anyone. She was frightened she had scared him away for good. When she spoke to him that Thursday night, he sprung the news that they were going to meet his family for dinner this weekend, only they were going to drive about halfway to Mountain City to meet up with his parents and then stay the night in the mountain town's only hotel.

She wanted time to slow down. She was not ready for the new semester to be starting in two weeks, and she definitely was not ready to meet Alex's parents for the first time and so quickly after they had dinner with her family.

She woke early that morning and went for a fifteen-mile run. She needed to work out some of the nervous energy before riding in the car for five hours to meet people she had never talked to before. She finished her run in about two hours. After her run, she showered and packed for the quick overnight trip.

She met Alex at their normal spot and hopped in his car. They sang along to the radio with the top down until it started to rain. They quickly pulled over on the side of the road and put the top back up. They finished their drive jamming to the oldies on the radio.

After what felt like forever, Alex finally pulled into an older motel. The sign in the window blinked No Vacancy. Sarah looked out of the car window while Alex got them checked in. This was a one-floor building with rooms whose doors faced right out into their parking spots. The spots right next to the building were all numbered, matching the rooms in front of them. The motel's office was right in the middle of the forty rooms it housed, twenty up front and twenty in the back. The building looked run-down, paint peeling from the siding and shingles missing from the roof. Sarah was skeptical about staying here for the night.

Alex hopped back in the car and drove around the back to the far corner of the lot. He got out and opened Sarah's door, helping her out of the car. He gave her the key to room twenty-one, and then he went to the trunk and grabbed their bags.

"Wait a minute," she said when she opened the door and saw only one king-size bed with an older style comforter on it. "You only gave me one key. Where is your room?" she asked as she continued to eyeball the room, taking in the old box television on a wobbly stand next to the old dresser. There were two nightstands, one on each side of the bed; the bathroom was at the back of the room with a toilet and shower/tub combination and the sink was just outside the toilet area. There was a rack hanging off the wall for guests to hang their clothes off the wire hangers. A small round table with two chairs on either side of it was just inside the door and an armchair on the opposite side of the bed.

"Well, funny story…"

"Don't you dare tell me that they are all sold out and we're staying in the same room! That's not funny! I only came up here because you said we would each have our own rooms."

"Well, Sarah, apparently my mother only booked two rooms, because she assumed we were already shacking up together. When I tried to get another room, the front desk clerk advised me that there is an old car show convention in town this weekend and that they are completely sold out. The next motel is another thirty miles away. She called, and they are also sold out because of the car show."

"Oh my god, how does this happen!" She threw her arms up in despair.

"Sarah, I promise, there are worse things that could happen then us having to share a bed together."

"Like what?" she asked. Just then, a giant spider came down from the ceiling and landed on the table.

"Well, like a giant spider landing on the table, for starters." He laughed as she panicked and ran behind him.

"No, no, no, no, this isn't happening! This hotel has the Bates Motel written all over it... We're gonna die up here," she said as she started hyperventilating.

"Sit down, take some deep breaths. Sarah, everything is going to be okay. I promise!"

She sat on the edge of the bed. "No, no, it won't be." She broke down in tears, pulling her feet up under her body and rocking herself back and forth.

He sat down beside her, facing her. He put a firm hand on the middle of her back and one on her shoulder, forcing her to stop rocking. She leaned into him and cried on his shoulder. She cried herself to sleep. Alex quietly got up from under her body weight and moved her up onto the pillows. He watched her sleep for about forty-five minutes before waking her to get ready for dinner.

"I know you took a shower after your run this morning, but I wasn't sure if you wanted to grab another shower before dinner after the long car ride."

"Are you saying that I stink?"

"No, you don't stink. I just know that sometimes after a long ride it is nice to take a warm shower."

She grabbed her bag and found a different set of clothes. She grabbed her jeans, tank top, and underwear and walked into the bathroom. She shut the door and took her shower. She felt refreshed when she got out and was redressed in her new clothes.

They walked across the street to the hole-in-the-wall steak house. Sarah was amusingly astonished at how nice the restaurant was inside. The dining area was lightly lit, with a sort of romantic ambiance. The bar area had limited seating but was stocked with multiple types of liquors. There were only tables and chairs in the restaurant, all hand-carved. The decorations and pictures on the walls were all antique pieces. She could not believe this place was just across the road from the Bates Motel, as she referred to it.

The host seated the two in a corner table. They each got an unsweetened tea while they waited on his parents to arrive. Ten minutes later, Sarah heard a very high-pitch squeal from behind them. Alex leaned over and said, "That would be my mother." He then got up from his chair and turned around to give her a hug.

"Oh, my Alexander whoopsie poo. I can't believe how long it's been since I last saw you." She grabbed him into another bear hug before he shook her off.

While Alex was in his mother's embrace, Sarah grabbed a quick look at Alex's parents. His mother, Anna, was about five feet tall and was as round as she was tall. She had reddish-brown hair that was pulled up into a bun. His father, Arthur, was tall and lanky, like Alex. He had the olive-toned complexion, and Sarah instantly recognized Alex in his father; they could easily be mistaken for twins. Behind Arthur was another lanky young man. He appeared to be her age and again looked just like Alex.

"Mom, Dad, Abe, this is my girlfriend, Sarah. Sarah, this is my mother, Anna, my father, Arthur, and my little brother, Abe."

They exchanged pleasantries before sitting down across from each other. Sarah felt uneasy around Anna, like Anna disapproves of her. It was only minutes later that Anna voiced her disdain.

"So, Sarah, my son says you haven't had sex yet. Are you really that much of a prude?"

Sarah nearly choked on her onion ring. "E-excuse me?"

"Oh, I know you heard me, are you a prude? What makes you think you deserve to be with my son?"

"Mom!" Alex and Abe said at the same time.

"Mom, don't be rude. If Sarah has decided to save herself, what business of that is yours?" Abe interjected.

"Oh, hush, Abe. This doesn't pertain to you. This little hussy thinks she's too good for my son. Well, she ain't. I hate to break it to you, you little hussy, my son is way too good for you."

"Mom!" Alex said, this time getting red in the face.

"Anna! That is enough!" Arthur spoke in a quiet, harsh tone. "If you can't behave yourself, we will leave."

"I asked you a question, Sarah. Why haven't you had sex with my son yet? Do you think you're too good for him?"

"Not that it's *any* of your business, ma'am, but no, I do not think I'm too good for Alex. In fact, half the time I wonder what it is that he sees in me."

"Now that I see you in person, me too," Anna interjected over Sarah, cutting her off.

"Anna, that is about enough of that," Arthur said again. "If I have to say it again, I will drag you out of this restaurant. I don't care."

Sarah looked over at Alex. He was completely red, and for the first time ever, she saw rage in his eyes. It actually scared her slightly. "Mom, you don't need to put my girlfriend down. I am in love with this woman. If you don't like it, that's too bad. I'm not here to get your approval. I'm just here to allow you time to get to know my girlfriend."

They quickly ate their dinner, making small talk after the interruptions and the threats to leave for the night. Anna kept trying to pick at Sarah, but Alex, Abe, and Arthur kept shutting her down every time she started in on Sarah. Sarah felt Alex squeeze her knee reassuringly under the table before they finished their dinner. As soon as she finished eating, Sarah excused herself to go to the bathroom. Once she was locked in, she sat down and started rocking herself, hyperventilating. Her panic attack worsened when she heard Anna start beating on the door, screaming at her, "The boys can't save you now, you little hussy. Get your ass out here and talk to me like a woman, not a coward."

"Please go away, Mrs. Clark."

"I'm not going anywhere until you tell me why you are such a prude."

"Go away!"

Just then, Sarah heard Anna scream outside the bathroom door, "Get off me, Arthur!"

"Sarah, I'm sorry about tonight! We will be leaving now. I hope you don't take this out on Alex. He really is a good man."

As soon as she didn't hear Anna's voice outside the bathroom door any longer, she opened the door and walked back to the table.

Alex stood up to greet her. "Sarah, I'm so sorry about my mother's behavior. I cannot believe she treated you the way she did tonight."

She faced him squarely. "Alex, how could you have ever told her that we haven't had sex yet? That is intimate, and no one outside of you and me should ever know about our sex life."

"You're right, Sarah, I should never have said anything. In my defense though, I was talking to my father when I said it. I never told my mother. She must have overheard my conversation with my dad."

"I-I don't know if I can continue with this relationship," she said as she collapsed into the chair.

"Are you breaking up with me?"

"I—how can I trust that something like this won't happen again? Alex, I'm stunned right now. I-I don't even know what to say to you right now."

"Sarah, I promise that I won't ever break your trust like this again."

"I need to go for a run and clear my head."

"Would you like me to go with you?"

"No, I think I need to go by myself."

"Are you sure you want to run on a full stomach?"

"I'll be fine, don't worry about me."

"But you don't know the area, Sarah."

"I'm pretty sure it is safe. Otherwise, I would like to hope you wouldn't have brought me up here if it wasn't."

"You're right, it is safe here."

"Can I please have the key so I can go change now?"

"I'll walk back with you to the room."

They walked back across the street in silence. Alex tried to hold her hand, but she pulled away. She quickly dressed in her running gear and left the room. She went out to the sidewalk at the street's edge and turned left toward town.

The sound of her feet hitting the pavement in rhythm helped her to lose her all thoughts of the events from the evening. She focused only on her breathing and her footsteps for the next hour. When she felt completely calm, she went back to the hotel.

Alex greeted her at the sidewalk with a towel, a bottle of water, and a dozen orange and yellow roses. She smiled, knowing that it could not have been easy for him to sit there waiting on her.

She took a drink of water. "Thank you. This is very thoughtful." She took another mouthful of water, swished it around in her mouth, and then spat it out on the ground.

She saw Alex intently watching her. Before she knew what had happened, she leaned into Alex as he leaned down to kiss her. The kiss lasted only five to ten seconds, but there were instant electric sparks between the two of them. He reached down and pulled her into him and kissed her again, this time more passionately. She melted into his grasp, almost forgetting everything around them until he squeezed hard enough that they both got pricked by the rose thorns. Sarah jumped back a couple of steps before giggling.

"I guess we better go get those into some water before they really do some damage," he laughed as he took her waist in his arm and pulled her close to him and walked toward the room.

Once the roses were down and could not harm anyone, Alex picked Sarah up; she wrapped her legs around his waist. Their lips met. Sarah was a bit shocked when he put his tongue in her mouth for the first time but enjoyed the way this new sensation felt.

Alex sat down on the edge of the bed, Sarah on his lap. He reached up under her tank top and fondled her breasts. Sarah stopped for a minute, freezing at the touch. Alex felt her body slightly tense at the touch, so he stopped. "Are you okay? Is this too fast for you?"

"I-I don't know. It's all so new to me."

"Tell me if you get uncomfortable or want to stop. I don't want you to feel pressured into anything."

She leaned back into him, kissing him. He reached down and pulled her top off, exposing her pink sports bra. He rubbed at her nipples under the fabric. This sensation was exhilarating; it hurt but at the same time felt so good. She did not want it to stop. After a couple of minutes, Alex unzipped her bra, exposing her chest. She pulled his shirt off, staring at his toned physique. She traced his abs with her finger.

Alex moved his hands down to Sarah's thighs. He reached under her running shorts and played with the edges of her underwear, rubbing his fingers gently across the material. Sarah could not help it when she let out a soft coo at the new feeling.

Alex stood back up and gently laid Sarah down on the bed. He pulled her shorts and underwear off, leaving her completely exposed. He pulled his own pants off and hovered over her.

"Is this okay?" he asked.

She reached up and kissed him in response. Her body ached with anticipation of what would come next.

When Alex finished, he lay down beside her on the bed, completely out of breath and panting heavily. Sarah stayed where she was. Her mind immediately started racing: *How could I have been so stupid, getting caught up in the moment?*

OMG, that felt amazing! I never imagined it could feel so wonderful.

Sarah, that was the dumbest thing you've ever done. Now your husband will hate you for giving in to your inhibitions instead of waiting.

She got up and went into the shower. When she came out, she crawled into bed. "Good night!" she said as she reached over and gave him a quick peck on the lips.

He threw on his shorts and T-shirt and then curled up in the bed beside Sarah. He put his arm around her waist and pulled her in tight. They quickly fell asleep.

Sarah was suddenly awakened by a loud banging on their door around one in the morning. Alex jumped up to see what was going on. Sarah could hear a young male voice on the other side of the door, "Alex, wake up, I need your help!"

Alex jumped out of bed and opened the door. "Abe, what's going on? Why are you beating on my door at one in the morning? This had better be good!"

"Alex, it's Dad. I don't know what's going on, but I need you to come now. He fell onto the floor and started shaking uncontrollably. He finally stopped shaking after about four minutes, but now we can't get him to wake up."

Alex quickly ran after his brother to the room where Arthur started having another seizure. Alex ran to his father's side and started to hold him down.

"Stop!" Sarah yelled. "Just move everything out of his way. Anna, call 911 and get the paramedics here as quickly as possible. Let them know that he is having clonic seizures and that his previous one lasted four minutes and he started having another seizure within five minutes of the first seizure."

Anna said, "Abe, you need to get something and put it in your father's mouth. He's going to bite his tongue with all that thrashing about."

Sarah put her arm out to block Abe from getting close to Arthur. "No, you don't want to put anything in his mouth. He could choke on it and make things worse."

"Abe, don't listen to her. She doesn't know what she's talking about. Do you want your father to bite his tongue off?"

Just then, Arthur's body stopped jerking around. Sarah rolled Arthur onto his side until the paramedics arrived and put him on the gurney. Anna went in the ambulance with Arthur to the small county hospital an hour away. Alex, Abe, and Sarah got in the car and followed them.

They arrived at the hospital emergency room and waited to find out what happened. Anna sat in the corner by herself. Sarah tried to go over and comfort her, but Anna pushed her away. The young very pretty resident came and found them in the waiting room.

"Well, we have good news, and we have some bad news."

"Why would you even say that?" Anna yelled at her. "We're here in the hospital and we don't know what caused Arthur to have a seizure. Wouldn't you say that is all bad news?"

"Ma'am, the good news is that we have your husband currently sedated and he is doing much better. He has not had another seizure since we got him medicated."

"Well, then what is the bad news, little Miss Know-It-All?" Anna retorted with a scowl on her face.

"Mrs. Clark, it appears as though your husband has a tumor that has formed on his brain."

"How does it 'appear' to be a tumor?" she asked, using air quotation marks when she said the word *appear*. "Are you imbeciles not smart enough to diagnose whether it is or is not a tumor?"

"Mom, that is enough." Alex stepped in and pulled her back from the resident's face.

"Alex, I knew we shouldn't have let the ambulance bring your father here. I should have forced them to take him back to Mountain City to the hospital there. These people are imbeciles and do not really know how to practice medicine." She turned and gave the resident a dirty look.

"Your father bit his tongue because Sarah wouldn't let us put anything in his mouth to prevent him from biting his tongue during the seizure. She's a fucking idiot who had no idea what she was doing." Anna turned on Sarah and got in Sarah's face.

"*Mom!*" Alex and Abe both stepped up and got in front of her.

"Sarah kept Dad alive, didn't she?" Alex asked her. "The resident also helped make Dad comfortable, right?"

"I don't know if I would call this a great success story, Alex." She then turned on the resident and Sarah. "What are you two bitches still doing here? You both need to leave. This is a family matter, and neither of you are welcome."

"Mom, you need to sit down, shut up, and take your medication. You are being a bitch to everyone," Abe told her.

After she calmed down and sat back in the chair, the resident came back a little closer to the group; Sarah stayed against the corner of the room. "Arthur isn't out of the woods yet. He will need to find a neurologist as well as an oncologist to help him get more definite answers. As long as he does well the rest of the night, Arthur should be released late Monday morning or early Monday afternoon."

Anna decided to stay the rest of the night in the hospital with Arthur. The hospital staff brought in a rollaway bed for her to sleep in his room next to him. Abe, Alex, and Sarah drove back to the hotel.

As soon as Abe went back into the room he was supposed to be sharing with parents, Alex and Sarah went back into their room. Sarah put on her spare pair of running clothes.

"Where are you going, Sarah? You need to get some rest. It's five o'clock and you haven't slept much."

"Alex, you and Abe need to go be with your mother and father. I am going to message my father and ask him to come up here and pick me up and take me back to my truck in Spring City."

"Sarah, you don't have to do that. You're welcome to stay with me. In fact, you'll be my excuse not to have to stay up here all day and then drive him back to Mountain City with my mom in the car. If you leave, then I'll be forced to drive to them back to Mountain City."

"Alex, I'm sorry, but I can't spend another minute around your mother today. She managed to ruin the trip up here, and I can't shake the fact that she hates me. She doesn't even know me."

"Sarah, please don't go. I need you here with me."

"Alex, you need to be with your family right now in this time of crisis. Your mother made it very clear that I am not welcome, I am not a part of your family. I will not subject myself to being around someone who is that cruel to me when I didn't do anything to deserve it. I don't care how much I love you. I cannot be around that negativity."

"Sarah, please don't go. I love you, and I need you to be here with me."

"I have to go. Even though you may not want to, you need to be there for your father's sake. Now, go in and take a nap. I have a feeling it is going to be a long day for you and Abe."

She heard him say, "Sarah!" as she walked out the door. She knew her father would already be up so she texted him and told him what happened. He agreed to come get her.

Sarah ran out to where the car show was going on. She decided to take some time to look at the classic cars sitting on the vacant lot before turning around and going back to the motel. When she got back to the room around nine thirty, she found the room locked. Alex's Camaro was no longer sitting in the parking lot, and neither was the Clark's family car.

She went to the front desk and got the spare key from the clerk to let herself in the room. She saw Alex's clothes laying in a heap on the floor near the foot of the bed. She took her shower and got dressed. While she waited for her father to arrive, she sat down and wrote Alex a quick note.

Alex,

I know you are probably mad at me for not coming back with you back to the hospital, and I am truly sorry that I could not be there with you. I put myself out there twice for your mother, and she was nothing but nasty and hateful to me.

I feel like it is time for me to bow out of this relationship. I cannot come between a mother and her son. I cannot ask you to pick me over your mother. She bore and raised you; you are a part of her and you always will be.

It is with a heavy heart that I ask you not to contact me when you find this letter. I need to move

on with my life, a life that you and your family
will not be in.

Sarah finished writing when she heard a light tap on the door.
"Chipmunk, are you in there?" her father's voice asked through the
door.

"Hi, Daddy. I'll be right out." She folded the letter, stuck it in
the envelope she found in the nightstand drawer, and wrote Alex's
name on the front. She opened the door and gave him a great big
hug. "Thank you for coming to get me. You don't know how much
this means to me."

Sarah got in the car and immediately fell asleep. Matthew
Jackson looked over at his daughter and saw how peaceful she was
curled up in his front seat. He turned on the radio and headed south
back to Spring City.

Arthur was released from the hospital later in the afternoon on
Sunday, a day ahead of when doctors originally anticipated his going
home. Arthur got in the back of their Nissan Rogue and leaned back
to take a nap while Abe drove the family back. Alex followed behind
Abe until they got to the motel.

When Alex walked in the room, he walked right past Sarah's
letter on the table to his pile of clothes. He gathered them up and
placed them in his bag. He moved on to his toiletries and packed
those up as well. As he opened the door, a small gust of wind caused
the letter to fly off the table onto the floor. Alex bent down to pick
it up.

His heart started racing as he opened the sealed envelope. As
he read the letter, he knew that he could not let Sarah end the relationship this way. He ran out of the room and grabbed Abe. "Dude,
I have to get back to Spring City. You're going to have to make sure
that Mom and Dad get home okay."

"Whoa, slow down there, big brother. What is going on? Is
everything okay?"

"No, no, it isn't, Abe. The woman I love wrote me a letter,
dumping me because of our mother's actions. I need to go make this
right with her. I can't let her dump me because of mom."

"Are you actually in love?" Abe teased him.

"I never thought I would feel this way about anyone. I cannot stand the thought of losing her, Abe."

"Okay, well then, go get your girl! I'll get Dad home okay."

Alex got in the car and drove back to Spring City. He stopped by the coffee shop as soon as he got to town to see if Sarah's truck was out back. His heart sank into his stomach when he realized she was not there. He counted on her being at the one place he knew she always was whenever she was not out with him or at school.

Alex suddenly came to the realization that he might actually lose Sarah; he had no clue where she lived, and she was not answering his calls or texts. He went inside to ask Oliver if he knew where Sarah lived.

"Oh, hey there, fly boy," Oliver greeted him when he walked in the coffee shop.

"Have you seen Sarah?" Alex asked in a hurried tone.

"Not since she came in to pick up her truck. What's wrong, son?"

"Sarah dumped me. I need to talk to her, and she isn't answering any of my texts or calls."

"Oh, sounds like she's serious that she wants to cut off all communication with you. What did you do to piss her off, fly boy?"

"I didn't do anything, my mother did. I need to talk to Sarah right now. I need to win her back."

"Ooh, the classic 'momma bear getting involved in her son's relationship and ruining it' routine, huh?

"I think you need to let Sarah have her space. If I know anything about Sarah, once she makes her mind up about something, she is going to stick to it. I don't think there's anything you can do, fly boy, to change her mind."

"Well, I have to try!

"If I were you, I'd leave it alone."

"Look, Oliver, I really need to fix this with Sarah. She's the first woman I've ever loved with my whole heart. Knowing that I may have lost her is the most devastating thing in the world right now. I need her to at least know that I love her."

"She asked to work a double shift tomorrow, so she will be here from six in the morning until eight tomorrow night. We are generally slow after six in the evening when everyone heads home to their families after work, and with classes out for another two weeks, we won't have any students in here studying."

"Oh my god, thank you, Oliver. I really appreciate this information."

"Of course, Alex. I hope you can win her over. She's the happiest I've ever seen her since she started seeing you. Don't ruin that, fly boy!"

"I won't!"

Operation Proposal

Alex stopped by the base exchange on his way home from the base. While he was looking around for a thoughtful gift that Sarah would like, he found some new racer-back tank tops that had just come in. He went ahead and bought Sarah a couple of the tank tops, knowing she would be able to get a lot of use out them.

Alex was nervous about how he was going to win Sarah back. He knew that he needed to let out some of the energy, so he went over to Lauren's place. She was just pulling in the parking lot in front of him. She smiled and welcomed him inside. He had a drink with Lauren and then went into the bedroom with her.

He took a quick shower and changed into a new pair of clothes before he headed over to the coffee shop. He realized as he pulled in next to her truck that he was holding his breath in anticipation that she was not there. He let out a long deep breath and then grabbed the package from the passenger seat. He walked inside and his heart skipped a beat when he saw her with her back toward the door; he had butterflies in his stomach for the second time ever in his life.

She turned around to greet her new guest when she heard the doorbell ring. Part of her was excited to see Alex standing there in the doorway, but the other part of her was terrified. She stood there, frozen in place; her heart sunk into the pit of her stomach.

"H-hey, there," he said as he stepped up to the counter.

"W-what can I make you tonight, Alex?"

"How about you make love to me tonight?" He smiled, trying to break the ice the only way he knew how.

"Alex, I-I can't with you. I need to ask you to leave." She turned away so that he could not see the tears start to well up in her eyes.

"Sarah, I can't leave. As soon as I read your letter, I realized that you were the best thing that ever happened to me. I knew that I couldn't lose you. If I have to choose, I choose you over my mother. Sarah, I love you!"

Sarah turned around with a little bit of rage in her voice and her facial expression, which Alex was not expecting. "You what? You choose me, if you have to choose? Is that what you just said to me? Alex, I don't want you to have to choose. I want to be accepted by your family the way that my family accepted you. I am not dumb. Your mother will always win out. I mean look at the fact that she knew we hadn't slept together. How did she know that? Oh, wait, because you told her."

"Sarah, that's not fair. I made a mistake and I apologized for that. It won't ever happen again, I promise."

"You're damn right it won't. I'm not going to ever let it be an option again." She could no longer hold back the dam; the tears started flowing down her face.

"Sarah, as I realized that I most likely lost you, you are the most important person in my life. I don't know how I did it, but I fell head over heels in love with you. I know that sounds cheesy, but I did."

"Alex, I love you too. I know I shouldn't, but I do."

"Well, then don't give up on me, Sarah." He handed her the box. "Here, I found this for you. I know you will appreciate it."

She hesitantly took the box from him. She knew if she opened it that she was taking another chance with him. She contemplated giving it back to him but finally decided to open it. She smiled when she saw the tank tops: a blue one that had the Air Force emblem on it and the second one that said *I'm with him* on it. As she held this one up, he took off his button-up shirt and exposed his matching tank top that said *I'm with her* on it.

Sarah couldn't help but laugh. "I can't believe how cheesy you are, but I love them." She walked out from behind the counter and kissed him.

After she closed up the coffee shop, she followed him back to his apartment. She met his roommates, Michael and Jason. She and Alex sat on the couch and watched a romantic comedy while Michael and Jason left to go to the bar. Sarah leaned onto Alex's chest. He reached down and gently kissed her head. She reached up to kiss him. They went into his room where they made love to each other.

When they finished, he pulled her next to him, and they fell asleep. They woke when Michael and Jason came back from the bar around two in the morning. Sarah did not feel comfortable staying the rest of the night, so she dressed and went home.

The next two weeks passed very quickly, and before Sarah knew it, classes started back up again. She worked doubles every day to help put as much money into savings as she could before the semester started. Alex came by every night after he got off, and they went back to his place at least twice a week.

Once school started, she cut back her shifts to three nights a week and doubles on Saturdays. She loved working for Oliver because he was so accommodating to her changing schedule.

Sarah came in for her shift on Saturday, September 6, expecting the day to be very quiet in the coffee shop; the Spring City University Broncos were playing the Mountain City University Cougars in their season opening game. Everyone on campus was hyped for the game because the Broncos were expected to go all the way to the title game this year.

Sarah came in and opened the coffee shop like normal. That morning was busy with all the visitors in town for the game. Anyone who asked was directed into the Caffeine Blending House because Oliver had the best coffee in town. As game time approached, business slowed down.

Oliver came from the back office and asked, "Would you like to leave early so you can join the rest of the student body at the game?"

"Naw, I like being able to hear all the noise from here but not having to deal with all the people."

"Oh, I understand. I just thought you might enjoy an afternoon off from here. You've been working so hard lately. You need to take a break before you kill yourself. You're young and so full of life. Don't be like me and waste it all working all the time."

"I can't be accused of killing myself when I'm doing what I love!"

Oliver shook his head. He knew he was never going to win this argument with Sarah. "Hey, why don't you at least go to the back for an hour and work on that paper project I overheard you telling Alex about."

"I can't do that. That would be stealing from you."

"How do you figure?"

"I would be doing schoolwork while I'm here at work getting paid to work for you. I can't do that."

"You can if I tell you to! Now, scoot. Get your bag out of the truck and go to the office. I'll come grab you in an hour, deal?"

"Okay, okay. It sounds like you aren't going to take no for an answer." She laughed as she headed for the door to grab her bag out of the truck. She walked outside and grabbed her bag then walked back inside, completely missing the fact that Alex's car was parked in the back corner of the parking lot.

As soon as she walked to the back, Oliver texted Alex that everything was clear for him to come into the coffee shop and execute *Operation Proposal.*

Oliver disabled the doorbell and let Alex in before putting the bell back over the door. Alex showed Oliver the ring he picked out, a half-carat princess-cut diamond ring set in a fourteen-carat gold band. "What do you think? Think she'll like this?"

"Alex, you do realize Sarah is a simple girl, don't you?"

"You think it's too flashy?"

"I think it's too flashy for who Sarah is, but then again, what do I know? I thought you were too flashy for Sarah, and here we are, sneaking around finding a clever way for you to propose to her," he whispered.

Alex laughed quietly, and the two of them quickly got to work opening a bag of coffee beans and placing the ring at the top of the bag. Oliver knew that Sarah would find the ring there when she went to add it to the grinder to grind up the coffee beans. Once the ring was hidden, Alex went back outside the coffee shop to wait for Sarah.

Sarah sat in the back office for a little bit and thought about what she wanted to write her paper on. Once she had a good outline for her research paper, she came back out to the front to get the shop cleaned up for closing.

The doorbell rang so Sarah looked up to greet the customer. "Hi, welcome to the Caffeine Blending House."

Alex walked in carrying a dozen red roses. "Hi there, beautiful."

"What are you doing here? Aren't you supposed to be out celebrating after the Broncos win with all your buddies?"

"I thought it might be nice to celebrate the win with my best girl tonight."

"Well, what are you having tonight?"

"Meh, why don't you surprise me?" He smiled as the door opened and Sarah's family walked in.

"Wow, to what do I owe this honor?" she asked as she looked from her Grams to her Pops, to her mother to her father to her twin brothers and her sister-in-law, Brenda. Sarah started to get confused and looked around the room at the group standing in front of her. "What's the occasion that brings everyone together here in the coffee shop? Did someone die?"

"Wow, what a rosy outlook on life, Sarah," Harrison retorted.

"Hey, beautiful, how about that coffee?" Alex asked, interrupting the banter between Sarah and her brother.

"Oh, yeah, while I'm at it, what is everyone else having?" She wrote down their orders and went to the coffee beans to start grinding them. As she reached down to pull out the first scoop, she saw something shiny in the beans.

"Hey, Oliver, where did this bag come from?"

"Our supplier, why?"

"Well, there's something in the bag. Did you happen to see anything shiny in here earlier when you grabbed some beans out of the bag?"

"Nope, can't say that I did. Well, what is it? Do I need to call and yell at the supplier?" Oliver asked her.

As Sarah went to scoop the shiny object out of the beans, Alex walked behind the counter to kneel right behind her. She looked down at the scoop and pulled the ring out from the beans. Alex grabbed the ring and held Sarah's left hand out, placing the ring on her ring finger. "Sarah Jackson, I have never known a woman who could make me as crazy as you do. I can't stop thinking about you, even when we're not together. Will you make me the happiest man alive by becoming my wife?"

She was in shock and could not believe this was actually happening. Sarah looked down at Alex, kneeling there before her.

"Y-yes!"

Alex jumped up off the floor and grabbed her into a giant hug, spinning her around the back of the counter. When he stopped turning, he placed her on the ground and kissed her.

She smiled into the kiss, not able to believe that at nineteen she was now an engaged woman. Her family clapped and cheered for her. "Whoop, whoop!"

"Would you get over here so we can properly congratulate you, chipmunk?" she heard Gram ask.

"Yes, ma'am!"

Sarah walked around the counter and was greeted by her grandmother, Hailey, a beautiful silver-haired woman of small height but great stature in the family. "Oh, Sarah, I'm so happy for you. This young man seems to be a fine catch," she said as she smiled at Alex, pinching his cheek.

"Oh, Grams!" Sarah blushed.

Oliver made the family their coffees, and they all sat around together. They laughed at funny stories of their childhood; they interrogated Alex and tried to force Sarah and Alex to set a date for the wedding.

Once everyone finished their coffee, all but Alex left the coffee shop. "You two should go celebrate," Oliver said to the couple.

"I can't leave you here to clean up our mess." Sarah helped Oliver clean the tables; she washed the coffee cups and the remaining dishes. Once the place was spotless, Alex grabbed Sarah's hand and guided her to the truck.

"You wanna grab dinner and a movie to celebrate?" he asked her as he swooped in for another kiss.

She smiled devilishly at him. "Naw, why don't you hop in?"

"What are you thinking?" He smiled back at her, playing with her hair.

"You into late night adventures?" she teased.

"Let's go!" He smiled.

Alex helped her into the truck before getting in on the passenger side. Sarah drove to the outskirts of town and drove up the hill that looked down over Spring City. After about an hour of driving, they stopped at a secluded spot overlooking the city.

"Ooh, I like where this is going," Alex said as he slid over next to her.

Sarah hopped out and grabbed a blanket from the backseat of the truck. She pulled the tailgate down and jumped in the back. Alex joined her in the bed of the truck. They celebrated their new engagement by making love in the moonlight in the back of her truck overlooking the city.

Once they finished, they lay together staring up at the moon and stars. "I cannot believe this is finally happening," Alex said as he mindlessly played with her hair.

"What's that?"

"That you are going to be my wife, Sarah, that's what!"

She smiled at him and then moved to put her clothes back on. They picked up the blanket and folded it. Sarah put it back behind the seat and then got in the truck. Alex jumped in beside her.

"How quickly were you planning to have the ceremony?" she asked him.

"Well, if I thought I could get away with it, I would say let's elope and get married tomorrow!" he laughed.

She laughed in response. "No, seriously, did you have a time frame in mind?"

"Well, if we have to be serious, what if we get married in May."

"This coming May? As in 2009 May? Like nine months from now, May?"

"Yep, that would be the May I was referencing!" He squeezed her hand.

"Oh, my goodness, that doesn't give me a lot of time to get everything together!"

"We have plenty of time. Don't stress yourself about this."

"You do realize that nine months will come and go before you know it, right?"

"We'll be fine! I know you will make this the best wedding ever!"

They drove back into town, and Sarah dropped Alex off at his car. She then drove back across town to her apartment. She called her best friend, Jen, to tell her the news.

"Jen, you'll never guess what just happened." She kept her expression steady, not revealing the excitement she felt.

"Uh, let me guess, you just popped your cherry for the first time!" She laughed.

"Really, shut the hell up!"

"What, what just happened? I'm dying over here from excitement," Jen feigned excitement through the phone.

Sarah shook her head. "You are such a dork. You know that guy I told you I was seeing?"

"Yeah, what about him?"

"Well, he asked me to marry him tonight! He got my whole family to be there for the proposal."

"Sarah, why have I still not met the guy yet?"

"Well, because you never seemed interested in meeting him, dork. You're always too busy running around with Jordan and Jamie. You'd think that I didn't exist anymore now that you are going steady with Jordan and have a two-year-old daughter!"

"Now who needs to shut the hell up? Well, before you get married, I need to meet the guy. I can tell you if he's a winner or a loser."

"Oh, you can tell if a guy is a loser, huh? Just like you did with Jamie's father when you slept with him for the first and last time?" Sarah teased.

"Ooh, you're getting under my skin now!" Jen laughed. "So, when is the wedding?"

"We decided for the first part of May next year."

"Wow, that seems a bit fast, don't you think?"

"Well, when it feels right, it feels right. You ought to know that by now?"

"Well, I'm here to help you with anything you need."

"Weeeeeeeeeellllllll, that was part of why I called you... Jen, will you be my maid of honor, and can I get Jamie to be my flower girl?"

"*Oh my god*, are you serious right now?" Jen yelled into the phone, waking Jamie up, making her cry in the background.

"Yes, I'm dead serious. I need you to stand up with me and be my maid of honor."

"Sarah, it would be my pleasure! I need to go now that I woke my daughter up. We'll talk more tomorrow! Bye!"

Sarah picked up her laptop and started searching through different bridal websites. She found a bridal show that was actually happening in town for the following day. She picked up her phone and texted Jen.

Sarah

9:30 p.m.

Hey, I found a bridal show here in town that is going on at the fancy hotel & convention center in downtown tomorrow only. You wanna come w/ me to check it out & get some ideas for the wedding?

Jen

9:40 p.m.

I'd love to. Jordan already said he'd watch Jamie so that we can go have a girls' day out.

Sarah

9:45 p.m.

Please tell him that I really appreciate him doing this so we can have a day out together; something we haven't had in quite a while!

Jen

9:50 p.m.

He said you're welcome but that you owe his big time for being on diaper duty for you! Lol! What time are we meeting up?

Sarah

9:53 p.m.

The doors open at 9:00; how about I pick you up at 8:00?

Jen

9:55 p.m.

Sounds like a plan.
See you in the a.m.

Alex decided to go to the Springs Tavern after Sarah dropped him off at the car. He walked in and saw his favorite cocktail waitress waiting tables tonight. He watched as she left a table full of guys and strolled over to his table. Her eyes immediately lit up as she recognized him.

"Hey there, big boy, what took you so long to get your nasty ass back in here?" she teased, grabbing his crotch.

"I've been a busy boy!" he said as he followed her back to the corner office. "I got engaged tonight."

"Oh, aren't you just an ass. Shouldn't you be out celebrating with the lucky lady rather than coming in here and spending the night with me?" she asked him, still grabbing and squeezing him.

"Well, this ass needs to get a piece of ass. She'll never know that I came here tonight."

"What exactly is she doing while you're here celebrating with me?"

"She's probably at home right now starting to plan our wedding," he laughed as he followed her to the office. She grabbed his pants and pulled them down. "Here's for your celebration," she said as she took him into her mouth.

"Fucking aye, that feels amazing!"

C h a p t e r   2

2009

Wedding

Sarah found a small-town dress shop that opened in Spring City early in January. She went in and asked to set up an appointment. The receptionist looked at her and started making dress recommendations immediately.

"Ooh, you have the perfect frame for so many different types of dresses. Have you thought about what you are looking for yet?"

"I've looked at a couple of different shops and haven't found anything that I feel looks good."

"Well, even though this shop is small, we have a wide variety of dresses. We can also have a dress designed for you. When is the wedding?"

"The date is set for May 8."

"Ooh, cutting it kind of close, don't you think?"

"How long does it typically take to get a dress back after I find the right one?"

"Oh, Sarah, it can take anywhere from three months to a year, depending on the designer."

"Oh, I had no idea," Sarah said, frowning.

"It'll be okay, Sarah. We'll get you in this weekend to start looking for the right dress. How many will be in your party?"

"There will be six people joining me: my best friend, my second bridesmaid, my mother, my grandmother, my sister-in-law, and my future mother-in-law."

"I need you to really look at dress types that you think you want to wear for your wedding. It will help the appointment go faster."

"I don't think anything is going to make this appointment go very fast. I have two women who have never met each other coming to join me: one of whom is very particular about everything and one of whom hates me for no reason. It should be interesting."

Sarah finished setting the appointment and called everyone to let them know when and where to be Saturday morning at eight.

Saturday morning came faster than Sarah wanted. She had a nightmare the night before the appointment about how everything would work out. She dreamed that Anna would start a fight that would cause her to break down in tears, walking out of the store without a dress.

Sarah picked Jen and Jamie up before driving to the dress shop.

"You ready for the day?" Jen asked as she put Jamie's car seat in the backseat of the truck.

"No! Can you just shoot me now?"

"Absolutely not! It won't be as bad as you're thinking. Everyone is coming together to help you find a dress that will make you beautiful for your big day."

"I hope you're right, Jen."

They pulled into the dress shop. Sarah sighed and got out of the truck. She picked Jamie up and carried her into the shop. They started looking at flower girl dresses while they waited on everyone else to arrive.

"There are a lot of cute dresses here for your little flower girl! Did you have anything specific in mind?" the receptionist came up behind them and asked.

"I was hoping to have her dress match her mother's dress."

"You know, some brides have their flower girls' dresses match their wedding dresses."

"Well, I'm not like most brides. I haven't spent my entire life thinking about my wedding. Until three and a half months ago, I didn't think I was ever going to get married. I thought I was going to be single the rest of my life." Sarah laughed.

Sarah's mother, grandmother, sister-in-law and bridesmaid, Zoey, walked in the store. Sarah gave them each a hug. They continued looking at bridesmaid and flower girl dresses while they waited on Anna to arrive. Zoey and Jen both found their dresses.

"Hey, Sarah, my name is Sara-Beth. I am going to be your consultant today. Are you ready to get started?"

"Well, we wanted to wait for my future mother-in-law to arrive before starting."

"I don't want to be pushy, but if she doesn't show up soon, we'll have to cancel your appointment and you'll have to come back. We are booked up today, and we have a limited time for your appointment."

"I understand. Let's go ahead and get started then. I would say waiting an hour for Anna to arrive is long enough, especially since she isn't answering her phone or texts."

"Do you have any idea what style you want to wear?"

"I was thinking that an A-line might look best. However, I want to make sure that it has straps. I don't want the girls falling out."

Sara pulled three dresses and combined it with the two dresses that Violet picked out for Sarah to try on.

"Let's put you into one of the dresses your mother picked out first."

"Oh, boy! I can tell you already that I hate it." Sarah laughed.

Sarah stepped into the ball gown and put it on. She looked in the mirror. "I guess I don't hate it. It doesn't look horrible once it's on. However, I'm not in love with it either."

"Let's go show everyone and get their opinions."

Sarah walked out of the room and into the main lobby where everyone was waiting for her. She stepped up on the pedestal and turned around to face everyone.

"Oh, Sarah, this dress has to be the one! It is absolutely beautiful," Violet started clapping and jumped up from the couch to hug her.

"Sarah, what do you think about the dress?" Sara-Beth asked her, picking up on the fact that Sarah was uncomfortable in the dress.

"I don't think this is my dress."

Sarah gave the reasons she did and did not like the dress. She heard from the group who also agreed that this was not the right dress.

Anna came in as Sarah was walking to the dressing room. "That dress is u-g-l-y! Who picked that hideous dress out?"

Sara-Beth pulled out the next dress and helped Sarah into it. This dress was another ball gown with more beading on the top and straps. This time everyone was in agreement that this was not the right dress.

Sarah tried on five more dresses before finally putting her favorite dress on, each dress splitting the group more and more in their reactions. Anna became so mean and loud that the store owner came over from her own appointment.

"Ma'am, I'm going to have to ask you to leave if you can't be supportive in this process. Your future daughter-in-law asked you to be here to support her, and all you are doing is tearing her down. I honestly do not care if you approve of the wedding or not. You will either get on board with the dress experience, or I will ask you to leave."

"Who do you think you are speaking to me that way?"

"I own this store. That gives me the right to ask you to either get on board or leave."

As Sarah entered the dressing room, tears ran down her face. "Sarah, everything will be okay. I promise." Sara-Beth put her hand on Sarah's shoulder.

"I just can't believe that she is acting this way!"

"Take a minute, and we'll step into the last dress that you picked out."

Sarah stepped into the beaded A-line dress. She turned and faced herself in the mirror. The top had a straight neckline with wide-set straps to help keep her top supported. Lace appliques trailed from the bodice, past the slim waistband. Clear sequins were distributed throughout the top to subtly catch the light. Sara helped accentuate the waistband by using a floral sash that tied in the back. The back of the dress had a scoop back that laced up. The dress's train was a short eighteen-inch chapel train.

Sarah smiled immediately at the reflection staring back at her. "This is amazing! This is the dress!"

They walked back out to show the group. Within seconds, Sarah was in tears and running back to the dressing room.

"That dress is h-i-d-e-o-u-s, hideous," Anna said. "I still don't see what Alex sees in you. My son will never marry you, especially not in this dress."

"You are ridiculous. That dress clearly makes Sarah very happy. It accentuates her curves in all the right places and just makes her shine," Jen said.

"I agree with Jen," Zoey seconded.

"You two will say anything to make Sarah happy. This dress is absolutely *ugly*," Anna said.

"Anna, you need to quit being a bitch. Sarah didn't have to invite you to this appointment, but she did." Jen stood up and walked toward Anna. Zoey reached up and stopped her.

Sarah undressed and got back into her clothes. She sat in the corner of the dressing room, head in her hands, tears streaming down her face. Just then, there was a knock on the door.

"Hey, chipmunk, it's Grams, can I come in?" Grandma Hailey quietly asked.

Sara-Beth opened the door, and Hailey entered. She sat down next to Sarah and pulled her into a hug. "Chipmunk, what are you thinking?"

"I-I can't. I don't even know."

"Do you love the dress? Will wearing this dress make you happy?"

"Yes, I love it, Grams. I felt absolutely amazing in the dress. It's the best I've ever felt looking at myself."

"Then don't let Anna ruin this moment for you."

Hailey turned to Sara-Beth. "What do we need to do to get the seamstress in here to take her measurements and get this dress ordered?"

Sarah and Hailey walked out of the dressing room arm in arm, Sarah smiling. Hailey found the owner and paid for the dress.

"Grams, you didn't have to pay for the dress. I planned to do that," Sarah whispered in her grandmother's ear.

"Nonsense, chipmunk. Your Pops and I couldn't wait for the day you got married. I want your day to be everything you want it to be. You work very hard, and you deserve to have the day of your dreams. We want to do what we can to help contribute to making this be the night of your dreams."

Jen and Jamie got matching dresses. They both got royal-blue dresses, taffeta and tulle halter V-necks. At the top of the taffeta and tulle was a ribbon with a bow. Zoey got the same dress in silver.

The wedding was going to be in the Spring City Botanical Gardens. The ceremony would take place in the garden's atrium: exposed brick walls with a glass-enclosed cathedral ceiling and a large terrace overlooking the botanical gardens. This area comfortably sat up to two hundred wedding guests. Sarah was most excited about taking advantage of the different gazebos around the property to take pictures both indoors and outdoors. Alex and Sarah loved the fact that the botanical gardens had their own catering.

They selected the luncheon buffet to start around one after a twelve o'clock wedding. The buffet included finger foods, sandwiches, and vegetables.

Alex and Sarah picked out a three-tiered heart-shaped cake. Each layer was a different flavor of cake: the bottom layer was vanilla, middle tier was chocolate, and the top tier was a marble cake. The three tiers were covered in white fondant. Each layer had hearts intricately placed around the cake, and each tier was wrapped with a small silver ribbon.

The closer the wedding came, the more excited Sarah got about spending the rest of her life with Alex. They selected the corsages and boutonnieres for each member of their bridal party: silver roses for Jen, Jamie, and Abe and royal-blue roses for Zoey and Michael. Alex's boutonniere had both a royal blue and a silver rose in it; Sarah's arrangement consisted of six royal blue and six silver roses.

The morning of the wedding finally arrived. Sarah was so nervous that she could not sleep the night before. She went ahead and got out bed at four thirty and put her running clothes on. Without realizing it, Sarah ran just shy of ten miles in an hour.

She got home and showered. She made herself breakfast and then waited until six thirty before she headed to the salon to meet her mother, Grams, Jen, Jamie, and Zoey. Once all the women arrived, the salon owner set each of them up with their own stylist for the day. They started with pedicures before they moved on to manicures. Once their nails were all done, they each got their hair done. Sarah had her nails painted in a French manicure, while the other women got their nails painted in silver and royal blue. Sarah asked to have her hair put up in a sectioned twist style, her side pieces pulled back where they were twisted and woven together to create a braid while the rest of her hair was curled to accentuate her wavy blond hair.

Once they finished with their hair and makeup, the women got into a beautiful white stretch limo. They rode over to the botanical gardens to finish getting dressed and start taking pictures.

Sarah got into her dress, which fit her body perfectly. "Oh, Chipmunk, you look absolutely stunning!" she heard her Grams say.

"Aw, you're just saying that, Grams." Sarah blushed.

They moved out to the gardens and met the photographer. Alex, his groomsmen, and his family met them in the gardens. Alex came up behind Sarah and grabbed her waist, gently spinning her around. "God, you look beautiful," he whispered in her ear.

"You clean up pretty good yourself!" She smiled as she reached up and kissed him.

As they stood there looking at each other, Anna came up beside them. "Alex, don't you look handsome! You are too handsome to be marrying someone as plain and simple as this girl. You know it's not too late for you to walk away from this girl and go find yourself a super model, right?"

Sarah looked at Alex, tears forming in the corners of her eyes.

"Mom, don't start that shit today. I'm getting married today, whether you like it or not. If you don't like it, you're welcome to leave at any time."

"I'm just saying, you don't have to marry this girl. There are way better-looking women out there who would love to have you."

He looked down at Sarah and smiled. "I don't want any other woman. I want Sarah."

Just then, the photographer came over and broke up the discussion. "Hey, do you guys mind coming over with the rest of the group? We would like to get pictures started and wanted to break everyone up into groups to get started."

Alex and Sarah walked to where everyone else was standing, waited for instructions. "Okay, there are three other photographers here from our company, Berenthal Photography. We are going to break off in a couple of different groups to start. Alex... Sarah, do you have your running shoes on today?"

They looked at each other and smiled before replying in unison, "Nope!"

"Well, you two are going to be rushing between groups all morning. We're going to first start out with individual families before we do group photos. Sarah, you and your family will follow me over to the flower gazebo. Alex, you and your family will follow Olivia over to the wood gazebo. Bridesmaids, groomsmen, and little flower girl, I need you guys to go over to the wooden bridge with Billy. Sarah and Alex will be there shortly. If we have any family in the wedding party, please go to the family shots first and then move over to the wooden bridge."

Alex and Sarah started at the wood gazebo with Alex's parents. After they finished with Alex's family, they moved over to the flower gazebo to take photos with Sarah's family. They took pictures with her whole family, just her and her parents, her and her grandparents, and then they took the same pictures with Alex. Once they finished the family pictures, they took shots with the bridal party on the bridge.

Sarah and Alex then moved with David into the open meadow to take the couple's pictures. They took multiple different poses together in the meadow before moving back to the bridge overlooking the creek.

When they finished taking pictures, they split up before the ceremony. Sarah went back to the room designated for her, the bridesmaids, and her family. Alex went back to the room across from the ceremony space to be with his family and Michael.

"I need to go use the restroom. I'll be back shortly," Alex said as he left his waiting room. When he got to the restroom, he bumped into Olivia, who was just coming out of the women's restroom.

He looked her up and down. She wore a tight little sleeveless black dress that came just above her knees. She was a foot shorter than him. He quickly noticed her toned physique. She looked at him and smiled, daring him to take her right then and there.

Alex grabbed her by the wrist and pulled her into the men's room with him. He locked the door behind him. "Is this what you wanted?" he asked her as he grabbed her and put her up on the bathroom counter.

"You read my mind!" she laughed, biting at his ear. "Aren't you getting married today? What would the bride say if she knew you were in here with me?"

"I am getting married today, and I don't really care what she would say right now. How about we get you out of that little dress now?"

Alex finished and got himself straightened back out. He went back into his waiting room. Abe looked at him and shook his head.

"What are you shaking your head for, little brother?" Alex asked him.

Abe leaned in close so that only Alex could hear. "I knew you were a dirty shit bag, but I didn't think you would dip so low to do this to Sarah on your wedding day. You are disgusting, you know that, right?"

"I don't know what you're talking about, little brother."

"Don't play dumb with me. I see it all over your face that you just screwed the photographer's daughter in the bathroom. I should go tell Sarah what you just did."

"I wouldn't do that if I were you!"

"Or what? What are you going to do to me if I did tell her?"

"Don't test me!"

"You don't scare me, Alex. She deserves to know that you're a fucking dog. You aren't ever going to change, are you?"

Just then Pastor Dan came in and got their attention. "Is everyone ready to take their places? Please, come and follow me."

They got up to follow. Alex went to the front of the ceremony space, while Abe and their father, Arthur, walked Anna down the aisle to her seat, then Abe took his position next to Alex and Michael at the front, in between the two men. Hunter and Harrison escorted Violet and Hailey down the aisle to their seats.

Jen and Zoey walked down the aisle, followed by Jamie, who threw out her little royal-blue and silver rose petals on the ground. Sarah and Matthew got into place. Once Jamie reached her mother, the music queued for everyone to stand and look at Sarah and Matthew. She looked up at her father, and he reassuringly smiled back at her before taking a step toward where Alex stood waiting.

The ceremony was short but beautiful. Alex and Sarah recited vows that Pastor Dan had prepared for them. Sarah was pleasantly surprised when Anna did not speak up when Pastor Dan asked if anyone was opposed to the joining of her to Alex.

"You may kiss your bride," Pastor Dan turned to Alex as he said these words.

Sarah smiled at Alex, who leaned close to her, giving her a quick peck on the lips.

They walked together to the back of the ceremony space to the applause of everyone there to witness their union. They thanked everyone for joining them as they left the ceremony and headed toward the tables where lunch was being served.

Sarah and Alex grabbed their sandwiches and quickly ate before getting up to mingle with their guests. Sarah lost track of Alex after a few minutes when she got tied up with some of her family. She looked around for him but couldn't find him.

Alex did not want to visit with Sarah's family, so he wandered off a little ways. He bumped into one of the servers. He followed her to the empty coat room and had sex with her. When he finished, he went to the restroom to clean up before rejoining Sarah.

The couple cut their cake, being nice enough not to smash cake all over each other. They listened to the toasts and enjoyed their afternoon together. The event wound down around two thirty as guests left to go home. They helped pack all their gifts up into the van that Violet and Matthew rented to take back for gift opening the following morning at the city park.

Once gifts were packed up, the couple left to go to their hotel. Alex's Camaro windows were painted with *Just Married* and old cans tied to the exhaust and bumper. Alex pulled Sarah tight to his body and kissed her forehead. "Can you believe that you are now Mrs. Jackson-Clark?

"I think I need you to pinch me to make sure this is all real and not just a fairy tale," she laughed.

They got in the car and drove to the hotel. Alex had rose petals leading from the doorway to the bed. On either side of the bed, he had a vase of blue roses and another with silver roses. Sarah was in awe. She could not believe how romantic her husband was and reached up to kiss him.

He carried her to the bed and made love to her. "Sarah, you have made me the happiest man in the world!"

"Ditto," she replied, staring up at the ceiling, smiling to herself.

Things Change

Sarah and Alex went on their honeymoon to the Turks and Caicos Islands. They spent the week exploring the island and all that it had to offer. They enjoyed spending nights walking hand in hand down the beach after dinner and swimming in the ocean after breakfast. They stayed in the room when they weren't out on the beach.

Sarah was unaware that every night they had dinner and drinks that Alex dropped sleeping pills into her drink. This caused her to become overly tired. As soon as she was asleep, Alex snuck out of the room. He met another girl every night down by the pool and then joined her in her room.

When they got back to Spring City, Alex moved most of his stuff into Sarah's apartment. He left his bed behind in the apartment, along with the bedroom furniture that came in the furnished apartment he shared with Michael and Jason.

Alex came home at the end of his first day back to work and gave Sarah the news: "Hey, Sarah, I know that we just got settled here in the apartment, but I need to let you know that I'm being relocated to Bay Hollow, Florida. I have to report to my new command at the beginning of next month."

"Say what? When did you find all this out?"

"I've known it was a possibility for a while now, I just didn't think it would ever happen."

"Why didn't you tell me? We just signed a new twelve-month lease on our apartment when you moved in here with me. What are we going to do about that?"

"Well, good news is that the manager has to let us out of our lease. I just have to show him my military orders."

"Why didn't you tell me this was a possibility?"

"I didn't want to burden you with the news while you were stressing over your classes and the wedding. It's no big deal, Sarah."

"No big deal! You're asking me to pack up and move and be at peace about it."

"Sarah, it's really no big deal. You're going to need to get used to it now that we're married."

"Believe, me, Alex, I understand how this works. You forget that I am a military brat. But you also forget that I know how much advance notice they give you before the move. I'm upset by the fact that you didn't tell me there was a chance we would be moving so soon after we got married. I would have had time to adjust to the idea of moving away so quickly after the wedding."

"Sarah, you're being a baby about this. It's really no big deal. I have to report for training first, so it'll be a couple of months before I'll be ready for you to move down with me anyways."

"No, I'm not, but *whatever*."

"Don't be that way."

"Don't be what way, Alex? We're supposed to be in this together. This is a partnership. We're supposed to communicate with each other. This isn't where we hide secrets from each other." She turned and started to walk away into the living room.

He made a grab for her wrist. "Sarah. Sarah, don't be that way."

"I'm fine, just let go of me."

Alex left the next week to start his training in Florida. Sarah went to visit to get the lay of the land. They put in their request for base housing but also found an apartment just off the base that would work. While Alex went to class, Sarah learned her way around town and the base.

Sarah applied to the Bay Hollow University before visiting the area. Once there, she stopped in the office and looked at programs. Sarah made an appointment for the following day to meet with an advisor about the classes she needed to take to finish her bachelor of arts in American history.

Alex took leave to help Sarah pack and move from Spring City to Bay Hollow. They got settled into their one-bedroom apartment off base. Sarah had the apartment unpacked and put away within a day of their stuff arriving.

Once she started her classes, things changed between Sarah and Alex. Alex stayed out late after training and drank with the guys; he continued to sleep around with the girls in the bar. He started questioning everything Sarah did and everyone she talked to, and he started mentally abusing her and separating her from her family and friends.

The year came to a close, and Sarah felt alone, separated from everyone she loved and cared about. Class was all she had so Sarah made the best of her new life. She ended the semester with her 4.0 GPA intact.

Sarah and Alex went back to Spring City and Mountain City for Christmas. Sarah enjoyed the time with her family. She got to meet her baby nephew, Brennen Jackson, for the first time. She hugged and kissed on him every chance she got.

"You would be a great mommy, Sarah," Brenda said as she told her.

"Yeah, but that's not what I want. I don't want to ever have kids of my own."

"Why not?" Brenda asked.

"I just don't want kids."

Alex walked in during their conversation. "You really don't want any kids, Sarah?"

"No, I don't."

"Wow, how did I not know that?" he asked.

"You never asked. I didn't think you wanted kids either."

"I don't know, maybe someday."

They spent Christmas Eve with Sarah's family and got up early Christmas morning to drive to Mountain City to spend Christmas night with Alex's family.

When they arrived, Anna greeted Sarah, "I can't believe you two are still married. What does he see in you?"

Arthur walked out and grabbed Sarah into a hug. "Hey, kiddo, Merry Christmas."

"Merry Christmas, Arthur."

They got their stuff settled in Alex's bedroom and then came back down to help finish fixing dinner and do their gift exchange. Anna kept picking at Sarah all night, telling her that she was no good and would never amount to anything.

"Sarah, I can't believe how u-g-l-y, *ugly* you are! You'll never amount to anything!"

Tired of the harassment from her mother-in-law, Sarah walked outside the house; she sat on the stoop and put her head in her hands.

Arthur walked out and sat beside her. "Hey, kiddo. How are things in your world?"

"Do you really care?"

"I am nothing like Anna, Sarah. I see so much potential in you. I see how you've changed Alex for the better, kiddo. He's a better person when he's with you."

"Anna sure doesn't think so. She seems determined to tear me down every chance she gets."

They continued to talk on the stoop for another hour, Sarah filling Arthur in on her classes and how she was settling in with her new surroundings. Arthur filled her in on how his health was going. She found out sitting there with him that his cancer had spread to the rest of his body; he stopped chemotherapy to have more quality time with his family and that this was most likely the last holiday he would spend with his family.

Sarah did not sleep well that night. She was the most uncomfortable she had ever been in someone else's house. She tossed and turned, watching the door and listening for other noises outside in the hallway.

"Hey, babe, you okay?" Alex asked after a couple hours of her tossing and turning.

"I'm fine," she said as she rolled over.

The next morning, Sarah woke before Alex. She struggled with the thought of staying in bed until he woke, but she decided she needed to pee and get a cup of coffee. She walked down to the kitchen; Anna sat alone at the table.

"There she is, Ms. America," Anna started in immediately.

"Where can I find the coffee cups?"

"Who says I am going to share my coffee with the likes of you?"

Sarah turned to walk back to the bedroom to get dressed. Anna spoke up as she got to the doorway between the kitchen and the dining room, "Get back in here. The coffee cups are in the cabinet just to the right of the sink."

"Thank you." Sarah grabbed a cup and made a cup of black coffee.

She turned to walk back upstairs. Anna stopped her. "What kind of woman doesn't want to have kids?"

"Excuse me?" Sarah asked as she turned back around to face Anna.

"Oh, you heard me. What kind of woman doesn't want kids? Do you think you're too good to have kids with my son?"

"It has nothing to do with being too good for anyone. I have my reason for not wanting children, and I don't feel like I need to share that with anyone, especially you."

"What is that supposed to mean, Sarah? Do you think you're too good for me now too?"

Sarah stood up, washed her cup in the sink, and then walked toward the stairs. "Sarah, you aren't going to amount to anything. You're a lazy piece of shit who thinks she's better than everyone else."

When Sarah made it to the guest bedroom, she grabbed her running clothes and put them on. She went back downstairs and immediately out the door.

"Where are you running off to?" she heard as she started down the street. "How about you just don't come back? Alex would be better off without you."

Sarah wanted to run fast to forget everything that happened, but she decided she needed to run at a leisurely pace. She really wanted to forget about everything and just go home to Spring City, but she knew she could not go back home. As she reached the street, she heard a familiar voice beside her, "Where are you headed off to?"

She turned to Alex. "I'm headed out for a bit. I can't stay here, and as you know, this is my release, or have you forgotten that?"

"Sarah, what's wrong?"

"What isn't wrong is the better question."

She turned down the sidewalk and set off. She heard steps pace hers. They ran in silence. She listened as he struggled to control his breathing. "Think about it, eight counts in and eight counts out. Use your footsteps as your count."

They ran out six miles out and six miles back. She immediately did her cooldown walk when they made it back to the house and then went up to shower. Alex joined her in the shower. He gently turned her to face him. "What are you doing?" she asked as she swatted his hand away.

"I thought I would make love to my wife here in the shower. Let's put a little baby in that belly of yours."

She pushed his hands off her body. "What the fuck?"

"I want kids, Sarah. I want to put a baby in your belly."

"I don't want kids, Alex."

"Why?"

"I just don't. I've never wanted kids, and no amount of talking to me will change my mind. Why does your mother know about this?"

"It just slipped out, I'm sorry."

"Whatever. I think you enjoy her tormenting me and putting me down. That's the only reason you would tell her something private like this." She turned back away from him.

"Sarah! It's not like that."

"How is it not, Alex? How is it not? I think you enjoy your mother being rude and nasty to me. I now know where you get it from."

They finished out their trip and flew back to Bay Hollow from Spring City. The rest of the year was uneventful. Sarah enjoyed her time off from classes and found a new position at the coffee shop next to the university, thankful for a distraction to help pass the time while Alex worked.

To help Sarah cope with the changes to her life, she adopted three scraggly little female kittens. They were about eight weeks old when she found them on the street, separated from their momma, who had been captured in a humane trap by the Animal Rescue League. She brought them home and cleaned them up. Each kitten got a unique name based on her personality: her little gray-and-white kitten she named Pretty Baby because she liked to look at herself in the mirror, her little white-and-orange kitten she named Squirrel Bait because she did not have a long attention span and everything distracted her, and last but not least, her little gray tiger-striped kitten she named Artemis, after the goddess of the hunt, named for her love of stalking everyone and everything.

Chapter 3

2010

Arthur's Funeral

Alex and Sarah rang in the New Year with Alex's new friends on base. Sarah sat off by herself for the majority of the night while Alex mingled with everyone else. She was thankful when the night ended and they went home.

Sarah found out that her parents were moving away from Grams and Pops at the end of January. Her father took a new promotion, and they quickly found a new place in Mountain City. They kept the house in Spring City for her brother Harrison to live in and take care of.

Sarah's parents were not the only family on the move. Alex's parents moved to Spring City to be closer to the hospital and Arthur's doctors. They found a cute little two-bedroom bungalow to live in. Abe moved with them to help his mother take care of his father.

Alex flew back and forth to Spring City from Bay Hollow every other weekend to spend time with his family and left Sarah behind. Sarah enjoyed the quiet time. She was not under constant scrutiny while Alex was away. She could do what she want, eat what she wanted, and read or watch whatever she wanted without constantly having to explain what she was doing and why she was doing it. She did not have to worry about arguing or fighting with him because she knew while he was away that he would not call her.

When he got home, all that changed. He started going through her cell phone to see who she called or texted. He started to argue with her when she would leave the house to go on her runs or go to the base gym to work out.

"Give me your phone."

"Why?"

"Just do it!"

"What do you think you're gonna find?

"I know you're cheating on me. I'm going to find out who you're cheating with."

"That's going to be hard to do!"

"Oh, yeah? Why's that?"

"Because I'm not cheating on you!"

"Just give me your phone!"

She threw her phone at him. "Here, good luck finding anything!"

Sarah woke to the phone ringing on Wednesday morning, March 3. "Hello?" she answered.

"Sarah, where's Alex?" she heard Abe's shaky voice on the other end of the line.

"He's already at work. What's going on, Abe?"

"I need to talk to him, and he isn't answering his cell phone right now."

"What's going on?"

Abe started crying. "Sarah, they just took Dad to the ER. He was unresponsive."

"Where are you, Abe?"

"I'm at the hospital, waiting on the doctors to come in and tell us what is going on. Sarah, I don't know what is going to happen when he dies."

"Abe, I can't tell you that everything will be okay, because we both know that it won't be. What I can tell you is that Alex and I will be there for you as soon as we can be."

"O-okay, Sarah, I need someone to be here to help me with my mother. I can't handle her alone."

Sarah called over to Alex's command and asked to speak with Alex. A young female voice answered the phone, "Military Police, Senior Airman Taylor speaking, how may I help you, sir or ma'am?"

"Yes, ma'am, may I speak with Technical Sergeant Clark, please?"

"May I ask the nature of this call, please, ma'am?"

"Senior Airman, this is Technical Sergeant Clark's wife, Sarah. I need to speak with him about his father."

Alex came to the phone. "Technical Sergeant Clark speaking. How may I assist you, sir or ma'am?"

"Hey, Alex, it's me."

"Sarah, you know better than to call me here! Why are you calling?"

"Alex, I wouldn't call if it wasn't important, you know that. They put your dad in the hospital this morning, and the doctors don't think he's going to make it past the weekend. I told Abe that we would be there as soon as possible to sit with him and your mother."

"Okay, thank you for the information. I need to go now. I'll call you back shortly."

Sarah hung up the phone and started picking out their clothes for the trip back to Spring City. She grabbed enough clothes to be back for a week, not knowing how many days she should truly pack for. She grabbed Alex's dress uniform and a suit for him to have options. She then grabbed her dress suit and packed everything in the garment bag.

Alex called twenty minutes later. "Sarah, I need you to pack a bag with our clothes. I'll be home in twenty."

"Already on it. The garment bag is packed with suits and your uniform, and I packed a bag with a week's worth of clothing."

"Wow, I can't believe you worked that fast."

"Alex, I may not like your mother, but I do care about your father. Family is important."

Alex got home, and they drove to the airport. They made it through security without any problems and flew back to Spring City. The flight took them about three hours once they were in the air. Matthew met them at the airport to pick them up.

"Hey, chipmunk, how are you guys holding up?"

Alex spoke up, "We're fine. Can you just take us to the hospital please without a lot of talking? I don't feel like talking, and neither does Sarah."

Matthew looked at Sarah and back to Alex. "You don't need to look at her. I asked you nicely to just take us to the airport without a lot of talking. If you can't handle that task, then we can get a taxi."

"No, I can handle it just fine, Alex."

"Do you want me to pick you up later?"

"We'll find our own way back," Alex replied.

Matthew drove them to the hospital and let them out at the main doors of the hospital. They walked inside and found Abe waiting for them just inside the doors. Abe grabbed Alex and Sarah into a hug. "Thanks for coming."

"Of course."

They walked together until they made it to Arthur's room in the oncology wing. Anna was out in the waiting room, crying. "Alex, you made it," she said as she jumped up and hugged him.

"Of course I made it, Mom. Where else would I be?"

Anna caught Sarah out of the corner of her eye. "Why did you bring that bitch here with you?"

"Mom, don't start right now, okay?"

"What way is that? I don't want the bitch here. She's not my family."

"Well, like it or not, she is my family, Mom. She stays," Alex replied.

Abe motioned for Alex and Sarah to follow him through the waiting room into Arthur's room. When they arrived, Abe took the chair in the corner of the room while Alex and Sarah took the chairs closest to the bed. Sarah reached out and grabbed Arthur's hand in hers.

The doctors were in the room next door. The nurse came in and asked one of them to go grab Anna before the doctors arrived in the room. Abe ran out and grabbed her.

Anna and Abe came back in the room just ahead of the doctors. "What happened to my husband? Why is he unresponsive?"

"Well, your husband's body can't handle the cancer anymore. Ma'am, I don't expect him to make it past the next twenty-four hours. I would recommend you start preparing yourselves for the end."

Anna left the room again crying. Alex walked out with her. Sarah and Abe stayed in the room with Arthur. Sarah listened as Abe told stories of his favorite childhood memories with his father. She got an insight into Alex's childhood and had a better understanding of why he was the way he was: Anna was abusive both mentally and physically; Arthur was the one who picked up the pieces. Abe loved his father very much and was scared of his mother. He knew that he would have to stay behind and pick up the pieces after Arthur died; Anna would fall apart, and Alex had his own life now away from home so it would all fall on his hands.

Three days later on Saturday, March 6, Arthur slipped away in his sleep. Sarah was left alone with him in the room while Anna, Abe, and Alex all had breakfast in the hotel cafeteria. Sarah called Alex's cell phone to let him know.

Sarah went back to the hotel while the Clarks went down to the funeral home and made the funeral arrangements. Arthur was laid to rest on the following Wednesday morning. The church altar was lined with flower arrangements from family and friends. The sanctuary, which seated two hundred people comfortably, was half full.

After the service, they got in the funeral home's Lincoln Town Car and rode out to the cemetery. Sarah got in the car last. "Where the fuck do you think you're going?" Anna turned on Sarah when she sat down.

Sarah turned around and looked over to Alex for help. "Mom, not here, not now."

"I'll do whatever I want whenever I want. What are you going to do to stop me?"

"Mom, stop!" Abe begged her.

They rode the rest of the way to the cemetery in silence. When they arrived, Sarah sat on the opposite side of the tent as Anna. Alex sat with his mother; Sarah expected that he would and was slightly hurt but not all that surprised. Abe joined Sarah at the end of the graveside ceremony.

"Abe, you should probably not be over here with me if you don't want any problems after we leave."

"Sarah, I'm sorry that my mom is so cruel to you."

"It is what it is. Now, you should probably go before you get yourself into trouble."

Alex and Dana

Sarah and Alex left Spring City on Friday, March 12, and went back to Bay Hollow. Sarah quickly settled back into her life: spending time between school, working out, and work.

Sarah worked most weekends at the coffee shop. She received an unexpected visitor to the coffee shop a little over a week after they got back home.

"Welcome to the university coffee shop, how may I help you?" Sarah asked as she turned around greeted her only customer of the afternoon.

"Is your name Sarah Clark?" the young woman asked her.

Sarah looked the girl up and down. The girl was Sarah's height and approximately her same weight. She also had blond hair and looked to be about a year or two older than Sarah.

"Well, it's actually Sarah Jackson-Clark, but yes, I'm Sarah Clark, how can I help you?"

"Can we go somewhere and talk?"

"I'm the only person on shift right now so I can't really leave the counter. What can I help you with?"

"Is there any way you can close up shop for a little bit? I really need to talk to you, but I don't want anyone to walk in on us."

"I can't close up right now, but if you aren't in a hurry, my coworker comes in to start her shift in about forty-five minutes. I can go on break at that point, in which case you'll have about thirty minutes where we can talk."

"I'll wait. This is important."

The girl ordered a cappuccino and went to a corner booth to wait. About forty minutes and another cappuccino later, Sarah joined this mystery girl in the corner booth.

"Okay, I'm here, what is it that I can help you with?"

"Sarah, my name is Dana Taylor. I need to talk to you about something super important."

"I kind of figured that when you chose to stay versus leaving. What is so important that you came to my place of employment to talk to me?"

"Sarah, I don't know how to tell you…"

"How about you just come right out with it? That's where one usually starts."

"Sarah, this is not easy to say, and it won't be easy for you to hear." Dana paused. She put her head in her hands, and she looked back up with tears in her blue eyes. "I'm so sorry! I need you to know how sorry I am, but you need to know."

"What is it that I need to know, Dana?"

"Sarah, I unknowingly had an affair with your husband."

"What do you mean you unknowingly had an affair with my husband?"

"Sarah, Alex came on to me at the office about nine months ago, when I joined the Military Police unit. We started sleeping together that day. When I asked him if he was involved, he told me that he wasn't. He told me that he was single."

"The ring didn't give it away?"

"Sarah, he doesn't wear his ring at the office. I swear that I didn't know. He was very forward when he came on to me."

"I see. You just couldn't resist, huh?"

"I found him very flattering, Sarah. I've never had a man treat me the way that Alex did, and I got caught up in the whirlwind that is Alex."

"Well, how did you find out about me?"

"Sarah, after about two months of sleeping with Alex, I found out I was pregnant. He seemed like he was ecstatic to be a father. When I lost the baby a month later, he quickly lost interest in me. It broke my heart. I was completely in love with him, and he broke my heart. I was completely in love with your husband." Dana started crying again.

"I still didn't know you existed at that time," she continued. "I found out about you when you called the office that day to tell Alex about his father. I was the Senior Airman who answered the phone that day. I knew I needed to talk to you once I found out about you. I knew you needed to know the truth. I'm not the only that Alex had an affair with."

Sarah sat there and just stared through Dana in complete shock. "Y-you must think I'm so dumb," she finally stammered.

"No, Sarah, I don't think you're dumb. I think we've both been played."

"Thank you for telling me, Dana. I know this couldn't have been easy for you."

Dana got up and gave Sarah a hug. "It wasn't, but I thought you needed to know."

Dana left, and Sarah went back to finish out the rest of her shift. When she finished, she drove home to the apartment. Alex was not home yet, so she took a shower and got into her oversized T-shirt and running shorts. She opened up her Civil War history book and tried to concentrate on the words written there on the page but found that she could not concentrate; her thoughts kept circling back to her conversation with Dana as tears slid down her cheeks: *What are you going to do now, Sarah? How could you not know that he was cheating on you? How could you be so fucking dumb? How could you let a man like this into your life? How are you going to exit this marriage now? Oh my god, Sarah, you are so fucking dumb! You said, 'Till death do us part.' You can't go back on that promise you made to God in front of all of your family and friends. You need to just leave... He clearly doesn't love you if he's cheating on you! I'm sure God and your family will forgive you if you divorce Alex. You can't just walk away!*

He's become abusive... Walk away while you still can!

Alex finally arrived home an hour later and interrupted her thoughts. Sarah stayed in the room until he came in to find her.

"Why didn't you come out to greet me?"

"Oh, I didn't hear you come in," she lied to him. "Where were you?"

"I was at work," he replied.

"You should have been off over two hours ago."

"I got caught up with the paperwork after a domestic violence arrest."

"Oh, is that why you smell like another woman and have lipstick on your neck?"

"I don't know what you're talking about, Sarah. You must be imagining things."

"Is that so?"

He walked over to the bed and sat down on the edge next to her. "Sarah, the woman I saved from her husband hugged me and kissed me on the neck as a way to thank me for taking her husband to jail. It was no big deal, and you shouldn't make a big deal out of it."

"How long have you been cheating on me, Alex?"

"What are you talking about?"

"Alex, you're not a dumb man. I know that you've been cheating on me, and I want to know how long it's been going on. I deserve that much."

"What exactly do you think you deserve, Sarah?"

"Honesty. I've been nothing but honest with you since the day we met. I trusted you, and now you've ruined that trust. I think it's time we end this now."

He turned and looked her in the eyes. "What did you just say?"

"I think it's time we just walk away from each other. You've lost my trust, and I don't think that we can ever rebuild that. Better to walk away now while we still can. I need to build a new life, one where I can trust the people in it, one where I don't have to wonder about my partner being faithful, one where I am not constantly being emotionally and mentally abused on a daily basis."

"What are you talking about, Sarah?"

"You know exactly what I'm talking about, Alex."

She got up and moved toward the closet. She started picking clothes off their hangers and shoving them into a bag. She grabbed her toiletries and walked everything out to her truck. She came back in and grabbed the bags she used to transport her cats in and put them in their bags.

Alex got up off the bed and walked toward Sarah. He gently put his hands on her shoulders and turned her around to face him. "Sarah, don't do this. We can make it work."

"How can we?" she asked.

"I love you, Sarah. I want to make this work. I promise not to ever cheat again!" Alex broke down in tears.

"Alex, I don't know if that's enough."

"Can you at least try? Sarah, I'm not ready to end this. I know we can have a bright future together."

"How can we?"

"Sarah, let me make this right. Please give me another chance."

"I'll give you another chance, but you have to promise to stop cheating. The first time I think anything is hinky, I will pack up and I won't give you another chance. I need you to be serious about this."

Justin Stewart

The rest of the semester went by fairly quickly for Sarah; she ended up on the dean's list for her 4.0 grade point average. When Sarah was not at school, she was at work. Alex came home immediately after work every night, and he laid off with the mental and emotional abuse.

Sarah received a knock on the door on the afternoon of Monday, May 24.

"Hello?" she asked as she opened the door. Once the door was fully opened, she saw two Air Force officers dressed in their dress uniforms standing on the front stoop.

"Mrs. Clark?"

"Yes, where is Alex?" she asked as they stood there. She felt her body start shaking, her legs became Jell-O, and her knees felt as though they were about to collapse on her.

"Mrs. Clark, your husband was shot apprehending a suspect earlier this afternoon. The doctors aren't sure if he is going to pull through. We need you to come with us to the hospital."

Sarah locked the door and got in the back of the car. She felt the tears stream down her face as she rode in silence.

Sarah, how did you get to this point? I guess you do still love him after all, huh? Why though? Why do you love him? He doesn't deserve your love! Oh my god, Sarah, what are you going to do if he really does die? He can't die! I'm not ready for him to die. He has to pull through.

I'm not ready to be a widow. I need him to survive this and pull through.

Sarah got to the hospital. When she arrived, the nurses escorted her to the surgical waiting room. The doctor came in the waiting room about an hour later.

"Hi, Sarah, my name is Lieutenant Colonel Simon Russo. I just came from the operating room with Alex."

"How is he, sir?" she asked as tears flowed from her eyes involuntarily.

"Mrs. Clark, your husband was shot in the chest. Fortunately, for him, the bullets missed any vital organs, and we were able to recover the bullets. Alex's road to recovery will be long and painful. He will be released from the Air Force under a medical discharge. As long as he takes it easy, he should be back to himself with no long-term complications." He paused for a moment before asking, "What questions do you have for me?"

"How long before I can go in and see him?" she asked.

"You can go see him right now, Sarah. Follow me."

Sarah followed the colonel into the hallway and down the corridor. They turned left down the first corridor, and then went down about a hundred yards before turning right down the next hallway. They walked another two hundred yards before finally coming to the hallway with Alex's room.

Colonel Russo pointed to the last room on the right of the hallway. "Your husband is in here. He is still heavily sedated so it may take a while for him to wake up."

Sarah sat down beside Alex and took his hand in hers. She gently caressed it and talked to him about all her hopes and dreams as well as all of her fears; she felt safe doing this while he was sedated.

When Alex woke and was coherent, Sarah called Anna to let her and Abe know what happened. Anna advised her that she would not come to Bay Hollow to visit him in the hospital.

A couple of days after Alex woke, they came to the decision to move back to Spring City to be closer to their families once he was fully discharged from the Air Force. They discussed the idea that Sarah would attempt to join the Marine Corps as an officer.

Sarah and Alex made the move back to Spring City in the middle of June. They quickly found a one-bedroom apartment to move into, not far from her Grams and Pops. They settled in, and Sarah went back to work at the Caffeine Blending House with Oliver and started the summer semester back at the university. Everything seemed to be getting back to normal; Sarah started to feel like she could maybe trust him again.

Alex quickly betrayed this trust. He took the first opportunity he could to cheat on Sarah while she was in class. He brought a woman into their bed. Sarah immediately smelled the girl's perfume the minute she opened the door and walked into the apartment. She decided not to say anything even though she wanted to. She went inside and put her stuff down in the corner. She went to the stove and started cooking dinner. She contemplated her revenge and how she would get back at him for making her hurt so badly, betraying her trust again.

Sarah went to her women's history class for the first day of class from eight until ten in the morning. She was immediately drawn to a fellow student two rows in front of her who was her age, tall, dark, and handsome. She got his name, Justin Stewart, from roll call. He had brown hair, a tan complexion, and brown eyes. She became easily distracted and could not keep her eyes off him during the first part of the class; she started daydreaming and losing focus on the discussion, like a little schoolgirl. She could not be sure, but she thought she caught him staring at her after she countered his argument in the class discussion.

The following morning, Justin moved to the seat next to Sarah. He started passing her notes, agreeing or disagreeing with what their classmates were saying. The notes eventually started getting off topic with him telling her that he would like to take her out to lunch sometime and asking if she would enjoy that. Sarah was ashamed to admit it, but she enjoyed this attention from Justin.

At the end of the first week of class, Sarah found herself agreeing to meet Justin for lunch off campus in between her classes. She drove over to the university diner, right off campus. She parked and went in, grabbing a table for two. Justin arrived moments behind her and quickly joined her at the table.

Their conversation started out around the class and quickly moved on to other topics, more personal topics. Justin admitted that he just ended a two-year relationship with his girlfriend and that he was on the rebound. Sarah advised Justin that she was married, and they talked a little bit about Alex.

Sarah looked at her watch and got up to leave. Justin stood up as well and walked her out to her truck. He opened her door for her, and without thinking, she reached over and kissed him. She was pleasantly surprised when he did not reject her and instead kissed her back.

She got in her truck and went back to campus for her next class, completely distracted by the events at lunch. She struggled to stay tuned in to the discussion and eventually just gave in to the daydreaming.

Alex and Sarah spent Independence Day with her family: Grams and Pops, her parents, and her brothers with their wives and girlfriends. The group started the day watching the Spring City Parade. Sarah always enjoyed watching the different floats go by; it made her feel like a kid again. After the parade finished up, Sarah and her family went back to Hailey and Tanner's place. They ate sandwiches and picnic foods for lunch.

They played games in the yard and enjoyed each other's company. Sarah helped Brenda put Brennen down for his nap while the boys all played corn hole and drank beer.

"Oh my goodness, Brenda, he's getting so big! Where has the last year gone?"

"I ask myself that every day. I can't believe he's walking and starting to talk. He's come such a long way considering the start he had and that the doctors didn't think he'd make it."

"He sure looks like his daddy and his uncle Harrison."

"Yes, he does. He's going to be a handsome little man when he gets older."

"Have you and Hunter talked about having more kids?"

"Yeah, we've thought about it. We want to wait a little bit though. Maybe when Brennen is three, we'll try again. What about you and Alex? When are you guys going to have kids of your own?"

"If I have my way...never. If Alex has his way, we'd already be pregnant."

"Really, Sarah? Doesn't that cause problems between the two of you?"

"There are other things causing problems, but that isn't an issue right now."

"You know I'm always here for you if you ever need to talk."

"Thanks, Brenda. I'm good though."

Abe and Anna came over to join the festivities at Grams and Pops' place. They came over around four thirty to enjoy Pops' barbeque. Abe joined the guys out in the yard playing corn hole while Anna joined Violet and Grams in the kitchen.

After they ate, they packed up in the cars and went to the local baseball diamond to watch the city's fireworks display. The display started just after it got dark and lasted an hour. Sarah could not believe all the different combinations of the fireworks; it was beautiful and terrifying all at the same time.

Sarah woke up the next morning and left for class. She found her normal seat in the auditorium and sat down about fifteen minutes before class started. A couple of minutes later, Justin came in and sat next to her.

"Hey, wanna talk about what happened last week?"

"What about it?" she teased.

"I don't normally let girls kiss and run. Wanna finish what we started?"

"What are you talking about?"

Just then the research associate came in the room, completely ignoring the fact that they were in the back of the room. She grabbed a dry erase marker and wrote *Class cancelled—enjoy another day to celebrate our country's independence*!

"Well, ain't that a bitch. I could have stayed in bed longer," Justin said.

"I hear that," Sarah said.

"Well, we could always finish what we started last week."

She contemplated for a minute and then gave in to her desires. "Sure, we gotta go back to your place though. My husband is home so we can't go there."

She followed Justin out to the car and hopped in with him. She went back to his place with him. As soon as they walked in the door, he pulled her into a passionate kiss. They quickly stripped out of their clothes. Justin picked Sarah up and carried her into the bedroom where they slept together.

"Damn, that was fun!" he said.

"Was it now?"

"You don't agree?"

"It was fun! Thanks for making my day!"

"No, you made my day, Sarah."

Sarah put her clothes back on and left Justin's place. She went back to campus and prepped for her next class. She could not stop thinking about what just happened with mixed feelings of excitement and guilt.

What did you just do! That was fun but very wrong. I can't believe you just did that. I can't believe how sexy Justin is! I would love to do that again! Sarah…you are a whore. Alex cheated on you multiple times, so you are justified in what you just did with Justin. You aren't that naive, are you? You know better, Sarah! Two wrongs do not make a right!

She tried to put the feelings of guilt behind her, but she could not. She knew that she had to tell Alex but was not sure how she was going to tell him. She decided to tell him the next morning.

They woke up around nine. She tossed and turned all night; she could not sleep. She felt so guilty for what happened the day before. They got dressed and then went out to the living room. As they sat down on the couch, she decided she needed to tell Alex.

"Hey, I need to tell you something, but I don't know how to tell you."

Alex turned to face her. "Oh, this is gonna be good, isn't it, Sarah?"

"Alex, I don't know how else to tell you, so I'm just going to come right out and tell you... I cheated on you yesterday."

"You *what?*"

"I had an affair. I cheated on you. I needed to get this off my chest and to tell you."

"How could you cheat on me?"

"The same way you continue cheating on me, even after you promised to stop cheating on me."

"I should leave you over this, Sarah."

"Go ahead, it'll make my life so much better if you did," she replied.

She got up and went back into the bedroom, ending the argument.

Staff Sergeant Miller

Sarah went online and signed up for information on joining the Marine Corps Officer's Candidate program, keeping her word to Alex that she would attempt to join. Alex watched as she entered her information into the Marine Corps' website.

"You better try your hardest to make this work, Sarah. Otherwise, I will walk right out the door."

"Are you threatening me, Alex?"

Two days later, Sarah received a phone call from a number that she did not recognize.

"Hello?"

"May I speak with Sarah Jackson-Clark?" the deep raspy male voice with a mild Southern drawl asked.

"This is she. How may I help you?"

"Do you mind if I call you Sarah?"

"That is fine, how may I help you?"

"Sarah, my name is Staff Sergeant [SSgt.] Ethan Miller. I am calling you on behalf of the United States Marine Corps. I received your request for more information on joining the Marine Corps Officers' Candidate Program. Do you have time to speak right now?"

"I do."

"Sarah, I need to ask you a series of questions before we set an appointment to meet. You good with that?"

"Sure, fire away."

"How old are you?"

"I just turned twenty-one. My birthday was the same day that I entered my information online."

"Happy belated birthday."

"Thank you!"

"Are you married or single?"

"I'm married, have been for about a year and a half, but that was already in my bio you got from the Marine Corps website."

"Is your husband aware that you went online and signed up to join the Marine Corps?"

"Yes, in fact, it was at his request that I did so."

"Are you telling me that you don't want to join or that you are being forced to join?"

"No, that's not what I'm saying, Staff Sergeant."

"What are you saying?"

"Staff Sergeant, I signed up to join for many different reasons. I grew up as a Marine Corps brat for the first seventeen years of my life. My father served twenty-seven years in the Corps. He retired as a sergeant major of the First Marine Division. My brothers chose not to follow in my father's footsteps, so this is my chance to do so."

"What is the highest level of education you have?"

"I am currently finishing up my senior year. I will have my BA in December. I plan to start my master of art's degree in August, unless I make it through OCS."

"Have you ever done drugs?"

"No."

"It's okay, you can be honest. The Marine Corps no longer disqualifies candidates because they tried marijuana, so if you've experimented, please make sure you're honest with me."

"Staff Sergeant, I have never done drugs, outside of taking prescription medications prescribed by a doctor."

"It's okay for you to be honest with me. I won't judge you, I promise."

"Staff Sergeant, I was what they called a Goody Two-shoes in school. I'm twenty-one and have never even tried alcohol."

"Are you serious?"

"Yep, never had a drink a day in my life."

"You are a Goody Two-shoes. Can you come in Friday morning to meet?"

"What time?"

"How does eighty thirty sound?"

"Roger that. See you Friday morning at eight thirty."

"Please make sure you bring your husband, if he can come with you."

Sarah hung up the phone smiling. She could not believe this man she did not know, had never met, had her smiling like a little schoolgirl. She could not wait to meet him.

Sarah and Alex got up Friday morning and got ready to go meet with Staff Sergeant Miller. "Are you ready for this?"

"I am."

They drove over to the address that Staff Sergeant Miller gave her. They walked up the exposed staircase to the second deck. They followed the walkway to the right and came to the office suit that she wrote down. She opened the door and they walked inside.

Once they opened the door, Sarah looked inside to see a bare space. There was a large outer room with two desks set up but no one manning them. She noticed that each desk had a giant dry erase board hanging from the wall behind it. There were two red leather couches set up in a U shape and a television set up close to the front of the office. At the back of the big room, Sarah saw two doors, obviously leading to two small office spaces. There were Marine Corps recruiting posters scattered throughout the space. A pull-up bar sat in the corner just outside of the offices. Sarah also noticed a pull-up machine next to the bar and a sit-up bench in the corner behind the desk. There was a hallway that led to the utility area behind the office space.

They were immediately greeted by Staff Sergeant Miller. Sarah was immediately drawn to his roguishly handsome looks. He stood a foot taller than her. He had chestnut brown hair, kept in the typical Marine Corps high and tight, and he had these gray eyes that cut right through her. His nose looked as though it had been broken at some point, possibly multiple times. Sarah was surprised to see that he came to the meeting in his civilian attire versus wearing his uniform of the day.

He reached his hand out toward her. "Hi, you must be Sarah?"

"That's right, and this is my husband, Alex."

Ethan quickly shook Sarah's hand and then extended it to Alex. "Hi, Alex, I'm SSgt. Ethan Miller. How are you guys doing?"

Alex answered, "We're fine. Can we just get this over with?"

Ethan walked toward the offices in the back of the space and opened the door in the corner. "Please follow me." He pulled two chairs out of the other office for Alex and Sarah to sit in and then sat in his own chair behind the desk.

They walked through all the physical fitness standards that Sarah would be required to meet to be accepted into the Officers' Candidate School (OCS). Sarah was confident that she could master physical fitness test (PFT), which included a timed three-mile run, a hundred crunches in two minutes or under, and a ninety-second flex arm hang without any problems. What concerned her was the combat fitness test (CFT). This test would require that Sarah be able to sprint 880 yards in less than three and a half minutes in full battle dress uniform, lift a thirty-pound ammunition can over her head from shoulder height sixty times in two minutes or under, and then perform a maneuver-under-fire event, which included a timed three-hundred-yard shuttle run in which she would be paired up with other Marines her size and required to perform a series of combat-related tasks in under three minutes.

They looked through different military occupational specialty codes to see which jobs interested Sarah. She looked at the specialties but could not make a decision right away. She could not decide on trying to become a pilot, go into admin, or try to get into intelligence. Sarah scheduled a time to come in and run a practice PFT with Staff Sergeant Miller for the following week and then Alex and Sarah left the office.

Sarah prepared herself for her practice PFT. She thought she had this aced and went into the office a little cocky. Staff Sergeant Miller greeted her at the door.

"Welcome back, Sarah. You ready for this?"

"This should be a cakewalk. Yeah, I'm ready."

SSgt. Miller walked her over to the pull-up bar. "We'll start out over here with your flex arm hang. Have you ever done a hang before?"

"No, I have only ever done pull ups."

"How many can you do?"

"I don't know, I've never really stopped to count."

"Well, then the flex arm hang should be fairly easy for you, once you get the concept of it. When you do your pull-ups, do you have someone assist you or do you do jump up on your own?"

"My father taught me to start from a full arm extension and then pull my body weight up. He always treated me just like one of the boys and expected that I keep up. I wasn't allowed to fall behind just because I was a girl."

"This should be easy then. Go ahead and hop up there on the bar. Once your chin is above the bar, I will start the time. You have to stay up for no less than seventy seconds. Your time stops once your arms lock out, so you don't have to keep your chin above the bar the entire seventy seconds.

You have your choice of grips. You can grip the bar with your hands shoulder width apart and place your palms either facing away from you or your palms facing toward you or you can hold your arms closer together, palms facing you."

"All right, let's do this then," she said as she walked up to the bar. "Do you mind giving me a boost? This bar is up a bit higher than I'm used to."

He put his hands together and cupped them so that she could step into them with one foot. She did so, and he gently helped her up so that she could reach the bar. As her body got close to Staff Sergeant Miller's body, she felt a rush come across her. She was embarrassed and hoped that her face did not flush the way she felt it had.

Once Sarah had the bar, she pulled her way up to where her chin was about four inches over the top. She steadied herself and tried to think of other things to help keep her focused. She did not realize that she slipped down until the Staff Sergeant called time. "Forty-five seconds."

"What? You've got to be joking. It felt like I was up there *forever!*"

"That's the difference between pull-ups and the flex arm hang. You can easily lose yourself in the hang and lose track of time. Next time you run this, you need to count to yourself; it will help you ensure that you stay up long enough. Like your pull-ups, you need to practice, practice, practice.

"Let's move on to your crunches. How many crunches can you do in two minutes?"

"I can get a hundred in less than two minutes."

"Alright, there's the mat, put it down. Now, I need you to lie back and put your knees up. I'm going to sit on your feet and put my arms through the V in your legs."

"You forget that I had to do these regularly with my dad growing up. I know that we only have to do a crunch, but I can do a hundred sit-ups in the two-minute time frame."

She sat down on the mat and then lay back. Staff Sergeant Miller sat down on her feet; she was surprised at how light he felt when he sat down. He grabbed her legs tight with his arms. She again felt a rush come over her at his touch.

She was easily distracted and missed him asking her, "Are you ready?"

He gave her a minute before asking again. "Earth to Sarah, you ready?" he asked her, grabbing the stopwatch in his right hand.

"Ready when you are."

"Time starts when you raise yourself up off the floor. If you need to take a break, you can take a break."

She lifted herself up and put her elbows to her knees and then moved back down, her shoulder blades hit the mat. She continued this, counting every full rep once her shoulder blades touched. "Ninety-eighty, ninety-nine, one hundred," she said as she finished out her set.

"Damn, Sarah! You weren't lying when you said you could do a hundred sit-ups in less than two minutes."

"How fast did I finish?"

"You completed those in a minute fifty-five."

"Damn, I got slow. Guess I need to really work on that more when I go to the gym."

"Ready for the run?"

"You going to run with me or wait for me at the stopping point?"

"Depends, how fast are you going to run your three miles?"

"Well, I can either run six-minute miles or I can run seven-minute miles. Which pace are you going to keep up with me at?"

"Can you really keep a six-minute pace through all three miles?"

"Staff Sergeant, I can keep a six-minute pace for over ten miles. I've been practicing this since I could walk. My father always wanted me to be able to keep up with the boys and outshine them. That's why he insisted I do full sit-ups and not just crunches. That's also why he insisted that I do pull-ups and not the flex arm hang."

"Well, knowing that, I think I'll hold off running with you today. I'll stay here and wait for you to finish."

"Chicken," she teased him.

"Promise you this, by the time you leave for OCS, I'll be back to running three six-minute miles with you."

"I'll give you three months."

They walked across the street to the track. Sarah quickly stretched her legs and then walked to the starting line. "I'm ready whenever you are," she turned around and told him.

She put one foot in front of the other. She counted out the laps. She was rounded the last quarter mile and gave it everything she had. When she hit the finish line, she collapsed.

"*Damn, girl!* You weren't lying that you could finish in six-minute miles. Do you know what your final time was?"

"No clue, but from the look on your face, I would say it was pretty good."

"How does fifteen minutes and thirty seconds sound?"

"Dang, that is pretty good. I had no clue."

"I think it was that push for the last quarter mile. You gave it your all, left nothing on the track. How did you build your endurance to run that pace for so long?"

"I didn't have a choice. My father expected the best from me. He treated me like the men and women in his unit. I ran every day. He gave me conditioning drills to run and I ran them. On the weekends, I ran in long-distance races with my brothers."

"Would you be willing to run these conditioning drills with the rest of the candidates?

"Sure...how much of a discrepancy are we talking about?"

"What do you mean?"

"What are our fastest and slowest run times?

"We have a couple of male candidates who are running seven- to seven-and-a-half-minute miles. Our female candidates are running around eight-and-a-half to nine-minute miles. I want to make sure that every candidate knows that it is possible to increase his or her time by thirty to sixty seconds."

"I will work with you to help condition these men and women. They are going to need to be willing to work hard and practice every day."

"Anyone who doesn't will be released from the program."

Sarah went home and cleaned up from her morning with Staff Sergeant Miller. She planned to meet Jen for lunch before going to her afternoon class. She met Jen at the Spring City Burger & Steak House.

"Hey, Sarah," Jen said as they walked in the door together.

"Hey, Jen, long time no see. Whatcha been up to?"

"Oh, you know, just trying to handle a two-month-old baby and a four-year-old. I'm lucky if I get to sleep or take a shower. What have you been up to?"

"Oh, you know, just living life."

Jen and Sarah enjoyed lunch together. Sarah told Jen about her meeting with Staff Sergeant Miller. Jen wanted all the juicy details. She asked multiple times for Sarah to describe Ethan to her. As she described Ethan to Jen, she realized just how attracted she was to him. She found it very easy to talk to Jen about the problems going on in her marriage, classes, and OCS journey.

"What else is going on in your life?" Jen asked.

"Oh, you know, not much. Found out recently that my husband is a cheating dog."

"Oh?"

"He had a girlfriend he got pregnant while we were in Bay Hollow. He got so bold as to have sex with another woman in my bed while I was in class. I have no clue how long he's actually been cheating on me."

"What a dog! Why are you still with him?"

"Some days I don't know, but other days it's because I can't break my vows to stay married."

"You're a fool, Sarah. He's not going to change."

"Well, I had a one-night stand and cheated on Alex... I guess you should say one-day stand. I felt like I needed to get my own revenge."

"Ooh, do tell!"

"It was a mistake. He was a classmate. It was way better than sex with Alex, but it can't ever happen again!"

"Why do you say that?"

"It just can't! I'm still married, and I can't go around cheating on my husband. Let's change topics: what's going on with you and Jordan? How's my little princess, Jamie, and her little sister, Julia?

Jen told Sarah all about how Jamie was doing, and they talked about motherhood. They laughed, and they teased each other. As they left the restaurant, Sarah realized how much she missed her conversations with Jen.

As promised, Sarah went into the OCS office every morning at seven and ran with the different candidates who were willing to get up that early and put the time in. Staff Sergeant Miller ran with the group every morning. Sarah looked forward to seeing him and hated when he was out of the office. She found very herself attracted to the staff sergeant and even fantasized what it would be like to have sex with him or, better yet, marry a man like him.

Sarah woke up during finals and knew this was it. She went in and took her tests. The information came easy to her, and she finished all four finals in record time.

She woke up the morning of the ceremony and looked at her grades online; she was excited and scared to death at the same time. She closed her eyes and waited for the site to load.

What am I going to do if I don't keep my 4.0? My parents will be devastated. Fuck, I'll be devastated! I can't stand not knowing. I can only imagine what Alex will say if I don't come out ahead on this. I don't think I can stand his ridicule if I don't come out with the 4.0.

She opened her eyes a minute later and noticed the screen loaded. She looked at each class individually… Each class showed an A next to her final grades.

Hell yeah, way to go! Nice work, Sarah!

Sarah picked up her robes and her cords from the university bookstore the morning of the ceremony. Her parents came to town for the festivities, and she met everyone at Pops and Grams' house for the graduation celebration the following afternoon. She went over to the recruiting office to run with the other candidates.

"Hey, Sarah, don't you graduate tonight?" Staff Sergeant asked her.

"I sure do."

"Well, what are you doing here?"

"I needed to get some pent-up energy out, so here I am."

"Everything okay?"

"Yeah, everything is fine. Thanks for asking."

"Well, kick ass tonight at your ceremony! You having a party tomorrow?"

"Yep, over at my Pops and Grams' place. You're welcome to come join us for some great food and games. Festivities start around one."

"I might just take you up on that!" He smiled at her.

Sarah met her family at Pops and Grams' place around three. Alex met them there around four. They helped Sarah get dressed in her robes and then drove over to the university's basketball arena to get lined up with the rest of the December graduates.

She sat in her seat alphabetically in between Christy Clark and Warren Clark. Sarah got bored with the speeches before they started handing out diplomas. She smiled when she heard her name called; her family clapped loudly for her. As she walked back to her seat, she saw Staff Sergeant Miller sitting in the aisle. He gave her a high five as she worked her way back to her seat.

They celebrated with dinner at Zippy's after the ceremony, and then everyone went home. The next morning, Sarah got up and went over to help Grams and her mother decorate the house and garage.

Chapter 4

2011

OCS

The New Year started off very strong for Sarah. She started her master's program and continued working with Staff Sergeant Miller, helping potential candidates improve their fitness through specified fitness programs for each candidate.

"Hey, Sarah, wanna hear some good news?" Ethan greeted her when she walked in the office door that early March morning.

"Sure, what's the news?"

"Well, you've been accepted for OCS. You ship out in sixty days."

"Are you for real?" she asked as she stared at him.

"Dead serious! Did you really doubt yourself?"

"Well, you never really know," she said as she shrugged her shoulders.

"Sarah, you were a shoo-in. You were the only one who didn't see it."

"Just because I can run a PFT and my father is a retired first sergeant, doesn't mean that the commanding officer [CO] wants to take a chance on me. I could see why he might actually not want to take a chance."

"Well, Sarah, you're the only one who doubted yourself. I knew from the minute you walked in the door that you were going to make it."

Sarah held her excitement back because she knew not everyone coming through the door would get the same news she received. She worked out with the group, taking them on a fartlek run mixed with some different circuit workouts for six miles. They ran for about two hours before they all left the office.

Sarah left and went home to shower and change clothes. When she walked in the door, Alex was standing there in his jogging suit.

"Where have you been?" he asked her.

"Out running with the OCS candidates on our morning run. You look like you're ready to hit the streets. You wanna go get a light run in and stretch out your muscles?" she asked him.

"What makes you think I want to go run?"

"Nothing in particular. I just thought I would ask while I'm still in my running gear."

They stretched together and walked outside to the end of the parking lot. "Hey, I got good news today."

"Oh, yeah, what's that?" he asked, a hint of sarcasm in his tone.

"Staff Sergeant Miller advised me that I will be receiving orders soon to ship out to Quantico in May."

"Okay."

She was hurt by Alex's reaction, or lack thereof. She could not let him see this because she knew he would feed on this and would antagonize her and make her feel unworthy. They jogged the rest of their two miles in silence. When they got back to the apartment, Sarah showered and went to class.

Sarah worked hard between her classes to finish her work early to make sure she could spend the last two weeks before her departure date without classes consuming her. Sarah left the Thursday after finals for Quantico.

The morning she left for Virginia, she woke up early. She felt a mixture of emotions—excitement, fear, and anxiety. She was excited to go try her hand at becoming a Marine and following in her father's footsteps; she was fearful of what could happen with her marriage, and she was anxious about failing at the Officer's Candidate School and having to come back to face her family and, worse off, Alex. She knew he would not let her live it down if she did fail and come back before the end of the ten weeks.

Her parents met her at the apartment and hugged her. "Chipmunk, you can do this. There will be times you want to give up and quit, but just remember why you are there and then dig deep. No matter what happens just know that I am proud of you!" her father whispered in her ear.

"Thanks, Dad!"

Alex drove her to the airport where she met the other six candidates who were leaving with her and their families. Staff Sergeant Miller and Captain James Butterfield met the group.

"Okay, the staff sergeant and I will be flying out to Quantico tomorrow to join you guys. However, we will have limited contact with you. There will be other candidates who will still be coming in to Quantico through Saturday night. At some point either tomorrow afternoon or Saturday morning, you will go pick up your gear. Does everyone have their five hundred dollars to pay for all your essentials?"

He waited for everyone to nod and then moved on, "At some point on Sunday, you will run your PFT. Some classes have done this first thing in the morning and other classes have gone to get their uniforms and boots as well as going through medical before running the PFT. Every commanding officer is different in how they like to handle this. Any questions?"

Everyone shook their heads no. The captain and staff sergeant took each candidate aside for a quick pep talk. Before the captain could grab Sarah, Staff Sergeant Miller took her aside. "Okay, Sarah, this is your time to shine. You know that you can master the PFT, and you will do well in your CFT. You need to remember to stay out of your own head. You can do this!"

"Thank you, Staff Sergeant," she replied back to him. He handed her the folder with all the paperwork she needed once she got off the plane and to the bus. It had her official military orders and all her other medical paperwork.

The Staff Sergeant moved on to the next candidate, leaving Sarah alone with Alex. "Are you sure you're going to be okay for the next ten weeks while I'm gone?" she asked him.

"I'll be fine." He smiled and gave her a hug. She tensed in his grip because she was not prepared for the hug. "Sarah, if there is anyone who can go through ten weeks of Marine Corps boot camp for officers and come out a success story, I know it is you. I know I haven't told you lately, but I am proud of you."

She did not know how to respond; she wondered who replaced her husband with this alien standing there in front of her. "Thank you, Alex."

Sarah got on the plane, followed by everyone else. As the only female of the group, she sat by herself, a couple rows ahead of the males. She stared out the window, the panic creeping up deep into her thoughts:

What are you doing, Sarah? What makes you think you can do this? You won't amount to anything. Even if you do succeed at this, do you think that your husband will be there waiting for you? Are you sure you're making the right decision? Your counselor didn't seem to think so—he thought this could damage your already failing marriage even more than it already is. Although, would that be a bad thing? Aren't you tired of being cheated on? Wouldn't you like to be with a real man, someone who will treat you right?

The plane landed at Reagan International Airport. She waited for everyone else to exit before they went to the baggage carousel. They collected their bags and met the bus driver waiting to pick them up.

The first couple of days went exactly as Captain Butterfield told them it would. They sat in a big auditorium doing nothing but staying quiet, reading the manual they were given, and drinking salt-laden water.

They were fed lunch and dinner in the auditorium. The food was good, but Sarah could not get over how much salt was in it; she was used to a lot of salt from the way her mother prepared food for her father growing up, but this was really loaded with salt.

A group of staff sergeants came into the auditorium after lunch and called out roll call. When a person answered, they were assigned a letter A through D. She was assigned the letter C.

After dinner, the group picked up their stuff and followed the enlisted Marines assigned to babysit the group outside the auditorium. Directions were given to the group to line up in formation based on the letters each individual was assigned earlier in the day. Sarah moved into the middle of the formation to avoid sticking out. Once everyone was accounted for in roll call again, she followed a female corporal and sergeant back to the barracks.

When they walked in the corridor to the barracks, Sarah felt like she was moving back in time. The walls were concrete with no paint on them. The bedroom she was assigned to had metal framed bunk beds on both sides of the room with a walkway big enough for four people to pass through comfortably. She counted twenty-five sets of beds on each side of the room, totaling a hundred beds in the room. At the base of each set of bunk beds was a small footlocker.

As they moved into the room, Sarah saw the gap in the inside wall that led into the female showers, toilets, and sinks. She noticed that there were about twenty-five toilet stalls, all missing their doors, hitting her that she was no longer in Colorado living her normal life. Her life was about to flip upside down on her.

At the end of each room, there was a stairwell that led to other floors (decks) of the building. The second deck was occupied only by women. The north wing of the building housed three male units: Alpha, Beta, and Delta, who occupied all three decks.

After the brief tour, the sergeant said, "Listen up, ladies, lights will go out in thirty minutes so find a bed. This will be your bed while you're here at OCS. You do not have to go to bed when lights go out, but there will be absolutely no talking out here. You are free to stay up as late as you would like, just remember, five comes awfully early when you haven't slept. You will not be late to roll call in the morning, do you understand me?"

"Yes, Sergeant," all twenty-five women shouted in unison, snapping to attention.

Sarah put her sea bag under the bottom bunk about a quarter of the way into the room. She knew that she did not want to be closest to the drill instructor, but she also did not want to be right outside the bathroom either. She took off her shoes and tucked them under the bed. She used the restroom, brushed her teeth, and then went back out to her bed. She fluffed the pillow and then lay down.

"Aren't you going to get under the covers?" the girl next to her asked, looking at Sarah in confusion for lying on top of her bedding. Sarah looked at her before responding. She was Sarah's height, weighed about 150. This girl had jet black hair cut into a pixie cut.

"Absolutely not!"

"Wait, why?"

"Because, I don't want to have to remake the bed any more times than I have to. It is currently made the way a military bed should look. I guarantee most of the girls in here did not look at the way the sheet and blanket were folded before ripping it up to lay down. You will find at five that the oh-so-friendly sergeant who is currently lounging around in that office down there will not be so pleasant in the morning while she waits for beds to be made properly."

"What do you mean?" She looked a little frightened by Sarah's response.

"Well, the Marine Corps likes their barracks to look a certain way at all times. They want everything to be perfect, nothing out of place. Racks need to be uniform and tightly pulled, no bunching in the middle of the mattress. If it isn't perfect, you could potentially spend a lot of time putting your bed together until its right."

"Oh. But I don't want to freeze, so I need to sleep under the blanket."

"You'll get really good at making that bed every morning before we leave for formation then."

Sarah rolled over and closed her eyes, wondering what Alex was currently up to.

As soon as he left the airport, Alex went over to his old apartment and found his old roommates, Michael and Jason. "Hey, you guys wanna go out?"

"Dude, did you forget that we still work for a living?" Jason asked.

"We just finished up with our PT for the morning, now we're headed back to actually police the base."

"Oh, I got it. Guess I'll have to go out by myself then and see what kind of trouble I can get into."

He left and went to the Spring City Diner where he hit on the waitress. He stuck around the diner until the end of her shift and then followed her back to her parents' house where they had sex together. They watched television for a little while together before he left and went back home. He took a nap and then went out to the bar to find his favorite cocktail waitress.

Sarah woke the next morning at four forty-five to use the head. She took a quick shower and got dressed before the majority of the girls got up and started moving around. Things turned sour fairly quickly when a fight broke out in the shower between two of the girls in the group. Sarah stepped in to sort things out.

"You bitch!" Sarah heard from the girl she heard referred to as Morley; her name was Shari Morley. Morley was a tall, lanky girl with short chestnut brown hair.

"Who are you calling bitch, bitch?" Karly Evans screamed at Shari. Evans was about three inches shorter than Morley; she was very muscular with blond hair.

"Whoa, what's going on, ladies?" Sarah asked as she stepped in the shower room.

"That bitch just shoved me," Evans responded. "She's lucky that I have self-control, or I would kick her fucking ass right here right now."

"She stole my towel and won't give it back," Morley responded.

"Okay, ladies, we are all adults in here. Grab a towel and get dried off, then get into your clothes. If the drill instructors come in here, we will all pay for you two."

"What do you care?" Morley yelled at her.

"I don't want anyone getting kicked out before OCS even starts. Just get dressed and out on the deck before you get busted by the sergeant."

The girls went ahead and got dressed, ignoring each other. They were all ready when the sergeant came out and instructed them to get down to the parking lot to formation. They went through roll call before marching off to the chow hall. Sarah sat off by herself once she got through the breakfast line. After clearing her tray, she went back out to the parade deck to wait for everyone else to finish up their breakfasts.

Instead of going back to the auditorium, they marched to the supply store. The store had everything lined up with enough space for one person to walk through single file. They were advised to shuffle through the aisleways with side steps rather than facing front. Each compartment had a tag that stated how many of each object the candidate was required to take.

Once through the warehouse, candidates were expected to go back out to the parking lot to get information and wait. Another scuffle broke out between candidates Morley and Evans. Morley pushed Candidate Evans from behind when she got into formation. This sent Evans flying forward into the girl in the front row. Sarah shook her head but stayed out of the scuffle.

Once everyone paid for their items they marched back to the auditorium. The group was instructed to pull out the marking kits from their new bags of gear. As soon as everyone held up their kits, the staff NCOs showed everyone how to quietly mark their gear while they waited for lunch to arrive in the auditorium.

The chow hall brought lunch into the auditorium. Lunch consisted of goulash. The goulash was saltier than Sarah could tolerate, but she knew she had to eat it all if she did not want to put a target on her back with the drill instructors. She finished her goulash, green beans, and brownie. She took her empty tray to the clearing station. She got in line behind Morley.

"What the fuck, candidate? Did we not cook the chow to your satisfaction, candidate?" one of the male drill instructors yelled at her.

Morley kept walking forward to the trash can. "Stop walking, candidate!" Sarah saw the gunnery sergeant step in front of Morley, blocking her way, causing the rest of the line behind her to come to a dead stop.

"You were asked a question to which a response is required, candidate. I need an answer now," he yelled at her.

"Aye aye, sir."

"What is your answer, candidate? Are you too good to eat our chow, candidate?"

"No, sir."

"Then why didn't you eat your food, candidate?"

"It was too salty, sir."

"Oh, so you don't like it then, huh, candidate?" he taunted her.

"That's not what I said, sir."

"You're too good to eat what you're given?"

"No, sir!"

"Go back and eat the rest of your food, candidate."

Morley stood there defiantly staring at the gunny. "Are you deaf, candidate? Do I need to get you some Q-Tips to clean your ears out?"

"No, sir."

"Why are you still standing here, candidate? I told you to move it."

"Aye, Sir."

After Morley moved out of the way, the line moved forward. Sarah moved in front of the staff NCOs. "Good afternoon, sirs." She put her empty tray on the stack and walked outside.

New candidates joined the group later in the afternoon. They walked over to get their toiletries and the rest of the group started helping them mark their gear with names.

They ate dinner in the auditorium again and then marched back to the barracks. They were released to have some free time before lights out. Some of the women finished marking their gear while others wrote letters home. Sarah went into the shower to get freshened up before getting into her rack.

As she got dressed, she heard two familiar voices yelling at each other again. Sarah walked out of the head and found Morley and

Evans wrestling around in the middle of the deck, pulling each other's hair. She noticed that none of the other girls moved to help stop the fight.

"ENOUGH!" Sarah forcefully told both ladies. "Get up and act like adults. Stop acting like children."

The girls stopped immediately and looked up at her.

"What the fuck, Clark? Who the fuck do you think you are getting in the middle of this?" Morley turned on her, finger stuck out in Sarah's face. "This isn't any of your business, bitch!"

"I'm the only one who seems to be an adult here. Do you really want to be kicked out of OCS before you've had a chance to prove yourself?"

Morley moved closer to Sarah, hands balled up in fists. At that time, one of the girls knocked on the drill instructor's door. Sergeant Baker walked out of the drill instructor's room. She pulled Morley and Evans into the office. Before long, Sarah watched the two ladies come back out. Morley glared at Sarah and Evans before going into the shower.

Sarah hopped into her rack and fell asleep before lights went out. She woke up an hour before reveille to the sound of sudden movement. She looked up and saw Morley get out of her rack and move toward Evan's footlocker. Sarah watched without letting Morley know she was awake and watching. Morley took all of Evan's gear out of her footlocker and put it in the shower. Sarah heard the water start running. She quietly got up and knocked on the drill instructor's door.

"Enter."

Sarah gently opened the door and shut it behind her.

"What are you interrupting me for, candidate?"

"Ma'am, I just wanted to let you know that Morley is currently in the process of destroying Evans's property."

"Are you a tattletale, candidate?"

"No, ma'am."

"Thank you for the information. Now, go back and hit the rack. Say nothing to nobody," Staff Sergeant Crane told her.

Sarah went back to her rack and went back to sleep. About twenty minutes later, Sarah heard the door to the office open. She saw Staff Sergeant Crane walk down the deck into the head.

She came out two minutes later. "Wakey, wakey, ladies. Everyone out of your racks right now." She yelled across the deck, "Get up and get dressed then out on the parking lot. You've got ten minutes. Now MOVE, MOVE, MOVE!"

Sarah grabbed her toothbrush and quickly brushed her teeth. She dressed and ran down the stairs. Sarah got in formation and waited for everyone else to join her.

Staff Sergeant Crane came down after everyone was out of the barracks. "Ladies, I cannot believe how many issues we've already had with this group. I should just go to the CO and have you all sent home right now."

After breakfast, they marched to chow hall and then went back to the auditorium. Staff Sergeant Crane had the group wait until the other platoons joined them in the parking lot. Once everyone was in formation and roll call done, they marched to the auditorium. Once they were all seated and roll call done, the announcement was made that they were going to run their PFTs later in the afternoon, before evening chow.

"Candidates, due to some unforeseen circumstances, we had to change the plan for today. Instead of starting the morning out by splitting the group in two and sending one group to get uniforms and the other to go through medical for shots, we are going to sit silently in the auditorium until you are given further instructions. At that time, we will have you all go back to your barracks and change into your PT gear. We will then run your first PFT. This PFT will determine whether or not you are allowed to stay here at OCS or whether you will be leaving us before the first week is out. Do you understand?"

"Yes, sir," the group yelled out.

While they sat, all the female candidates were pulled out of the auditorium two or three at a time. After a couple of hours of waiting, Sarah heard: "Candidate Clark, front and center."

"Aye, ma'am." Sarah got up from her seat and moved to the front of the auditorium to where she came face to face with Gunnery Sergeant Shore.

"Follow me, candidate."

"Aye, ma'am." Sarah walked behind the gunnery sergeant into an office just outside of the auditorium.

As she walked in the room, she saw Colonel James McDougal sitting in the room. She came to attention, "Good morning, sir. Candidate Clark reporting to Commanding Officer Colonel McDougal as ordered."

"Sit, please."

"Aye, sir."

"Do you know why we are meeting, candidate?"

"Not entirely, sir," she replied. She had a good idea of what she was meeting with the CO for but wanted to make sure before she answered.

"Well, candidate, it has come to my attention that at least one candidate destroyed the property of another candidate. Do you know anything about this, Candidate Clark?"

"Yes, sir."

"What do you know, candidate?"

"Permission to speak freely, sir?"

"Go ahead, candidate," he said as he nodded.

"Well, sir, we have two candidates who have done nothing but fight with each other since they got here. I was startled this morning and woke to witness Candidate Morley take all of Candidate Evans's gear out of her footlocker. Once she had everything together, she walked into the shower room. I heard the water start running and then I heard her laughing from inside the shower."

"Did anyone else witness this happen?"

"I cannot be one hundred percent certain that anyone else witnessed this behavior, sir. I did not want to let on to Candidate Morley that I knew what she was doing because I did not want to start a fight with her."

"What did you do, candidate?"

"I woke Staff Sergeant Crane up and reported what I saw to her. I then went back to my rack and went back to sleep as instructed, sir."

"Have you witnessed any other misconduct?"

"Yes, sir."

"What have you witnessed, candidate?"

"I witnessed Candidates Morley and Evans fight on two different occasions, sir. I attempted to break up both fights to be able to avoid a situation like this where we would be called into your office to report the misconduct. The first fight started in the shower because Candidate Evans inadvertently used Candidate Morley's towel in the shower. I do not know what caused the second fight. I just broke it up when I got out of the shower."

"Is there anything else, candidate?"

"No, sir."

"Okay, thank you, candidate. You are under strict orders not to discuss your conversation with anyone once you leave this room. Do you understand, candidate?"

"Yes, sir."

"If you were to be caught talking about this with anyone, you will be dismissed from OCS immediately. Do you understand, candidate?"

"Yes, sir."

"You're dismissed, Candidate Clark."

Sarah stood up into attention before turning and leaving the room. She returned to the auditorium and took her seat. The next candidate was called out of the room.

Around three in the afternoon, everyone was ordered to go out and get into formation. They marched back to the barracks where they changed into their PT gear. Sarah could not wait to do some physical activity after doing nothing but sitting around for the last two days.

Once dressed, all the candidates marched out to the physical training field. The men moved over to the opposite side of the field, and the women stayed closest to the barracks. Sarah stood in formation awaiting instruction.

"You'll all need to break up into groups and stand next to the pull-up bars. Once everyone is in groups, the first candidate in line will be assisted with getting up on the bar. Once your chin is above the bar, time will begin. Time will stop once your arms lock out or once you've reached seventy seconds. Does everyone understand?"

"Yes, ma'am," they all yelled in unison.

Sarah managed to end up in the middle of her group. She patiently waited her turn, watching as the majority of the other candidates came down before their seventy seconds and watched as the drill instructors wrote down their results.

Sarah stepped under the pull-up bar when it was her turn. "Name?" asked the corporal standing on the opposite side of the pull-up bar holding the clipboard with the list of names on it.

"Candidate Clark, ma'am."

"You ready, Clark?"

"Yes, ma'am."

"Candidate, move over here next to Candidate Clark. Cup your hands together so that Candidate Clark can step into it. You will then lift her up to the bar. Understood?"

"Yes, ma'am," the candidate responded.

Sarah looked at the height of the bar; it was within her reach if she were to jump and grab the bar. "Ma'am, this candidate would like to know if it is okay for this candidate to jump up and grab the bar without assistance?"

"Are you sure you can grab the bar, candidate?"

"Yes, ma'am."

"Okay, Candidate, if you are confident you can grab the bar without assistance, you may proceed."

Sarah took a deep breath and let it out slowly. She then jumped up and easily caught the bar with her hands. She pulled herself up into a chin up and waited to hear the sound that time had begun. As she held herself above the bar, she slowly started counting to seventy. She knew that time would be called before she got there herself. As she got to the count of fifty-five, she started very slowly allowing her chin to drop below the bar. When she counted sixty-two, she heard, "Time. You can drop now, candidate."

"Aye, ma'am."

She waited for the rest of the candidates to finish their flex arm hang. Once everyone finished, they all moved to the center of the field. "Now, we will break off into partners. One candidate will lie on her back while the other candidate moves into position to hold her partner's legs steady. Break up into partners and decide who will go first and who will go last. Do you understand?"

"Yes, ma'am," they yelled out in unison.

Sarah paired up with a girl she saw only one other time. "Do you mind if I go first?" the girl asked Sarah.

"Sure, that's fine," Sarah responded.

"I just want to get this done and over with. I'm so nervous about this."

"Don't be nervous. Just do your best and don't give up. You'll do great, candidate."

"How can you be so sure?" she asked Sarah.

"Well, you can either fail or perform. I have faith that you will perform, even if you don't have faith in yourself."

"No one has ever said that to me before."

"Well, you wouldn't be here if you couldn't pass the requirements to get here, right?"

"True!"

"If you did it once, you can do it again."

Just then, Sarah heard the instructions to get ready to start. Her partner lay down flat on her back with her arms folded across her chest, her knees drawn up into a triangle. Sarah sat down on her feet and tucked her arms in behind the back of the girl's legs. "This okay or too tight?" Sarah asked her.

"No, that's perfect."

Time started, and Sarah started counting the girl's crunches. The girl struggled after she hit fifty crunches. She lay back on the ground and stopped.

"Don't stop now, you're halfway there. You still have at least a minute to get those last fifty. Don't give up and get sent home! You have it in you to finish this out."

The girl grunted and started again; this time the crunches came a little slower. Time was called, and all candidates stopped trying to get more.

"Nice job! You ended up with eighty-five crunches in two minutes. What was your highest before you came?"

"Seventy-five crunches... This isn't my strongest area of the PFT," she replied back to Sarah as they switched positions.

"*Nice!* That's awesome, candidate. How did you do on your flex arm hang?"

"I was able to hang on the bar for sixty-five seconds before my arms gave out. Before I came here, I was able to get to seventy seconds twice but typically stayed around sixty-five seconds."

"That's still good!"

The same instructions that were given to the first candidates were given to the second candidates now lining the ground waiting for time to begin. Sarah lay back and waited. Once it was time to begin, she focused on her breathing like her father taught her.

Sarah hit a hundred before the two minutes time was called. "Damn, girl!" her partner exclaimed. "That was amazing. How did you do that?"

"Lots of practice over the years. My father is a former sergeant major, and he insisted that my brothers and I train with his unit and we had to keep up. He did not allow us to fall behind."

"That's hard-core!"

"It was, but it helped me develop a love for being physically fit."

The two minutes ended, and the instructors walked around asking each pair for their names and the number of crunches each candidate performed.

Sarah could not wait to get to the run. Her legs needed to be stretched out after all the sitting she had done over the last couple days; she wasn't used to just sitting around not doing much.

The men joined the women in the middle of the field where they were given instructions on how the run was going to be performed: they would run on the roadway that circled the parade deck, the PT field, the barracks, and the auditorium three times; each loop was a mile. They were instructed that about a quarter of a mile of the path was loose rock behind the barracks.

They lined up at the starting point and stretched for five minutes. After five minutes, they were instructed to line up where the fastest starters were to be at the front of the group while those who typically ran slower were asked to move to the back of the group to avoid anyone being tripped at the start of the run. Everyone arranged themselves accordingly and waited for the gun to be fired.

Sarah lined up at the front of the group. She knew that she wanted to run a solid first run.

"You think you can keep up, honey?" she heard a random male candidate ask her.

"You sure you want to challenge me, candidate?"

The gun went off, and Sarah took off with the rest of the group. She followed the signs and the men in front of her who were leading the pack. She focused on her breathing and listened to her footsteps hitting the pavement. She lost herself in this routine; this was the first time she felt free to be herself since arriving.

She looked at the giant clock to see how she was doing as she finished her first lap.

Okay, perfect, Sarah. You're right on target with that first lap to be six minutes. You need to keep this pace for your second lap. You got this! This is a piece of cake.

As Sarah finished her second lap, she looked at the clock again and saw that she was now at eleven minutes and fifty seconds. As she started her third lap, she heard a familiar voice beside her, "Oh, you think you're a runner, huh? Just finishing up your first lap, slowpoke?"

Sarah ignored Candidate Morley's voice and just kept running. She felt a bump against her right shoulder and she briefly lost her footing, but quickly recovered and continued running. She tried to move away from Morley, but every time she sped up or slowed down, Morley matched her pace.

Once they were on the back side of the course, out of the instructors' eyesight, Morley reached over and shoved Sarah to the ground. Sarah slightly turned as she felt her legs give out from underneath her, trying to stay loose. She tucked and rolled into the impact, which helped her quickly get back up and kept running.

Morley became angry at seeing Sarah bounce back so quickly, so she reached out and purposefully tripped Sarah. This time Sarah went down hard on the ground. It all happened so quickly that Sarah did not have time to relax her body. She heard the loud crack underneath her body as she fell with her leg pinned underneath her body. This time she felt a sharp pain instantly and immediately threw up on the ground. She tried to get up but immediately passed out from the pain.

Before she passed out, she heard Morley's voice taunting, "Snitches get stitches, bitch, and today you get stitches."

When she woke up ten minutes later, she saw Colonel McDougal standing over her along with a couple of Navy Corpsmen holding smelling salts to wake her. "Candidate Clark, do you know what happened?"

"Yes, sir," she answered him.

"Please fill me in, candidate."

"Sir, yes, sir," she replied. "As I was running my third lap, I heard Candidate Morley's voice taunting me. I tried to ignore her and kept running, but she shoved me. I fell but was able to quickly recover and continued running. The next thing I remember after getting up was feeling my leg getting tripped up, causing me to fall. This time I fell right on top of my leg. I heard a loud crack and felt a sharp pain, which caused me to vomit."

"Did Candidate Morley do this, Candidate Clark?"

"Yes, sir. Before I passed out, I heard her say, 'Snitches get stitches, bitch, and today you get stitches.'"

"Thank you, Candidate Clark." The colonel turned to the corpsmen and told them to take her to the hospital.

Sarah went in for surgery to have the bone reset and pins placed in her leg. She stayed in the hospital for two weeks before being discharged and sent back home to Spring City. Sarah felt absolutely defeated that she did not get to finish out OCS.

Move to Fair Falcon

Sarah got home from her OCS experience. Everything went back to normal when she got home; she and Alex fought all the time about everything. Sarah poured herself into her classwork while she was home on bedrest. She did everything she could to keep the peace in the house when Alex was home.

Sarah woke up early on the Fourth of July, excited about her family's annual festivities. Alex came in the bedroom after taking a call out in the living room.

"Sarah, we need to pack up everything and be ready to move by the end of the week."

"What are you talking about?"

"I was offered and accepted a position with the Fair Falcon Police Department into their detective unit. I report for duty starting next Monday."

"When did all this happen?"

"I just accepted the offer today."

"Were you going to loop me into this at all? It doesn't just impact your life you know!"

"I figured you'd be okay with it, seems as though you couldn't cut it in OCS. Where else are you going to go except with me?"

"It would have been nice to know all this beforehand. I could have mentally prepared myself for this transition rather than having it dumped on me right before we're supposed to go meet my family."

"Well, you have a couple of hours to prepare yourself before you have to go tell your family. Figure it out."

"Have you already found a place for us to live?"

"No, that's your job. Guess you better figure it all out. You've got four days to get everything lined up."

"What exactly are you going to do to help me with this transition?"

"Nothing. This is all on you, darlin'. Ticktock."

Alex and Sarah went over to Grams and Pops' place to meet everyone for the parade. They got into cars and left for the parade.

Brennen was super excited because he was riding on one of the floats with his daddy.

"Daddy, go now!" Brennan said, tugging on Hunter's leg.

"Hey, Buddy, we're headed that way now. We've got plenty of time to get there and meet everyone else."

"Daddy!"

"Hey, Brennen, are you going to make sure you throw your favorite uncle all your candy?" Alex squatted down to ask Brennen.

"No way, Unkie."

"Why not, buddy?"

"Cuz I can't, Unkie."

Alex stood up and tussled Brennen's hair; "It's okay, buddy. I understand," he said as he smiled.

When they got to the parade route, they let Brennen and Hunter off at their float before going to find a good place to sit and watch the parade. They enjoyed the parade and jumped up and down shouting to Brennen when his float drove past. Brennen perked up and waved back.

After the parade, they went back to the house for lunch. "Chipmunk, you've been awfully quiet today, what's going on? Everything okay?" Grams asked, looking from Sarah to Alex.

"Everything is good, Grams," she replied back, weakly smiling.

"Out with it, kiddo! What's going on?"

Sarah looked over at Alex and back at Grams. Alex spoke up and said, "Well, we might as well come out with the news now, Sarah. It's going to come out at some point today, why not tell them now?"

"Well, Alex took a position with the Fair Falcon's Detective Unit, so we will be moving there before the end of the week."

"What are you going to do, Sarah?" Violet jumped in.

"What do you mean, Mom?"

"How are you going to finish your masters' degree? What are you going to do for work?"

"The university opened the master's programs to be done online or in class. I elected to do my classes through the online program, so I could start back right after I got back from OCS. I can continue doing that in Fair Falcon, so the move won't affect my ability to graduate. I started looking for jobs in Fair Falcon and applied this morning for a few different positions. I am positive that I can easily find something that won't impact my ability to finish my master's program."

"When did you find all of this out, chipmunk? Why didn't you tell us before this?" Matthew asked her, a look of concern on his face.

"I found out this morning and was advised that I need to be there by Monday," Alex advised everyone.

"Well, I think it's a great chance for you two to continue growing up together," Pops jumped in.

They finished eating lunch before they went out into the yard and played games. Brennen could not make it to the fireworks display, so they stayed at the house and watched them from the back deck.

The next morning, Sarah looked through the internet for apartments and moving companies that could pack them up on such short notice. She found a two-bedroom apartment on the outskirts of Fair Falcon that might possibly work and actually had an apartment open for them to pick up the keys on Friday morning. The rent and the security deposit were reasonable, so Sarah went ahead and got everything situated. She also found a small moving company that was willing to give them a discount on their moving costs for Alex's military service and could get their stuff packed before Friday.

Ocean Sun Bank

The moving company came in and packed up all of Sarah and Alex's belongings two days after their Fourth of July festivities. Sarah packed up the items that they needed to get them through until their furniture arrived. She put the girls in their bags and loaded them up in the truck. Sarah followed behind Alex as they drove the eight hours to their new home.

They unloaded the cats and their stuff and put it all away once they picked up the keys to the new apartment. They grabbed lunch at the Falcon Diner before driving over to the police department where Alex and Sarah met his new command.

A week after arriving in Fair Falcon, Sarah received a phone call. "May I speak with Sarah Jackson-Clark, please?" she heard an unknown female voice on the other end of the phone.

"This is she. How may I help you?"

"Sarah, my name is Sally Shore. I work for the Ocean Sun Bank as an associate director in our customer service department. I saw your resume and application to become a customer service representative and have a couple of questions for you. I see that you were a shift supervisor at the coffee shop. How many people worked under you in a shift?"

"I had anywhere from one person to ten people who reported under me at any given time."

"What would you say was your biggest success in the coffee shop?"

"I was able to help the owner market the coffee shop to bring in more clientele. We took the business from where he only needed two to three people to run it a day to where we needed a staff of up to ten people at any time throughout the day."

"What did you like most about being a supervisor?"

"I love watching people succeed in their goals. I loved working with the public, making them happy when they came in the doors. I also enjoyed watching a business that was struggling to keep its doors open become very successful, looking to open another shop in Spring City and possibly up in Mountain City."

"What did you dislike most about your job?"

"Ooh, that's tough to answer. I can't really think of anything right off that I disliked. I guess I would have to say the thing I disliked the most was when I had a customer walk away unsatisfied with his or her coffee or service. I aim to please, so it really affects me when I can't make someone a hundred percent happy."

"How did you handle escalated situations?"

"Can you tell me what you mean by that?"

"Did you ever have a customer, or an employee, yell or get upset in the coffee shop?"

"I did from time to time, but I tried to make sure that did not happen often."

"How did you do that, Sarah?"

"I listened to what the customer or the employee was telling me and then I responded with empathy or sympathy when I felt the situation warranted it. Afterward, I came to a satisfactory resolution that would appease all parties involved. An example of this would be where I had an employee who wanted time off to go to a concert. She gave me notice after the schedule was posted. When I advised her that she would have to work the scheduled shift because she did not give enough notice about the concert, she started yelling about how unfair I was. I related to her that I also enjoyed going to concerts, but then I pulled out the employee handbook that she signed and reminded her where she signed that she understood she needed to give at least two weeks' notice for time off requests and that once the schedule was posted, it was her responsibility to find a replacement. I worked with her by giving her a list of potential employees who might be willing to help her out on such short notice, and we were able to find someone to cover her shift. She was happy that she got to go to the concert and I was happy that the shift was covered."

"Thank you, Sarah. Can you come in tomorrow morning and meet with the call center director for a face-to-face interview?

"Yes, what time?"

"How does nine thirty sound?"

"That sounds great."

Sally gave her the address for the building. She also gave Sarah the instructions on how to get security to open the doors and let her into the building. Sally advised Sarah that she would meet her down in the lobby and would personally escort Sarah to the director's office for the interview.

Sarah woke up early and went for a quick run. She only ran three miles; she wanted to make sure that she had plenty of time to get cleaned up and drive over to the address that Sally gave her the day before. After her shower, she dressed in a charcoal-gray pants suit with a pink camisole under the jacket with a pair of black dress boots with a chunky heel. She pulled her hair up into a French braid.

She drove over to the Ocean Sun Bank and sat in their parking lot for about twenty minutes before plucking up the courage to go inside. She followed the instructions that Sally gave her the day before: she parked in the parking lot marked as South lot. She walked in the set of doors closest to the parking lot. She easily found the button for the intercom system, which she pushed and waited for an answer on the other end.

"How can I help you?" the deep male voice asked her.

Sarah looked in the glass doors and saw two older men, around her father's age, sitting at a big desk in the middle of an open floor. There were multiple hallways that branched off in different directions from the security desk. She saw a set of stairs off to her left and two elevator doors off to her right. Above the security desk was a walkway that connected the three wings of the building together at a centralized point, exactly like the first floor.

"How can I help you?" the voice asked her again.

"Oh, sorry. I am here for a meeting with a Ms. Lisa Chapman."

She heard the door buzz and the lock disengaged. She pulled it open and walked toward the security desk where she handed her driver's license to the man closest to her; he had black-and-silver hair with brown eyes. He wore glasses and had a five o'clock shadow where he chose not to shave that morning.

As the security guard handed Sarah her visitor's badge, Sally walked out of an office just to the left of the elevators. She greeted Sarah with a firm handshake. Sarah was drawn to this woman; she was very beautiful. Her figure was very petite; she stood around four feet, ten inches. If Sarah had to guess, she would have guessed that Sally weighed around 120 pounds. She had brown eyes and silky black hair that flowed all the way down her back. She wore a black skirt that went down to her knees and a purple button-up shirt.

"Hi, you must be Sarah. We spoke yesterday on the phone, my name is Sally Shore. It's such a pleasure to finally meet you."

"The pleasure is mine. Thank you for the opportunity to meet with you today," Sarah replied as she took Sally's hand in her own.

"Sarah, today you will be meeting with the call center director, Lisa Chapman, but before I take you to her, I want to have a quick word with you in my office."

"Okay," Sarah replied as she followed Sally across the atrium to a set of doors just off the lobby. Sally used her badge to gain access to the floor behind the locked doors. They walked another 250 yards or so before stopping at an enclosed office at the back of the room. Sally unlocked the office with her key and then invited Sarah to sit down in a chair opposite her chair. Sarah was drawn to the view the office had, looking out over the river and part of the cityscape.

"Sarah, I was not completely upfront with you yesterday when we spoke."

"What do you mean, Ms. Shore?" Sarah felt butterflies creep up in her stomach.

"Sarah, I know that you applied for the customer service representative position, but I need you to know that Oliver Peterson is a dear friend of mine. He and I had a very lengthy discussion about you once I saw your resume pop up from our human resources department. After speaking with Oliver and then our conversation yesterday, I feel like you would be a great addition to our team, but not as a representative…"

She could see the confusion spreading across Sarah's face, so she finished, "I think you would make a great supervisor here on our team, which is why you will now be interviewing with Ms. Chapman here in a couple of minutes."

"Wait, what?" Sarah stammered, confused and taking everything in.

"Sarah, I used our conversation yesterday as a chance to interview you for the supervisor position. One of my colleagues, Dennis Massey, was in the room with me while we spoke. He agreed with me that we should move you on to the next round of interviews for this position. What questions do you have for me?"

"Wow, I am in shock right now," Sarah said.

"Don't be nervous. Lisa is very easy to talk to. She will most likely ask you a lot of the same questions you've already answered. Just take a deep breath and have a conversation with her. She doesn't like things to always be formal, she really prefers things to be pretty relaxed. I think the two of you will get along. You ready?"

Sarah took a deep breath and stood up from her chair, "Let's go get this position."

"That's the spirit." Sally laughed as she led Sarah back down the hallway at the edge of the call center floor through the doors and back out into the lobby. They then walked through the wooden doors next to the elevator. "Here is where I leave you, Sarah. Glennis will let Lisa know you're here and will escort you into the office once Lisa is ready. I will meet you here after you're finished to get your license back from security. Good luck!"

"Good morning, Sarah. Please feel free to have a seat. Ms. Chapman will be with you momentarily." Sarah felt like she recognized Glennis from somewhere but could not place her before her thoughts were interrupted by a buzz on the intercom.

"Glennis, can you please show Ms. Jackson-Clark into my office? Thank you," Sarah heard over the intercom.

"Please follow me," Glennis said as she showed Sarah into an office that had two giant oak desks butted up to each other to make an L shape. This office also looked out over the river, into the woods beyond the bank.

Sarah was immediately greeted by a woman who stood about three inches taller than she did. This woman had a very pale complexion, with short blond hair, blue eyes, and glasses. She wore a flowery dress and black pumps. She reached her hand out. "Hi, Sarah, please sit."

"Thank you for having me today."

They sat and talked for a while; Sarah was surprised at how informal this process really was. The questions that Lisa asked her had nothing to do with her knowledge of the banking industry or even about being a supervisor. They were questions that helped Lisa understand Sarah's thought process, but more about her favorite period in history. After about thirty minutes, Lisa stood and ended the interview.

"Thank you for coming in, Sarah. It's been a pleasure getting to know you better. We will be in contact by no later than the end of the week."

"Thank you, Ms. Chapman. I appreciate the opportunity to come in and meet with you today. I look forward to joining your team, not only learning more about the credit card industry but also helping customers with their customer service experiences."

Sally walked Sarah outside. "Good luck, Sarah! Have a great day. I'm sure we'll talk again soon." Sarah grabbed her license and went home.

As Sarah walked in the door to the apartment, she heard the phone ringing. She walked into the kitchen and answered the phone.

"Hello?"

"May I speak to Sarah?" asked a familiar voice.

"This is she."

"Hi, Sarah, this is Sally. Do you have a minute?"

"Yes, ma'am. How can I help you?"

"Well, Sarah, I don't know what you and Lisa chatted about, but she was super impressed with you. We would like to offer you a position here at Ocean Sun Bank as a supervisor. We would like to offer you forty-five thousand dollars a year, along with full benefits, which include health, dental, eye care, and a 401k.

"We realize that this is your first time in this specific industry, so we would like to put you through seven weeks of training and five weeks of taking calls before we assign you a team to ensure we set you up for success. The next class is scheduled to start on Monday, July 25. The class starts at eight and ends at five, with an hour for lunch.

"We understand that you may need some time to think this over and talk to your husband, so we ask that you let us know by Friday."

"Thank you. I will talk this over with my husband tonight and will let you know as soon as possible."

"You have a great night! We will talk soon."

Alex got home after seven. Sarah grilled pork chops, mashed potatoes, and green beans for dinner. She had everything plated and on the table by the time he got out of the shower and joined her at the table.

"How was your day?" she asked.

"It was long. What did you do all day?"

"I had that interview over at Ocean Sun Beach this morning, remember?"

"No, not really. Well, how did that go? Are you going to finally start contributing to our income and start paying for your education?"

"First of all, you haven't paid a cent toward my education, my bachelor's degree or my master's degree. Second of all, I do contribute in many ways to this family. Thirdly, not that you seem to really care, but I went into the interview thinking that I was interviewing for a customer service representative position only to find out that they wanted me to join the company as a supervisor. They called me less than an hour after I left and offered me the position."

"Well, did you take it?"

"They wanted me to talk it over with you first and would not accept my answer until I did."

"Are you going to take it?"

"Yes. I planned to call them back tomorrow to accept the position."

"What all did they offer you?"

"Health benefits, retirement fund, and a starting salary of for-ty-five thousand dollars."

"I guess that's pretty good."

"Pretty good? It matches what you're making a year. You're no longer the bread winner. We have the same income."

They finished their dinner in silence, and then Sarah cleaned up the remaining dishes before moving into the bedroom to go to sleep.

Alex came in an hour later and lay down next to Sarah. She felt him start rubbing her back. He then reached down and started kiss-ing her before reaching down into her pajama bottoms and pulling them off. She tried to pretend like she was asleep but that did not stop him from forcing himself inside her. She lay there completely motionless until he finished. She got up and went into the bathroom to cry silently into her hands.

Sarah spent the next two weeks getting her background check and her hiring paperwork done and turned in early. She showed up early on the first morning of training. Sarah walked into the south entrance and waited at the security desk to be greeted by the trainer. The remaining nineteen applicants showed up and lined the lobby and waited with her.

Ten minutes after eight, the trainer finally showed up in the lobby to collect the group. He was tall and fairly skinny with a slight beer belly forming. He wore wire rimmed glasses that accentuated his baby-blue eyes. His head was completely shaved. Sarah could tell that he was no stranger to the outdoors because his skin was naturally tanned. He wore musky cologne that was very strong and overwhelming.

"Hi, my name is Nick. I will be your trainer through the next seven weeks of classroom training. Your training supervisor, Amanda, will be joining us throughout the classroom experience, but she will also be staying with you through the remaining five weeks while you are out showing off your skills and everything you learn in my classroom." He pointed to a young woman with long blond hair pulled into a ponytail who stood about Sarah's height. Sarah guessed that Amanda probably weighed twenty-five to thirty pounds more than she herself did. She looked to be about three years older than Sarah.

"Hi, ya'll, my name is Amanda. I'm excited to have you all join us."

Nick and Amanda escorted the group up the staircase to the second floor. When the group got to the top of the stairs, they made a left hand turn down the hallway next to the stairs and then stopped at the second doorway. Nick unlocked the door and asked everyone to find a seat at one of the computers. Sarah sat near the front of the room in the corner opposite the trainer's station. The rest of the group filtered in and sat as well.

They played a few games to help break the ice and introduced themselves to one another. They went on a tour of the building where Sarah learned that each of the three wings held different parts of the business. Nick made the gym, pool, recreation, and relaxation areas for last on the tour. She was excited to learn that they could use the gym and pool for free from the hours of six in the morning until nine in the evening. The bank also had an indoor and outdoor track.

Harrison's Accident

The first seven weeks of the training went by in the blink of an eye. Sarah watched as some of her classmates struggled with the information while others got it right away. Every week they had to take tests on the material they learned. Sarah helped those struggling with extra study sessions as they could not fail more than two of the seven tests. By the time they made it to week seven, the group lost two of their teammates for attendance.

The remaining eighteen students graduated from training on Friday, September 16. They celebrated with a tailgating themed potluck. The entire leadership team met the training group down into the conference room. Nick and Amanda had a fun slide show they put together to introduce everyone and talk about their training room accomplishments.

Sarah enjoyed taking the calls once they got out onto the floor. She loved talking to people and found it easy to relate to her customers. Her classmates came to her as a natural leader to help them with deescalating their calls and help with finding information. She knew that she would easily transition into the supervisor position.

Sarah got home from taking her phone calls on Friday, October 14. Alex was home when she got home from work. They went out and grabbed dinner at the Fair Falcon diner. When they got back from the diner, they turned on the television and watched Julia Roberts and Richard Gere in *Pretty Woman*. Sarah fell asleep on the couch; Alex left her and moved back into the bedroom.

Sarah woke up around two in the morning to the phone ringing. She groggily answered the phone, "H-hello?"

"May I speak with Sarah Jackson, please?"

"This is she. Who is this, and why are you calling me at two in the morning?" she asked.

"Sarah, are you Harrison Jackson's sister and power of attorney? Do you know if he has a DNR or letter of direction?"

"Who is this? What's going on?"

"Sarah, this is Dr. Maura Williams from the Spring City General Hospital surgical staff. Your brother Harrison was just brought into the hospital. He was in a head-on accident. Sarah, I need to know what Harrison's medical wishes are. He is completely unresponsive and needs to go into surgery. I need to know if there is any medical directive against this."

"What do you mean?"

"Sarah, your brother needs immediate medical attention, but I don't have anything on file on how to proceed."

"If he goes through surgery, is there a chance he will be a vegetable?"

"If he recovers, he should recover without any issues. However, there is a chance that he could remain in a vegetative state. Sarah, Harrison's injuries are very severe. I need you to know that there is a good chance that he may not survive the surgery. What are his wishes in this regard?"

"He has a DNR in the event he will be in a vegetative state. Otherwise, he wants everything done medically to help keep him alive. Please do everything you can to save my brother! I cannot bear the thought of being the reason he doesn't get the surgery he needs to survive."

"We will take him to surgery and will keep you posted through-out the night. Do you have a cell phone in the event we need to get ahold of you and you aren't answering at this number?"

"My cell phone number is 719-555-2055. Please keep me updated with his progress, and Doctor, whatever you do, please don't let him die!"

"Sarah, I won't make any promises. There is a chance that we can bring him back, but I need you to know that the next forty-eight hours are the most critical. We'll be in touch."

Sarah hung up the phone and fell to the floor in a heap. She started sobbing uncontrollably. Alex came out of the bedroom while

Sarah was on the phone with the hospital. He stood over her and asked, "Why are you crying? Who was that on the phone?"

"That was Dr. Williams from the Spring City General Hospital. Harrison was in a head-on collision and was taken into the hospital. They don't know if he will make it through the surgery. If he does make it through surgery, they don't know if he will pull through. We need to drive to Spring City. I need to be there." She got up and started to head to the bedroom to pack.

"Whoa, where do you think you're going?" Alex asked as he grabbed her wrist, stopping her in her tracks.

"I'm going to pack our stuff so that we can head to Spring City. We need to go now. The hospital said there is a good chance that he won't make it, and I want to be there to either be able to say goodbye or to be there when he wakes up."

"We aren't going anywhere. We are going to wait to see what happens. I have a shift in a couple of hours. We can leave after I get off work tomorrow morning."

"There is a chance he won't make it that long. Alex, I need to go be there with my family. Outside of my grandparents, we're the next closest to Spring City. It will only take us eight hours to get there versus taking my parents or Hunter over ten hours to get there. I'm Harrison's power of attorney and his executor of his estate. I need to be there to make those tough decisions, God forbid they have to be made. We need to go now."

"I'm putting my foot down. We aren't leaving until late tomorrow morning when I get off from my shift. We'll be there before eight." He turned around and went back into the bedroom, ending the discussion.

Sarah sat back down on the couch and cried. The phone rang again; this time it was her father on the phone. They talked about the game plan on when everyone was going to be able to get to town to be at the hospital. Her parents would leave at seven to head down to the hospital, Sarah and Alex would leave around eleven, and Hunter would meet them the following morning.

Sarah lay back on the couch and put her head in her hands. She quietly cried herself to sleep, wanting desperately to be there for her brother, her truest best friend. She loved him fiercely and could not stand the thought of being without him. She woke up in a dead sweat a couple of hours later, as Alex started moving around in the bedroom to get ready for his partial shift.

She got a call from the hospital that Harrison was through his surgery:

"Sarah, this is Dr. Williams. We just finished Harrison's surgery. It took longer than we expected, and there were some complications."

"What kind of complications, Dr. Williams?"

"Your brother had bleeding in his abdomen from the impact of the accident where he got caught up on the seat belt. We had to remove his spleen and one of his kidneys. Good news, he still has his other kidney and it appears to be functioning correctly after the surgery. He lost a lot of blood both before we got him to the operating room and while he was in surgery."

"Doctor, I need him to survive until I get there. I won't be there until around seven tonight. I can't lose him before I get there. I can't let him be alone. Please do anything and everything you can to keep him alive."

"We will continue to do everything we can to keep your brother alive as long as he's willing to fight."

She received a call from the Spring City Police Department:

"May I speak with Sarah?"

"This is she. How may I help you?"

"Sarah, my name is Captain Anthony Cassidy. I am Harrison's commanding officer. Do you have a minute we can chat about Harrison's accident?"

"What have you found out about Harrison's accident?"

"Well, what we know is that Harrison stayed late that night to fill out the case file on a missing person's case he and his partner, Tim Black, closed earlier that evening. He stayed to file the paperwork so that Tim could get to his daughter's recital. Harrison finished the paperwork around eleven and left to go home. He took Highway 20 south between Spring City and Spring Grove, the same road he took every night for the last three months to his new house.

"The driver of the other car was speeding, doing about fifteen miles over the speed limit. Turns out, he was also distracted by an argument he was having with his wife via text message. He veered into Harrison's lane, and Harrison didn't have time to react. The impact of the crash caused Harrison to lose control of his car. He hit loose gravel on the side of the road, which caused him to slide off the edge of the road. Harrison's car rolled multiple times down the embankment before coming to rest on its roof at the bottom of the steep hill.

"First responders were not able to quickly get to Harrison due to the steep incline of the embankment. When they did, they had to cut him out of the mangled car."

Tears rolled down Sarah's face. "W-what about the other driver, Captain? Did he survive?"

"No, Sarah. He was killed on impact."

"Please tell me that he didn't have kids."

"His wife is six months pregnant with their son. He left behind a two-year-old daughter."

Sarah got up and packed clothes and called Sally to let her know what was going on.

"Hello?" Sally answered.

"Hey, Sally, this is Sarah Jackson-Clark. I need to talk to you about a family emergency. I just found out that my older twin brother was in a car accident. The doctors don't think he's going to make it."

"Sarah, I'm sorry to hear this. Go be with your family, take as much time as you need. We'll throw you into another class when you get back. Don't worry about your job, just worry about taking care of things at home. Keep me posted on what you need from me."

When she finished her conversation with Sally, she cleaned up the apartment. She packed a couple of sandwiches so that she and Alex could eat on the road and only stop for gas. As soon as Alex came home, he took a quick shower. Sarah put the cats in their bags and packed the truck.

They got in the truck and headed East for Spring City. She drove the entire way while Alex lay back and napped. She only stopped twice for gas. She went directly to the hospital.

"Good evening, can I help you?" asked the older woman at the information desk in the middle of the hallway corridor.

"Can you please tell me how to get to intensive care unit to my brother, Harrison Jackson?"

"It looks as though Harrison is in room 12. Go down this hallway until you get to a hallway where you can only go left or right. Once you reach the main corridor, you'll turn left. Follow this hallway down past the children's hospital wing and past the maternity wing, both on the right side of the hallway. You'll come to another dead end at the end of the hallway. You can only go up the staircase or the elevators, I would recommend taking the elevators because you're going to go up to the sixth floor. Once you get off the elevators or stairs, you'll take a quick right and the doors will open into the intensive care unit waiting room. You'll go to the desk and they will buzz you into the unit and will give you instructions on how to get to the room from there."

"Thank you, ma'am," Sarah replied before she turned down the hallway.

"Sarah, slow down," Alex said.

"I can't! I need to get up there and be with my brother. He's always been there for me. He came to help take care of me when I got back from OCS."

She got to the waiting room and went to the desk. "I'm here to see my brother, Harrison Jackson."

Sarah heard beeping and people rushing around in the background. "Code blue in room 12" came over the intercom behind the desk.

Sarah's heart sunk in her chest. She could not believe she got to the hospital only for her brother to pass away. "Ma'am, I need to be in there. I am Harrison's durable power of attorney. Please let me in there with him."

"If the doctors tell you to step out, you'll need to come back out here." The receptionist turned to Alex. "You'll need to stay out here, Sir."

"Gladly!"

The receptionist buzzed Sarah into the ICU lobby and then escorted her back to the room. Sarah moved to the front of the room, out of the way of the doctors. She reached out and whispered in his ear, "I need you to stay with me, Harrison! I need my bestie. You help keep me sane. I need you to be okay, big brother."

The doctors pulled out the ventricular defibrillator (VF) to try to restart Harrison's heart. "Sarah? Is that you?"

"Yes. Dr. Williams?" Sarah asked the woman standing next to the VF.

"Correct. Sarah, things aren't looking good for Harrison. I don't know how much more his body can handle."

Sarah moved back up to Harrison. She kissed him on his forehead, tears streaming down her face. "Twinkie, I can't believe I'm telling you this, but I know that you're tired. You can never truly know how much I love you and how much you mean to me. I can only hope you know how much I love you and always will!"

She hesitated and broke down in sobs. "Twinkie, if you are waiting for my permission to let go, then I want you to know that you have my blessing. I hope you know that you will always be in my heart and that a giant part of me will be lost when you go. I love you, Twinkie! You have always been my best friend and always will be. Let go now, your watch is over. Let the new guard take the next watch."

She leaned down and kissed him again, and with that he slipped away. She felt cold and lonely when he left. She fell to her knees and put her head in her hands. The doctors left the room, giving her some time alone.

The door opened, and Sarah's parents and Alex entered the room. Violet collapsed; Matthew caught her and put her into a chair. Sarah pulled a chair up next to her mother and leaned in, embracing her mother. They sobbed together, grieving Harrison's early departure from the world. Alex reached out and put his hand gently on her shoulder.

After a few minutes, Sarah stood up from the chair and went out to the main waiting room to call Hunter.

"Huntee," she said when he answered the phone.

"I already know. I felt him leave this world when my connection to him was severed. I already know, chipmunk," he cried through the phone.

Sarah spent the next few days in a fog, just going through the motions. She planned Harrison's funeral with her father's help. She closed out all his accounts. The family helped her clean out his house, and Sarah put it up on the market, agreeing that once it was sold that part of the money from the sale would be put into a trust fund for Brennen and the other part would go to help wounded officers and their families.

Even though his death was not caused by an incident in the line of duty, the Spring City Police Department reached out for the family's permission to perform a formal funeral with full honors. Sarah knew how much being a detective was to Harrison, so she was honored that his unit wanted to be such a big part of remembering such a great man.

Alex left Sarah with her family the morning after Harrison's passing so that he could go back to work. They argued over this decision.

"You've got to be kidding me? Are you really going to leave right now and go back to Fair Falcon?"

"Sarah, I have to report back to duty. I don't have endless time off built up at this point."

"That's *bullshit*, and you know it. Your captain said he would grant you all the time off you needed to be here with me in Spring City. You forget that I overheard that conversation between the two of you."

"Look, you don't have to like it, but I'm going back to Fair Falcon to work the next four days. I'll be back on Friday before the memorial service."

"You know, this wouldn't have been acceptable if I had done that for your father's funeral. I was expected to be there at your side the entire time, taking your mother's abuse. My family doesn't abuse you, the least you could do is show my family the same respect I showed your family."

Just then the rental car company pulled up on the street outside Harrison's house with his rental car and honked to get his attention. "Whatever, Sarah. I'll be back on Friday. It's not like you're going to miss me anyways."

He turned and walked away. He opened the door to the Nissan Rogue and got in the passenger seat. The driver drove off. Alex did not even turn to look at her as they drove off. She stood there in shock; she could not believe that her husband had such little respect for her that he would walk out on an argument like that.

Sarah spent the week getting everything ready for Harrison's memorial service on Friday night and his funeral on Saturday morning. She could not believe how quickly his house sold. She had torn emotions when the realtor called her the day after they listed the house; she was excited to not have to deal with selling the house for an extended period of time once she left town, but at the same time, she was devastated that this part of her brother was going to be gone.

Alex got back to town early Friday afternoon. He was accompanied by fifteen other Fair Falcon officers. Sarah was shocked to see so many officers drive that distance with Alex. As Alex introduced her to each of the officers, Sarah enjoyed all the stories of how each of these men and women interacted with Harrison over the last ten years while he served on both the Spring City Police Department and the Fair Falcon Police Department before that. She laughed and cried; she loved the stories, but it made it her miss him so much more.

Sarah made it through the memorial service without collapsing into a crying heap. She mingled with all the visitors, laughed at all the funny stories about Harrison, and hugged all those who mourned his loss.

The following morning was a completely different story. Sarah could not stop the waterworks from the minute she woke up until after the luncheon at the church. She stayed behind at the cemetery after everyone else left; she watched as the cemetery workers lowered Harrison into the ground. As his coffin came to its final resting place, she felt empty inside; this was the end of a wonderful friendship:

Twinkie, you will always be my best friend. I don't know how you expect me to carry on without you, but you know that I will. I'm not ready to put you in the grave yet. I don't know what way is up and what way is down right now. I love you and always will.

Chapter 5

2012

Visitors

Sarah threw herself into work when she got back to Fair Falcon. She finished her last two weeks in training on the phones before she took over her own team of agents. She was excited when she found out her team would report to Sally; Sally was a good leader who was out to help her leaders be successful.

Sarah and her team started at the bottom of the stack rank but very quickly became the top team in the center. She found it easy to coach the agents to fine-tune their customer service and sales skills. She promoted friendly competitions among her agents and her peers and rewarded generously.

The New Year was a continued success of the end of 2011. Ocean Sun Bank did their yearly kick off the second week of January every year. They pulled all the agents off the phones for an entire day and bussed them over to the Fair Falcon Hotel and Conference Center. The senior leadership team gave a yearend review of the previous year's results and then gave the team the outlook for the New Year. After all the serious messages were covered, the leadership team celebrated the many successes for all levels of management from 2011: top sales, best overall results, and other miscellaneous awards before they broke for lunch.

Sarah and her team were recognized for the best fourth quarter results. Every single one of her agents received $3,350 in recognition for their sales and overall scorecards; Sarah earned $12,500 for her team's results in the fourth quarter. They pulled off better results in the last two months than other teams did the entire year. Many of her agents made more revenue for the company in three months than most of the agents in the center did in the six to twelve months prior to her team joining the company. She could not believe how well the company took care of her team.

After the meeting finished, the entire center went into the banquet hall. Ocean Sun Bank provided a very nice sit-down plated lunch to the entire center. Sarah enjoyed a nice plate of lasagna and garlic bread with a salad.

"Wow, does Ocean Sun Bank do this every year?" Sarah asked Sally after lunch.

"Yes, we sure do. Along with the yearly luncheon, we also do quarterly luncheons for the top fifty agents, ten supervisors, and two OM teams in the center. Quarterly award winners are given seven hundred and fifty dollars and supervisors are given two thousand five hundred dollars. Yearly winners get the quarterly awards times four."

"Wow, that's pretty amazing! I would never have guessed that companies do this sort of thing."

"Sarah, that's why people like me have been with the company for the last ten years."

After everyone ate their dessert, the festivities started. The bank brought in a bunch of gaming stations for the agents to play different games. They used this as a way to build rapport between the different departments and teams. They spent the afternoon playing games before they bussed the group back to the center and let them leave.

Sarah spent the next three months coaching her new team to be the best. She reached out to her peers and shared her best practices with them to help them improve their results. Sarah became a leader that her peers looked up to and reached out to for help with their outlier agents and other situations.

At home, Sarah tried to keep her life together. She and Alex fought on a regular basis. She wanted to go back to Spring City for

Christmas to spend time with her family, but Alex refused. They constantly fought over this decision, and it got really heated when Alex informed her in the middle of January that he invited his mother and brother to stay with them for a week in February.

"Sarah, you'll need to clean the house before my mother and Abe come visit for the week of Valentine's Day."

"Excuse me?"

"You need to clean the house next week so that it is clean before my mom gets here."

"It's *your* mother coming, you need to clean the house."

"It's your job to keep the house clean."

"Well, I could give two shits what the apartment looks like for your mother. If she doesn't like it, she can always go back to Spring City."

"Just get the place clean. They will be here on Saturday, February 12, whether you like it or not."

"Why is it we can bend over backward for your mother, but we can't go home and be with my family?"

"My family is more important than your family."

"Piss off, I'm glad you enjoy your mother giving me a hard time all the time. You're such an ass."

Sarah made sure the apartment was picked up but did not go above and beyond with cleaning. She was mad because Alex expected her to give up her bed for a full week so that his mother could sleep in their bed while they slept on a blow-up mattress in the spare bedroom and Abe slept on the couch.

Anna and Abe arrived around four Saturday afternoon. Alex and Sarah met them in the parking lot to help bring in their bags. Sarah could not believe Anna brought three bags with her for a week's stay.

Anna jumped out of the passenger side of the door and came running to Alex. She pulled him into a giant hug and then gave Sarah a dirty look. "Well, you're still around, huh? Why don't you make yourself useful and go get my bags out of the car?"

Sarah stood still and refused to move. "I'm sorry?"

"I told you to go get my bags out of the car."

"*Mom!*" Abe yelled from the back of the car. "Be nice and stop talking to Sarah that way."

"I'll talk to the bitch however I want to, boy. You just stay out of it."

"Anna, I realize that your son isn't going to speak up on my behalf, but I am done sitting here taking your bullshit. You're on my turf now. Keep disrespecting me and you can get back in your car and drive right back to Spring City. I will not allow you to disrespect me in the home that I pay rent for."

Anna turned and looked at Alex. "Alex, baby, are you going to let her talk to me like that? I did nothing wrong. You were witness to the fact that I did nothing wrong."

"Mom, you're right, you didn't do anything wrong. Sarah, you should apologize to my mother for being rude to her and then you should go get her bags."

Sarah turned and looked at Alex. "You have got to be kidding me. I won't get her bags. If she wants her bags, she can get them herself or you can go get them for her, but I won't be doing it." She turned around and walked back into the apartment, slamming the door behind her.

Sarah looked forward to going in to work every morning. She could not stand how Alex acted when he was back with his mother—like a child. Anna and Alex ignored Sarah when she did come home from work. Sarah made her own dinner every night and then went into the spare bedroom to be by herself.

Celebration Dinner

Sarah continued with great success at work. Sarah's team was one of the five teams who got to go out to lunch in celebration of their first quarter results on Friday, April 6. Lisa took the group out for Italian. Sarah received her $2,500 bonus after lunch. When they got back from lunch, Lisa asked Sarah to come into her office.

"Hey, Sarah, can you please join me in my office, please?"

"Sure, everything okay?"

"Oh, yeah, everything is perfect. I wanted to take a minute to thank you for being such a big part of our team," Lisa said to her.

"Lisa, I know that I haven't been here long, but I really love this place."

"Well, I love to hear that! Sarah, as you know, we've been expanding our center."

Sarah nodded. "Yes, I've seen that we have added a few new faces here."

Lisa laughed. "Just a few, huh?"

"Yes, ma'am."

"Well, Sarah, with that expansion, we need another associate director [AD] to lead the new team. I asked my current AD team who the next up and coming leader is. Your name came out of all twelve of their mouths. As such, I would like to ask if you would be willing to step into this role as an interim AD?"

"What exactly is an interim AD?"

"Your title and credentials would be changed to reflect that you are an AD. You will also get a partial pay increase to sixty thousand dollars to help compensate for the additional duties and responsibilities. This position will be six months, and at the end of six months we will evaluate how your team is doing. What do you say?"

"I would love to join the team as an interim AD."

"Great! It will take a couple of days to get all your credentials changed, but you will start on Monday. For the first couple of weeks, I would like you to shadow each of the current associate directors to make sure you understand the role, then from there, you'll be on your own. What questions do you have for me?"

"I don't have any questions at this time."

"Okay, great! Have a great weekend, Sarah. See you bright and early on Monday morning."

"You have a great weekend as well, Lisa!"

Sarah went home; she was in the mood to celebrate her meeting with Lisa. Alex was home on the couch in his underwear.

"What has you so happy? Who did you just screw?"

"I didn't screw anyone, but thanks for asking. I just got some big news at work, and I feel like celebrating."

"What news could get you wanting to go out? These days all you want to do is stay home and read self-help or leadership books."

"Well, I got my first quarter bonus, and I got asked to become an interim AD all in the same day."

"What does that mean?"

"It means that I would be an acting AD for at least six months. This is basically my chance to show Lisa that I can do the job. If I am successful, then I stand a good chance of getting the position permanently."

"I guess I should tell you, good job, Sarah. Let's go celebrate. Where would you like to go?"

"I want a nice big fat juicy steak. How about we go to the Wild Steer for dinner and dancing?"

"Okay, get us a reservation and then get dressed."

Alex held the door open for Sarah as they entered the steak house. The restaurant was dimly lit. The tables surrounded the dance floor. The bar was filled with top-of-the-line liquor. Sarah was drawn to the giant dance floor in the middle of the restaurant. It was filled with couples slow dancing to "You're Still the One" by Shania Twain.

Alex bent down and whispered, "Looks like we made it, look how far we've come, my baby. We mighta took the long way, we knew we'd get there someday. They said, 'I bet they'll never make it,' but just look at us holding on. We're still together still going strong. You're still the one I run to the on that I belong to. You're still the one I want for life, you're still the one I love, the only one I dream of. You're still the one I kiss good night."

Sarah had a couple of drinks with her dinner, which helped loosen her up. She ordered the ten-ounce prime rib with a baked potato and salad; Alex ordered the sixteen-ounce New York strip with mashed potatoes and sweet corn kernels.

After dinner, Alex grabbed Sarah's hand and pulled her out of the booth. He walked with her over to the dance floor. As they walked onto the floor, the DJ finished playing Kenny Chesney's "You Had Me from Hello" before switching over to Tim McGraw's "My Best Friend." Alex took Sarah's right hand in his left hand; he gently placed his right hand on her hip while she placed her left hand on his shoulder.

As the song started playing, Sarah kept her distance at first. As they danced a little longer, tears fell down Sarah's cheeks. The lyrics ripped through her.

This is such a lie. My only best friend is no longer here for me to talk to. He's the only one who loved me for who I am.

I hate feeling like my life is a lie. Has Alex ever believed in me? If he has, it sure doesn't feel like he's ever believed in me. Why can't he ever tell me that he's proud of me? Has he ever loved me?

She broke away from Alex and walked back to the table.

After they got home from dinner, Sarah hopped in the shower. She lost herself to her thoughts while she was in the shower; she thought about how much her life had changed over the last year and a half. She did not hear Alex join her; she jumped when he touched her. In her emotional state, Sarah gave in to Alex's caressing.

He rubbed her back and then slowly moved his hands around to her front as he gently kissed her neck. She moaned as he reached down and started rubbing in between her legs. She turned around and kissed him back. He tried to pin her against the back of the shower, but when that did not work, he picked her up and took her into the bedroom. He laid her on her back and climbed on top of her gently spreading her legs apart.

Six weeks later, Sarah woke up early to go for her morning run. As soon as she got out of the bed, she immediately ran to the bathroom. She barely got the toilet seat lifted when she threw up. She got up and took her shower. She made it into the office before throwing up again.

Sally came into her office after she cleaned herself up. "You okay?"

"Yeah, I'm just feeling a bit under the weather today. If it doesn't stop, I'll go to the doctor tomorrow."

Sally smiled and walked out of her office. Sarah made it through the rest of the day with only throwing up one more time. She went home and lay down on the couch. She closed her eyes and fell asleep.

After an hour, she woke up and ran to the bathroom. Alex walked through the door and found her throwing up.

"What's going on?" he asked.

"I must have caught a bug. I've been throwing up off and on all day."

He left the bathroom and came back about ten minutes later. He brought her a pregnancy test.

"Here."

"What makes you think I'm pregnant?"

"Just take the test."

She took the test out of the box and peed on the stick. Alex stood in the doorway and waited for the results. Sarah closed her eyes as a wave of nausea hit again. She assumed the position and got ready to throw up again.

Alex picked up the test and looked at it—*pregnant*. He picked Sarah up off the floor and grabbed her into a hug. "Oh my god, Sarah! I'm going to be a father!"

Sarah looked at the test. She held back the tears that wanted to erupt from her eyes.

I'm not ready to become a mother! Who in their right mind would bring a child into this relationship? All we ever do is fight, that isn't healthy for a child. How could I be considered a good mother letting my child see his or her father and mother always fighting? This would ruin him or her for life.

How can Alex be so excited to bring a child into this turmoil? How did this happen? How could I have been so fucking stupid as to let myself get into this position? You are a fucking idiot, Sarah!

Sarah woke up the next morning after just a couple of hours of sleep. She made an appointment at her primary care physician's office for the start of the morning. Alex took time off his shift to join her. The nurse came in and asked Sarah for a urine sample.

The doctor walked in the room about fifteen minutes later. Alex squeezed Sarah's hand tightly as they sat in the chairs. "Hi, Sarah, how are you feeling today?"

"Not good! I constantly feel nauseous, and I can't seem to keep anything down."

"Well, I can try to help you with that. Your pregnancy test came back positive."

"I told you, Sarah!" Alex beamed.

"Sarah, I need you to jump up here on the table for a minute. I want to do a quick ultrasound before you leave the office."

"Can I still run while pregnant?" she asked the doctor.

"Sarah, you can do whatever your body allows you to do. Just make sure you listen to your body."

"She won't hurt the baby by running or lifting weights, will she, Doctor?" Alex asked.

"Alex, exercise is actually good for Sarah and the baby."

"I just don't want her to jeopardize the baby."

"She should be just fine, Alex."

"Sarah, I'm going to set you up with an obstetrician-gynecologist [OB-GYN] to monitor your pregnancy." She gave them a list of things that Sarah could still do while she was pregnant because Alex was nervous that running and exercising would hurt the baby.

As they left the office, Sarah turned to Alex. "Hey, we need to keep this tight-lipped through the first trimester. That means we don't tell anyone, especially your mother!"

"I want Mom to know."

"No, it's bad luck to tell people before the first three months."

As soon as Alex dropped her off at the office, he called his mother to tell her the news.

"Hi, Mom."

"Alex, what's going on? Everything okay? Why are you calling me in the middle of the day when you should be at work?"

"Mom, I wanted to let you know that I'm going to be a father. I'm so excited!"

"Say that again?"

"Sarah's pregnant. I'm going to finally be a father!"

"Oh my god, Alex, that's great news! I can't wait to be a grandmother!"

Miscarriage

Sarah's first nine weeks of pregnancy were very tough. She threw everything up that she ate, even with the antinausea medications that the doctor prescribed her. She experienced random mood swings, which she hid while she was at work but could not hide when she was home; it hurt to wear a bra because her breasts were so swollen and tender, and her stomach became very sore to the touch. She had to move her cats off her stomach every night because it hurt for them to lie on her belly. She slept every chance she got and found it very hard to work out.

Sarah woke up on the morning of Friday, June 8, in extreme pain; her back hurt worse than she had ever felt. Alex rushed Sarah to the hospital. She was seen right away by the ER staff. Sarah started cramping, and then minutes later she started bleeding. The doctors did a quick ultrasound and determined that she had a miscarriage that had not completed itself. Her OB-GYN came in and scheduled a surgical curettage for later in the afternoon to ensure that Sarah's miscarriage did get completed.

The doctor released Sarah to go home and spend the weekend in bed. She spent the entire weekend curled in a ball in the bed crying. For someone who never wanted to have children, she was shocked at how devastated she was by the fact that the pregnancy ended.

Alex worked Saturday and Sunday, leaving Sarah home alone to grieve. When he got off his shift Saturday night, he went out with his partner and a few other officers. They went down to the Falcon Flyaway. Alex flirted with the cocktail waitress, Bethany Brown, a busty strawberry blonde with brown eyes. He was immediately drawn to her bustline, the opposite of his wife. Bethany was more submissive and did not shut down his sexist comments; instead she laughed nervously at them. She was like so many of the other girls he slept with, easy to overpower and dominate.

After a couple of beers, Alex's fellow officers left him there alone at the bar to go home their families. Alex stayed behind and had another drink. When Bethany came back to the table, he invited her to have a drink with him.

"Hey, gorgeous, you wanna grab a drink with me and see where things go?"

"Sure. I get off here in about ten minutes."

She sat down with him once she got off her shift. He immediately reached over and pulled her into a kiss. They started making out, and before long, he was helping her into the passenger side of his Camaro. He drove back to Bethany's place with her, where they had sex. When they finished, he got up and went home.

He walked into the bedroom, and Sarah immediately smelled Bethany's perfume on his clothes. She was instantly repulsed by the fact that he walked in and did not attempt to cover up what he had just done.

"*Really?* You've got to be fucking kidding me!" she yelled at him from the bed.

"What?"

"You just can't stop being a fucking man whore, can you?"

"I don't know what you're talking about Sarah."

"You think I'm really that fucking stupid, Alex? I fucking smell her on you."

"It just kind of happened."

"Yeah, sure it did. You mean to tell me that you just tripped, and your dick slipped right in the girl's pussy! I'm not fucking stupid, Alex."

"I was grieving the loss of the baby. It just happened, Sarah."

"You think I'm not fucking grieving? You should have been here with me, not out with another woman!"

"You didn't even want the child. I didn't think you'd want to grieve with me. I thought you'd be happy to be unsaddled from the baby and the changes it was doing to your body."

"My body did start to change, even if I wasn't all that far along. Even though I didn't want to, I became very attached to the baby. I am just as devastated as you are, if not more than you. That doesn't give me license to go out and fuck someone else."

"Well, you're right about one thing, Sarah. Your body did change, and not for the best."

Sarah threw a pillow at him and then curled back up in her ball. "Just get the fuck out of here. I don't want to see you in here again."

He left and went out to the living room where he fell asleep on the couch. He woke up, took his shower, and left for work early Sunday morning. He heard her crying into her pillow and thought about comforting her but walked out of the door instead. He called his mother, "Mom!"

"What happened, Alex?"

"Mom, Sarah lost the baby."

"What do you mean? Do the doctors know what caused it? How did she manage to sabotage the pregnancy? I think you need to bring her up on charges."

"The doctors say that the fetus never fully attached to the uterine wall. There wasn't anything that Sarah did or didn't do that caused the miscarriage, but I still feel like it's her fault because she was so against having kids for so long."

"How are you holding up, baby?"

"I don't know anymore, Mom."

"Well, I think you need to come home next weekend and let me fix you all your favorite comfort foods, baby."

"Okay! I'll let Sarah know."

"Oh, well, she isn't welcome."

While Alex was gone, Sarah got up and picked up the apartment. She did the dishes, vacuumed, and dusted. She lay down and cried, her emotions washing over her in waves.

Pull it together, Sarah. You didn't even want the child to begin with. Why are you so upset?

How could he go out so quickly after finding out that we lost the baby and cheat on me? Why can't I just be enough for him? What is it about me that he doesn't like and feels he needs to cheat? Am I not skinny enough? Am I ugly? I must be ugly. I've seen the pictures of some of the girls he's cheated on me with—they are missing teeth, cross-eyed, some are considerably heavier than me, some are taller, and some are shorter. I wish I knew exactly what it was that he was looking for so that I could try to fit that mold. I just want my husband to love me. He's showing me right now that he could only love me if I were to have his child... What kind of life is that? We would be horrible parents. I am going to go to hell for thinking this, but I'm glad the baby didn't survive. Our household is not the right place for a child to grow up. Our constant fighting—a child isn't going to fix that. Why can't he just love me for who I am?

Why do you stay and allow him to continue making you feel horrible about yourself? You're such a fucking idiot, Sarah. You will never amount to anything other than a complete failure. You can't seem to do anything right. You're allowing yourself to get fat and out of shape. How could you let yourself get to 140 pounds? You know that with a baby, you'd probably have gained anywhere from twenty to seventy pounds... How would you have gotten that weight off?

Sarah's thoughts were interrupted by the phone ringing... "Hello?" she tried to wipe the tears from her eyes and make her voice sound steady.

"Chipmunk, is that you?" her father asked from the other end of the telephone conversation.

"D-Daddy?"

"Chippy, what's going on? Have you been crying?"

"Y-yes, but that's not what you called about, is it?"

"No, no, it isn't, but now I'm worried about you. What's going on?"

"N-nothing. What's going on with you?"

"Well, I was just calling to chat with you and see what you guys think about possibly coming home in the next month or so. We want to see you guys, and I know Pops and Grams want to see you as well."

"I'll see what Alex says when he gets home from work and will call you back."

When Alex got home that night, Sarah broached the subject of going home to see her parents. "Hey, I spoke with my father earlier today. He wanted to know if we could go back home to Spring City for a long weekend next month. What do you think?"

"Why would we do that? What is it that your parents want?"

"Well, they just wanted to see us. We haven't been home together since Harrison's funeral."

"What's that supposed to mean?"

"Well, you've been home twice since the funeral to 'help' your mother out, but I've yet to be invited to go with you. Any time I ask to go home, you always make up an excuse as to why we can't go back, or you just tell me no."

"I'll think about whether or not we go back to spend time with your parents. Oh, and just so you know, I'm going home next weekend."

"What the fuck! What's the excuse now?"

"She wants to help me grieve the loss of the baby. She's going to spoil me while I sit around and do nothing but put my feet up."

"Okay, whatever. Well, whether you like it or not and whether you want to come home with me or not, I'm going home to see my family next month. I'm done and over this game you want to play."

She finished her dinner and then cleaned up the kitchen. She went back into the bedroom and cried into her pillows. She was tired of feeling like a failure and being segregated from her family.

Sarah found herself very emotional. She could not see herself as the tough girl who could handle anything any longer; she felt like an extreme failure. The only thing going good for her was her job; she looked to it as her escape from the rest of her life.

Two weeks after the miscarriage, Sarah woke up and looked herself in the mirror; she did not like the girl looking back at her.

Girl, you look fat. You aren't the same person you were way back. You've been through the ringer. You aren't worth anything. No one will ever love you. You aren't worth loving, Sarah. You need to lose weight. You look like a fat cow. Running, exercising, and eating right aren't help-ing me lose the weight. Maybe I should try fasting. It has worked for other people, maybe starving myself will help me lose weight as well. I guess it's worth a try.

She fixed dinner for Alex every night when she got home from work but would not eat anything herself. After three weeks of starving herself, she weighed herself—125 pounds.

Oh my God, Sarah you look amazing. I can't believe that you've lost an average of five pounds a week. This is amazing. Sacrificing food is worth the pain.

Sarah walked in to work and ran into Sally, who had been off for the last month for surgery. "Damn, Sarah, you look like you've been through the ringer. Everything okay?"

"What is that supposed to mean?"

"Sarah, you don't look very healthy. What's going on?"

"Nothing. I'm fine."

"Sarah, your skin tone is very pale."

"I haven't been feeling very well. I'll be fine though."

"It looks like you've lost a lot of weight in a short period of time."

"Sally, I'm fine."

"Okay, if you say so."

"I do say so. I'll be fine."

"You wanna grab lunch today? My treat."

"I think I'm going to have to pass, but thanks for the invite."

"Okay, we'll have to catch up later this week. I feel like I've missed out on so much over the last month. Thank you for taking care of my team! I really do appreciate you helping to keep my team running while I was gone."

"It was my pleasure. I enjoyed working with your leaders."

Collapse

Sarah continued to starve herself. When she did eat, she immediately went into the bathroom to throw up. She tried to work out; some days were easier than others. Over the rest of the year, she continued to lose weight. She woke up Halloween morning excited for the day; the bank was putting on a costume contest. She and Sally planned to wear tailor-made Twinkie outfits for the contest.

She put her costume on, and it fell right off. She picked it up off the floor and grabbed her regular clothes.

Sarah

6:15 a.m.

Good morning, Sal! Are you going to hate me forever if I tell you that I can't wear my Twinkie costume?

Sally

6:16 a.m.

WHAT?!? You can't not wear the costume! If you don't wear it, who else is going to be my Twinkie? Why wouldn't you wear it?

Sarah

6:18 a.m.

I just put it on and it fell right off. I don't know if we have time to fix it.

Sally

6:19 a.m.

Get your ass over here like yesterday! I'll fix it for you.

Sarah

6:20 a.m.

Be there in like 10.

Sarah got in the car and drove right over to Sally's place. She knocked on the glass door, and Sally immediately opened it for her, motioning her to walk inside. "What is going on with your costume, Sarah?"

"It doesn't fit. It fell off as soon as I put it on."

"Okay, get in here." Sally pointed to her craft room. Sarah saw the sewing machine in the far corner.

"Do we have time to fix this?"

"Just put it on so I can see how much I need to take it in."

"Do you have a bathroom I can change in?"

"We're both women. I promise you don't have anything I haven't seen before. Besides, you still have your white tank top and your shorts on. Let me shut the door and let's get to work."

Sarah stripped down to her tank top and shorts and then put the costume on. Sally caught a quick look at Sarah's body while she was in between her street clothes and her costume. "Woah, what is going on with you, Sarah?"

"What are you talking about?"

"Sarah, you're skin and bones. It's no wonder the costume fell right off. What is going on with you?

"Nothing."

"Sarah! Don't lie to me. As your friend I need to know what is going on with you."

"Sally, I'm fine. Nothing is going on. Let's just get the costume fixed and get over to the office."

"Sarah, I want it noted that I am worried about you!"

"I appreciate that, just know that I'm fine and you have nothing to worry about."

Sally fixed up the costume, and they got dressed. They both drove over to the office and walked inside. They immediately got comments about their costumes from everyone they walked past. The ladies walked around the call center trying to get votes from their peers.

Lisa had a warhead put on all incoming calls to allow everyone to get off the phones for two hours from eleven to one in the afternoon to have a potluck and to judge the costumes; all votes had to be in by noon to allow time to tally the votes and announce the winners. She had a DJ come into the center and had stations set up with games for the employees to enjoy.

Sarah was impressed with all the different costumes that the agents wore. Her favorite costumes involved two couples who were willing to dress up as condiment bottles: they wore ketchup, mustard, pickle relish, and mayo suits. The winners were announced: Sarah and Sally won second place, behind the condiment bottles. All winners received fifty dollars.

Sarah went home after work and got ready for her run. She made it about a mile from home when she lost her footing and fell. She hit her head on the sidewalk and passed out. She woke up to someone rubbing his knuckles on her sternum and a hard board underneath her. "Ouch! Stop!"

She looked up and saw a handsome paramedic crouched over her. He had dark warm brown hair that was slightly spiked; his eyes were dark brown, and his skin was sun-kissed. She was drawn to his square jawline with a slight five o'clock shadow. The rubbing immediately stopped. "Ma'am, do you know what your name is?"

"Sarah."

"What's your last name?"

"Jackson-Clark."

"Do you know what happened to you?"

"I don't know. I know that one minute I was running and the next minute you're rubbing my sternum, which hurt by the way."

"Well, we need you to come to the hospital with us."

"What if I don't want to? Do I have to?"

"Well, you don't have to, but I would definitely recommend it after a fall that resulted in a head injury."

"I really don't want to go. I think this is silly, all this fuss over me falling down."

"Well, Ms. Clark, I can't tell you what to do, but I would recommend you coming back with me to the hospital. We don't know what caused you to fall and hit your head. You should go see what the doctors have to say. You're lucky you didn't break your leg in this fall and you've lost some blood from the gash on your forehead."

She looked him back over again before replying, "Are you going to be with me the entire way?"

"Yep, I'll be in the back with you, making sure you don't pass out again."

"Okay, I'll go," she said as she tried to get up off the paramedic's board.

"Oh, no, you need to lie back down. I'm Carter by the way."

"I may have bumped my head, but I can still read your name tag."

"Oh, smartass much?" he laughed.

Sarah enjoyed the ride to the ER with Paramedic Carter Sanchez. He kept her laughing and relaxed. When he touched her, shock waves coursed through her body. She found herself not wanting to ever reach the hospital, but when they did, Carter slipped her his phone number. "I hope this isn't lost on you," he said in his deep, husky voice.

"It won't be lost on me." She smiled back at him. She gave him her number as well.

Just then, the ambulance doors opened, and Carter's partner stood there with two doctors and two nurses waiting to pull her out of the ambulance and whisk her into the hospital. "This is where I leave you." He leaned down and whispered quietly in her ear. "Don't be a stranger, Sarah."

As soon as they were inside, the doctors ordered many different types of blood tests to see what possibly caused Sarah to pass out and fall. They started an IV with fluids. "Hi, Sarah, my name is Dr. Lee Howard. Can you tell me what you know?"

"I honestly don't know, Doctor. I was running one minute and then the next thing I know I had someone rubbing on my sternum to wake me up."

"Any idea what caused this?"

"No, I don't have any idea what happened."

"Have you lost any significant amount of weight lately?"

"What do you classify as lately?"

"How about within the last six months?"

"I've lost a few pounds in the last six months."

"What exactly is a few?"

"I honestly don't know. I know I've lost weight, but I don't know exactly how much weight I've lost."

"What would you say if I told you that you're down to a hundred and five pounds?"

"I would tell you that I don't believe you. I have to be at least a hundred and thirty pounds."

"Well, you would be wrong. You're down to a hundred and five pounds, and if I had to guess, I'd say you are starving yourself and aren't taking in enough calories to sustain your basic life functions, let alone to sustain your running."

"What makes you think that?"

"Well, there are a few things that make me think that. The white marks on your knuckles make me think you've been forcing yourself to throw up, your skin looks pail, and you appear to be skin and bones only at this point. You look like a girl who used to have muscle tone, but you don't any longer. Sarah, you look sick. I think you need to work with a counselor about your eating disorder."

"I'm fine, Doctor."

"Do you know what you are doing to yourself, Sarah? This disease causes you to be more susceptible to heart attacks because your heart isn't getting the proper fuel to pump and circulate your blood. It can cause you to faint or have dizzy spells because your brain isn't getting enough energy to pump the blood through it. You could die."

"I'll be fine. Do you know if anyone has called my husband?"

"We reached out to him and let him know you are here. He said he will be here in the next ten minutes or so."

"Can we take this IV out now?"

"Nope, sorry, not until you're discharged. It's for your own good," he said before he walked out of her room.

Alex showed up about ten minutes later. He had never seen Sarah look so frail and helpless before as he did when he walked in and saw her hooked up to all the different machines. "Sarah, what's going on? What happened?"

"I don't know, I went for my nightly run and apparently passed out. The doctors are just being extremely thorough to make sure this doesn't happen again. Sounds like they are going to send me to get a CAT scan here in a few minutes to make sure that there isn't any damage to my brain after I hit my head on the curb."

Dr. Howard walked in right before the medical transport came in to take her for her CAT scan. She went up to the scanner. When they finished, they brought her back down to her ER room to wait to see if she was being admitted or released. After an hour of waiting, Dr. Howard came back in the room. "Hey, Sarah, looks like we have answers for you."

"Am I dying, Dr. Howard?" She smiled at him.

"No, you're gonna live. Looks like you ended up with a concussion, but nothing to be too concerned about."

"Sounds good, I'm outta here."

"Not too fast, Sarah. You're going to need someone to sit with you and keep an eye on you over the next twenty-four hours."

The doctor walked out of the room into the hallway to the nurses' station. Alex turned to Sarah. "I'm going to go get the car and bring it around to the front and wait for you."

When Alex left the room to go get the car, Dr. Howard came back in before she was wheeled out. "Sarah, I am concerned about you. I don't know what started this for you, but you need to get help with dealing with it before it kills you. Have you told your husband about your disorder?"

"Nope, and I don't plan to. Thanks for patching me up, Doc. Have a great day."

"Sarah!" he replied sternly.

"I'll be fine, thanks, Doc." She turned to the nurse. "Please get me out of here."

The nurse wheeled her out to the car. Alex opened the door for her and helped her get into the passenger seat. They drove home, and Sarah immediately went to the bedroom to lie down. She curled into a ball and fell asleep. Alex checked on her throughout the night.

Alex left the next morning for work before Sarah woke up. She heard her phone chime with a new text message:

721-555-8724

6:50 a.m.

Hey, Sarah, this is Carter. I just wanted to check on you to see how you're doing after all the excitement yesterday.

Sarah

6:55 a.m.

I'm okay, thanks for checking.

721-555-8724

6:57 a.m.

What did doctor say?

Sarah

6:59 a.m.

He said I'd live.

721-555-8724

7:00 a.m.

What else did he say? I would guess that he diagnosed you with a concussion; is your husband there with you keeping an eye on you?

Sarah

7:02 a.m.

Concussion & that I'll live.

No, my husband left for work this morning. He got called out on a new case w/ his partner, probably gone all day and into evening.

721-555-8724

7:03 a.m.

Wait, is your husband Detective Alex Clark?

Sarah

7:05 a.m.

Yes, does that make a difference on whether you continue to hit on me or not?

721-555-8724

7:06 a.m.

No, I just didn't you realize that you were his wife when we were talking yesterday.

Since I'm off today & you need someone to keep an eye on you, you want some company?

Sarah

7:07 a.m.

I'm sure I won't be a very good hostess.

721-555-8724

7:08 a.m.

How about this… How about I come over here in a bit & check on you & then make you lunch?

Sarah

7:12 a.m.

I don't think you're going to stop until I agree to let you come over to keep an eye on me.

721-555-8724

7:13 a.m.

You're smart! LOL

Sarah lay back down and fell asleep. An hour later she heard a knock on the door. She walked out to the door and opened it, coming face-to-face with Carter. She invited him in. She turned on the TV and sat down on the couch. Carter joined her at the other end of the couch.

"How are you feeling, Sarah?"

"I'm feeling okay. I have a slight headache, but otherwise I'm good. You know, you didn't have to come over and check on me."

"I know, but I wanted to check on you. Let's watch a movie."

"What would you like to watch?"

They agreed on a superhero movie. Sarah fell asleep about thirty minutes into the movie. Carter grabbed a blanket off the floor and draped it over her and then he went back to his side of the couch. He kept an eye on her, gently waking her from time to time to make sure that she was okay. She woke up around noon. She was hungry, so they ordered delivery pizza.

When they finished eating, Carter put a romantic comedy in the DVD player. They sat back down on the couch, only this time, Carter moved closer to her. She laid her head on his shoulder, and he gently played with her hair. This light touch felt magical and helped Sarah relax; she dozed off again.

When Carter thought she was asleep, he leaned down to kiss her forehead. Sarah pretended to sleep through it, but she could not believe how nice that touch felt. Ten minutes later, he leaned down again, this time Sarah met his lips with her own. The kiss started out very softly and gradually became more passionate.

Sarah pulled away from Carter. "I-I can't do this. I'm sorry if I gave you the wrong impression."

"Did I do something wrong?"

"No, absolutely not. It's just that I'm married, and as miserable as I am in my marriage, I can't cheat on my husband."

"As much as I can understand that feeling, I can't understand that feeling. If the rumors about your husband are true, he's a real man whore."

"What do you mean?"

"Sarah, he's a cheater, and he's not all that quiet about it. He's slept with a couple of the officers in the PD as well as a number of nurses in the hospital."

"How do you know that, Carter?"

"I am friends with one of the girls who slept with Alex, and she told me about him and the things they did together."

"Oh, I see." Sarah turned away from Carter as tears rolled down her cheek.

Carter gently pulled her back to face him and reached out to kiss her again. She rested her forehead against his. "I'm sorry."

"Sorry for what?"

"I hate crying, and I definitely don't enjoy doing it in front of people I barely know."

"You have nothing to be sorry for, Sarah. You are a beautiful woman. Why do you stay with him?"

"I take my vows very seriously... 'Till death do us part.' I cheated on him once and promised to never cheat again."

"Sarah, you don't deserve to be treated this way. You deserve to be with someone who will treat you right."

"I appreciate that sentiment, but I'm not sure that I can leave him right now. I want to try to work it out with him, if I can."

"Well, just know that you deserve a man who will be faithful to you. If you ever decide to you are ready to move on, you have my number."

"Thank you, Carter. I appreciate you. I know you want to see what could possibly happen between us, but do mind if we keep our relationship as friends?"

"Friends with benefits?" He smiled at her.

"Just friends." She laughed.

"I would be honored to have you as a friend, Sarah."

Carter reached down and kissed her on the forehead and then left. Sarah lay back down and fell back asleep until Alex got home.

Promotion

Sarah enjoyed her interim position and was successful. Her teams consistently ran top of the stack rank; she had a blast, and her teams worked hard for her. Sarah loved being out on the floor coaching and developing her supervisors and agents.

Sarah's hard work did not go unnoticed by her peers, Lisa and Lisa's bosses. Sarah arrived to work an hour early on Friday morning, November 2, after Dr. Howard released her to go back into work. When she got to her office, she set her bag down and plugged her laptop in to her docking station.

Ten minutes after she arrived, she received a phone call on her desk phone. "This is Sarah," she said when she saw that it was from an internal extension and not an external one.

"Hey, Sarah, this is Glennis. Can you please come downstairs and meet with Lisa?"

"I'd love to. When did she want me to meet with her?"

"Right now, please."

"Be right down."

She hung up the phone and went downstairs. She was a bit nervous about the reason Lisa wanted to see her.

Sarah got downstairs and walked into the office. "Good morning, Glennis."

"Good morning, Sarah. It'll be about five minutes, please have a seat."

"Anything bad that I need to be worried about?"

"I really don't know. I was just asked to call you and ask you to come down. Fingers crossed for you!" She smiled.

Lisa opened her office door and stepped out into Glennis's office. "Good morning, Sarah. Please join me in my office," she said as she motioned for Sarah to join her.

Sarah walked into Lisa's office. She saw Lisa's giant L-shaped oak desk with two computer monitors sitting in the corner, allowing Lisa to turn and easily face anyone sitting across from her; there was a high-back black leather office chair behind the desk. Her desk had pictures of her husband and twin boys on it, as well as a three-tier paper tray and pen holder. On the opposite side of the office was an oval oak conference table that seated up to eight people.

"Please sit down, Sarah." She pointed to the two stationary office chairs sitting across the desk from her own chair.

Sarah sat down nervously in the chair closest to the door. Lisa walked around the desk and sat down in her desk chair. She turned and faced Sarah who sat across the desk. "Good morning, Sarah."

"Good morning."

"I can see the concern on your face. You have nothing to worry about, Sarah."

Sarah visibly relaxed in her seat. "Is everything okay?"

"I have a couple of things I want to chat with you about, but first, I want to ask how you're doing after your accident two days ago."

"Oh, I'm fine. I just had a concussion. I'll be fine, thanks for asking."

"Sarah, there are a lot of people worried about you."

Confused, Sarah looked over at Lisa. "What do you mean? Are you saying that you don't think I'm doing a good job with my interim role?"

"Oh, no! You're doing amazing in your current position. I hear nothing but great things from your agents, supervisors, and peers."

"Well, then what would people need to be concerned about?"

"Sarah, we're concerned because we've all seen how much weight you've lost and how little you actually eat. We're concerned that you might have an eating disorder? Are you seeing anyone to help you with this?"

"I'm fine, but thank you for asking."

"Okay, well, I won't push it then. Please know if you need anyone to talk to about it, I'm here for you. You've made a positive impression on a lot of people here."

"If I need someone to talk to, I'll definitely reach out."

"Okay. Well, let's move on to why I really wanted you to come down this morning... Sarah, you've made so many changes to this center in such a short period of time and you are doing such a great job in your interim role."

"Thank you!"

"Sarah, I would like to offer you the position permanently."

"W-what?" Sarah stammered.

"Sarah, you have made huge strides with each one of your teams, and you've been willing to go above and beyond to help your peers get their teams performing better. Every single supervisor is ranked in the top fifty supervisors in their respective departments, with only five to ten other leaders in the mix. We would like to have you join the team permanently as an associate director. You would keep all your current benefits, but your salary would be increased to one hundred five thousand dollars. What do you say?"

"Are you serious?"

"Very serious, Sarah."

"How could I say no?"

"So, are you saying yes?"

"Yes!"

As Lisa stood up from behind her desk, Sarah also stood. Lisa extended her hand to Sarah, which she took firmly in her own right hand, "Welcome to the team as a full-time associate director, Sarah. We'll make the announcement on Monday morning, if that's okay with you."

"That sounds just fine. Thank you for this, I can't wait to see where we go from here!"

"You earned this all on your own, Sarah! I can't wait to see how things continue to change for our center over the next few months."

Sarah went back to her office and shut her door. She grabbed her office phone and called her parents. "Hello?" Matthew answered the phone.

"Hey, Dad, is Mom there with you?"

"Yeah, I'm here," Violet replied. "What's up, kiddo?"

"I wanted to let you guys know that I was offered a promotion here at Ocean Sun."

"*Really?*" they both said at the same time.

"I'm so proud of you, chipmunk!" she heard her father say. "I always believed you would do well there. You are a rockstar, chippy!"

"That's so awesome, chipmunk!" Violet said. "How did Alex react to the news?"

"I haven't called him yet. You guys were my first call. I plan to call Grams and Pops next and then I'll text Alex since he's on duty right now and on a case. Gotta go, love you guys."

"Love you too!"

Sarah called her grandparents who were just excited for her as her parents were. She had to make her call quick because her team started coming in and she did not want them to overhear the conversation.

She left her office to go out on the floor to greet them. As they sat in their desks and signed in, she walked around and said good morning to each agent as she gave them all a high five. She thanked them for coming in and told them to have a great day.

After she finished greeting every agent and supervisor on the floor, she went back into her office to text Alex. As she grabbed her phone, Sally walked in and shut the door. "I hear congratulations are in order!"

"Thank you!"

"You wanna grab lunch to celebrate?"

"Sounds like a plan! We have to keep this under wraps though so we can't make it too obvious that we're celebrating."

Sally left the office and closed the door for Sarah. She grabbed her cell phone out of her desk drawer:

Sarah

8:30 a.m.

Hey, Alex…just wanted to let you know that I was offered the full-time AD position.

Alex

9:00 a.m.

Does that come with a raise?

Sarah

9:03 a.m.

Yes.

Sarah was on cloud nine. It was hard to contain her excitement, but she remained successful. Sally and Sarah went to lunch at the Falcon Diner. When they sat down, they were the only two in the restaurant. The hostess sat them at the back of the restaurant, so they could have privacy, which gave them a direct line of sight to the front door.

They were in the restaurant about ten minutes when Sarah looked up and noticed that Alex walked in the door with a busty strawberry blonde on his arm. As they waited on the hostess to walk to the front to greet them, Sarah watched Alex bend down and kiss the other woman. The hostess seated Alex across the restaurant from Sally and Sarah. She was heartbroken that he was so open about taking his girlfriend out in public, but she was not in the mood to go over and confront him, so she texted him:

Sarah

12:20 p.m.

Whatcha doing?

Alex

12:25 p.m.

I'm at work.

Sarah

12:30 p.m.

Wanna grab lunch to celebrate w/ me?

Alex

12:32 p.m.

Sorry, can't...working a big case... I'm not going to be able to leave to get lunch at all.

Sarah

12:33 p.m.

Oh, I see.

Alex

12:35 p.m.

Sorry to disappoint; we'll have to celebrate over dinner.

Sarah

12:36 p.m.

Yeah, I guess we'll have to do that.

In the meantime, enjoy your lunch w/ that strawberry blonde sitting at the table w/ you.

Alex

12:40 p.m.

I don't know what you're talking about.

Sarah

12:42 p.m.

Keep playing dumb.

Alex

12:45 p.m.

I really don't know what you're talking about, Sarah.

Sarah

12:46 p.m.

Well, you can keep playing dumb, but I'm staring right at you w/ your tongue down your girlfriend's throat.

     Sarah excused herself from the table to use the restroom after she sent the message to Alex. As she stood up, she noticed Alex looking around trying to find her. When he spotted her, she waved at him and then walked to the restroom.

     As she reached the bathroom on the other side of the restaurant, she saw that Alex got there first. He forcefully pulled her inside. "What the fuck are you doing? Are you spying on me?"

     "No, I had absolutely no idea that you brought your girlfriends here where I could see you at any point. You're such a fucking idiot. Thanks for embarrassing me, now get the fuck out of here."

     She opened the door and kicked him out. She finished peeing and then went back out to join Sally at the table. They finished lunch and then went back to the office.

Chapter 6

2014

Fight

The first quarter of year was uneventful for Sarah and Alex. On Friday, April 4, Sarah's phone rang.

"Hey, Grams, how are you?"

"I'm good, chipmunk. How are you?"

"I'm doing good, Grams. What's new?"

"Hey, kiddo, I'm calling to let you know that Pops is going in for bypass surgery to clean up his heart. I know he would love to have you come home and be here with him."

"How serious is it, Grams?"

"It's pretty serious. They thought he was going in for double bypass surgery, but it looks like he's going to now have a quintuple bypass. It would mean the world to Pops and me if you were here."

"I will do everything I can to get there. I need to check with Alex, and I'll keep you posted."

Sarah called Alex.

"What are you calling for?"

"Hey, Alex, I just found out that Pops is going in next week for a quintuple bypass surgery to clean up his arteries. Grams asked that we come home to be a support system for her while Pops is in surgery. Grams didn't say it outright, but I got the feeling that she is extremely worried that Pops won't pull through. Is there any way you can get the time off from work to be there for me?"

Alex retorted, "Why do you always have to be there for your family? Why can't you ever tell your family no?"

"Oh my god, Alex, my grandfather has always been a major part of my life, the same way your mother is for you," Sarah yelled through the phone at him. "Why can't you ever just support me? Why do we always have to fight whenever it comes to my family, but whenever it comes to your mother, you always drop everything you are doing to run home to Mommy? She can just have a cold and you will run home to her, but whenever I ask for something you *always* give me a hard time."

"Give me an example of when I gave you a hard time about going home!" Alex challenged right back.

"Oh, is that the way you want to play things? Really? Okay, I can give you an example. When the hospital called after Harrison's accident, you refused to let me go home right away. You wanted to wait until later in the morning. I now have to live with the fact that he had to suffer longer than he needed to before I got there to be with him. One might ask, 'Why is that?' Because you didn't believe the doctor when it was said that my brother was in the bad shape, so you refused to get in the car and drive the eight hours home."

Exhausted, Alex asked, "Really, you want to bring that up again, Sarah?"

"You're *damn right*, Alex!" Sarah yelled at him. "You asked for an example, so I gave it to you. Why can't you just be as supportive of me as I am with you?"

"I support you."

Sarah couldn't help herself from chuckling a little bit when she asked him, "When? In what ways have you *ever* supported me?"

Alex stated, "I supported you when you tried to join the Marine Corps. When have you ever supported me?"

Sarah exclaimed, "I supported you when you moved us from Spring City to Bay Hollow. Once you were discharged, you wanted to move back home. I supported that move. When you couldn't make it into the force there, you moved us to Fair Falcon. I never complained once."

"I regretted moving us to Bay Hollow, which is why I moved us back to Spring City when I was medically discharged."

"Can you get the time off or not?"

"I will see what I can do. You may just have to go without me."

Sarah exclaimed, "SHOCKER! I am going to leave here on Sunday to drive home. Let me know as soon as you do know if you will be joining me by no later than Tuesday."

Sarah worked through Saturday, getting their apartment in order. She hated leaving the place anything but spotless when she knew she was going to be gone for more than a few hours. She reached out to her next-door neighbor, Susan, to see if she could watch her cats while she was going to be out of town.

"Hey, Sarah," Susan said when she opened the door. "What's going on?"

"Hey, Susan, I was swinging by to see if you would be able to watch my baby girls for a week."

"Sure, I would love to. Your girls are great and easy to watch. When do you need me to start?"

"I will leave tomorrow morning to head back to Spring City."

"Sounds good. I'll swing by Sunday evening to feed the girls."

"Thank you, Susan! I'll owe you one," she said as she smiled and turned around to go back to her own apartment.

Susan was the only person she trusted in the apartment when she and Alex were gone. Sarah and Susan hit it off right away; they were so much alike in so many ways. Susan enjoyed hiking and working out, she was also Sarah's height, and they could share clothes when needed.

After getting the apartment cleaned and ready for her to feel comfortable to leave for the week, she decided to get on her social media page, InstaChat, to let her friends know that she would be back in town starting Sunday night.

Found out that I'll be coming back to Spring City Sunday night and will be there through the week. Anyone want to grab a drink while I'm back?

Sarah leaned back on the couch with her laptop and scrolled through her InstaChat feed to see what was going on with all her friends. She started to doze off when her phone buzzed.

Jen

8:30 p.m.

I just saw your post on InstaChat; are you really gonna be home next week?

Sarah

8:32 p.m.

I am.

Jen

8:33 p.m.

Who died?

Sarah

8:35 p.m.

Pops is going in for heart surgery so coming back to be w/ Grams.

Jen

8:36 p.m.

Oh, Sarah, I'm sorry! I didn't mean to joke around.

Sarah

8:37 p.m.

You didn't know!

Jen

8:38 p.m.

You'll need to spend the entire time with your family; you won't have time to go out w/ anyone.

Sarah

8:40 p.m.

I'll make time to hang out w/ you.

Jen

8:41 p.m.

Keep me posted! TTYL.

Ethan

9:00 p.m.

Hey Sarah, I saw your post on InstaChat.

Did I see correctly that you're coming to town?

Sarah

9:03 p.m.

You read that correctly.

Ethan

9:05 p.m.

Is it just you coming?

Sarah

9:07 p.m.

Not sure.

I asked my husband if he was coming as well, but it's hard to say whether or not he'll come.

Ethan

9:08 p.m.

You up for a double date, if he comes back with you?

Sarah

9:10 p.m.

I can definitely ask & let you know.

Ethan

9:12 p.m.

Sounds like a plan.

Just let me know.

Sarah

9:15 p.m.

Sounds like a plan! TTYL!

After she got off InstaChat, Sarah immediately packed her bags into the car to hit the road Sunday morning to make the drive back to Spring City from Fair Falcon. She got into her 2013 panther black-colored Ford Edge that she bought three months before in the New Year sale to move out the old stock and make room for new. She stopped to get gas at the station that was two blocks from her apartment and then set her car's navigation to get her directions for the fastest drive back to Spring City. After being on the road for about two hours, Sarah got a call from Alex.

She answered the phone, "Hello?"

Alex responded, "I hope you're happy with yourself! I have to take three of my personal days in order to meet you in Spring City, but I got it worked out so that I can fly into Spring City early Tuesday morning. Are you going to come pick me up at the airport?"

Sarah was semiexcited when she heard this news, knowing that she wouldn't be going through this alone. She replied, "Yes, I will be happy to come get you! I know that you are mad at me because you have to take part of your paid time off in order to come be with me. I am sorry there is no other way for you to join my family and me at home to be there for my family. I'm sure we'll end up with your mother and brother at some point."

Exasperated, Alex replied, "I don't want to talk about it. Just be at the airport at eleven thirty Tuesday morning to pick me up."

Frustrated by his reaction, Sarah asked him, "Are you going to be able to hide your disdain for me while we're home? Because if you can't, then just don't even come! Why do you seem to hate me these days? It can't all be because I caught you with your whore, can it?"

"Oh, let me tell you since you won't let it go!" he replied. "*I hate you!* I hate that you make more money than me and especially because you lost the baby! You never wanted kids! It's all your fault! Had you wanted kids, you wouldn't have lost the baby!"

"Oh my god!" Sarah yelled into the phone. "You have gotten really good at blaming me for everything that goes wrong these days in your life. Can you ever start taking responsibility for your own behavior?"

"What do I not take responsibility for?" Alex asked.

"I'm tired of you constantly blaming me for losing the baby. I didn't do it on purpose! You always say that it is my fault that you keep cheating on me, but I am not at fault there," she replied back to him.

"Of course, you would bring that back up!" he retorted. "Don't forget that you cheated on me as well."

"You're damn right! I get tired of being blamed for *absolutely every little thing.* You made a decision to cheat on me, not just once but every week, multiple times a week. You continued to lie to me about what you were doing. Did you really think I was so dumb that I would believe that you were working fourteen-hour days five days a week? I am not as stupid and naive as you think I am! I got tired of being lied to, so I made a choice to cheat."

"Oh my god, when did I ever say you were stupid?" he cut in, trying to talk over the top of her, but she kept going.

"From the minute I came right out and told you what I did, I have always told you that I knew that it was the wrong choice. I also told you that I would never cheat on you again. You also committed at that time that you would never cheat again either, but guess what, you continued…continued not only to cheat but to lie about it. How can I ever fully trust you again?"

Alex replied, "I stopped trusting you the day that I found out you cheated on me. How do I know you didn't continue cheating on me after that?"

"How do you have the audacity to say that you don't trust me when you started cheating on me before we got married, and rumor has it that you cheated on me from the beginning? I have always been honest with you, I told you right after I cheated on you what I did because I knew it was a mistake. I wanted you to know what I did and how I felt. You told me that night you never truly cheated, but I wasn't dumb, I knew what you were doing."

"You're right, I told you three years ago on that night that you came clean that I had never cheated, but I lied. Apparently, you already knew or suspected that though. As you know, I continued to cheat on you, even had a longtime affair with one of my staff sergeants in my command that you were too dumb to see," he yelled at her, trying to make her feel even worse than she already did. "Oh, and by the way, that girl you saw me with at the diner, Bethany— she's pregnant with my baby."

"Oh, you think I didn't know? I knew… I just didn't feel like fighting with you over all of that. To protect myself from any and all the STDs you are carrying around on that nasty dick of yours, I just stopped having sex with you. Do you even remember the last time we were intimate? The last time we truly kissed? The last time we held hands?" she asked him.

Alex nastily responded, "I guess it wasn't memorable, so no, I don't really remember. Do you think I truly care?"

"Wow," Sarah replied. "I guess not. Why are we even still married?"

"I have no clue. Why don't we start talking about divorce after we get back from your grandfather's surgery?" Alex responded.

"Sounds like a plan!" she retorted. "I'm tired of you constantly lying to me. I'm tired of being faithful to a man who refuses to be faithful to me. Do you think you can at least pretend to still love me this week when we are around my family? I don't want to make this week any more stressful for my family than it already will be."

"I will pretend, but only because your grandparents don't need the distraction. I will put on my game face like we always do when we are around your family," he responded.

"Fine, thank you," Sarah said. "Can you do the same thing when we go out with Ethan and his wife, Grace?"

"What! Why would I want to go out with your old OCS recruiter and his wife?" he asked. "He's your friend, not mine."

Frustrated, Sarah replied, "You're such an asshole! Fine, if you don't want to come with me, I'll go by myself and meet them."

"I'll go, but know that I don't want to. I need to go now. Be there to pick me up at the airport Tuesday afternoon. Don't call me again before I get there on Tuesday."

"Which hoe bag are you going to bang now? Is she at least classy, or is she completely disgusting like the majority of them? Does Bethany know you're cheating on her with other hoes?" she asked. "You don't need to worry, I will not call you again. I will be at the airport Tuesday afternoon. Enjoy your bang! Here's to hoping she doesn't rip you off."

Seeing the Family and Making Plans

Sarah continued her drive to Spring City. After fighting with Alex for the last thirty minutes, she had to stop at the next gas station. She was not certain why she was crying.

Why are you crying, idiot? Are you finally facing all your unhappiness, or are you crying because your husband just told you that he hates you? When is the last time you remember truly being happy? Have you ever really been happy with him? Stop crying… He clearly doesn't deserve your love anymore. Pull yourself together! You're such an idiot for loving this man!

She started getting more and more upset with herself; she could not seem to stop crying no matter what she did. The more she cried, the more upset she got. Sarah took ten minutes to collect herself. Once collected, she got out from behind the steering wheel, topped off the gas tank, used the restroom, and bought a bottle of water, getting back behind the wheel. She called her mother to let her know that she was only about three hours into her drive and not to expect her back in Spring City until around six in the evening. She did not make any more stops on her journey and arrived right at six. Everyone was waiting on her to arrive so that they could eat dinner.

Sarah pulled up into Grams' driveway. As she contemplated whether to get out or to turn around, she looked up to see she had an entourage from the garage. She had no choice at that point; she had to force herself to smile and get out of the car and go inside to everyone waiting inside. She walked into the two-car garage right into the hallway leading from the garage into the kitchen, where Grams showed her all the new renovations that she and Pops made to the house. Grams showed loyalty throughout the kitchen with Whirlpool appliances, all in the stainless steel. She had a forty-two-inch French door refrigerator, six-burner stove, two ovens, and an island with three bar stools on the same side of the bar as the kitchen table. The kitchen had three open doorways; one doorway led directly into the hallway leading from the garage all the way through the dining room to the living room, one open archway led to the dining room, and the last archway from the kitchen led to the living room. The walls were lined with oak-stained cabinets. The countertops were Hawaiian granite. Grams' kitchen sink was a double basin drop-in sink.

As she walked into the kitchen, she immediately saw that her Grams and Mother had the island covered in food, ready for everyone to sit down and eat. Grams had the boys grill Sarah's favorite dinner, steak shish kebabs, while she and Violet worked on the baked potatoes and fresh sweet corn. Sarah also noticed that there was a vegetable tray with green, red, yellow, and orange peppers on it as well as cauliflower and broccoli.

"Why were you late, Chipmunk?" Grams asked.

"Accident on the interstate so everyone was gawking."

I hate lying! You can't be serious right now, Sarah. They don't need to know what happened. They will judge you and ask questions that you don't want to and can't answer right now. You don't even know what went wrong with your marriage. This marriage started out strong but quickly became toxic. Better for you to leave before the questioning gets worse.

"Earth to Sarah!" Hunter said as he kicked her in the shin.

"W-what's that?"

"When is Alex coming to town, or was he able to break away from his case?" Matthew asked.

"Oh, yeah." She looked up at her father. "He'll be here Tuesday afternoon. I have to go pick him up at the airport. What's the rest of the week look like? I've got a couple of friends who want to get together at some point while I'm back in town."

"Who wants to hang out with you, shrimp?" Hunter asked.

"Does it really matter?"

"Yep, now spill the beans, shrimp."

"Jen wants to meet up for lunch, and Ethan wants to do a double date with Alex and me."

Grams spoke up, "Well, Pops' surgery is Wednesday. Tomorrow afternoon is free if you want to meet Jen. Pops wants to go to Monday night's bingo game at the VFW. We can do lunch once Alex arrives on Tuesday. We'll all take turns sitting with Pops after he gets into recovery and have a buffet-style dinner Wednesday night, so anyone can grab food before turning in for the night. Thursday night should be free for you and Alex to go out on your double date."

Once she finished with dinner, Sarah went to into the living room to sit and listen to everyone in their different conversations, without interjecting into any of them. She continued to think about her fight with Alex, making her feel horrible.

Why did you say those mean and ugly things to Alex? You didn't need to do that, Sarah! You are such an ugly person. Why can't you just find a way to be happy and turn a blind eye to everything Alex is doing? Why should I have to turn a blind eye? Why can't he just be faithful? How is it my fault that he cheated on me? Why is everything always my fault? How is he so good at turning everything back on me even when it isn't my fault?

Why am I still in love with this pig? I hate him for everything he's put me through. What did I do to deserve this? How did I get into this mess? How do I get out of it?

She fought back tears because she did not want to explain what they were for to the family at this point. She had no idea why she was so torn up over this failed marriage. She had a husband who admitted to hating her and who consistently cheated on her... Her marriage clearly was over, so why could she not just admit it to herself? Instead of focusing on allowing her marriage to end, she decided she would try one more time to convince Alex to seek marriage counseling to see if there was any way to save their marriage.

After spending an hour listening to everyone else talking, she decided that she was tired and it was time for her to leave to go check in to her hotel room at the Spring City Inn and Suites. She got back in her Edge and drove the five miles to the hotel. She got herself checked in to the king-size room with a deep soaking Jacuzzi tub in the bathroom as well as a walk-in shower. She pulled out her phone and reached back out to Jen and Ethan to let them know what the plans for the week were. She sent them both a group text message to let them know that she was free for lunch or drinks Monday afternoon and then Thursday with Ethan and Grace.

Sarah

9:00 p.m.

Hey, guys, I just wanted to fill you both in on the plans for this week.

Jen: I can meet up w/ you for lunch or drinks tomorrow, if that works for you.

Ethan: Alex & I can meet you & Grace Thursday night for dinner, if that works for you both.

Jen

9:05 p.m.

The girls will be in school & daycare. I can meet you at Spring City Burger & Steak House around one, if that works for you!

Ethan

9:07 p.m.

Hey, Sarah, Thursday night at six thirty works for us, if that works for you. How does Zippy's Italian Restaurant sound?

Sarah

9:10 p.m.

Jen: One sounds good, meet you there tomorrow for lunch! Can't wait to see you!

Ethan: Six thirty will be fine & Italian sounds fantastic!

Jen

9:15 p.m.

Can't wait to see you tomorrow to catch up!

Ethan

9:17 p.m.

Be there or be square!

Sarah

9:18 p.m.

Can't wait to see you both! Have a great night!

After messaging and setting up plans with Ethan and Jen, Sarah felt much better. She hopped in the soaker tub to take a long hot bath with the jets running and sat in there for about twenty minutes. While she soaked, she let her mind wander back to the fight she had with Alex earlier in the day. She tried to think back to all the positive moments they had together over the last five years. All she could focus on was the negative because it was fresh in her mind after the fight. She got out of the tub as she felt herself drifting off to sleep.

Catching Up

Monday morning, Sarah woke up feeling slightly rested. She tossed and turned the entire night, waking throughout the night. When she got up, she threw her black running shorts, purple racerback tank top, and her running shoes on. She knew that nothing would clear her mind better than a long run, where it was just her and the sound of her feet hitting the pavement. She left her room and found a good sidewalk that she could run down. Before long, she was lost in the run and completely lost track of time and miles. She looked down at her Smart Watch and realized that she better get back to the hotel so she could get cleaned up before her lunch date with Jen.

Sarah arrived at the restaurant fifteen minutes before scheduled time to meet Jen. As she walked into the restaurant, she saw that it had been completely renovated since the last time she ate there. There were about forty tables and booths surrounding the restaurant. They removed about twenty tables from before to put a wraparound U-shaped wooden bar in the middle of the restaurant to pull in more customers. As the hostess seated her in the back booth next to the window, Sarah received individual text messages from both Ethan and Jen.

Jen

12:45 p.m.

Hey, Sarah, I may not be able to make it to our lunch date.

Sarah

12:46 p.m.

Oh, okay. Is everything okay?

Jen

12:46 p.m.

I have a sick kid & I'm trying to get Jordan to pick her up. Keep you posted.

Sarah

12:50 p.m.

Hate to hear that you've got a sick kiddo… Keep me posted on what's going on & if you need anything from me!

Ethan

12:45 p.m.

Hey, Sarah, whatcha up to?

Sarah

12:47 p.m.

I'm sitting at the Spring City Burger & Steak House, waiting to hear if my friend Jen is going to be able to meet me for lunch. Why, what's up?

Ethan

12:48 p.m.

I actually have the rest of the afternoon off from work & Grace is out of town for the night, so I wanted to see if you might like to grab a drink w/ my ass!

Sarah

12:49 p.m.

Isn't it a bit early in the day to start drinking? Lush much, LOL! :P Where is Grace?

Ethan

12:50 p.m.

You outta know that it's never too early to grab a drink! LOL! She's out of town for some training w/ her cosmetology business.

Sarah

12:51 p.m.

Feel free to swing by, I can hang out for a little bit... How long before your ass shows up?

Ethan

12:52 p.m.

Great news, I just drove by so give me a sec to flip a bitch & get there. I'll see you here in about 2 min.

Sarah

12:53 p.m.

Were you really texting & driving???!!!! Not exactly safe now, is it? You're such a dingbat!

Just as Sarah hit Send on her last message, she heard an old familiar deep, sexy voice with a mildly Southern drawl asking to be led to where she was waiting.

Stop blushing like a little schoolgirl. God, I forgot how fucking hot he is. Don't you dare let him see you like this. I could totally lose myself with him. You aren't even in his league, Sarah! He's so freaking hot! You need to stop! There's no way he'd ever be into you! I would love a chance to sleep with him! Stop! *We're both married, he'll never cheat on Grace, especially not for the likes of you!*

She could see this tall handsome man walking down the aisle toward her. Her stomach got butterflies, and her heart skipped a beat.

As she reached up to give Ethan a hug, her phone beeped with an incoming message from Jen.

Jen

1:00 p.m.

I have some great news! Jordan is going to pick up both Julia & JoyJoy from daycare so that we can hang out! Isn't that great? ☺

Sarah

1:01 p.m.

That's AWESOME! Hey, my friend and old recruiter, Ethan, texted so I invited him, not knowing that you were going to be able to join me! Do you mind if he hangs out w/ us for a bit?

Jen

1:02 p.m.

WHAAAAAAAATTTT????!!!!???? Wasn't he that tall extremely hunky recruiter from way back in the day? You still keep in touch w/ him? That's awesome!

Sarah

1:03 p.m.

Yes, he would be the 1 & only, but please don't say anything to him. I don't want to complicate things between us! He's married, I'm married... Just won't work out, so no point in even going there w/ him!

Jen

1:03 p.m.

OMG, I CAN'T WAIT TO MEET HIM!!!!!! I want to see just how hunky he is for myself! ☺ I'll be there in about 5. Where you sitting?

Sarah

1:03 p.m.

We're in the back corner. You'll probably see us through the window from the parking lot.

"Hey, everything okay over there?" Ethan pulled Sarah back out of her phone and put her attention back on him. She stood there silently for a minute, looking him up and down, taking in the eye candy in front of her. He had not changed much in the two and a half years since she last saw him. He still had that tan chiseled body she remembered. He was clean-shaven, with his light chestnut hair still cut in a high and tight. His shirt accentuated every muscle in his upper six-foot-four-inch-tall body. "Hey, I asked you if you were okay! You going to answer me or just sit there and stare at me?"

"Who said I was staring? Huh? I was thinking, you just happened to be in my line of sight!"

"Oh, it's okay! I know I am hot!" Ethan replied with a wink and a devious smile.

"I see you haven't changed a bit in the last two years." She laughed. "You're still as cocky as ever!" But as she said it, she found she just could not take her eyes off him.

"What was that with your phone just a couple minutes ago?" he asked.

"Oh, my friend Jen is going to end up making it after all. I hope you don't mind meeting her."

"Any friend of yours is a friend of mine!" Ethan replied, helping to put her at ease.

Just then, Sarah caught Jen out of the corner of her eye out in the parking lot walking in. Within a matter of seconds, Jen made her way back to Ethan and Sarah. Sarah watched as Jen quickly checked Ethan out. As she pulled Sarah into a big bear hug, Jen whispered into her ear, "Damn, girl, you need to find an excuse to hit that ass! Now, I know why you are so infatuated with him."

After Jen released Sarah from the bear hug, Sarah introduced Jen and Ethan. "Hey, Jen, this is Ethan, my former recruiter from back in the day. Ethan, this is my friend, Jen." The two of them shook hands, and then Ethan motioned for everyone to sit down. Sarah crawled into the side of the booth with her back up against the back wall, facing the front door of the restaurant. She moved to the inside of the booth so that Jen could sit next to her but was shocked when Ethan slid into the booth next to her. Jen sat across from them with a devious smile on her face.

The server came over and took their orders. While they sat there waiting for their food, Sarah, Jen and Ethan sat around trading stories about their families and what they had going for them in their personal lives. The conversation between the three of them came so naturally that they all jumped a little bit when their server came back with their food about fifteen minutes later. They started laughing at their reaction and then dug into their sandwiches.

As they finished eating, Sarah excused herself to use the restroom. She felt anxious and nervous. She did not want to leave Jen alone with Ethan because she was not sure what would come out of her mouth, but she could not fight the desire to purge any longer. Her mind raced as she walked to the restroom: *Oh god, are you sure you should do this... You know Jen can't keep her mouth shut when she's excited. I really hope that she doesn't spill the beans about how I feel about Ethan! I will die if she tells him that I had a crush on him.*

Sarah, you need to go purge to feel better. I guess you'll just have to trust Jen to stay quiet. You have this down to a science so you can be in and out of the bathroom in less than four minutes.

As soon as Sarah was out of earshot, Jen turned to Ethan. "Sooooooo," she started.

"So what?" Ethan smiled.

"So, I see the way you've been looking at my girl since I joined you two. What are you thinking?"

"What do you mean?"

"Don't play stupid with me. I have three girls, and I didn't get them by not being able to read a man's body language."

"And?"

"I can see the look in your eyes when you look at Sarah that I see whenever Jordan looks at me... You wanna screw her."

"E-excuse me?"

"You aren't denying it! I knew it!"

"Okay, busted! But you know she won't ever cheat on her husband. She's totally in love with him."

"How do you know she wouldn't cheat on Alex?"

"I just don't get that feeling from her."

"She will probably kill me if she knows that I told you what I'm about to tell you, but I think you need to know that Sarah isn't above cheating on Alex. She did it once before."

"What do you mean?"

"Alex is a dirty dog who cheated on Sarah. Sarah had a moment of weakness and gave in to the seduction of a classmate. She also told me that she had a crush on you way back when. She used to fantasize about being with you."

"Oh, really."

"So, now that you're armed with that information, what are you going to do with it?"

"I would have to hear it directly from her before I would be comfortable making a move."

"Well, you know she won't ever just come right out and say anything. We'll have to find a way to trick her into it," she said as she smiled at him.

"What do you have in mind?" He laughed.

"Well, I'm pretty sure I can get her to admit to it. What if I called you while you stepped away from the table and got her to admit that she wants to fuck you? Would you then make your move?"

"That's for me to know and you to never find out."

"Good to know that you wanna tap Sarah's ass! She'll be thrilled. Now, what's your phone number so I can call you when she gets back?"

"It's 555-231-5579."

"Whatever you do, don't hurt my girl! I don't see a ring on your finger. Are you married?"

"Technically, I am still married, but the divorce will be finalized in the next six months."

"If you hurt her, I will kill you, Marine!" Jen said quickly and quietly as she saw Sarah walking down the restaurant from the bathroom.

When Sarah rejoined them at the table, Ethan got up and let her back inside the booth. "Now that you're back, I suppose I should run and use the head."

As soon as he was clear of the table, Jen quietly reached for her phone and dialed Ethan's number and waited to see the call connect before she started in immediately on Sarah, "OMG, GURRRLLLL, when you told me he was good-looking, that was an understatement of the century! He is sooooooo fine, girlfriend! Not only that, he is COM-PLETELY into you. You need to get him to tap that ass of yours! He wants to, I can tell he does!"

Sarah just looked at Jen, rolled her eyes, and then started smiling like a little schoolgirl.

Oh my goodness gracious, why does she have to know me so well? She's such a monster but completely right! I hate her for this but love her at the same time!

"I told you he was good-looking, I wasn't lying about that! But there is no way he is into me. He's married with kids. I'm married. There is no way anything will ever, EVER happen between the two of us. I am nowhere near his league! Why are you smiling like that at me? I'm telling you that I am not his type!" Sarah exclaimed as she saw the smile continue to widen on Jen's face.

"What if I told you he was in the process of a divorce?"

"I would say you're lying! I'm *definitely* not buying it. I'm telling you he's devoted to Grace, and I'm not his type."

"Girl, I'm telling you, he told me that he's six months away from divorce and you are completely his type. He wants to hit that ass of yours, the same way you want him to hit it."

"Oh my god, would you stop already? He does not! Just because you're horny and getting a piece of ass anytime you want it doesn't mean that everyone else is that horny!" Sarah could feel herself blushing and getting flustered. It was hard to hear Jen spill the truth about how badly she really wanted things to escalate between herself and Ethan. She knew that this just would never happen. She tried rationalizing the fact that both she and Ethan were both married and that he would never cheat on Grace, with her of all people.

"Let me ask you a hypothetical question then."

"What's that?" Sarah asked.

"Well, let me finish! If Ethan came back and told you that you were his type and that he wanted to move things to the next level with you, would you? Would you have sex with him?" Her face no longer smirking, her devious grin was replaced with a serious look on her face.

"I... I honestly don't know! Do I want to, yes! I mean you hit that nail directly on the head. I want to, oh Lordy do I want to! But—and this is a GREAT BIG BUT—we are both married, and you know that I promised Alex that I wouldn't ever cheat on him again. As much as I would love to be with Ethan, I can't!"

Jen contemplated Sarah's response for a couple of seconds before responding back, "Why are you worried about staying faithful to Alex? You know he hasn't ever been faithful to you! He cheated on you before you got married and continued to cheat immediately after you walked down the aisle and said, 'I do.' You said it's been over two years since you last slept with him and you can't remember the last time you were truly intimate with him... Take this time to get intimate with a man who is *totally* head over heels for you! You owe yourself this. Now, I ask you again... If Ethan asked you to make love to him *right now*, would you do it? Be honest with yourself and with me, damn it!"

"OMG, you're relentless, aren't you! You aren't going to let up until I say yes, are you?"

"Nope," Jen laughed.

"*Fine*, yes, yes, I would have sex with Ethan if he made the first move and made it extremely clear that was what he wanted to have sex with me!"

Sarah was so flustered that she did not notice that Jen made the call when Ethan walked away from the table so that he could hear the entire conversation between them. She found herself starting to wonder: *What the hell happened to Ethan? Did he fall in, or did he run away based on the conversation that he had with Jen while I was gone? I wouldn't blame him for running away. That girl can be relentless when she thinks she's onto something. Maybe I should text him and make sure he's okay and didn't leave.*

Sarah

2:30 p.m.

Did your ass fall in?

Ethan

2:31 p.m.

If I did, are you going to come in here & rescue me? :P

Sarah

2:32 p.m.

Uh, NO! Get your ass out of the shitter & get back out here!

Ethan

2:33 p.m.

I'll get out there when I'm damn good & ready. You can't rush a person!

Sarah

2:34 p.m.

Don't forget to wash!

Ethan made his way back to the table and slid in next to Sarah again, this time she thought that he seemed to be sitting closer to her than he was before he left for the restroom. Jen must have noticed as well because she started smiling at Sarah and kicked her under the table. Ethan, Jen, and Sarah started chatting again; however, after five minutes of the group getting back together, Jen's phone buzzed. She informed Sarah that she needed to leave to go home and help take care of her daughter, JoyJoy, who was sicker than the daycare originally thought she was.

Ethan moved out of the booth so that Sarah could stand up to give Jen a hug. Once Jen turned to leave, Sarah sat back down. Rather than sitting across the table from her in the empty side of the booth, Ethan sat back down right next to her, pushing her into the corner of the booth. He took her left hand in his right as he turned slightly to face her. She shivered a little bit as he made physical contact with her. She realized just how well her hand slid right into his and how nice it felt to have Ethan's fingers interlocked with hers. She shivered again, wondering what was next, where this was going to lead next.

Oh my god! What is he doing? Please, please, please let this go where I think it's going. I feel like I'm blushing... Stop blushing! Don't make it so obvious that you want to jump his bones. I wonder what he would do if I just reached out and kissed him.

As she sat there wondering, lost in her own mind, she missed the fact that Ethan was staring at her, soaking in her every expression. When he could no longer sit there without advancing the interaction, he reached out with his left hand and cupped her chin in his hand. He pulled her face closer to his and reached down to kiss her lightly on her lips. She could not believe how soft his lips were and how much she longed for that touch on her lips again after they separated. As he pulled back from her, he saw the desire in her eyes that he felt, and before she knew it, he reached back down and had her lips covered with his own in a more passionate kiss.

She felt herself slowly part her lips to deepen the kiss. He quickly took advantage of this opportunity she made for him and moved his tongue into her mouth to engage hers. They both slightly shivered at the chemistry that this new touch created. She found her hands reaching out and under Ethan's shirt as he wrapped his hands into her hair, pulling the back of her head closer to his mouth. They were so engaged in their kissing that they did not hear the server come back to the table, so when she cleared her throat to get their attention and said, "You two need to get a room," they both jumped in the booth and hit their knees on the bottom of the table, kicking out their legs and hitting their feet on the other side of the booth. They started laughing like children at being caught.

As they waited on the server to bring the check back, Ethan reached back in for another quick kiss. Sarah could not believe how badly she wanted this kiss to linger and how much she wanted to see where this could potentially lead with Ethan. After they pulled away from this quick kiss, Ethan looked Sarah up and down. He then asked, "What are you doing for the rest of the afternoon? Did you have plans, or are you free?"

"I am free until late tomorrow morning. Why do you ask? What did you have in mind?" Sarah replied back to him, slowly tracing her lips with the tip of her tongue.

"Well, I was hoping by your reaction to being interrupted meant that you enjoyed yourself and was wondering if you wanted to go somewhere private. We could finish what we started." Ethan looked at her longingly.

"Well, I would love to, but first, I need you to know a few things," she replied.

"Can it wait?" he asked with a scheming smile.

"Probably, but I want you to know a few things before we move further."

"Such as...?"

"Well, for starters, I cheated on Alex once, a long time ago, and I promised him I would never cheat again."

"Okay, as I recall, he cheated on you, and knowing the type of guy he is, he is still cheating, am I right? It was only the one time, right?" he asked her.

"Yes, that would be correct to both questions."

"Okay, so why do you feel bad about seeing where this leads us?"

"I don't like breaking my promises."

"If it makes you feel any better, Grace has been cheating on me."

"Well, two wrongs don't make a right, goofball."

"That is true, but I won't hold this against you or think any less of you. What else?"

"Secondly, I haven't had sex in over two years. I obviously suck at it because Alex hasn't tried to have sex with me and the other guy never contacted me after our rendezvous."

"Okay, so far I'm not hearing anything horrible here. I would love the opportunity to see just how great you are in the sack for myself," he replied. "Anything else I need to know?"

"The other thing, I can't give blowjobs. Also, I have never had sex in any position other than missionary, and I want so badly to try something different with you. I hope this isn't a deal breaker."

"Well, that's it, now you've gone and done it. I'm going to go home right now and masturbate," he teased her. "It really sounds more to me like you're trying to weasel out of this. Here you go getting me all fucking horny, wanting to see where this leads, and now you're trying to be a dick tease." He winked at her.

"I can be a dick tease if you'd like." She winked back at him and started laughing. "I just wanted you to know where I stand before we get too involved."

"Well, Sarah, these confessions did not turn me off. In fact, they had quite the opposite effect. Now, I want you more than I did before. If I could take you here in this booth without our being arrested, I would do so."

"Haha, you're so funny."

"No, I'm dead serious right now. I can feel some apprehension though, so why don't we do this? Why don't we go back to your hotel room and just take things nice and slow? See where things lead, unless you really don't want to do this now."

As Sarah realized how badly she wanted to see where the chemistry would lead the two of them, she found herself agreeing to head back to her hotel room for the afternoon. They drove back to the hotel separately, to avoid one of the two vehicles being towed for being left in the restaurant's parking lot. Sarah was so excited at the possibilities that she found herself thinking that this was the longest seven-minute drive back to the hotel that she ever endured.

When they got to the hotel, Ethan parked right next to Sarah. He jumped out of the car as soon as he turned the engine off and rushed over to her side of the car where he picked her up and spun her around, before pinning her up against her car door and enveloping her in another passionate kiss. She responded by immediately wrapping her legs around his waist as he picked her up to make it easier to kiss her. As she wrapped her legs around him, he reached up with his right hand and started rubbing her left thigh, moving further and further up her leg, moving her shorts along with it, until he was only about an inch from her the seam of her black lace panties. As he pulled back from her embrace to catch his breath, Sarah breathed heavily but could not help herself reaching up and whispering in his ear, "How about we take this inside before we get arrested for indecent exposure?"

"Oh, you think they would do that? They only arrest ugly people for indecent exposure, and as we are both beautiful specimens of the human race, we have nothing to worry about… Let's stay out here and take our chances!" Ethan teased as he moved to put her back down on the ground.

"Follow me!" Sarah excitedly said as she walked toward the backdoor of the hotel, leading him inside. They walked down the hallway about ten feet before making a sharp right into another hallway. Her pace picked up in her excited state, and she quickly made the distance to the room at the end of the new hallway. As she searched for her key, Ethan playfully grabbed at her butt with his right hand and pulled her closer into him with his left. As though this was not enough to distract her from getting her key out of the bottom of her purse, she had to keep wiggling away from him while he nibbled at her ear. After what felt like an eternity, Sarah finally got the door open. Before she could turn to face Ethan, he picked her up and turned her around. She wrapped her legs around his waist. His lips immediately closed the distance to her parted lips, where he slid the tip of his tongue into her mouth.

He sat down on the sofa with her legs wrapped around his waist still. He continued to kiss her passionately. "How is this?"

"Perfect! Now, how about you lose the shirt," she replied.

"Only if yours goes off at the same time."

"You've got yourself a deal!" she said as she reached down and tugged at his shirt. They took turns getting their shirts off each other. He sat there soaking in the sight before him. Her breasts were contained behind a black lacey bra. He noticed that her ribs and shoulder blades were protruding just under the skin. He reached out and unsnapped her bra, letting her breasts out of confinement. He immediately took her left breast in his mouth and fondled her nipple with his tongue. "Ooh," she moaned, "that feels amazing."

As he switched to her right breast, she pulled her legs out from behind his waist and straddled his lap as he sat there. She reached down, unbuttoned, and unzipped his blue jeans. She took quick note that he was not wearing any underwear or boxers. "I see you decided to free ball, do you do that every day?" she teased him.

"It depends," he replied as he pulled her back in for another kiss. She reached down and pulled his testicles into the palm of her hand. She started slowly stroking them and then moved up his shaft. "Oh, holy shit! That feels amazing," he said as he kind of sat back allowing the wave of pleasure to overcome him.

She then stood up over him and waited for him to unbutton her shorts and pull them off, revealing the matching black lace panties to her bra, which was thrown on the floor with their shirts. She quickly stepped out of her shorts and then sat back down, straddling his lap again. She slowly started rubbing herself back and forth on his penis, then started rubbing a little faster. He reached down and started fingering her while she reached back with her right hand and continued fondling his balls. Short of breath, he pulled away just enough to look into her eyes before asking, "Are you sure you're ready to move on?"

"Oh my god, yes!"

She continued to rub on him and moved her hand from his balls to his shaft again, and as she came back down, she gently pulled his penis away from his body to where he could easily enter her. They stayed on the couch for a couple of minutes before Ethan stood up and made quick work of the ten-foot distance from the sofa to the bed, where he carefully laid her back onto the feather comforter. As they parted to catch their breath, he looked deeply into her eyes before he rested his forehead against hers.

She felt herself losing control as Ethan moved his right hand from her chest down to her right thigh. She heard herself quietly moaning as she longed for more of his touch. He pulled out and put his hand down in between her legs. Sarah found herself taking Ethan's hand and positioning it exactly where she wanted it; he gladly obliged. He started slowly sticking his index and middle fingers into her soaking wet vagina and then pulling them out again. As she started rocking with this motion, she found that he started thrusting faster and faster until she was moaning loudly. Sarah quickly found herself clutching his rock-hard penis in her hands, stroking it slowly between her fingers. Ethan bent down and started kissing her neck again. "Oh my god, would you just take me now. I don't want to just feel your cock in my hands, I want it inside again!"

"Oh, *really*?"

"Oh my god, did I just say that out loud?"

"You sure did! Where did you say you wanted my cock again?" he asked as he climbed back on top of her.

She was so elated that she couldn't speak; all she could do was open her legs and pull him into her body as she sat on the edge of the bed. Ethan slid his rock-hard throbbing penis into her. He started thrusting slowly. "How's this?" he asked her.

"Ooooohh, that feels AMAZING!" Sarah exclaimed with a smile on her face.

He started kissing her again, and as his tongue found her mouth again, he started thrusting faster and faster, her hips thrusting in fluid motion with his. As he was just about ready to climax, Sarah motioned that she wanted to be on top. She positioned her legs around his waist, lowering herself back down onto him. As she took control, she slowed down the thrusting. She started slowly rocking her hips back into his, sliding his penis slowly up and down inside of her, allowing them to feel all the motion together. He moaned in ecstasy as she made this transition. She teased him by slowly picking up the speed of her thrusting, and as he started to climax again, she slowed back down to get him to last longer. "Oh my god, this feels amazing! I don't know how much longer I can hold off."

"I'm ready for you to come now!"

That was all it took: he flipped her back over on her back, and he ejaculated inside her. After he finished ejaculating, he gently lay down on top of her, leaving his penis inside her. She felt him go flaccid.

She expected him to get up and get dressed at this point, because that was what Alex had always done right after having sex with her; however, Ethan did not do that. He lay there, still inside her, his face beside her neck in her hair. About a minute after finishing, he started kissing her neck again, down her collarbone, connecting with her breasts before moving back up to her lips. He started fondling her breasts again, her nipples still hard from before. She felt his penis slowly harden again. She thrust her hips back into his. He finished more quickly, and she did not tease him this time. He came inside of her for a second time. As he collapsed back on top of her, she started laughing at how sweaty they both were.

"What are you laughing about?"

"I feel like a little schoolgirl right now!"

"Why's that?"

"Can't explain it, just do!"

Ethan lay there another minute before he pulled out of her and got up. "You want to go sit in the hot tub with me for a few minutes?"

"Sure!"

She splashed him in the face with water as she joined him in the tub and cuddled up next to him, resting her head on his chest. Ethan pulled Sarah from beside him into his lap, positioned her in between his legs, pulled her back up to his chest, and wrapped his arms around her, gently massaging her shoulders with his fingers. She melted into his touch.

After enjoying the hot tub together for fifteen minutes, they both got out and dried off. Sarah dressed in a strapless purple sun-dress that flowed down just past her knees. Ethan dressed back in the clothes he was wearing when he met her at the restaurant, a button-down short-sleeve shirt and his relaxed cut Wrangler jeans.

After they dressed, they drove to Zippy's Italian Restaurant, where they enjoyed dinner, dancing, and wine before they headed out for a stroll along the outskirts of the city's central plaza. The pair could not keep their eyes or hands off each other through dinner or the park.

They lost track of time as they walked the park. When they realized how late it was, they moved to the west side of the park to sit and watch the sun set over the mountains. Once they found a quiet place to sit, they sat down and faced each other. Sarah looked up into Ethan's eyes; they locked their gazes on each other for a minute before he reached down and pulled her closer into his warm embrace and kissed her passionately. As they pulled away from each other, mildly out of breath, she snuggled closer to him, and he wrapped his arm around her shoulders.

This feels so comfortable! Why couldn't I have found Ethan right away versus finding Alex? I thought I was happy with Alex when I first found him. How stupid was I? Why couldn't I have just come clean with Ethan back when he was my recruiter? How would life have been different if we had gotten together immediately versus waiting until now? When did things go bad with Alex? We used to have moments like this. Why was he not happy with me?

I haven't been this happy in... I can't even remember the last time I was truly this happy. I can't believe we just had sex so many times tonight. Being with Ethan makes me happy! Is it possible to actually be happy? I wonder how many more times we can make love tonight!

She was so deep in thought that it made her slightly jump when Ethan brought her back to reality by asking, "Hello in there, you still with me?"

"Oh my god, I'm so sorry!"

"I thought I lost you there for a moment. Anything you feel like talking about?"

"Not really, haha. There is a lot of racing around up there, and it is like a winding corn maze to get around inside there," Sarah said.

"You aren't having any regrets about us, are you?" he asked her, concerned she was having second thoughts about the events of the evening.

"Oh my god, no! I have enjoyed today more than I think you will ever know or understand, probably more than I should."

"Are you sure? You looked like you might have been regretting what transpired earlier. I just want you to know that you can talk to me, tell me anything. I promise I won't judge."

"I can't tell you how much I needed today. I don't remember the last time I had sex with my husband at this point. It's been over two years."

"I know you said that earlier. I thought you were just joking around."

"Nope, not joking."

"Is he a fucking idiot?"

"What do you mean?"

"I mean you're a beautiful woman, not just on the inside but outside as well. You are such an amazing person who seeks to make people happy. You have a smoking hot body and an infectious smile. When I am around you, I can't help but smile, just because you are smiling."

Sarah nervously giggled at Ethan's response. "Well, that's what I was reflecting on...where it all went wrong in my relationship with Alex. I can't really remember the turning point in our marriage where it went from decent to what it is today. Can I ask what the story is with you and Grace? I remember back when I was your recruit you would never have thought about stepping out on your first wife, even when she kept accusing you of cheating with all the cute college girls."

His face completely changed as he reflected on what exactly to tell Sarah about his relationship with Grace. Sarah immediately regretted asking him, so before he could say anything, she spoke up and told him, "If you aren't ready to talk about this, then I'm fine with that. I'm sorry I asked. I don't want to get into something that makes you uncomfortable."

"No, it isn't that at all. It's just that as much as I remained faithful to both of my wives, neither of them could seem to remain faithful to me. I married Sherry, my first wife, right out of high school before I left for boot camp. As you know, we had two boys, Elijah and Emmanuel. However, as soon as I found out Sherry cheated, I divorced her. I then found Grace, and we dated for about a year before we moved in together.

"I found out about two months ago that Grace has been cheating on me the entire time we've been together. I filed for divorce from Grace last month. However, we are still living together only because I don't want my daughter to be living on the streets."

"Oh, Ethan, I'm sorry! I could say the same thing to you that you just asked me about Alex... How could they do that to you? You are an amazing person, and I truly feel blessed to have you in my life, even if just as a friend... Although, it wouldn't hurt my feelings if we could at least be friends with benefits from here on out." She smiled and winked at him.

Ethan effortlessly picked her up from the bench and put her on his lap. She straddled his waist with her legs. He gently pulled her lips in to meet his. Within seconds his tongue was inside her mouth. She started unbuttoning his shirt so that she could rub her hands on his bare chest. She pulled away temporarily, long enough to whisper in his ear, "Take me now! I don't think I can wait until we get back to the hotel!"

He saw the lust in her eyes. She made quick work of his zipper, pulling his already erect penis out of his pants. He ripped her panties to get them out of the way. She moved her skirt around them as she lowered herself onto him. They moved their hips up and down in perfect rhythm. After they finished, she rested her head on his sweaty chest. "Is it bad that I don't want this moment to end?" Sarah asked him.

"*Absolutely not!* I'm not ready for it to end either. Although it is starting to get chilly now that the sun has gone down. Are you ready to go back to the hotel?" Ethan asked.

She looked at him before replying, "Yes and no. I am starting to get cold as well, but I'm also afraid to go back."

"What, why?"

She looked down and couldn't meet his gaze, so he asked her again, "Why? What's going on?"

"I'm just worried that you will leave once we get back to the hotel and won't ever want to see me again, that I was just a one-night stand."

"Oh, Sarah... I can't imagine ever not seeing you again! You *definitely* are not a one-night stand! Can I tell you a secret?"

"You have secrets?"

"Maybe!"

"Haha, what's your secret?"

"I wanted to do this with you since the day we first met."

"What, are you SERIOUS?"

He looked at her with a smile on his lips. "Is that a bad thing?"

"Absolutely not! I remember the first time we spoke on the phone thinking you were absolutely adorable. Then when we met the first time when I came into the office, I was infatuated with you.

The more closely I worked with you, the more I thought about what I would do if you ever mentioned that you wanted to have sex. I was willing to break my promise to Alex that I would never cheat on him again to see where things would lead with us."

"Wait, what?"

"What what? What are you saying what to? The fact that I wanted to cheat with you all those years ago or that I cheated on Alex?"

"I guess both."

"Like I started to tell you earlier, I found out about a year into our marriage that Alex had been cheating on me since early on in our relationship. To make him feel as broken as I felt, I slept with a classmate of mine when class was cancelled. He flirted with me in class, and we went back to his place, where I gave in and had sex. When he never called me back, I began to feel like it really had to be my fault that Alex had been cheating on me for so long. I must have been a really shitty lay. I told Alex the following morning what happened. He threatened to leave me, and in order to save my marriage, I promised him that I would never cheat again that day. To this day, I still feel horrible for cheating on my marriage. Until today, I have remained faithful to him."

"Oh, Sarah! You are definitely not a shitty lay! I can attest to that!"

"I really hope that this isn't a deal breaker between the two of us! I know that most people think once a cheater, always a cheater… I promise, I am not that type of person. Although, that could be hard to picture as I just cheated on my husband for a second time with you."

"This is definitely not a deal breaker! Knowing what you've dealt with for so long, I honestly can't blame you for cheating on Alex. I know that our situation is precarious due to the fact that we're both married, and we live so far away from each other, but I want to enjoy what time we can sneak away together this week while you're in town to be just be with you."

He picked her up as he got up from the bench. He gently put her on her feet. He buttoned and zipped his jeans, and then they slowly walked back to the east side of the park, hand in hand. They made their way to the car and headed back to the hotel. When they got back to the hotel, Sarah expected Ethan to leave her. Her face showed a look of surprise when Ethan followed her back to the room. "I told you I didn't want the night to end!" he said when he saw the look on her face.

"I have just come to expect people to lie to me and tell me what I want to hear but then do the complete opposite. Can I ask you a question?"

"You just did! Haha, shoot."

"What was your favorite part of today?"

"That's a great question... Can I pick more than one thing?"

"You pick... It can be more than one thing."

"I am having a hard time picking just one thing, but I would have to say our time in the park was at the top of my list. What was your favorite part?"

"Realizing that you still want to try to make things work knowing about my history with Alex would have to be at the top of my list. Am I a horrible person if I said that I really enjoyed our intimate times and the fact that we had sex three times today? I've never done that before!"

"No, you're not a horrible person because I have to say that I enjoyed the fact that you kept up with me and weren't afraid to tell me what you wanted! Are you good with me staying the night with you?"

"Do you really even have to ask? Of course, I want your sexy ass to stay with me. Just know that I may possibly snore."

"That's a deal breaker... I don't sleep with women who snore!" He laughed. She playfully punched him in the arm.

"Well, you may have to take your chances and see if you can tolerate my snoring. But I don't want to force you into anything you aren't comfortable with."

"Oh, whatever! Get your tight little ass over here!"

"Oh, you think, huh?" She laughed and took a couple steps backward smiling at him with her devious smile. "If you want me, you're gonna have to come get me!"

"Oh, I think I can handle that. Are you sure you can get away?"

She ran to the opposite side of the room laughing, as he closed in on her. She jumped up on the bed to get away. He caught her midjump. They fell onto the bed together, laughing, tangled in each other's arms and legs. He reached out and kissed her. "Oh my god, you are so beautiful. I can't believe we were able to finally make this happen. I am thankful that Jen gave me the push to pursue this with you!"

"Say that again?"

"You are absolutely beautiful!"

"Why does it not shock me that Jen said something to you? She tried to push me into this as well. That crazy girl! I guess I'm glad she gave us the push we both needed. You are such an amazing person, Ethan."

He smiled at her, pulled her into him, and then showered her with kisses. "You make me so horny! I don't understand how Alex doesn't get this same feeling when he's around you. I want to have sex with you all night long!"

"You know, I'm not going to be able to walk right tomorrow. I'll be walking bowlegged. I haven't ever had sex more than once a day or night. You did that to me! I hope you're proud of yourself, mister."

"Oh, I am definitely proud to be the reason you're going to be walking bowlegged." He laughed. "Now, you never answered my last question."

"What question was that again?" she asked him, smiling deviously.

"Oh, you want to be that way, huh?" He smiled and winked at her.

"Maybe, whatcha gonna do 'bout that?" She smiled as she tugged at his shirt buttons.

He obliged her by taking his shirt off, then he said, "Now, then, I will have to punish you for being a naughty little girl."

"Maybe, have I been naughty here?"

"Oh, for sure! Now, what would you like for your punishment? A spanking?" he asked as he flipped her over gently and pulled her dress up over her buttocks and gently slapped her exposed flesh.

She started laughing. "Laughing isn't allowed here, young lady. I am going to have to continue your punishment if you continue laughing," he said with a smile on his face.

"Oh, no, what ever shall I do?" She wiggled out of his grasp and pulled at his pants again. Ethan quickly obliged by taking them off. He pulled her sundress and her bra off, and they stood there briefly staring at each other. Ethan reached down and kissed her. She gently pushed him backward onto the bed. He looked up at her from the edge of the bed. She jumped up to join him, pushing him onto his back.

Sarah and Ethan climaxed together. As she slid off him, he pulled her closer to him. She put her head on his chest and snuggled in close to him. They lay like that until they fell asleep.

"I hope you enjoyed last night as much as I did." He smiled and winked at her.

"Oh, I enjoyed myself very much! It's too bad we need to get up, shower, and head out for the day. I don't know how I'm going to face this week now."

"You're a strong woman. You'll make it through just fine. My biggest concern is making sure that Grace and Alex do not find out when we all meet for the first time on Thursday night."

"Oh, yeah, there is that. It's going to be hard pretending like we haven't seen each other in years when we just spent an amazing night together. I guess we'll have to cross that bridge when we get to it. For now, let's hop in the shower together before we part ways."

As Sarah got ready to hop in the shower, her phone beeped with an incoming text message. She grabbed her phone to see who it was.

Jen

6:30 a.m.

So, what all did you two do after I left you?

Sarah

6:31 a.m.

I don't know what you're talking about, Jen.

Jen

6:32 a.m.

Sure you don't! Did you hit that ass hard-core yesterday?

Sarah

6:33 a.m.

I don't know what you're talking about!

Jen

6:34 a.m.

Don't play stupid w/ me, girlie! I watched him scoot closer to you after I left & then he went in for the kiss! I know how badly he wanted to have sex w/ you!

Sarah

6:35 a.m.

How exactly do you know that?

Jen

6:36 a.m.

He told me while you were in the bathroom.

Sarah

6:37 a.m.

Jen! I asked you not to talk to him about it!!!!! I can't believe you right now. :'(

Jen

6:38 a.m.

But now you know where you stand w/ him! Is he as good in the sack as he looks? ☺

Sarah

6:39 a.m.

I'll never tell!

Jen

6:40 a.m.

Rude! Come on, you can tell me!

Sarah

6:41 a.m.

Gotta run! Gotta go join Ethan in the shower! ;)

TTYL

Sarah put her phone down and joined Ethan in the shower.

Picking Up Alex

After they showered and dressed, Ethan gave Sarah one final kiss before he left her there in the hotel room to finish getting ready to go meet Alex at the airport. She was nervous about how he would react to her when she got there after their huge blowup Sunday. The only contact she had with him on Monday was when he sent her a text with the time of his flight and the terminal he was flying into so she could pick him up out front with the rest of the passengers.

As she sat there reflecting on the events of the last two days, she became saddened by the fact that she had more passion with a man she had not seen in five years than she had with her own husband. She could not remember when the passion died.

There had to have been passion at some point because I was especially drawn to him, but when did it die? Why was he drawn to me? He was clearly a player when we started dating. If he had a sex addiction, why did he stay with me? I remember enjoying all our dates. When did spending time with Alex become so painful?

She started crying thinking about that memory and then thinking about the first time she found out he cheated on her.

Why do I still have feelings for a man who clearly doesn't reciprocate the feelings? Why, after spending an amazing night with a fantastic man, am I still thinking about trying to make things work with my husband? I can't give up on my marriage. I did say, 'For better or worse, till death do us part,' in front of all my family and friends. I need to honor that promise. I guess I should really try to make it work, if Alex is willing to continue working on our marriage.

Alex seems to like women who show skin. I've always been a modest dresser. Maybe I should try something I haven't ever really done before… Let me wear this new halter top and pair of skinny jeans I bought to show off my abs and ass. Let's see if that grabs his attention. If anything is going to get his attention, this will be the outfit to do it.

She grabbed a sweater she could throw on while they were at lunch with her family and walked down to the front desk.

The young woman at the desk smiled and asked, "How may I help you this morning, ma'am?"

"Um, yes, can you please ask housekeeping to strip my bed, including the comforter, when they come in to clean my room this morning? Also, can you make sure they clean up all the towels and replace those as well?"

"I would be happy to ask them to do this for you, ma'am. What is your room number?"

"Oh, yeah, it would help if I gave you that information, wouldn't it? I'm in room number 126. Thank you for ensuring that all the bedding and towels get replaced today before I get back here in about two hours."

"We will be happy to get this all done for you! You have a nice day, and we'll see you in a little while, Ms. Clark."

Sarah left the hotel and walked out to her car. She instantly remembered the events of the afternoon before. She smiled as she thought of this memory, then she became instantly sad because she knew that would not be Alex's reaction when he got into the car with her.

Driving the forty-five minutes from the hotel to the airport, Sarah tried to think of other ways to win Alex back over. She decided that she would park in the garage and would go in and greet him at the baggage claim. That way he could see the outfit she picked out to meet him in.

Arriving at the airport, Sarah parked the car on the same deck of the garage as the baggage claim carousels. She took a deep breath and got out of her Edge. She walked into the airport, turning heads as she walked through the doors. She heard people she walked by make comments: "Oh, wow, did you see her abs?" "I'm jealous!" "Who would wear an outfit like that? What a skank!" "Look at her collar bones and ribs sticking out, that's disgusting!'"

She continued walking to the correct carousel and waited for Alex to join her, amidst all the comments and stares.

Within ten minutes of her arrival at the carousel, she looked up and saw Alex walking toward the carousel, his eyes down in his phone so he did not see her at first, smiling and slightly waving at him. She saw that whatever he was looking at on his phone had him smiling the way she secretly hoped he would when he saw her. When he arrived at the carousel, his smile immediately faded, and he growled at her, "What the hell are you doing here? I thought I told you to wait for me at the curb. Who told you to bring your skanky ass in here?"

"I thought it might be nice to help you grab your bag."

"I honestly don't want to see you at all, but I told you I would come in because I like your grandfather. I will put on the fake smile and happy face when we are with your family and your friends, but don't expect me to do that when it is just the two of us together. I don't want to talk to you, I don't want to hear your voice, and I especially don't want to see your body."

They walked out to the car in silence after Alex's bags arrived. Once inside the car, Sarah turned on Alex and asked, "What the fuck is your problem? I know for a fact that your hoe, Bethany, dresses this skanky and you seem to swoon over her when she dresses this way, and the clothes don't fit her right because she's pudgy with fat rolls galore. Why is it okay for her to dress this way but not me?"

"You don't dress this way, you never have... Are you sleeping with someone new? Is that why you decided to dress this way, you little whore?"

"If anyone is the whore, it is you, not me, putting your dick into anything with a vagina! I dressed this way because, like a dummy, I had hoped that this might help us get back to who we used to be. You used to beg me to wear clothes like this and praised me when I broke down on special occasions and did. I had hoped we could possibly mend things, but I see that isn't the case here."

"What the hell ever made you think we could mend fences? You're so fucking dumb, you dumb whore! I hate you! You're just so fucking dumb," he scoffed at her from the passenger seat. "Now, are we going directly to lunch, or do we have time to stop by the hotel first so I can change?"

Trying to keep herself composed, she looked away and put the car into drive; she headed back to the hotel so he could change clothes and take a quick shower. "I'll take you to the hotel first so you can shower before we meet my family for lunch. You fucking smell like her, and I don't want my family to smell that skank on you." They rode the remaining forty minutes back to the hotel in complete silence. Sarah stared at the road as she drove, trying not to notice him texting Bethany out of the corner of her right eye. Every few minutes she would hear him laugh a little bit as he texted back and forth with her; Sarah could only imagine what he was telling the bitch he was cheating on her with.

They made it to the hotel. She walked him to the room and let him in so that he could shower and change. While he was in the shower, she quickly changed into her regular clothes, a baggy T-shirt and her baggy carpenter-style blue jeans. After she changed, she went back outside to wait on Alex to appear.

Sarah

11:30 a.m.

Just wanted to let you know that I just got Alex picked up and he wanted to go back to the hotel to shower and change before we meet everyone for lunch. We will just meet you at the restaurant at noon rather than meeting you all at Pops & Grams' place & riding in w/ everyone else.

Mom

11:31 a.m.

You know that Pops & Grams are going to be very disappointed you didn't come over 1st so that we could all ride over to the restaurant together, don't you? ☹

Sarah

11:32 a.m.

Yes, Mom, I'm fully aware of how they are going to react. ☹ Alex got on a flight after working an overnight shift, and he wanted to make sure he looked & smelled his best before meeting everyone. He didn't want to smell like he'd been riding on a plane for the last 2 hrs. Can you really blame him?

Mom

11:33 a.m.

Is everything okay?

Sarah

11:34 a.m.

Things are fine. We'll see you in a little bit.

Mom

11:37 a.m.

Okay, I get it, I'll let everyone know so that we can go ahead & get in the cars & head that direction. We'll see you in about 20 mins. Love ya, kiddo!

Sarah

11:40 a.m.

Luv u 2, Mom <3

Sarah

11:30 a.m.

I can't stop thinking about last night!

Ethan

11:32 a.m.

Me either! I'm getting horny just thinking about you! What are you wearing?

Sarah

11:33 a.m.

Skinny jeans & a halter top.

Ethan

11:34 a.m.

Ooh, sexy! I feel like I need a cold shower now!

Sarah

11:35 a.m.

Gotta go! Know that I miss you & wish I could be with you right now rather than with my husband!

Ethan

11:36 a.m.

Bye, sexy! Have a good day! I'm gonna run to the bathroom & jerk off now!

Sarah

11:37 a.m.

Don't get busted, Gunny! ;)

Sarah deleted the text chain between her and Ethan and finished her last text to her mother as Alex walked out of the hotel. As they got into the car, he saw she had her phone out and asked, "Who you texting, whore? Your new boyfriend?"

"No, I was texting my mother, if you must know. You're welcome to come over here and look, if you would like to. I'm not the one cheating in this marriage."

"Whatever! I don't know why I even asked, it's not like I truly give a shit about what you are or aren't doing with your life these days. Our marriage can't end soon enough. I can't wait to get back to Fair Falcon and find a divorce attorney who is going to help me take you to the cleaners in divorce proceedings!"

"Did you ever love me?" she blurted out before she realized she was saying it out loud.

"What?"

"You fucking heard me, I just asked you if you ever loved me? If you did, when did that all change for you? When did you stop loving me? If you didn't love me, then why string me along for all this time in a loveless marriage?"

He looked her straight in the eyes and said as maliciously as he could, trying to inflict the most damage, "No, I never loved you."

She knew he wanted to get a reaction out of her so she knew she could not allow herself to show any emotion. "How do you ask someone you don't love to marry you and then follow through with the wedding and the marriage for five years, wasting their life and your own?"

"Are you *serious* right now? You *really* want to have this conversation right now, as we are on our way to meet your family for lunch?" he yelled at her.

"You know what, forget it." They rode the remaining ten minutes in complete silence, which seemed to be what they were best at these days.

They pulled into the restaurant just behind the rest of her family. They put on their game faces and got out of her Edge and walked toward the rest of the family, who was crawling out of her Pops' Ford Expedition. Before they could enter the restaurant, Sarah and Alex had to give everyone a hug. Once the hugs were finished, they all walked inside to greet the hostess, who walked them back to their table at the back of the restaurant.

Lunch went well. Everyone enjoyed their meals. As they took their last bites, Grams got everyone to quiet down so they could discuss the events for the rest of the day and the following couple of days. Alex mentioned that he wanted to take some time before dinner to go over to his mother's place, since she lived in Spring City, about twenty minutes from the restaurant and Sarah's grandparents. Sarah and Alex excused themselves from the table, thanked Pops and Grams for lunch, and gave their hugs. As Sarah came to her mother in the hug line, her mother asked, "What's going on? Is everything okay between the two of you?"

Sarah quietly replied, "Everything is fine, Mom. Now isn't the time to talk about it."

"Are you sure?"

"Yes, I'm sure. We'll be back over to Pops and Grams' by no later than four thirty tonight to help get everything ready for dinner. Do we need to stop and pick anything up before we get to the house?"

"Not that I know of, but if that changes, I've got your number. I'll text you to let you know. Have fun and stay safe! We'll see you here in a little bit."

Sarah and Alex got back in the SUV and drove over to Anna's house in silence. When they arrived, Anna came out to meet them in the driveway. She gave Sarah a dirty look and then moved on to embracing her son. "Damn, kid, you look good. You look happier than I've ever seen you. I can't believe you're finally going to be a daddy! You'll make a great daddy! How's Bethany doing? Is she starting to show?"

"You told your mother about Bethany?" Sarah looked at Alex and asked.

"I sure did. Why wouldn't I tell my mother about the woman who is carrying my child and whom I am madly in love with?"

"Wait, come again? She's carrying your child? How far along is she?"

"Oh, silly girl, she's about four months along. How did you not know that?" Anna asked her, smiling. "I'm going to finally be a grandmother! I can't wait!"

Turning back on Alex, Sarah asked, "You think you're in love with her? Do you think she will still be in love with you when she finds out that not only are you cheating on me with her, but that you are cheating on both of us with multiple women? Do you think she will let you see your child then? Wow, you're even dumber than I imagined!"

Alex turned away from Sarah and turned back to his mother. They continued their conversation there in front of her about Bethany and the baby.

Don't you dare cry, Sarah! You'll just be giving them a reason to dig at you if they see tears. You need to be stoic! Why do you even care? You've known for a while that he no longer loved you. Why is it impacting you so much that he told his mother that he got Bethany pregnant?

After a while, she excused herself from the conversation and went outside to take a walk. She did not want to hear any more about the woman carrying her husband's child in her womb.

She thought back to all the arguments they had over the years about her not wanting to have children. She thought about the pain of losing her own baby.

Lost in her thoughts and memories, she stopped paying attention to what she was doing and almost walked out in front of a car. Thankfully, the driver was able to stop before hitting her. He honked his horn, and she immediately sprung back to reality. She waved and apologized to the driver as she walked in front of him.

"Hey, lady, pay attention to what you're doing! I could have killed you."

"Again, I'm sorry! It won't happen again!" she said as she waved and finished walking across the street. As she said it, she thought to herself, *Maybe I would have been better off if he hadn't stopped and had just hit me.*

She looked down at her WalkBit and realized that she had walked for about an hour. The time was nearly three o'clock. She decided she better turn around and walk back to Anna's house; although, she knew that Anna and Alex had not missed her. She cleared her head of all thoughts, put in her right ear bud, and put some tunes on. She did not want to put both ear buds in so that she could stay alert to anything happening in the street. She got back to the house without any issues. She was right, Alex and Anna did not miss her; they acted as though they did not realize she had left and was now back. She sat and listened to them talk for another half hour before finally speaking up, "Alex, it is time to leave to get back to Grams and Pops' place."

Both Alex and Anna looked at her with extreme disgust for interrupting their conversation. "How dare you interrupt my conversation with my son!" Anna yelled at her.

This verbal abuse from Anna was nothing new to Sarah. She had always quietly put up with it in the past, trying not to upset her marriage with Alex; however, with recent revelations and knowing that their marriage was over, Sarah yelled back at her. "How dare you! You treated your son like shit his entire life, and now all of a sudden because he is going to give you a grandchild, you want to start treating him right. You're such a two-faced hypocrite. The two of you deserve each other. You're both abusive narcissists. I hope for Bethany's sake she realizes this before it is too late. You can go to hell, Anna. Alex, are you coming or not?"

"What gives you the right to speak to my mother like that?" he yelled at her.

"Five years of quietly putting up with her bullshit and biting my tongue is what gives me the right. In six months or so, I won't have to worry about her feelings ever again. I won't have to listen to you bitch about how horrible a woman she is, how controlling and manipulative you think she is. Neither one of you will be my problem once the divorce is finalized. That day can't get here soon enough for me at this point!"

"Alex, are you going to let her speak to us that way?" Anna shrilly screamed.

"You either come with me or stay here with her. If you stay with her, I will bring your shit from the hotel sometime tonight and then the two of you can figure out your travel arrangements. I will have absolutely nothing to do with you, other than to sign the divorce documents, ever again if you stay with her. Once I get home next week, I will throw your shit out on the lawn, so you better ask Bethany to come pick it up. I'm done and over this shit. Are you fucking coming or not?"

Alex stood there, staring at Sarah. She had never stood up to him like that before in front of other people, and it took him by surprise. She turned and started walking toward the car. She heard the door shut behind her and was shocked when Alex got into the passenger seat beside her. He continued to stare at her as she started the car and pulled out of his mother's driveway.

"What? Why are you fucking staring at me?"

"I can't believe you did that. Are you out of your goddamn mind? You know I will never hear the end of this now, right?"

"It's like I told you back there, I no longer give a damn about you or your mother. I wanted to try to make this work, but after this morning, I knew that wasn't possible. After finding out that you got Bethany pregnant, I knew you couldn't have ever loved me. I still don't understand why you would have dragged this out for so many years if you never loved me or why you told me you couldn't live without me. I guess I'll never understand that, and at this point, I don't really care anymore. You're now Bethany's problem to deal with, not mine. I'll put on a happy face for my family while we're here together and Thursday when we go out with Grace and Ethan, but when it's just the two of us alone, I don't want to hear a peep out of you, got it?"

He just continued to stare at her.

In the last six years, I've never seen Sarah come close to her breaking point. She usually lets everything slide off her back like water rolls off a duck, but lately she's no longer afraid to let me have it. I kind of like this side of Sarah and it kind of turns me on. I wonder why that is? I also can't believe she thinks she can talk to me that way. What a bitch! She wonders why I no longer love her!

Pops

They pulled in the drive at Tanner and Hailey's house around four thirty. When they got there, they found Sarah's father, Matthew; mother, Violet; her brother and sister-in-law, Hunter and Brenda; and her five-year old nephew, Brennen, all out in the yard playing or watching on the sidelines. As they exited the car, Brennen came over and pulled on Alex's shirt. "Uncle Alex, will you come play catch with me? Daddy says he's tired."

Alex looked over at Hunter, who was doubled over breathing heavily, fighting bronchitis. He then looked at Sarah before finally agreeing to play catch with his nephew. Even though he knew his marriage to Sarah was over, he wanted to enjoy all the time he could spend with Brennen.

I am going to miss this once Sarah and I are divorced. I really hope that Bethany and I have a little boy so I can go out and play catch with him once he's big enough. I hope he wants to play baseball or football. I don't know if I could handle him wanting to do anything else.

Sarah went inside the house to help Grams finish getting the final touches on dinner, while her Father and Pops finished grilling the meat. When she entered the gigantic kitchen, Grams put her knife down and came over to embrace her in a giant bear hug. She whispered so that no one else in the house could hear her, "Kiddo, I know that things haven't been good between you and Alex in quite a while, but I want you to know that Pops and I really appreciate the fact that you are both here for his surgery in the morning. It means a lot to us that you are here, even if you are putting on a front for us."

"Wait, how did you know? I haven't told anyone, not even Mom?"

"Oh, kiddo, we're not blind. We have seen it in your face for a couple of years now that you weren't happy. I just wish that there was something we could do to make it all better for you!"

She walked away before Sarah could answer, picked her knife back up, and continued cutting the vegetables for the veggie tray. Sarah grabbed a paring knife and joined her at the kitchen sink. Together, they made a colorful vegetable platter, full of colored peppers, cauliflower, broccoli, and radishes. They finished boiling the corn and set the table. Grams went outside to hand the boys a meat platter and to call everyone in to wash their hands for dinner. Everyone came in, sat down at the table, and grabbed the hands of the person sitting on either side of them. Pops led the family in a brief prayer: "Thank you, Lord, for this food that you've provided. Bless it to nourish our bodies so that we might do your works. Thank you for guiding my surgeon's hands tomorrow morning when he has my heart in his hands. Thank you for a speedy recovery. I also pray that everyone here in this room find the happiness they seek. I pray these things in your name, Amen!"

"Amen" rang out around the table.

After dinner, Sarah excused herself from the table. She cleared empty plates from those who were finished and took them to the sink. She started rinsing them before putting them into the dishwasher. Alex joined her at the sink, taking rinsed dishes and placing them into the dishwasher. She never looked at him, just handed him dish after dish until the dishwasher was full and the table cleared.

Once the dishes were ready to go, she started her "goodbye tour" as Alex called it, giving everyone hugs and kisses. She made sure to give Pops his regular hug and kiss, but she also gave him a "Good luck, see ya on the back end" hug and kiss because she knew she wasn't going to see him before he went into the operating room in the morning. She then walked to the car, Alex closely following behind her.

When they got to the hotel, she went into the bathroom and changed into her pajamas—an oversized T-shirt and jogging pants. She stuck her finger down the back of her throat and quietly threw up everything she had just eaten for dinner into the toilet. She brushed her teeth before she opened the door and walked back out to the bed. She crawled up into the bed where she and Ethan spent the previous night together, turned off her light, and started to go to sleep.

Alex watched her get into bed. He realized he had not paid any attention to just how skinny Sarah was these days; she hid it well by keeping her body in good shape with exercise. He had no clue that she was hiding her eating disorder from him and everyone else in the family. He went into the bathroom, took another shower, and then crawled into the bed beside her.

She felt his eyes staring at the back of her head; however, she had already decided before he joined her that she was not going to look at him. She felt Alex start to reach out to touch her, but she immediately recoiled from his touch as soon as his fingers made contact with her shoulders.

What makes him think he has the right to touch me with all the horrible things he said to me this week, not to mention the last couple years? I do not want this man who does not love me touching me. I wish he would just go sleep on the couch. I don't even want to be in the same room as him right now.

After being rebuffed, Alex pulled his hand back under his side, rolled over, turned off his light, and started snoring instantaneously. She let out a sigh and then closed her eyes.

The next morning, Sarah woke up to find the bed empty and Alex nowhere to be found. She heard the door as it quietly opened and closed as he came back into the room. She rolled over to see that Alex brought two plates of breakfast food from the hotel restaurant. He looked at her and said, "I brought you your favorite: a Belgian waffle with melted butter, smothered in maple syrup. I hope you enjoy."

"Thank you. You didn't have to do that!" She smiled at him as she took the waffle from him.

She ate half the waffle in silence as Alex got showered, shaved, and dressed. Once he finished in the bathroom, she took her clothes into the bathroom and shut the door. She did not want to let him see her fully naked. She turned on the shower to cover the sound of her purging. When she finished purging, she hopped into the steaming shower and lost herself in the water. She felt a little light-headed, and before she could sit down, everything went black. She felt herself falling backward. Sarah came to with paramedics checking her vitals. "W-what happened?" she asked as she searched the room.

"Ma'am, it appears as though you passed out in the shower. Your husband heard you fall, and when he couldn't get you to wake up, he called us in."

"Where is he?"

"He was asked to step out of the room so that we had room to work on you, ma'am."

"I'm feeling better. You can go ahead and leave now."

"I'm afraid we can't, ma'am. We have to transport you to the hospital to have you checked out by a doctor."

"I'm fine, I promise! I don't need to go to the hospital. Well, I guess technically I do need to get to the hospital, but I have to be there with my family for my grandfather's surgery. I'm just a little stressed right now, and it got to me. I'll be fine, really!"

"Are you refusing medical treatment, ma'am?"

"Yes, I am. Do I need to sign a waiver so that you can get on to the next emergency?"

"The only way we leave without taking you into the emergency room is if you sign the waiver. Let me go grab that right now for you to sign. I'll be right back."

As the cute paramedic got up to grab the form, Sarah saw Alex walk back into the room out of the corner of her eye. He came over to her as she lay on the bed, head propped up on two of the pillows. "What happened? Why am I hearing that you are refusing medical treatment?"

"Well, I don't need medical treatment, that's why I refused it. I'll be fine. It's just stress. We need to get to the hospital to be with the rest of the family. We'll leave as soon as the paramedic comes back with the form for me to sign stating that I refused to be transported to the hospital. Clearly, I can't drive, so you'll need to do that. Grab my keys and bag, please."

Alex started to protest, but then thought better of it.

What is she hiding? Why does she not want to share what is really going on with me? Why can't she just let me in? I can see she isn't healthy. Why would she refuse medical treatment? I guess the best thing to do right now is just to keep an eye on her and let her talk when she's ready. If there's one thing I know about Sarah, she's stubborn and won't talk if I push her.

Sarah signed the form, and the paramedics left. Alex grabbed her clothes from the bathroom and then turned around so that she could get dressed without an audience. He helped her to the car, where he lifted her into the passenger seat. He drove the thirty minutes to the hospital, where the rest of Sarah's family was waiting in the surgical waiting room for news about Pops.

Grams came over and threw her arms around both Sarah and Alex. "I'm so glad you guys could make it. Everything okay with you two lovebirds?"

Alex started to tell the family what happened but was quickly silenced by "the look" Sarah gave him from the other side of Grams' embrace. "Oh, yeah, everything is fine. We just slept through the alarm this morning. I'm so sorry, it won't happen again while we're here visiting," she told Grams.

Grams eyeballed them both suspiciously, but then she let go and walked back over and sat back down, waiting to hear anything back about how surgery was going. Just then a young man, about six feet, three inches tall, came into the room.

"Hi, Dr. Wylie, how is my husband doing?" Grams asked the good-looking young doctor with a fit physique, blue eyes, and an obviously shaved head.

"Well, Mrs. Anderson, there was a bit of a complication once we got Mr. Anderson's chest open, so the surgery is going to take a little longer than expected. I wanted you to know so that you don't stress. We expect everything to turn out just fine. Hold tight, and I'll be out shortly with another update for you all."

Sarah saw the fear in Grams' eyes, even though she tried to keep a stoic look on her face for the rest of the family, who reacted very poorly to the news. Sarah looked at Grams and mouthed, "He's a tough cookie, he'll pull through just fine! I love you!"

Grams smiled back at Sarah and mouthed back, "I know you're right! He'll pull through, he has to!"

"He's too tough to do anything but pull through this! He told me last night that he's not ready to go yet, he still has things on his bucket list to get done. We don't need to worry about him."

They all sat and watched as Brennen played quietly in the middle of the waiting room. Sarah was glad they did not have to share the room with any other families; there was enough stress in the room waiting for Dr. Wylie to come back in the room without adding stress from another family in there with them. About an hour after his first visit, Dr. Wylie rejoined the group again to give them the great news:

"Mrs. Anderson, Tanner pulled through his surgery with flying colors. He is currently in the recovery room. Once we ensure that he has pulled out of the anesthesia, we will move him to his own private room in the ICU, where you will be able to visit him two at a time for about thirty minutes at a time. Mrs. Anderson, you will be the only person allowed to stay with him as long as you would like."

"Thank you, Doctor, we really appreciate that you were able to pull him through this surgery safely. You were the answer to our prayers!"

While they waited for Pops to move to his own room, they took the opportunity to create a timeline to ensure everyone got to spend time with Tanne and still got to spend time doing whatever else they wanted to do. They all agreed that Brennen did not need to go in the room right away and that they would wait until Pops was out of the hospital before Brennen would spend time with him, not wanting to scare him with all the tubes.

Sarah and Alex waited their turn to go in and see Pops. They spent their thirty minutes in the room making Pops laugh with jokes. When their time was over, they walked back into the waiting room. Sarah told everyone she was tired and was going to go back to their hotel room to rest until it was their time to come visit again later in the afternoon. Grams looked at Sarah with concern, but Sarah dismissed it by saying, "It is nothing to worry about Grams, I just didn't sleep well last night, so I want to go back and take a nap to make sure I'm refreshed for my afternoon visit."

They walked out to the car after saying goodbye to everyone. Alex turned to her when they got into the car and asked, "Do you want to tell me what is going on with you?"

"I'm fine, just tired. I just want to go back to the hotel to rest. You can do whatever or whomever you want while I rest, I don't really care what you do."

"Sarah, I know you're hiding something from me. You don't lie very well. I know all your tells, you forget that."

"Think what you want to think, Alex. At this point I don't really care anymore! You made it clear that you checked out of our marriage years ago, so you no longer deserve to know what is going on with me. Please just drive me back to the hotel."

They drove the rest of the way back to the hotel in silence. Alex parked the car, got out, and walked into the room. As she fumbled to get the door unlocked, she could feel the light-headedness returning. She was terrified that she was going to pass out again, knowing that if Alex found her like that again, he would either leave her or would force her to go to the hospital, and she did not want either to happen. She got the door open and made it to the bed before the blackout happened again.

Five hours later, Sarah woke up to someone beating on her hotel door. She groggily got up and opened the door to find her mother, Violet, standing outside the door.

"Mo-om, what are you doing here? What time is it?"

"Spill it, kiddo, what is going on with you?"

"W-what do you mean? What are you doing here?"

"Sarah, you missed your second visitor's session with your grandfather. Where is Alex? Why is he not here making sure that you are okay?"

"I'm f-fine, Mom. I must have been really tired and lost track of time."

"Enough with the shit, I've always been able to tell when things aren't right with you. I need you to be honest with me. What is going on with you and Alex?"

"What makes you think there is something going on between us?"

"Chipmunk, it is written all over your face when he is around you. Now, out with it already!"

"Things are over between the two of us. We decided to contact a divorce attorney once we get back to Fair Falcon."

"Are you sure? Is this what you really want?"

"Yes. I'm done and over being married to him. Now, can we drop it? I will get ready, and you can take me back over to the hospital."

"Oh, we're not going to the hospital. We're going to go grab a late lunch, chipmunk. Let's go."

Sarah grabbed her wallet and a sweater. As they exited the room, Alex walked up the hallway toward them.

"Hi, Violet, where are you two ladies going?"

"We're going to grab lunch. Are you able to pull yourself away from whatever it is you are doing to join us?"

"Anything for you, Violet." He smirked.

The three of them went to lunch and made small talk about many different things. After they finished eating, Violet took them back to the hospital so that they could visit with Pops again. Pops' face lit up when they walked back in the room. They sat and reminisced about her childhood; Pops told all sorts of embarrassing stories of the trouble that Sarah, Harrison, and Hunter got into when they were little.

"Well, Pops, looks like you are feeling better already!" Sarah exclaimed.

"I will be up chasing Brennen in no time! It will be nice to be able to get up and run again without any worries."

"I can't wait to see videos of that, Pops!"

The family decided they needed to let Pops get his rest, so when Sarah and Alex finished their visit in the room with him, they all got back into their vehicles and went to the Spring City Burger & Steak House for dinner. Alex noticed that Sarah only ordered a side salad for dinner. He leaned over and whispered, "Is that all you're going to eat tonight? Don't you think you need something more than that to eat?"

"I'm still full from lunch. You realize we only ate about two hours ago, right? Now, leave me alone and focus on your own meal, will ya?"

They finished eating with everyone, and then Violet dropped Sarah and Alex back off at the hotel. They said their goodbyes and agreed to swing by the hospital tomorrow in the late morning to spend time with Pops and Grams before meeting Grace and Ethan for dinner. They went into the hotel room. Alex immediately turned on the television to an action movie, a movie he knew that Sarah hated. She sighed, shook her head, and then took her pajamas into the bathroom before she slid into the whirlpool tub.

Alex heard the jets come on and asked, "Are you sure that's a good idea with the fact that you've passed out twice and hardly ate anything today? I won't know if you pass out again."

"Why are you acting like you care about what happens to me all of a sudden?" she yelled back out to him. She finished her bath, got dressed into her pajamas, and crawled into the bed.

Lunch with Abe and Anna

Sarah woke up early Thursday morning and got dressed for her morning run. She left the hotel and took a right out of the parking lot, following the six-mile route she took Monday morning. Her time was about ten minutes slower than usual. When she got back to the hotel, Alex was already up and dressed. "Where have you been?"

"I went on my morning run. You were asleep and I was wide awake, so I decided to take advantage of the beautiful morning."

"That was fucking stupid. What if you had passed out?"

"Well, it didn't happen. Again, I have no idea why all of a sudden you care what I do. You made it clear you don't love me when we were with your mother on Tuesday."

"I may not love you anymore, Sarah, but I also don't want anything to happen to you. You want to get showered and dressed so we can go to the hospital?"

"Give me twenty minutes and I'll be ready to go."

"What are we going to do between the hospital and dinner tonight? Do we have time to go back over and see my mother? Abe is in town."

"Are you going to keep your mother in check? If she starts anything with me, I will leave. I am not going to put up with her shit today. I don't have to and I'm not going to, do you understand me?"

"I will let her know. I really want to see Abe."

Sarah got showered and dressed. They swung by the hospital and spent time with the family before leaving to go back to Anna's.

"Remember, I'm not playing with your mother today. If she starts in with anything, I am out. If you don't come with me, then you're on your own to get back to the room for dinner."

They pulled up to Anna's house; Abe came bolting outside and gathered Alex into a giant bear hug. He turned and looked at Sarah then said, "Good to see you."

"Good to see you too, Abe. Hope you've been doing all right."

"Doing better than you are these days."

"What's that supposed to mean, Abe?"

"Well, for starters, look at you."

"Look at me, what?"

"Sarah, you look like a twig. Where is all your muscle? You look sick. What is going on?"

"I'm fine, thanks for asking, but you won't have to worry about me much longer."

He looked at her. "What do you mean?"

"Don't worry about it. That sort of slipped out, and it shouldn't have. Let's just go inside, your brother wants to catch up with you."

They walked into the house where Anna was putting lunch on the table for the four of them. She was not the best cook, so Sarah was not looking forward to whatever meal Anna had prepared for them to eat. Anytime they came to visit, Alex and Sarah always went out to eat immediately after.

Anna ushered them all unto the table, where there were four plates already dished up with meatloaf, mashed potatoes, overcooked carrots, and broccoli all covered in brown gravy. Sarah was not excited at all because these were all items that she could not stand to eat, but then to have it all smothered in gravy made it ten times worse for her. Anna sat down last and asked how they liked their lunches. Sarah mindlessly pushed the food around on her plate, lost in thought.

I can't wait to see Ethan tonight! How am I going to hide my excitement? I am going to have to find a way to contain my excitement. I wonder what Grace is like. I've never met her before. I hope she isn't as uptight as Sherry used to be. I really hope Alex can keep himself composed, especially if Grace is half as beautiful in person as she is in pictures.

I would hate to be embarrassed by him if he decides to flirt with her in front of Ethan.

"Are you too good to eat what I spent time preparing for you?" Anna pulled her out of her thoughts with her snide comment.

"I'm just not that hungry," Sarah replied.

"Yeah, uh-huh, I bet. Don't think I don't know that you think you're too good to eat here at my place."

Sarah immediately shot Alex a look letting him know if he did not stop his mother, she was going to get up and leave. Alex knew she was serious, so he turned to his mother and said, "Mother, if you don't want us to leave and not come back this weekend, you need to stop insulting Sarah right now."

Anna glared at Sarah. She did not like being given an ultimatum. She hated Sarah and always had, but she wanted her boys to spend some time together, so she stopped being nasty to Sarah.

After lunch, Sarah emptied her untouched plate into the garbage disposal and then washed and dried all the dishes while Alex, Abe, and Anna sat in the living room chatting and catching up on life events. When Sarah finished with the dishes, she joined the other three in the living room.

Sarah curled up on the floor at the corner of the room; she managed to stay out of the conversation. She lost herself again in deep thought about Monday's events.

I still can't believe how great a time I had with Ethan Monday night! He is such an amazing man. What would possess Grace to cheat on him? I really wish I could just skip meeting Grace and enjoy a night alone with Ethan. What I would give to feel Ethan's touch right now! He sent electric sparks through my entire body with just one touch. I don't remember ever feeling that with Alex.

How am I going to pretend that I didn't see Ethan Monday and spend an amazing night with him when we get around Alex and Grace? I sure hope I can pretend well that I didn't just see him. Man, this is going to be tough tonight!

Sarah looked down at her watch and realized that it was four thirty. She knew that it would take them at least twenty minutes to get back to the hotel. She wanted to change clothes before they left for Zippy's Italian Restaurant, and that it would take about fifteen minutes to get from the hotel to the restaurant. She decided that she could give Alex another half an hour before they needed to leave.

"I hate to break up this family reunion, but Alex and I need to go. We had other arrangements we made before we knew that you were going to be in town, Abe."

"Do you really have to go? Are you sure I can't join you?" Abe asked.

"Yes, we really have to go. You wouldn't want to join us. We're meeting a friend I haven't seen in years and meeting his wife for the first time. I'm sure you would be bored."

"Oh, okay. I suppose we'll just have to catch up some other time."

"Catch ya later, Abe," she replied as she gave him a hug.

"Take care of yourself, Sarah."

Meeting Grace and Ethan

They made it back to the hotel to change. Sarah picked out her outfit and went into the bathroom to change. She came out in a halter style purple and pink sundress that accentuated what was left of her shoulder muscles and her golden tan and her black sandals. The dress hit her just above her knee. Alex wore a pair of khakis and a purple polo. As she walked out of the bathroom, he started in on her, "Are you trying to impress Ethan tonight? Is that why you're wearing a dress?"

"No, I'm not trying to impress anyone tonight. This is the only dress you ever picked out for me."

"Uh-huh, sure I did. I don't remember every picking that ugly dress out for you. Why haven't you worn it before tonight?"

"Well, because you bought it too small for me when you bought it, so I had to wait until I could get into it. Apparently, you thought

I was too fat at a hundred and thirty-five pounds, size six, so you bought it as a size two as a way to tell me I was too fat to ever wear it."

"Whatever, let's go get this over with."

They arrived at Zippy's Restaurant and waited for their table to be prepared for them. Just as they were about to be seated, Ethan and Grace arrived. Sarah introduced Alex to Ethan. Ethan then introduced Grace to both of them. Sarah noticed that Grace was shorter than she was, approximately five feet one inch; she had short brown hair that she dyed with a rose hue to it and brown eyes. If Sarah had to guess, Grace probably weighed around 135 pounds. Grace wore a short black mini skirt and a bright pink tank top. Ethan wore a nice T-shirt with khaki cargo shorts and flip flops.

After the introductions, they followed the host back to the back of the restaurant in the empty banquet room. The table they sat at was square with a chair on each side of it. Sarah sat with her back to the window, Alex on her left side and Ethan on her right. She immediately felt Ethan's knee touch her own knee as he tried to adjust his chair at the table to accommodate his long legs. As soon as he was situated, he positioned his left foot under her right foot, and then he started slowly moving his toes in a rubbing motion under the arch of her foot. The touch felt good and sent a shiver down her spine.

The server came around and asked everyone for their drink orders. Sarah rarely drank alcoholic beverages, but as this had been a long and stressful week, she ordered a mojito. Grace ordered the same thing, and the two men ordered a double shot of whiskey on ice. The server left to go get their drinks. They continued to look over the menu, deciding on what to order. Sarah felt Ethan gently move his foot so that he could rub her leg without being noticed by the other two at the table. She relished his touch, and to show him, she reached down to adjust her napkin in her lap and let her fingers brush over his bare knee.

Grace broke the silence after they ordered their food. "So, Alex, what is it you do for a living?"

"Oh, well, it's not all that exciting, but I'm a detective with the Fair Falcon Police Department."

"What do you like most about being a detective? I'm sure it's scary work, isn't it?"

Sarah saw the lust in Alex's eyes as he stared at Grace's chest—DD implants which overflowed from the tank top she wore. "Hands down, it's meeting beautiful women like you."

She giggled as she winked at him. "Awe, how sweet that you think I'm beautiful. Aren't you just a flirt?" She batted her eyes, licked her lips, and played with loose strands of her slightly pulled back hair.

Sarah kicked Alex in the shin and glared at him.

I can't believe this man. Does he not care how embarrassing this is?

Angry at his behavior, Sarah leaned over and whispered in his ear, "Are you really going to do this right now?"

"I would love to get to know you better, Grace," Alex told her as he continued to openly flirt with Grace in front of Ethan and Sarah without a care in the world. The two ignored their spouses completely.

When they finished eating, Grace excused herself from the table. "Excuse me, I need to use the little girls' room, then I'm going to go smoke. Alex, would you care to join me?"

"Are you fucking kidding me? You do realize that you and he are both married, right?" Sarah asked as Alex jumped right up from the table, knocking over his chair, to join Grace.

"Your point is?" Grace asked as she turned and walked to the bathroom. Alex looked at Sarah then followed Grace.

As soon as the door closed, Grace locked it and then turned around on Alex. "What took you so long? I thought from all the looks you kept giving me that you were going to invite me in here much earlier than this. Are you a scaredy-cat?"

"Just shut up and get that skirt off," Alex replied back to Grace.

He bent her over the bathroom sink and fucked her right there. She moaned loudly so that anyone near the bathroom could hear. "Oh, you know how to make a woman happy, big boy."

When Alex finished, they got dressed and went outside the restaurant for Grace to smoke. "That was fun now, wasn't it?" she asked as she reached up and lit her cigarette.

"Wanna go again, right out here?" Alex asked her as she reached her hand into his pants and played with him behind the restaurant.

"I have an even better idea—why don't we go back inside and tell the other two that we're going to swing for the night, maybe the rest of the weekend?"

"You want to swing?" he asked her.

"Yes, dummy. As in I want to sleep with you all weekend and in exchange, Ethan and Sarah can sleep together all weekend. It's only fair, don't you agree?" Grace asked as she coupled his balls in her hand and squeezed them.

"Sarah would never sleep with Ethan. She's too much of a prude to go along with this plan."

"Oh, you obviously don't know your wife very well, then do you?" Grace asked.

"What do you mean?" Alex replied.

"I see the way Ethan looks at Sarah. He wants to fuck your wife as badly as you wanted to fuck me. I can't get a read on your wife, but I think with a bit of peer pressure that she would give in to the idea, and if not, they can just do whatever they want while we spend the weekend fucking. I don't really care what they do. What do you think? It's only fair, isn't it? I mean, we can't go back to my place if Ethan is there, and we can't go back to the hotel if Sarah is there. It doesn't make sense to pay for a second hotel room, so we might as well get them to agree to this arrangement."

"I'm game if you are, but I highly doubt that Sarah is going to agree to this, and if she doesn't, then we'll just have to get a second room because I'm going to fuck your brains out this weekend!" Alex replied back to Grace. As Grace finished her cigarette and put it out, Alex reached down and unzipped his pants. He pulled his penis out right there and said, "In order for me to sell this to Sarah, you're going to have to suck me off right here."

Grace smiled and immediately got down on her knees. She took him into her mouth. She heard him say, "Deeper, woman, deeper.

Faster! Deeper. Oh, that's good," as she took him deeper into her throat and moved faster, wrapping her tongue around his shaft as she did this. She finished, got up, and then kissed him.

"How was that, big boy? Did you enjoy yourself?"

"Oh, you know I did, and I have plenty more where that came from. Let's go in now and sell this plan of yours to the other two idiots. I can't wait to fuck your brains out all weekend!" They made their way back into the restaurant.

Meanwhile, as soon as Alex and Grace were out of earshot, Sarah turned to Ethan and said, "I am terribly sorry for the way Alex is acting tonight. I knew he had no regard for our marriage, but I never imagined he would be so disrespectful to your marriage as well."

"Hey, not a whole lot we can do about them. They are both selfish and self-centered. It would never work between the two of them the way it could work between us. Is it bad that all I can really focus on is how badly I want to take you into the bathroom, rip that dress off you, and take you right here in the restaurant?" he asked her with a mischievous smile on his face.

"No, but I can tell you right now that I don't care how clean the bathrooms are. I'm not having sex here. However, I do feel myself getting all worked up thinking about next Monday when we can be together again!" She smiled back at him and winked.

"Just how worked up are you getting?" he deviously asked. As he asked, she felt his hand pushing the bottom of her sundress further up her thigh under the table. She shivered at his touch and started to moan as he reached the inside of her thigh.

"Oh my god." She leaned over and whispered in his ear, "I wish we could leave and go back to the hotel right now!"

In answer to her comment, she felt his fingers gently pull her lace panties out of the way. He felt how wet she was as he slowly pulled his hand back down her thigh. "Oh my Lord, you are so amazing, but aren't you afraid they are going to come back and catch us?"

He reached over and kissed her. "Nah, we've got time. Grace doesn't ever just smoke one cigarette. She always smokes at least three, and it usually takes at least fifteen minutes. However, with

Alex out there, it'll probably take a little longer because I'm sure that she is all over him right now out there at the smoking area."

She reached over and kissed him slightly on the lips. "I better go freshen up before those two come back in from smoking."

Sarah left Ethan there while she walked to the restroom. She decided she would take her time with freshening up as she was in no rush to go back out to watch her husband embarrass himself. She stuck her finger down her throat and threw up her dinner before grabbing her toothbrush out of her bag. She lost track of time while in the restroom but was pulled back to reality when she received a text message.

Ethan

7:30 p.m.

Hey, earth to Sarah...you still alive or did you fall in?

Sarah

7:30 p.m.

I'm still freshening up, be out here in a couple min. Sorry, got lost in my thoughts. Be right out.

Ethan

7:31 p.m.

These 2 have a crazy proposition; they are going to ask you if you would be interested in swinging partners for the rest of the weekend... Act surprised when you get back out here, I don't want them to know I mentioned anything to you! I want it to be their surprise to you.

Sarah

7:32 p.m.

Wow!

Okay.

Sarah rejoined the table as the three of them sat there impatiently waiting for her to get back to the table. She looked around at the three of them. Alex and Grace could not keep their hands off each other, and Ethan sat there in shock.

"Okay, because someone has to come right out and say it, while we were outside, Alex and I decided that we want to propose swapping partners for the weekend. As I'm sure you heard, Alex and I fucked in the bathroom, and then I gave him one hell of a blowjob outside. We've decided that we're going to lock ourselves in a room together and continue to fuck like rabbits all weekend. We thought you and Ethan might enjoy some alone time together as well."

"You want to what?" she asked, looking stunned.

"Oh, don't play dumb, I know you know what swinging is. Alex and I would go back to the house and have sex together all weekend, and you and Ethan can hang out together. We wouldn't interrupt you in the hotel room, and Ethan wouldn't be able to come home to interrupt us. What do you think? Good plan?"

Sarah could not believe what she was hearing. She looked around the table at each person individually, starting with Alex. She saw from the look on his face that he was completely in favor of this idea, as was Grace. Ethan was a bit harder to read; he tried to keep his poker face.

She turned back to Alex. "I promised you three years ago that I would never cheat on you again. You made that same promise back to me, and while you've not kept up your end of the bargain, I've kept up my end. I have not had sex with anyone since that one-night stand. Now you're asking me to break that promise I made so that you and Grace can have sex together. What happens if I say no?"

"Well, Grace and I are going to have sex no matter what you choose to do. We just thought you and Ethan might enjoy a chance to do the same, but I don't really care what you choose to do. I'm going with Grace," he triumphantly replied.

She turned on Ethan and asked, "Obviously, these two are on board with this because they came up with the plan. What are your thoughts to this whole crazy idea?"

"Personally, I think it is a crazy idea, but I do find you beautiful and sexy. I would be willing to give it a try, but only if you are a hundred percent on board with it. If you aren't, well, then I'll find someplace else to spend my time as these two will be taking up my bed for the weekend."

This is the perfect excuse for me to spend the entire weekend with Ethan without Alex throwing a fit. He can't say anything when it was his idea. I can tell that he's going to leave this restaurant with Grace no matter what I say, so I might as well enjoy myself too! If the rest of the weekend is like Monday night, I won't be able to walk straight at all. I guess I might as well agree to it.

Everyone looked at her expectantly. She finally responded, "I promised you that I would never cheat again. This technically is cheating, however, as our marriage is about to end, I don't see how it could hurt me to spend the weekend with Ethan since you two are so hell-bent on banging each other. I will only agree to this under one condition."

Alex glared at her and asked, "What's that?"

"No matter what, no one questions their spouse at any point in the future on what happened during the weekend. I do not want to be interrogated after the fact with what may or may not transpire between Ethan and me, and I *definitely do not* want to hear all the crazy things that the two of you end up doing. As long as we all can agree to that, then I guess I will give this a shot."

They all looked at each other and then went around the table saying, "I agree to this rule."

Once everyone was in agreement, they got up from the table and moved to the front of the restaurant to pay their checks. Sarah reminded them that she and Ethan would need to swing by the house first so that Ethan could get some clothes for the weekend and that Grace and Alex would need to do the same thing. They agreed to take about fifteen minutes at each location so that they would not run into each other again.

Grace and Alex walked out before Ethan and Sarah. As they walked to the car, Sarah reached up and put her arm around Ethan's waist, and he drew her in closer by wrapping his arm around her shoulder. She looked up at him and smiled. "I can't believe this is actually happening! I thought we were going to have to sneak around again to get a moment like this."

"Oh, Sarah, you don't know how happy I am to see you so excited about this. This is like a dream come true." They stopped walking when they reached her driver's side door. He looked down into her eyes and smiled before he reached down and enveloped her in a passionate kiss. They stood like that for a couple of minutes before they broke away from each other breathless. "I suppose we better get going so we can get to the house to pick up my clothes before it's too late for us to get there."

He opened her door for her and helped her get in before closing the door and walking around to the passenger side of the car and getting in himself. As soon as he was in the car sitting beside her, he grabbed her hand and interlocked her fingers with his. Sarah could not get over the fact that she could be with Ethan for the night. They pulled out of their parking spot and headed toward Ethan and Grace's place. At every red stoplight, Ethan reached over and pulled her into a kiss. They were honked at on more than one occasion for taking too long to start driving once the light turned green. They arrived at the house, and he quickly showed her around. He picked out his regular clothes as well as running attire so that they could run together in the mornings.

They left the house and drove back to the hotel. Ethan immediately jumped out of his side of the car and ran around to open her car door for her. He picked her up, and she wrapped her legs around his body. He shut the car door, and then he turned and pressed her back up against the car door where he reached down and met her lips with his. She parted her lips slightly, giving him just enough room to maneuver his tongue into her mouth. He pulled away to catch his breath just as someone walking by yelled out, "Get a room already!" They both laughed.

Sarah replied, "We already have one. Mind your own business."

Ethan carried her inside, her legs wrapped around his waist and her arms around his neck. He put her down when they got back in the room, and she smiled before she bolted across the room chanting, "Catch me if you can!"

"Oh, you better run. When I catch you I'm going to punish you!" he teased back.

"Oh, yeah? What kind of punishment are you going to give me if you catch me?"

"You just wait and see."

She weaved this way and that way wiggling out of his grasp for about a minute before she finally let herself get caught. "You've been a really bad girl! Now, it's time for your punishment!"

"Oh, no, please don't punish me." She tried to be serious and not laugh. "I promise to be a good girl from now on," she said as she winked and smiled devilishly at him.

"Oh, I don't believe that for a second," he replied back as he tickled her. She tried to wiggle free but could not so she turned and started tickling him back. "Uncle, Uncle! I give up!" he laughed.

"You're not getting away that easily," she told him. She pulled him closer and made quick work of getting his shirt over his head, all the while passionately kissing him. She then reached down and made quick work of the button on his jeans. She pulled back and said, "Oh, that's a great look on you," as he stood there in his birthday suit staring back at her.

"Not fair!"

"Life's not fair. You either get over it or you don't," she teased him.

"Oh, is that so?" He reached out to pull her in, and she teasingly swatted his hands away and took a step back, just out of his reach. "Get that ass of yours over here right now, little missy."

"What happens if I don't?"

"Please don't make me beg! If I have to stand here in all my glory, then you should be too!" He reached out, and she stepped into his grasp. She let herself be pulled up next to him; he started kissing her neck and collarbone. She could feel his body through her dress, and she longed for him to take her right then and there.

"Ethan!"

"Yes!"

"Don't stop! Take me now!"

"Your wish is my command, my lady." He made quick work of the zipper on the back of her sundress and pulled it over her head, then unfastened her bra and pulled that off, exposing her breasts. He gently laid her on the bed climbing on top of her. He took her breast in his mouth, circling her nipple with his tongue! He felt her shiver as he reached down between her legs and gently pulled them apart, putting his body in between them. He started kissing his way down her stomach until he reached her legs.

He knelt down at the edge of the bed and pulled her gently to the edge of the bed so that her legs hung over his shoulders. He got down on his knees and continued to gently kiss up and down her sweet spot, causing her to moan in pleasure. As she started rocking her hips into his touch, he switched from kissing to licking up and down her lips. He enjoyed the sounds of pleasure she displayed. She could not help herself as she screamed out in ecstasy. "OH...MY... GOD, fuck me! Fuck me harder! Don't stop!"

He picked her up from the bed and slipped her over the edge of the bed so that her feet were on the floor and her chest was on the bed. He took her from behind, wrapping his right hand around her waist, and played with her clit while he thrust himself into her. They rocked their hips back and forth together until they both climaxed.

He reached back down with his tongue and started licking again. She felt her whole body shudder as she climaxed again for the second time that night. Her legs gave out, and she sank to the floor. He picked her up from the floor and put her in his lap as he sat back on the edge of the bed.

When he caught his breath, he asked, "Everything okay?"

"That was AMAZING!" she quietly exclaimed. "I've never experienced that before."

As soon as they could both stand, they made their way into the hot tub. She wrapped her legs around his waist and her arms loosely around his neck. She sat there staring at him, lost in her own thoughts.

How is it that this man can drive me so wild? I haven't wanted to have sex in years, but this man makes me so fucking horny. He brings out feelings I've never had before. What did I ever do to deserve a man like this? When is the other shoe going to drop? This has to be too good to be true.

She was brought back to reality when she heard Ethan say, "Hello, earth to Sarah, anybody in there?"

"Oh, yeah, sorry!"

"Whatcha thinkin' 'bout?"

"Oh, it's nothing."

"You're not fooling me, woman. That's not nothing going on up there in that beautiful head of yours! Wanna fill me in?"

She contemplated for a minute and then said, "I should really keep it to myself. I don't want you to think I'm being dumb."

"I would never think that! I promise!"

"Pinky swear? Cross your heart, hope to die, stick a needle in your eye, swear?"

He grabbed her right pinky with his right pinky and gently shook it as he said, "Cross my heart, hope to die, stick a needle in my eye swear." She laughed and relaxed a little bit. "Now, out with it!"

"I don't know where to start."

"Just start wherever you want to."

"I have had so much fun with you between Monday night and so far tonight, but I can't help but wonder about not being good enough for you and that after I leave to go back to Fair Falcon, you won't want to keep in touch with me. I need to protect myself from rejection. I don't know if I can handle it, so I need you to tell me now so that I can prepare myself for the rejection that is coming."

"Whoa, slow down, Sarah! Who said anything about rejection?"

"Well, no one exactly, but it's inevitable. I feel like I'm destined to wind up alone in this life with everyone rejecting me."

"No one is rejecting you here! You are the smartest woman I know, beautiful on the inside, which makes you beautiful on the outside. I don't know where things are headed between the two of us, but in just the few short hours we've spent together, I know that you make me want to be a better man for you."

"Really? You're not just saying that to get me to sleep with you again, are you?" Tears welled in her eyes.

"Really, that's the way I feel. From the moment I met you way back then, I felt a special connection to you, Sarah. You've always been very easy for me to talk to. I never felt like you judged me, no matter how stupid I must have sounded to you. You've helped me keep a level head when my first wife accused me of cheating on her and when she logged into my account and tried to have my paychecks routed into a new checking account instead of our joint account. You were always there for me. I can never truly repay you for your kindness. I know our situation is precarious and that it won't be easy, but Sarah, I want to see where things lead with us. I don't want our relationship to only be a sexual one, although, I must say that the sex I've had with you is amazing. Five times in one night is a record for me!"

"That makes me feel better to hear that you want more than just sex out of our relationship and to hear that even when I go back home that you want to try to make things work."

"Desperately!"

She wrapped her hands around the back of Ethan's head and gently pulled him closer to her. She leaned into his kiss. When he pulled away, he grinned mischievously and said, "If we keep this up, I'll have to play hide the salami again! You up for that again so soon?"

She smiled and said, "Not right this minute, but maybe later. Right now, I think we should get out of the water before we become wrinkly prunes. Let's go cuddle up and watch a movie, if that's okay with you?"

"Sounds like the perfect ending to a perfect night!"

They picked a romantic comedy to finish out their night. Sarah rested her head on Ethan's chest while he wrapped his arm around her shoulders, mindlessly playing with her hair while they lay curled up together. They dozed off to the movie. Ethan woke long enough to turn the TV off when the credits appeared on the screen. He then curled back into Sarah, finding it very comfortable to lay on his back while she rested on his chest, something he did not often do.

The Run

Sarah woke up around five thirty in the same position she fell asleep in, her head resting on Ethan's chest with his arm tucked around her, keeping her safe and protected. It was the best night's sleep she could remember having in years. She carefully moved his arm from around her body so that she could get up to use the restroom and get ready for her run. He was so peaceful that she did not want to wake him; however, the slight movement caused him to wake up. "Wha-what's going on? Where do you think you're going? Trying to sneak out on me, are you?" he teased her.

"No, but my bladder isn't being very nice right now. Unless you can pee for me, I better go do that before I have an accident right here in the bed." She got up and went into the bathroom, Ethan's eyes on her naked body the entire way into the restroom. "Whatchu staring at?"

"Oh, nothing other than the most beautiful woman in the world!"

"Whatever! Are you going to get up and go run with me this morning or you going to lay there like a bag of lazy bones?"

"How far are you planning on running this morning?"

"Oh, I don't know. I usually wait to determine that until I'm out on the run. Some days I just get into a rhythm and don't want it to end. I don't like to plan anything. Is that okay with you, or do you need a plan before running?"

"I'm game for whatever, you take the lead and I'll follow you."

They dressed in their running gear; Sarah wore a pair of black jogging pants and a light blue racerback tank top, Ethan wore a pair of basketball shorts and a T-shirt. "Why aren't you wearing your Marine Corps issued PT gear?"

"I don't want anyone else to see me in my short shorts—other than you, that is!" He winked.

They left the hotel and went out to the parking lot to stretch before starting their run. She took them for a warm-up jog down in front of the recruiting station, which was only four blocks from the hotel. They stopped and stretched again and grabbed a quick drink of water from inside the office before hitting the path they took so many times together when she trained to become a Marine Corps officer. "Brings back old memories, doesn't it?" Ethan asked as they started out at a seven-minute-per-mile pace.

"Sure does! Think you can keep up with me, old man?" she teased as she took off on him, leaving him in her dust.

His long legs helped him easily catch up to her. They ran side by side in complete silence for about two miles before she felt that familiar light-headed feeling overpowering her body. She slowed her pace to a nine-mile-an-hour pace hoping that would prevent her from passing out or having to stop to let the feeling pass. "Everything okay? You don't look so good!" she heard him ask as she felt her body collapsing on her.

Ethan easily caught her falling body in his arms. He laid her on the cool grass and tried pouring water on her, thinking she overheated and needed to cool down. When she did not come to after two minutes, he called paramedics for assistance. The paramedics took only a couple of minutes to arrive on scene.

"Hey, you're a different guy than who was with her the last time this happened. What were you doing when she collapsed?" the lead paramedic asked Ethan.

"What do you mean this happened before? When did this happen before? Where was she the last time you saw her in this condition?" Ethan asked.

"Who are you, sir?"

"I'm a friend. Now please answer my questions."

"She passed out in the shower of her hotel room just two days ago and hit her head as she went down. She refused medical treatment and said she was fine. Now, how could you let her exert herself like this after an episode like that only two days ago?" the paramedic demanded.

"I-I didn't know. She didn't say anything about passing out and hitting her head. She insisted on running this morning. Had I known, I wouldn't have let her get up and go running."

The paramedic team worked to get Sarah to wake up, but the smelling salt did not work this time. He looked at Ethan and said, "We're taking her to the hospital. You're welcome to join us in the ambulance, or you can meet us at the hospital. Your choice but make it quick."

Ethan jumped in the back of the ambulance with an unconscious Sarah and rode in silence as he watched the paramedic team work on her. He felt helpless. Why had she not told him what was going on? As Ethan watched the heart rate monitor, he saw her heartbeat stop entirely.

"She's flatlining, get the paddles charged and ready."

Ethan watched as they shocked Sarah's lifeless body there in front of him. He talked to her quietly in her ear. "Sarah, please don't go. You can't go yet. We still have so much to figure out. Come back to me!" After the second charge, her heart started beating again. Ethan let out a long deep breath at this change.

"How much longer to the hospital, Justin? I don't know how if she's going to make it if we don't get her there soon," the lead paramedic, Adam, said to Justin from the back of the ambulance.

"We're pulling in now. Medical staff is waiting for us."

They pulled into the ambulance bay just as Sarah woke up. She started pulling at her IVs and the blood pressure cuff. "Where am I? What happened? Who are you?" she fired off these questions in rapid succession.

She heard Ethan's voice. "Sarah, calm down. I'm right here with you, baby. You passed out while we were out on our run. I couldn't get you to wake up, and you were barely breathing, so I called the ambulance. Your heart stopped beating, and they had to shock you twice to restart it. You are at the hospital where we are about to meet the medical staff who are going to take care of you and figure out what happened."

She became agitated. "I am not stepping foot inside that hospital! I'm fine. I feel fine! I want you to take me back to the hotel. I just need to rest. I DO NOT WANT TO GO INSIDE THE HOSPITAL, DO YOU HEAR ME?" she started yelling, pulling at her IVs again.

All the commotion caused her heart rate to drop again, and she passed out. The medical staff wheeled her into the trauma room. They sedated Sarah, helping to take the pressure off her heart while they ran bloodwork and tests to figure out what caused this sudden drop in her heartbeat.

The emergency staff called Dr. Wylie from the cardiology unit to come down for consultation. He recognized her right away, and after initially examining Sarah, he went out to the waiting room to look for Alex. "Alex Clark?"

No one came forward. "Who is here with Sarah Clark?" Dr. Wylie called out.

"You aren't Sarah's husband, Alex. Who are you?" he asked when Ethan stepped forward.

"My name is Ethan. I'm a friend. I was out running with her this morning when she passed out."

"Where is her husband?"

"Her husband wasn't with her when it happened, I was. If I can get her phone from her belongings, I can call him and have him come down here. What is going on? What happened that caused her to pass out like this?" Ethan asked Dr. Wylie.

"Get her husband down here, please. I cannot release anything to you because you aren't family."

One of the nurses in the room brought Sarah's phone out to Ethan and handed it to him before she went back in the room and shut the door. Ethan went to the waiting room to wait. He opened her phone and found Alex's number. He took a deep breath and dialed the number.

When Alex finally answered the phone, Ethan was greeted with the response, "What the fuck do you want this early in the morning, Sarah? It's six thirty in the fucking morning. I'm going to hang up now."

Ethan took another deep breath as he wondered how Sarah put up with an ass like that for so long and then wondered what exactly Grace saw in this guy before saying, "Alex, it's Ethan. Don't hang up. Sarah passed out this morning when we were out on our run. I couldn't get her to wake up, so the paramedics brought her in to the emergency room. They won't tell me anything because I'm not family. I need you to drag your ass down here as soon as possible."

"What the fuck? Why did you let her go running this morning? Didn't she tell you that she passed out twice on Wednesday like this? What are you, a fucking moron?"

"Hey, asshat, don't forget who you're talking to. I'm not your wife. I will throat punch the life out of you if you don't stop speaking to me like this. Do you really think I would have let her go for her run this morning if I had known that she passed out and possibly had a concussion from it? Just get your ass down here now." Ethan ended the call and went back to find Dr. Wylie.

"I just got off the phone with Sarah's husband, Alex. Sounds like this happened earlier in the week, only when it happened before, she hit her head in the shower on her way down. I was not aware that she passed out and hit her head, or I would never have let her run this morning."

"It isn't your fault that she didn't tell you, son. Now, if you'll excuse me, I know that her mother and father are upstairs visiting with her Pops, who just had heart surgery Wednesday morning. I'm going to go fill them in on what I know up to this point. They can decide if they want to keep you abreast of what is happening or not. Please excuse me."

Ten minutes later, Ethan saw a couple who looked exactly like Sarah walking down the hallway toward him with Dr. Wylie right beside them. They were not close enough for him to hear their conversation, but he saw Dr. Wylie point at him.

"Who are you? Where is Alex?" the woman asked, clearly Sarah's mother because she had the same eyes and cheekbones as Sarah.

"Ma'am, my name is Ethan. I am a friend of Sarah's. We got up to go for a run this morning, for old time's sake. We were about two miles into our run when Sarah passed out, and I called the ambulance to bring her here."

"My name is Violet, Sarah's mother, and this is her father, Matthew. Do you know if this has ever happened before to Sarah?" she asked him.

"I spoke with Alex on the phone, and he stated that she actually passed out twice on Wednesday, the first time she hit her head in the shower. She apparently refused medical treatment so that she could spend time with your family while you all waited on her grandfather to come out of his own surgery."

"Where is that little prick of a husband? Did he say when he was going to be here?"

"He did not. I did let him know that this was an emergency and that he was needed to help tell Dr. Wylie what happened earlier in the week. I hope he gets here soon."

Just then, Dr. Wylie came back out of the room again. "Are you okay with my discussing this in front of Ethan since he isn't family?" he asked Violet and Matthew.

"He is the one who brought her in, so yes, I'm good with him hearing whatever you have to say."

"Okay, we are going to wheel Sarah up to get a scan of her brain. We need to see if there is any bleeding after her fall the other day. We also see that her enamel on the back of her teeth is decayed due to vomiting. Do you know if Sarah is on any medications or has any medical conditions that could be causing her to throw up like that?"

"No, nothing that I am aware of," Violet responded.

"I am going to run some more tests, but I should have a better answer for you soon." Dr. Wylie left them there in the waiting room. As Dr. Wylie strode away, Ethan looked down the hall to see Alex and Grace coming toward them. Violet saw him at the same time, and she got up from the seat and closed the distance. Ethan could not hear the entire conversation, but he heard enough to get an idea that Violet did not like Alex and was not impressed that he walked in with Grace on his arm.

"Just who the fuck do you think you are? Why was Ethan there with her when this happened and not you? Were you out with this whore all night? And why the *fuck* did you not force her to get medical help when she passed out Wednesday morning?"

"Who do you think you are talking to me like that?" Alex retorted.

Violet reached up and smacked him across the face. Ethan saw Alex's face turn red, and Grace cowered a little bit. "I'm only going to ask you one more time: why did you not bring Sarah into the hospital Wednesday when she passed out and hit her head? Why did you not at least tell anyone in the family what happened?"

Alex relaxed a little but was still visibly upset at the fact that Violet smacked him. "Your daughter is as stubborn and bullheaded as you are. She did not want to tell anyone because she knew you were all concerned about Pops. To be honest, she isn't really talking to me much these days, so I don't know what is going on with her, and she refused to tell me when I asked."

"You really shouldn't be here. You obviously don't care about my daughter if you're willing to bring your whore down here with you to flaunt the fact that you're cheating on my daughter."

"There's more to it than you think, but of course, like always, your daughter can do no wrong."

"Boy, do you want to get smacked again? You better shut your mouth right now!"

Dr. Wylie came back down to the waiting room, so everyone gathered around to hear what was going on with Sarah. "I see the amount of people here has increased. Violet, Matthew, would you like me to tell you this news in private, or are you okay with everyone getting the news at the same time?"

Violet and Matthew looked at each other then in unison replied, "Go ahead and tell everyone."

"Well, it looks like Sarah got a subdural hematoma when she hit her head the other day. The bleeding stopped on its own the other day, but it formed a clot. I consulted with the head of neurosurgery, and they agreed that they need to go in and remove the clot to prevent it from increasing in size and putting too much pressure on her brain. Everyone with me so far?"

They all nodded and said, "Yes."

"After further examination, we think we know what caused her to originally pass out, but I want to first ask if you've noticed anything different with Sarah lately? Is she eating okay?"

"She seems to eat every time I've seen here this week, why do you ask?" Violet asked.

"Actually, Violet, she appears to be eating, but if you've paid attention, she has really just been moving the food around on her plate and not really eating. When I asked her about it the other night when she only ate a salad, she got upset and told me to mind my own business. Then I noticed yesterday afternoon at my mom's she didn't touch her food and again last night at dinner she really only ended up eating about a quarter of her dinner, salad included," Alex spoke up.

"Have any of you noticed her throwing up after eating her meals?" Dr. Wylie asked.

"No, I would have heard her if she had been. Why do you ask?" Alex asked.

"We noticed the enamel on the back of her teeth has been eaten away by acid, and it appears as though the lining in her esophagus has been worn down from all the acid. We can see that Sarah tries to stay fit, but her muscle is breaking down, which tells us that she has an eating disorder. We ran all of the tests we could run to rule out anything else that would be causing these symptoms, and this is the only explanation."

"What do you mean she has an eating disorder? She looks healthy to me?" Violet asked.

"Do any of you know how much Sarah weighs right now? If you had to guess, what would you say her weight is?"

Violet and Matthew both answered, "About a hundred and fifteen pounds."

Alex answered, "A hundred and twenty-five pounds."

Ethan answered, "A hundred pounds."

"Ethan wins as he's the closest to her weight with his guess. She currently weighs about ninety-five pounds. At her height, five feet, four inches, she should weigh between a hundred ten to a hundred and forty-five pounds. She is currently fifteen pounds underweight. She is not taking in enough calories or keeping the calories she does eat to keep her body functioning, so it is breaking down, hence, the passing out. Her heart is too weak to pump blood through her body, so she passes out. Any ideas when this started for her and how long she has been doing all this?"

"I don't have any idea. She never said anything to me about this. I can't believe she's been hiding it from us," Violet responded.

"Alex, do you know when it all started?" Violet turned and asked him.

"No clue, she isn't on speaking terms with me right now."

"We're going to have to keep her sedated until we can see if we can get her to pull through this, but I need you all to know that there is a real likelihood that she might not pull through and could die."

Violet broke down in tears, while Matthew hugged her to his chest. He started crying into Violet's hair at the possibility of losing his daughter. Alex and Grace did not seem to have any sort of reaction on their faces. Ethan was devastated.

I don't know if I can handle if Sarah is ripped out of my life as suddenly as she came back into it. Sarah is such a wonderful person. I haven't ever felt so strongly about a woman as I do with Sarah. How could I have been so stupid to get up and run with her this morning? I knew something wasn't right when I saw how skinny she was. Please, God, don't take Sarah home yet!

The surgeons took Sarah to surgery immediately to get the clot drained. Dr. Wylie kept a close eye on her heart to see if once the strain of the extra blood in her brain was removed if it would help her heart heal. They pumped protein and electrolytes into her system to help make her strong again while she was sedated. Ten days after she was admitted to the hospital, Dr. Wylie came into the intensive care unit (ICU) waiting room and asked Violet and Matthew, "Where's Alex?"

"He had to leave to go back to work. He was working a case back in Fair Falcon that needed him."

"Okay, well, I wanted to let you know that we feel that Sarah's heart and body may be strong enough now to bring her out of the sedation. We need you in there with us to help keep her calm when she wakes up. We don't want a repeat of what happened in the ambulance."

"Okay, when do we do this?"

"Right now, follow me."

They slowly woke Sarah up. She tried to speak but could not because her throat was still raw from the ventilator tube that had been in her mouth the last few days. She was too weak to write so she sat in silence as she watched her family react to her condition. Violet caught her up on what all transpired over the last fifteen days or so while Matthew sat there holding her hand, piping up when needed.

I can't believe that Alex stayed as long as he did before he left to go back to Fair Falcon. Part of me hoped that I ruined Alex's weekend with Grace, although I'm sure he didn't let this impact that. Why was the hospital so strict in only allowing family in? As far as I'm concerned, Ethan is family! On the flip side, I'm glad to hear that Pops is home. I hope he takes it easy and doesn't over do his recovery.

When Violet tried to ask Sarah questions about her disorder, Sarah shut down and refused to talk about it. Eventually, Violet stopped pushing and decided that Sarah would tell her when she was ready.

The doctors were all happy to see Sarah's speedy recovery. They expected her to be in the hospital a couple of months after all she had been through, but Sarah was determined to be back up within just a couple of weeks of her admission. Dr. Wylie came in exactly three weeks after she was admitted to the hospital to discharge her. "Hey, Sarah, are you ready to get out of here?"

"I sure am! I can't get out of here fast enough!"

"Well, I will let you out of here only if you promise to get the help you need."

"What do you mean? I'm fine!"

"Sarah, you're not fine. You have an eating disorder that nearly killed you."

"I'm fine, Dr. Wylie."

"From what I hear, you used to be very fit and muscular. What caused you to stop eating and start binging?"

"It doesn't matter."

"Sarah, you're wrong. It does matter. You need to see a counselor. Good news, I already have you scheduled to see Dr. Tracy Jackson once you get back to Fair Falcon."

"You really didn't have to do that! I'll be fine, thanks."

"You agree to see Dr. Jackson, or I keep you here in my psych ward. You choose."

"Fine, I'll agree to see Dr. Jackson.

Big News

Sarah returned to Fair Falcon the day after Dr. Wylie discharged her from the hospital. It felt good to be home, sleeping in her own bed with her cats. She felt bad for leaving her three precious babies with Susan for so long. She knew if she was going to truly recover from her illness she needed them with her; they were the babies she would never have.

The trip home was uneventful. She stopped to get out and stretch her legs every two hours, stopping a total of three different times on her drive home. She followed Dr. Wylie's orders and drank a nasty protein supplement shake at every stop. She knew if she wanted to return to working out she needed her body to heal from the trauma she put it through.

As she pulled in her driveway, her phone buzzed with a new message. She looked at the phone to see who it was.

Ethan

6:30 p.m.

Did you really leave w/o saying bye? :'(

Sarah

6:31 p.m.

I didn't know what to say. ☹

Ethan

6:32 p.m.

How about for starters: Bye, I'm headed back to Fair Falcon, then you could say, I enjoyed the time we got to spend together.

Sarah

6:33 p.m.

I thought I made it clear while we were together that I enjoyed every min we spent together. ☺

Ethan

6:34 p.m.

How're you holding up?

Sarah

6:35 p.m.

Oh, you know, 1 day at a time

What about you, what're you up to?

Ethan

6:36 p.m.

Oh, you know, 6'6"

Sarah

6:37 p.m.

Aren't you just so funny that I forgot to laugh. ;)

Ethan

6:37 p.m.

Did I at least get a smile from that beautiful face of yours?

Sarah

6:38 p.m.

Maybe. ;)

Ethan

6:39 p.m.

I'm worried about you! I just want to make sure that you are okay. I know I'm six hundred miles away, but I want you to know that I will be there in a heartbeat if you need me!

Sarah

6:42 p.m.

I am so grateful to have you in my life! I hope you know just how much you mean to me.

Ethan

6:43 p.m.

Good to know ;-)

After being w/ you, I don't know how I can stand to stay w/ Grace.

Sarah

6:44 p.m.

I know how you feel! At least I know where I stand w/ Alex... We're done & over. He made that clear when we went to see his bitch of a mother & she knew that he knocked some bimbo up & then when he brought Grace to the hospital in front of my parents

Ethan

6:46 p.m.

He WHAT?

Bet Grace would love to find out that he has another side bimbo! Should I tell her & see what her reaction is?

Sarah

6:47 p.m.

I'll leave that up to you! You decide how much drama you want to cause. I'll just be over here minding my own business, trying to get back in to shape—gotta get my guns and abs back!

Ethan

6:48 p.m.

Wow, slow down over there, tiger! Gotta take it 1 day at a time, don't push yourself or you'll end up back in the hospital.

Sarah

6:49 p.m.

Awe, you don't have to worry about me! I'll be fine.

Ethan

6:50 p.m.

I do worry though!

Sarah

6:51 p.m.

Thanks, Ethan!

It's been a long last few weeks & a long drive home; think I'm gonna turn in for the night! TTYL.

Ethan

6:52 p.m.

Okay, sweet dreams! Sleep tight & don't let the bedbugs bite!

She smiled as she walked in the door and saw her three babies waiting anxiously for her at the door. They started rubbing on her legs, each begging to be picked up and cuddled. She quickly obliged them, picking one up at a time, giving them a good scratch of the ears and a kiss before putting them down. She took her shoes off and placed them on the shelf next to the door of the apartment. She moved the twenty feet from the door to the couch and sank into the soft microfiber cushions. Her girls curled up in her lap, purring contentedly as she absentmindedly rubbed their chins and ears. She woke up about four hours later and moved from the couch to her bed.

She thought about the events of the last few weeks:

God, I am a lucky woman to have been able to spend time with Ethan. I would love to have him lying right next to me—wish he was here with me so that I could cuddle next to him. How is it that I felt more safe and secure with him in the two nights I spent with him versus the entire time I've been married to Alex? I feel like Ethan looks at me more in a way I've never been looked at before. He doesn't just look at me as a way to get sex, but I feel like he looks at me like I'm a whole person... He didn't just want to have sex with me, he wants to really get to know me. I wish I could have more time with Ethan right now. I feel like this is a man I could easily love and live with. I enjoyed his body and the way he made my body feel. I can't believe we had more sex in one night than I had with Alex in a year.

She fell asleep with the memories of her time with him at the forefront of her mind.

She woke the next day around noon when her girls would not stop pestering her to get up and feed them. She looked at her phone and saw twenty missed calls from Alex and a new voicemail from Ethan, so she picked up her phone and played the message: "Hey, Sarah, I just wanted you to know that you were the last thing, or I guess I should say person, I thought about as I fell asleep last night and the first person I thought of when I woke up this morning. You put a smile on my face. I miss your touch, your laughter, and your smile. You are beautiful—just know that you are missed!"

She quickly lost her smile when she received a call from Alex. "Hello?"

"What took you so long to answer the damn phone? I've been trying to call you all morning?"

"I was sleeping and didn't hear the phone. Can I help you with something?"

"I need you to come over to the police department and pick me up."

"Why do you need me to come pick you up? Why can't you get a cab? Or why not have someone else bring you back here?"

"Bitch, you know that shit is expensive, just get your ass in the car and come get me! My car is in the shop."

"I thought you were staying with Bethany. What did she do, kick you out?"

"Just shut up and come get me. I'm tired of Bethany's constant nagging, and I need a break."

"Whatever, I'll get there when I get there. You know once we're divorced this won't ever happen again!"

She hung up with Alex and got ready to go pick him up from the station. She had no idea why he had come home and honestly did not really care to know. She found herself annoyed at the prospect of spending the weekend with him. She still was not feeling 100 percent well and did not want to spend the weekend fighting with him; she wanted to relax but knew that it would be anything but with him in the apartment with her.

She pulled up to the curb of station, and Alex got in the passenger seat. She looked at him, expecting some mean words to come out of his mouth. She was pleasantly surprised when he asked her, "How are you doing? You look better than the last time I saw you."

"I'm fine," she answered and then drove in silence back to the apartment. She felt his eyes on her the majority of the drive home but did not acknowledge him in any way. She kept her eyes on the road and never once looked over in his direction to see what he was doing. After a little while, she no longer felt his eyes on her, so she sneaked a peak to see him silently staring out the window. When they got back to the apartment, she said, "I'm still exhausted. I'm going to go lie down and take a nap. Please try to keep it down out here while I sleep."

They kept their distance from each other throughout the weekend, saying very little to each other. She wondered why he had come home. She drove him back to the mechanic to get his car Saturday morning.

Sarah woke early Monday morning to get ready for her day. Dr. Wylie set up an appointment with a psychotherapist first thing every morning before she went to work. Even though she did not want to go, she grabbed the therapist's address from the card Dr. Wylie gave her and punched it into her phone's navigation program. She arrived at the office about fifteen minutes ahead of the appointment time. The office was not at all what she expected. She figured it would be in a rundown old office building, but it was in the new wing of the Fair Falcon Hospital. The clinic spared no expense when it came to decorating the walls and providing a comfortable place to sit and wait.

Sarah's therapist, Dr. Tracy Jackson, came and greeted her, taking her back to her office; the office was massive, approximately fifty feet by fifty feet in dimension. Sarah looked around and saw a giant oak desk set up with a nice configuration of dual monitors and a docking station for Dr. Jackson's laptop to the right of the door. Behind the desk was a matching five-shelf oak bookshelf, full of books and magazines. The walls were lined with nature pictures to help soothe patients. To the left of the door she saw four very comfortable chocolate-brown microfiber oversized chairs, set in the shape of a square with a glass coffee table set up in the middle of the configuration. Dr. Jackson pointed to the chairs and said, "Please pick out whichever seat you would like to take, and I will join you momentarily."

Sarah chose the seat in the back corner, facing the doorway. She continued looking around the room until Dr. Jackson sat down across the coffee table from her in her own chair. "Good morning, Sarah, my name is Dr. Tracy Jackson, but please feel free to call me Tracy. I like to be informal with names because I feel that it helps me develop a stronger relationship with my clients. I know this is not something that you want to do with your time, but it is important for us to sit down and talk about the events that led you to this disease in order for us to help you heal. Let's start out talking about whatever you would like to talk about to break the ice a little bit, how does that sound?"

"It sounds like I don't really have a choice now, do I? I don't really have anything that I care to talk about. I'm here because it was the only way Dr. Wylie would release me from the hospital."

"I completely understand your hesitation and reluctance to talk about things. Let's start out with this... Tell me about your family and your home life."

Sarah sighed before replying, "Both sets of my grandparents are still alive. My parents have been married for thirty-three years. I have an older brother who is married with a five-year-old boy and another baby on the way. My brother's twin, and my best friend in the whole world, was killed in a car accident."

"I understand that you are married. Tell me more about your husband."

"I'd rather not!"

"Amuse me, please. I'm not here to judge you. However, I need to know more about you in order to help you get better."

She sat and contemplated just what to say. Tracy could see that she was really fighting talking about Alex, so she said, "Tell you what, let's talk about something else and then you can tell me more about your family situation when you're comfortable, deal?"

"What do you want to talk about?"

"Tell me more about what you like to do in your free time. What are your hobbies?"

"Well, I am what most would call a gym rat. During the week, I tend to be in the gym working out and helping others who are new to weightlifting."

"Have you ever thought of making it a career?"

"What's that? Personal training?"

"Yeah."

"No, well, I thought about it for a while until I realized I would be a giant hypocrite if I tried to tell people that they should eat better in order to lose weight when I knew I wasn't losing weight the healthy way myself. So, I knew that wasn't something I could ever pursue. All I could do was to help give exercise advice and be a spotter when needed."

"Well, maybe that is something we can work toward with your recovery, if that is something you would still like to pursue in the future."

"Maybe, I guess I hadn't put much thought into it lately. On my weekends, I usually am up in the mountains hiking. I love to be out in nature, taking in all the sights and sounds. I love hiking the mountains and looking out over the city. I generally go up the trails twice a month."

"That sounds nice. Do you like to camp, fish, or hunt?"

"I enjoy camping. I used to hunt with my dad and my brothers, but once I got married and moved out, I stopped hunting. I also enjoy doing a little bit of free climbing, but I don't do that very often. I'm also a runner. I don't ever run races, but I run anywhere from one to fifteen miles a day."

"So, you enjoy keeping in shape and being active. What else do you enjoy?"

"What do you mean?"

"Do you enjoy time with your family? Do you enjoy the arts such as theater or art museums/festivals?"

"I enjoy spending time with my nephew, Brennen, when I go back home. I don't go home very often because it makes me miss Harrison. I also hate going back home with Alex."

"Why's that?"

"We always have to go see his mother, the same woman who openly berates and belittles me."

"Tell me more about Alex."

"Alex is a very selfish person, always only thinking about himself. Everything is always about him or his mother. He also has a way of turning everything back on a person to make them feel like something he did wrong is actually their fault. He never takes ownership for his actions, and nothing is ever his fault."

"You seem the complete opposite, very caring and gentle."

"I was when I first married Alex. Now, I have no idea who I am. I wonder what my purpose in life is. I want more from my life than just going to work and working out all the time. I want to matter to someone, to be important. I want someone to care as deeply for me as I do for him."

"What drew you to Alex?"

"To be honest, Tracy, at this point I don't even remember. He used to make me happy and spend time and energy on me. Now, all I feel is resentment, anger, and hatred toward him."

"That's good."

"No, that's not good. No one should ever feel resentment or hate their spouse. I have these feelings toward him, and then I started hating myself because I feel that way, when I know I shouldn't feel that way. I am just a confused, messed-up person who feels like life is spinning out of control."

"You are not alone, Sarah. There are many people who feel this way. I'm not going to say it is normal, because it isn't, but you are not a horrible person for feeling this way. Tell me more about when you started with the binging/purging and the just not eating at all. What happened that caused this to start?"

Sarah paused and thought back to the moment her life completely spiraled out of control, leading her down the path of her eating disorder. She shuddered as she remembered the memories she tried so hard to repress.

Dr. Jackson saw the agony in Sarah's eyes. She moved chairs to be a little closer to Sarah and then reached out to touch Sarah's arm. "Sarah, this is safe place. No one can harm you here in this room."

"I never told my family this, but I think they always suspected. I found out after Alex's father passed away that he was cheating on me and had been since before we married. To top it all off, I found out that he cheated on me with our photographer's daughter the day of our wedding. I was so young and naive and so in love that I missed all the red flags. I cheated on him not long after I found out to get back at him. I immediately felt guilty, so I told him what I had done. He called me a whore and told me that I was horrible person. He then turned the fact that he's cheated the entire length of our relationship around on me. I felt so guilty that I cheated on him that I took the abuse and started to believe that I was a horrible person. I promised him that I would never cheat again, which I didn't do, until a couple weeks ago, but that's a completely different story.

"Alex was medically discharged from the Air Force, and we moved back to Spring City, where I finished up my history degree. He moved us here from Spring City when he took a position with the Fair Falcon's Detective unit. After I graduated, I took a job here at the Ocean Sun Bank's call center. I received multiple promotions with the bank and was making considerably more money than Alex was at the time. He continued to cheat on me, making me feel like an ugly person. The cheating got worse after I got pregnant and then lost the baby. He blamed me for losing the pregnancy. He told me that I was fat and ugly. Although, I saw pictures of the people he was sleeping with and wondered how I could be considered fat when I was physically fit, had flat washboard abs, and weighed about a hundred and thirty pounds. He told me so frequently that I was fat and ugly that I started to believe it myself. I felt worthless and uncomfortable in my own skin. I made myself believe that if I could get skinny enough, he would start to love me again and would want to have sex with me.

"It was hard at first to starve myself. I knew my body needed fuel to make up for the calories I burned during my runs and my workouts, but I knew that I was not going to lose weight by eating. Then I got to the point where I needed the calories, so I would splurge and eat, but then when I was done, I had to go purge because I just knew I was going to get fat. I cycled through that for three years and no one ever noticed, not my husband, my coworkers, and my family."

"Do you know what your weight was when you were your smallest?"

"According to Dr. Wylie, I was ninety-five pounds when I was admitted into the hospital. I don't know how much I weighed before that. I don't own a scale. I refuse to look in the mirror because I know I am going to see a giant fatty staring back at me."

"Do you know what you weigh now?"

"No. All I know is that I that I look and feel fat. My size zero pants are too snug, and I've had to move up to a size two waist. If I am forced to keep drinking these nasty protein shakes, I'm going to end up a size four and then I really will be fat. I don't know how much more I can take of gaining weight. I'm terrified. I don't want to get fat. No one will ever love me if I do!"

"Sarah, we need to get you back to a healthy weight so that your body doesn't shut down on you again. Chances are you won't survive if your body shuts down again. Do you understand this fact? How do you feel about that knowledge?"

"I don't know… Some days I feel like it would be best if my body just shut down and I didn't survive. My family would be better off without me, and I would be out from under Alex's abuse. I would also be with Harrison again, which wouldn't be a bad thing at all! Other days I know that I'm not ready to die yet. I have so much I still want to do. I want to climb all ninety-six fourteeners in the US before I die. I am terrified at the thought of not accomplishing this goal."

"Tell me more about what happened when you cheated on Alex and then what you meant by the statement you hadn't cheated on him until a couple weeks ago. How did cheating make you feel?"

"Oh, boy! I was raped by my high school's star quarterback as a freshman in high school. From that moment on, I vowed that I would not sleep with anyone until my wedding day. Until I cheated on him in 2011, he was the only man I had ever been with voluntarily. Alex always wanted to be in control of everything, so sex was no different for us. He always had to be on top, and it was always in missionary position. I read magazines that showed other positions, but he got angry if I mentioned wanting to try any other position than missionary. He become more violent during sex after I brought that up.

"I was devastated when I found out what he was doing, but I got really good at blaming myself because he blamed me so much that I started to believe him. I met Justin Stewart in a summer history class. We flirted back and forth until things progressed from there. I went back to his place with him. I gave in to my inhibitions at that time and slept with him. When I left his house, I never heard or saw him again, so I figured that I must be the problem, which is why Alex cheated on me. After I told Alex, he yelled and screamed at me. He even threatened to divorce me over it. I convinced him not to get a divorce by promising to never cheat again; however, that didn't stop him from constantly accusing me of cheating on him and calling me a whore.

"I remained faithful to this man for the last four years, even when he completely stopped having sex with me two years ago…that is, until I was home in Spring City."

"What happened in Spring City?"

"I went home to be there for my Pops' surgery. I told a couple of friends I would be in town and asked if they wanted to meet me for drinks or what not. Originally, I was supposed to meet my girlfriend Jen for lunch and then my old recruiter, Ethan, and his wife, Grace, later in the week once Alex got to town. However, Ethan ended up eating lunch with Jen and me. While I was in the restroom, Jen was able to get out of Ethan that he had feelings for me and wanted to attempt a relationship, as long as that is what I wanted as well. When I got back, Ethan left to use the restroom, and unbeknownst to me, Jen placed a call to his phone so that he could hear our entire conversation. When Ethan came back, the little matchmaker herself left, leaving the two of us to finish our drinks. One thing led to another, and he ended up back in my hotel room with me, where we shared a very sexually charged evening.

"I picked Alex up at the airport on Tuesday. He berated me and made me feel like a skank because I tried to dress cute for him. We went about our activities Tuesday and Wednesday. We planned to meet Alex and Grace for a double date Thursday night after we spent time with his mother and brother earlier that afternoon.

"Alex was immediately smitten with Grace when we were introduced, and the two of them started flirting immediately. Alex and Grace made no bones about going into the bathroom to have sex, leaving Ethan and me alone at the table. While they were gone, Ethan and I enjoyed each other's company. Alex and Grace came back in from smoking and asked if we wanted to try swinging because they wanted to continue having sex. They made it clear they were going to spend the weekend together whether we agreed to the swinging or not, so we all agreed to the arrangement. It kept us from having to go behind their backs again to be together. When we got up the next morning to run, I passed out for the third time in a few days. I was hospitalized, and the rest is history from there.

"I don't see how this is going to help me recover, but I hope you got what you need from all this. I need to go now because I need to get back to my team. They've missed me over the last month."

"This is a good break through. We will continue to work together, and I promise, we will get you past feeling like you are worthless and fat. We will get you believing in yourself again, I promise."

"Don't make a promise you can't keep, Tracy!"

Sarah left the office and shut the door behind her. She did not want to admit it to Tracy, but she did feel a little better after just talking. She knew she still had a long road ahead of her to recovery, but this made her feel more hopeful than she had been in years. On her way to the office, she also set up an appointment with her friend, Zack, to start the paperwork for the dissolution of her marriage with Alex for later that same day.

Sarah made it to the office where all her coworkers hugged and welcomed her back. They had a cake in the afternoon that Lisa purchased. Sarah worried about how the first day back would be but quickly realized that she had worried for no reason; everything went smoothly, as though she had never left. She enjoyed getting back into her routine; she had a certain peace of mind knowing that she had the papers for the dissolution of her marriage to Alex, and all she needed to finalize everything was his signature throughout the document stating that he wanted to end their marriage as well. She planned to give him the papers the next time he came home from Bethany's. Things were looking up in her world.

Two months passed, and Sarah reflected on how smoothly everything had been, easily getting into a new routine. She stayed busy between going to see Tracy every morning, working at the office, going to the gym, and chatting with Ethan every night. She was deep in thought when Lisa interrupted her, "Hey, Sarah, do you have a minute where we can chat?"

"Yeah, sure, what's up? Is everything okay?"

"Everything is great, Sarah. I couldn't be happier with the way you transitioned back here at work, as though nothing ever happened, and you didn't miss a single day of work. Your team is a well-oiled machine and has rubbed off on the rest of the center. The center has consistently been at the top of the stack rank, thanks to your hard work and dedication. That's actually what I wanted to chat with you about."

"What, that I did my job? Isn't that what anyone would do?"

"Sarah, you aren't just anyone. You are amazing! I have an awesome opportunity, and you were the first person I thought of."

"Me, why would you think of me?"

"Hear me out—you don't even know what it is yet, goofball! I received word that we are opening another call center in Spring City in the next couple of months. They broke ground on the building earlier this year, and it will take about six months to get everything built and ready for staff to come in. They are going to need someone there who can help train the new staff on our systems and ensure that they are following the rules and regulations of the bank. You are an amazing AD, and I thought you would be perfect for the job. Plus, I know that it would get you closer to your family for a little while. You'll be out there for no less than six months getting the call center up and running, which could possibly lead to full transfer depending on how the center does under your management. You will have a furnished apartment to stay in while you are there, paid for entirely by the company, and you will be able to take your cats with you. I made sure they put you in a pet-friendly apartment complex."

"Wow, Lisa, I don't know what to say. Thank you for this opportunity! I am so excited. I'll be able to spend some time with my nephew and help out with the new baby once he or she makes his or her appearance!"

Sarah was so excited at the opportunity to spend time back in Spring City that she had to share her news with Ethan. She called him up, but he did not answer. She left him a message: "Hey, Ethan, I have some news to share with you. Please call me back as soon as you are able to. I can't wait to hear from you."

She dreaded her next call, but she knew she had to make it; she would not be able to get away with not telling Alex what was going on, and she really needed him to come home and sign the divorce papers before she left town to go back to Spring City. She sighed heavily as she found his contact picture in her phone, hoping he would not answer the phone because she did not want to fight with him. "What the fuck are you bothering me for? Don't you know that I'm fucking working?"

"Well, hello to you too. I called because I need to tell you something. Do you have a couple of minutes?"

"What could be so important that you're calling me while I'm working?"

"I need you to know that I have been told I need to go back to Spring City to open a new Ocean Sun Call Center. I have about a month before I go, and I'll be there for at least six months. I need you to come back to the apartment before I leave so that we can clean it out of all your crap and so that you can sign the divorce paperwork so we can move on with our lives."

"Just what the fuck, Sarah? Do you really think I have time to talk about this right now? You're so fucking stupid."

"I needed you to know so that you can call me after you get off work. Otherwise, I know I won't hear from you until you're ready to contact me. Just call me when you get done working." She hung up before he could yell at her again.

Later that night, Ethan called her back. As she answered the phone she heard, "Well, hello there, beautiful. I had this message on my voicemail left by the most beautiful voice in the world. I couldn't wait to call and find out just what exactly this good news really is! Do share!"

"ETHAN, oh, you don't know how badly I needed to hear your voice. I need someone to ground me and keep me sane right now. I'm about to lose my mind."

"What's going on?"

"Well, how do I say this?"

"Just come right out and say it! Spill the beans!"

"I found out today that I have been chosen to open and be the acting site director to the newest call center with Ocean Sun Bank there in Spring City!"

"You WHAT! OH! MY! GOD! That is AMAZING news! When? When do you start?"

"Well, they haven't quite finished construction, so it'll be at least a month before that is finished. Then I will be out there for at least six months training the staff and running the center."

"That is AWESOME news. I'm so happy for you, and I can't WAIT to have you back in town."

He heard her sigh into the phone. "What's wrong, beautiful?"

"It's Alex. I called to tell him, and he was a complete asshat. He is the one who wanted this divorce, so I went and had the papers drafted, and the asshole hasn't been home to sign them yet. I just want my life with him to be over, and now I feel like he is purposefully dragging it all out to make me miserable."

"We'll get through this! I know you are ready to close this chapter of your life, but everything happens for a reason. I have some pretty awesome news myself, wanna hear?"

"Nope, absolutely not," Sarah replied with a laugh in her voice.

"Really? You're breaking a guy's heart over here." She heard his pout in the phone.

"Of course, I want to hear your news!"

"Well, you can't tell Alex I told you this, promise?"

"Pinky promise!"

"Grace and Alex decided that they want to get together again, so it looks like we are going to be coming out to Fair Falcon this time to spend a whole weekend with you!"

"Say WHAT! *That is amazing news*. When? When are you guys coming out here?"

"This weekend! You think you're up to a whole weekend with me? Last time we spent a night together, you had too much of me and it caused you to collapse," he teased her.

"That's not very nice to tease me about!"

"I'm sorry. Forgive me?"

"You're going to have to make it up to me, that's for sure!"

"I think I'm up to that challenge! I can't wait to see you in person! Phone sex just isn't the same and doesn't compare to being able to touch and hold your body in my arms. I'm so excited, I can't wait to take you all over your apartment! Do you have any lingerie that I can rip right off your body?" He smiled as he asked her.

"I'll see what I can manage to find! I can't wait to have you all to myself again!"

"Just thinking about everything I am going to do to you and with you this weekend has me hard as a rock. Guess I should get off here so I can go fix that problem! Dreaming of you! Sweet dreams tonight!"

"I'll be dreaming of you myself and all the things I want you to do to me! Sweet dreams yourself! Talk to you later." She slept peacefully that night.

On her way out the door to go see Tracy for her daily meeting, Sarah received a call from Alex.

She sighed deeply because she knew it was going to turn into a fight. "Hello?"

"I will be coming back to the apartment this weekend. I should be there Thursday afternoon. Think your dumb ass can manage to clean up?"

"I am working Thursday and Friday at the office."

"I don't care if you're working or not. You'll need to let me in the apartment Thursday night."

"What if I say no because I don't want to deal with your ass this weekend?"

"Oh, I guarantee you'll want to let me in this weekend. I heard that you and Ethan got along pretty well on our trip back to Spring City, so I'm sure you'll be happy to hear that Grace and Ethan are coming out this weekend."

"What, why? When did this all transpire?"

"Grace and I decided it, so Ethan is tagging along with her. We figured you two could try again at a weekend together—that is, if you can avoid passing out again."

"Before they get here, we need to talk about splitting up our property and signing the divorce documents."

"I don't want to talk about that right now. We'll talk about it later."

"For someone who said he hated me and no longer wanted to be married, you sure are dragging your feet on signing these documents. I can tell you that I want this to be done and over with so that I can move on with my life. You've moved on and now you are juggling two other women, and I do not want to be a part of that any longer than I have to!"

"Did you not hear me? What I had said was we would talk about this later! What are you, fucking deaf, bitch?"

"Whatever, I have to go now. Goodbye," she said as she ended the call.

Weekend in September

Sarah got off the phone with Alex and drove to her daily appointment. She had tears welling up in her eyes as she walked in the door. Tracy could see things were not good and was worried that Sarah would relapse back into old behaviors. She knew she needed to confront this right away. "Hey, what's going on this morning, Sarah?"

"It's nothing."

"The look on your face doesn't say nothing, it says that something is going on. Dish the deets."

"I really don't want to talk this morning. Can we find something else to do to take my mind off everything?"

"Sorry, kiddo, I need to know what's going on so I can help you get through this and avoid a relapse. I need you to spill the beans, even if it's tough and you don't wanna talk about it." Tracy gave her a look telling her that she understood the situation but also made her realize that Tracy only had her best interest at heart, so she decided she would talk it out with her.

"Well, I've been talking to Ethan either via text or via video calling every night since I got back to Fair Falcon. I look forward to our chats, and it makes me truly happy. He makes me happy. He tells me I am smart, funny, beautiful—all the things a woman needs to hear. He told me last night that he and Grace are coming out to Fair Falcon for the weekend. Don't get me wrong, I'm super stoked because it means I'll have a weekend with Ethan, but it also bothers me because that means that Alex will be here too. I feel like I've done very well because I've had very limited contact with him since I got out of the hospital. I'm afraid that his constant barrage of telling me how worthless I am will send me into relapse. I know I'm probably just being dumb, but it really has me worried."

Tracy gently put her hand on Sarah's arm to comfort her. "You are not dumb. You are being smart to worry about that. You are in a delicate place right now in your recovery. You can't afford a setback because I don't know if we'll be able to bring you back again if you do. Where are you guys on finalizing the divorce?"

"Well, I went to see my friend Zack, who practices family law. He drafted the paperwork for me, but I haven't talked to Alex until this morning. When I brought it up before I came in here, he told me he didn't want to talk about it. I just want this marriage to be over with. I am so miserable when I am with him. I just don't think that I am strong enough to keep confronting him about this!"

"You are strong—you're one of the strongest people I know. There aren't many people who could survive what you survived. You are an amazing person who deserves happiness."

"Thank you for the vote of confidence!"

"When is he coming back to the apartment?"

"Thursday night, so I have three days to figure out a way to confront him and get this process started. I just don't understand why he is dragging his feet on this when he's the one who told me this is what he wanted and he couldn't wait to move on with his life."

"Sarah, you can't focus on his motives and thoughts. All we can do is focus on you. We need to get you stronger and healthier in both your mind and your body. We will take the next couple of days to help you prepare for this conversation. Deal?"

"Deal! Now, I suppose, I should probably get to work."

Sarah worked the rest of the week and saw Tracy every morning. Thursday came and went. Sarah went to lunch with Sally and then went home after her shift. Alex waited for her on the apartment building's front stoop. She expected a fight based on his body language when she got out of the car, but he did not say anything to her. They walked inside, and Sarah sat on the couch.

"We need to address the elephant in the room," Sarah said when they made it inside. "You said you wanted a divorce, I obliged you by getting the paperwork ready. I just need you to sign it so we can take it to the attorney before Grace and Ethan get here tomorrow."

"Whatever, I'll get to it when I get to it."

"Why are you dragging your feet? You clearly don't love me and haven't for a while. You've moved on with Bethany and have started a family with her. Now you want to do the same thing with Grace."

"Not that it's any of your concern, but Bethany kicked me out."

"Oh? So, you think that because you're no longer with Bethany that I want you back? I'm tired of living in a loveless marriage where my husband thinks it is okay for him to cheat on me whenever he wants and I have to stay faithful. I'm over you and our marriage."

"I'm just not ready to give up on us yet. I… I think we can still make this work. I promise I will stop cheating on you."

"Nope, not good enough! You said that before, and look where we ended up. I know what furniture and clothing I brought into this marriage, and that is all I plan to take with me. You can have the rest of the stuff in here. I don't want anything that is going to remind me of you once the paperwork is finalized. I don't know what you plan to do with it all though. Our lease is up in a month, which is convenient for me because I will be in Spring City at that point. You have a couple weeks to figure out where your stuff is going or else I will leave it here and the landlord will take it all."

"*God, you're such a bitch!*" he yelled at her. "I can't believe you would throw me out like this. What are you going to do? *You can't survive without me. No one else will ever want you. You're a worthless waste of space.* I'll sign those papers and will take you to the cleaners. When the divorce is finalized, you won't have a penny to your name."

"Think that all you want. Don't forget we signed a prenup before we said, 'I do.' You won't walk away with a single penny of my money, but even if I ended up without a penny, I'd still be better off because I won't be with you."

"Whatever, you won't last a month without me!"

"I'm done talking to you about this. I'm going to bed now. We'll go to the lawyer in the morning before they get here."

Sarah walked into the master bathroom to change into her T-shirt and running pants. When she came back out, Alex was in the bed with the TV turned on. She looked at him and sighed. She did not have to sleep next to him and was not going to, so she grabbed her pillows from her side of the bed and went out to the couch to sleep for the night. Her girls looked at her with confused looks on their faces, but they jumped off the bed and followed her to the couch.

The next morning Sarah got up and got ready. Out of habit, she made breakfast for herself and for Alex, and then she cleaned up the dishes before getting in the car to head over to Zack's office.

Alex was shocked when he met Zack, who greeted them at the door and ushered them inside. Zack was only about five feet three inches tall and was already balding. He had amber-colored eyes hidden behind his black-framed glasses. After meeting Zack in person, Alex could not believe that Sarah was friends with this man.

They both signed the divorce summons paperwork. "Well, now that I have both signatures, I will file the paperwork with the court before they close today. This process will take between ninety and a hundred and eighty days before the divorce is finalized," Zack informed them both.

Before they turned to leave, Alex asked Zack, "How do I ensure I get everything that is Sarah's? I want all her savings and her trust fund."

"Well, you have the option to go to arbitration, but know that chances are you won't get everything you think you should get. The judge will look the prenup you both signed. Based on the prenup, he will make a decision on how to split your assets and debt. He will split things between the two of you or may possibly lean toward giving Sarah more because when it comes out that you were unfaithful to her for your entire marriage, the judge may likely side with her being the victim here. Sarah advised me when she had me draft the paperwork that she was willing to give you everything that wasn't already hers or that was purchased with your joint checking account when the two of you married. Why would you want to risk losing all that by going into arbitration?" Zack asked Alex.

"Whatever."

"If you want, Alex, we can go the way of arbitration, but you will lose. This way, you walk out of the marriage with most of the items the two of you purchased together. It's your choice. Arbitration will also take longer."

"Just file the damn paperwork and let's get this over with," Alex growled at Zack before heading out the door.

They got in the car to head back to the apartment. Alex got a call from Grace telling him that they were about an hour out of Fair Falcon. He turned to Sarah. "You need to get us home now so that you can pack your stuff to go to a hotel with Ethan for the weekend."

"Why do you think that you get to stay in the apartment for the weekend? Are you going to take care of the cats?"

"No, you're going to take them with you."

"No, either you get the hotel or you take care of the cats. None of the hotels in town allow pets, and I'm not paying penalties. Your ass can get a hotel room."

"Fine, whatever. Grace and I are going to leave as soon as they get here."

"Good, I hope the two of you have fun together."

Alex stormed away from Sarah in order to go pack his bag for the weekend. As soon as he finished packing his bag, Ethan and Grace pulled in the driveway. Alex walked over to the driver's side to Grace and told her they were going to spend the weekend in a hotel. She smiled and agreed that would be fun. Ethan grabbed his bag out of the car, and Alex hopped in the passenger side. Like before, they decided that they would not contact each other over the weekend but would have breakfast together Sunday morning at the Falcon Diner around nine in the morning. Grace waved out the window as they pulled out of the drive. "Have fun, you two, I know we will!"

As soon as they were down the road, Ethan grabbed Sarah up into a giant bear hug and swung her around in a circle. He put her back down and kissed her. She leaned into his kiss and quickly turned up the heat. She paused and said, "We should probably take this inside before all the neighbors start asking questions."

Ethan picked her up and carried her into the apartment. She guided him to the bedroom, where he gently put her down on the bed. He sat beside her and just stared at her in silence, soaking in the changes she had made over the last couple months. He could not believe just how healthy she looked, back around the weight she was when he first met her four years ago. "Damn, you are beautiful. I am almost intimidated by all those muscles. I think yours may be bigger than mine now. Amazing what feeding your body can do for it." He winked at her.

"Well, I guess when you feed them what they need, they definitely pop!" She giggled. "You wanna see all my muscles?"

He reached down and kissed her. She put her hands under his shirt, grabbed his back, and pulled him closer to her. "God, I missed this," he moaned, and he tugged at her shirt. "How about we lose this?" he asked as he started pulling it off. "I think we need to let the ladies loose from this horrible titty torture chamber," he said as he unsnapped her bra.

"Not fair, it's your turn to lose some clothing," she said with a pout on her face.

He laughed a little as he helped her take his shirt off. She tugged at the button and zipper on his pants. He stood up, and she slid them right off his waist. "Oh, I see you went commando today." She smiled at him as she took in all of him there in front of her.

He helped her out of her jeans and then pulled her into his lap as he sat on the edge of the bed. They stared at each other, longing desire in their eyes. "God, I can't even begin to tell you all the times I wanted to do this since the last time we were together. Watching you play with yourself isn't the same as me playing with you!" he said to her as he leaned in to kiss her again.

"Don't just talk about it, put those words into action." She smiled at him.

"Oh, is that how you want to play this then? Do you think you can handle me?" He stood up, picking her up with him. He gently put her back down, bending her back over the bed. He then stood behind her and took her from behind. She arched her back to help him get the best angle. She yelled out, "*Oh. My. God! Keep going, don't stop!*"

After he climaxed, he lay down next to her on the bed, staring into her eyes, fondling her nipples absentmindedly. They lay there speechless for a few minutes, trying to catch their breath. Ethan finally spoke first, "You are truly amazing, you know that, right?"

He got up from the bed and ushered her into the shower. "I am famished. We didn't eat the whole way here because Grace just wanted to hurry up and get here. Wanna go grab something to eat here in town?"

They enjoyed the rest of the weekend together, alternating between watching movies and making love. On their last night together, they sat on the couch watching a romantic comedy together, with Sarah's favorite actors, Tom Smith and Natasha Beauregard. Ethan put his back against the arm rest and extended his body the length of the couch. He pulled her in between his legs, and she rested her head on his chest and shoulder; he wrapped his arms around her chest, pulling her in tight against his body. He reached down and kissed her on the crown of her head. She looked up at him begging him to kiss her. He indulged her desire and passionately kissed her. When they momentarily separated lips, she heard him say, "God, I love you!"

He looked down at her, searching her eyes and face for her reaction, afraid he may have said this too early in their relationship. She pinched herself. "Ouch."

"Why did you just do that, goofball?"

She smiled and said, "I just had to make sure I wasn't dreaming. This seems too good to be true!

He looked down and smiled at her. "You aren't dreaming, Sarah. I told you that I love you, and I mean it with my whole heart. You are the sweetest, most caring person I think I've ever met. You make my heart skip a beat whenever I think about you."

She smiled, reached up, and kissed him briefly on his lips and then said, "I love you too! I don't want this weekend to end!"

"Me neither!"

Back to Spring City in October

Alex came back to the apartment with Sarah after their breakfast with Ethan and Grace. They stayed quiet on the car ride back. She saw Alex reply to a text message, which slightly annoyed her, but then she quickly remembered he was no longer her problem. When they got back to the apartment, Alex grabbed his bag. "I'm outta here!"

"Okay! Don't let the door hit ya where the good Lord split ya!"

"Don't you want to know where I'm going?"

"Honestly, I could care less where you go as long as you leave me alone. Take care!"

"If you were wondering, I'm headed back to be with Bethany. She's taking me back."

"Good for you. Good luck!" Sarah shut the door behind him and locked it. She went back to the couch and flipped on the television.

Man, without Ethan here, I feel so alone. I can't believe how complete I feel when I'm with him. He makes me feel so peaceful and comfortable. I now know what it feels like to be truly in love! Why couldn't I have had this all along?

She jumped when a loud commercial came on the TV, which caused her to laugh at how silly she was. She reached down and grabbed her cell phone. She needed to communicate with Ethan, even if she couldn't talk to him on the phone:

Sarah

11:00 a.m.

OMG, I miss you already! Come back! ☹

Ethan

11:01 a.m.

I was just thinking the same thing! ☺

When do I get to see you again?

Sarah

11:02 a.m.

Probably not until I am back in Spring City next month. ☹

Ethan

11:03 a.m.

That is too long!

I just want you to know that I had a lot of fun with you this weekend!

Sarah

11:04 a.m.

Me too! I didn't want it to end. ☹

Ethan

11:05 a.m.

Me neither!

Hey, I hope I didn't freak you out when I told you that I loved you last night while we were on the couch together. :-/

Sarah

11:06 a.m.

ABSOLUTELY NOT! I know we haven't been together long, but I feel the same way about you! I just didn't want to scare you away by telling you too early in our relationship.

Ethan

11:07 a.m.

You're stuck with me for as long as you want to be stuck w/ me!

Sarah

11:08 a.m.

That's good to hear!

I can't wait to come back to Spring City to see what is in store for the next chapter of my life. ☺

I also can't wait until my divorce is finalized so I can move on!

Ethan

11:09 a.m.

I can't wait for you to get back to Spring City as well.

I wonder if Alex knows that Grace is sleeping with every Tom, Dick, and Harry she meets?

Sarah

11:10 a.m.

Hard to say… I can almost guarantee that Grace doesn't know that Alex has a baby on the way w/ another woman & that along w/ the other woman & Grace, he's slept w/ probably ten other women in the last month or so!

They truly deserve each other!

Ethan

11:12 a.m.

You are so right! They do deserve each other!

Sarah

11:13 a.m.

Well, I suppose, I should probably clean up the apartment a bit & take a nap since I didn't get a whole lot of sleep this weekend. ;)

Drive safe, my love! Let me know when you guys get back to Spring City!

Ethan

11:15 a.m.

Get some rest! I'll keep you posted when we get back.

<3 u!

Sarah put her phone down on the end table and curled up on the couch. She thought back to all the events from the weekend. She smiled as she thought of the moment Ethan told her that he loved her. She pinched herself again to make sure that this had not all been a dream. She fell asleep thinking about all the possibilities.

The next month passed by like a whirlwind. Before Sarah realized, it was time for her to start her new adventure back in Spring City. She and Alex were in the process of finalizing their divorce from each other; Alex packed up all but her belongings and moved them out of the apartment. She put the finishing touches on packing her possessions and put them in her Edge. She came back in and put the cats in their carrying bags and then took them out to the car as well. The manager came and did his walkthrough of the apartment and told her everything looked good, so she would get her full deposit back within thirty days.

Sarah got in the car and started the drive back to Spring City. She called Lisa, "I can't say this enough—thank you for this opportunity."

"Sarah, you deserve this. You've worked hard to get this chance. Make the most of it like I know you will!"

"Thank you!"

When she got off the phone with Lisa, she called Ethan, "Hey, panda, I'm leaving now. I should be in town by six thirty."

"I can't wait to see you! I have the boys tonight, but I can come over and meet you in the morning to help you get everything out of the car and into the apartment. Sound good?"

"I'm pouting!"

"Don't pout!"

"I would love to be able to see you tonight, but the boys are the most important thing. Enjoy your time with them, and I'll see you in the morning!"

"Drive safe, chipmunk! Love you!"

"Love you too, panda!"

She settled in for the long ride home, which was uneventful. She turned on her radio and switched between oldies and today's hits. Sarah stopped about halfway between Fair Falcon and Spring City to top off her gas tank, use the restroom, and grab some snacks for the rest of the trip. She arrived in Spring City thirty minutes earlier than she expected.

She found the apartment building she was to call home for the next few months; the building did not look like anything special, but she was okay with whatever Ocean Sun Bank was willing to put her up in at this point since she was not responsible for the costs. She walked inside, and the doorman greeted her. She quickly noticed that he was about five foot ten inches, probably in his mid to late fifties. He was a little overweight with graying hair. She greeted him, "Hi, my name is Sarah Clark. I am supposed to be moving into one of the units here for the next couple of months."

"Hi, Sarah, my name is Greg. I was told to expect you in tonight. The apartment manager, Mark, is unable to meet you tonight due to a last-minute emergency in another complex, so he asked me to give you the tour and let you in tonight. He will be by tomorrow to go over all the paperwork, as long as you are okay with that."

"Sounds good to me. After driving all day, I just want to get my girls all settled in and then grab something to eat before crashing."

"Well, let's get you upstairs so that you can get settled. Follow me," he said as he handed her a key fab and walked her toward the elevator. "If you don't mind, we'll take the elevator up to your unit. You're up on the top floor, and I am in no shape to walk up ten flights of stairs. Once we get up there, I'll show you where the stairs are so you can decide if you want to take them or not from here on out."

"I'm good with the elevator for tonight. I'm too tired to climb ten flights of stairs, haha."

"Oh, that is fantastic, Sarah. You'll need to use that key fab I gave you to access your floor in the elevator. Let me show you how you access your unit," Greg said as he took back her key fab temporarily. He held the fab up to the elevator panel and the doors closed behind them. The elevator immediately started to climb and did not stop at any of the other floors. Once the elevator stopped, the doors opened to reveal a huge penthouse suite, overlooking Spring City.

"This is your stop, Ms. Sarah." Greg snapped her back to reality when he spoke to her. "Isn't it an amazing view from up here?"

"It is breathtaking. I never realized how beautiful this city really is. Surely, there are more people who live on this floor though, right?" She looked around the room and then back to Greg.

"No, ma'am. This whole floor is yours, which is why you needed special access to get up here. You don't have to worry about anyone else bothering you while you are staying here with us. Now, if you would like, I can take you on a quick tour, and then I can help you get your stuff unpacked so you can settle in for the evening."

"You are too sweet, Greg. I would love a tour."

"Well, as you can see, the elevator opens directly into a huge living room. You can overlook the city on three sides via the huge pane glass windows. The tan microfiber couch and love seat are both new. You should find them very comfortable. Should you find you would like a different color, just let Mark know tomorrow, and he will get them switched out for whatever color you would like. He also picked out the wooden coffee and end tables. If these are not to your satisfaction, please let him know and they can easily be switched out as well to ensure that you are comfortable in your place while you are here."

"Oh, that isn't necessary. These are just fine the way they are." Greg continued to show her around. In the living room she saw a beautiful baby grand piano in the west corner. When she faced north, she saw a hundred-inch 4K television. She walked through the huge doorway, which led from the living room into the amazing dining room and kitchen areas. There was a fully stocked bar with bar stools in the east corner of the room.

"You shouldn't have any problem with space if you want to entertain guests up here," Greg said to her.

She noticed a huge wooden dining room table, placed directly under a beautiful old-fashioned chandelier. She saw that the table sat at least twenty people comfortably. As intriguing as the dining room was, she was drawn to the huge kitchen with brand-new stainless-steel appliances. This kitchen was as large as her living and dining rooms put together at the apartment back in Fair Falcon. The cabinets were all oak, and the countertop was made out of granite. The kitchen sink was a triple basin sink with two Gangang LED kitchen touch-free faucets in both outer sinks.

They walked past the kitchen down the hallway. The first door on the right opened into a beautiful spare bathroom. She noticed that there was both a shower and a soaker tub for any guests she had over to enjoy. They continued walking down the hallway away from the kitchen and walked into the second door on the right. "Ms. Sarah, this room here is your guest bedroom. It has a king-size bed in here as well as a king-size pull-out sofa in the corner. The closet is a nice-sized walk-in closet where you can store all sorts of clothes."

She was completely in awe of the room. This guest bedroom was double the size of her old master bedroom in Fair Falcon. "If you think this is amazing, just wait until you see the best room of the place."

"I can't believe there is more. This is way too much for one person, especially someone who is only supposed to be here a couple of months!" she exclaimed.

"I don't know what to tell you. This is an amazing place, Ms. Sarah. We are lucky to have you joining us." He walked her back into the hallway a little way. He stopped her at the only door on the left side of the hallway. "Are you ready for this?" he asked her.

"I don't know if I can handle any more amazing rooms, but I'll try," She laughed. Greg opened the door to the master bedroom. She felt her breath catch in her lungs a little bit, and she just stood there staring in complete amazement. "Oh my god! Greg, you were right, this *is* the best room in the entire unit, and I didn't think that was possible after seeing the kitchen and the living room."

This room alone was as large as her previous apartment. She noticed the California king-size canopy bed in the middle of the room with a deep purple sheet set. Off to the left, there was a small sitting area with the identical couch and love seat to what was out in the living room. There was another one-hundred-inch 4K television in the master suite. To the right of the bed were two doors. The furthest away from the hallway led into a gigantic walk-in closet, filled with clothes and shoes but left with plenty of space for her own clothes and shoes.

The second door was into the master bathroom: almost identical to the guest bathroom, except that it had a dual sink with marble countertops, and instead of just having a soaker tub, she noticed this one had jets to make it into a whirlpool tub and was big enough to comfortably seat two adults.

She heard Greg quietly snicker behind her. "Are you sure you're going to be able to ever leave this room?"

"I don't know, Greg! This is pretty amazing and has *way more* than I could ever have imagined."

"Well, I have one last surprise for you, Sarah. Follow me back through the unit to the elevator. We will need your key fab again."

He took her key fab from her and swiped it on the unit. The doors closed and went up one more floor. When they opened, she looked out onto a pool the size of her entire unit. "This pool is for your enjoyment and the enjoyment of your guests. Again, no one else in the building can get up here without your key fab. What do you think?"

"How is this even possible? I cannot believe that Ocean Sun would go through all this trouble to put me up in this amazing place. Thank you, Greg, for giving me the tour. Now, I just need to know where I can park so that I can bring my girls up here and we can get settled in for the night."

"I would be happy to show you. Follow me back to the elevator and we'll head down to the parking garage below the building."

Sarah grabbed her three girls and everything she needed to get them settled in and took them upstairs. Once she had the litter boxes set up and a place for her girls to eat, she sat down on the couch and messaged Ethan:

Sarah

5:00 p.m.

OMG, Ethan, you won't believe the place they put me up in while I'm here in the city! I can't believe it myself!

Oh, yeah, I made it to the city & got the girls all settled in for the night. I need to go find food now. I'm starving!

Ethan

5:02 p.m.

That nice, huh?

Sarah

5:03 p.m.

Let's just say that we could play hide & seek in here & you might never find me, lol!

Ethan

5:04 p.m.

Sounds like a challenge! I'm up for it, if you are!

Sarah

5:05 p.m.

Haha, looks like we'll have to play soon. ☺

Gotta go get food now, I'm starving & that's the 1 thing they don't have in here.

Ethan

5:06 p.m.

Where you going to go?

Sarah

5:07 p.m.

Haven't decided, but thinking I'll probably just go to Spring Burger & Steak House

Feeling like a big fat juicy steak tonight.

I hope they aren't too busy this time of night on a Monday night!

Ethan

5:09 p.m.

Enjoy! Sounds like a great meal!

They shouldn't be too terribly busy.

Sarah

5:10 p.m.

Not waiting that long…headed there now, should take about 10 min for me to get there.

I'm so hungry I could eat a horse right now!

Ethan

5:11 p.m.

Wow, that's pretty hungry! You better get going!

Sarah left the apartment. On her way out the door, she said goodbye to Greg, "Bye, Greg. Thank you again for the tour and helping me get my girls upstairs. I appreciate you!" She hopped in the car and drove the ten minutes to the restaurant. She pulled up in the parking lot and was so focused on getting in the building that she completely overlooked Ethan standing next to the door waiting on her.

"You just going to walk right on by me, little lady?" she heard the familiar drawl ask her.

"Oh my god, what are you doing here!" She squealed when she looked up and saw him standing there. He reached out and grabbed her into a big hug. She reached up and kissed him as he placed her back onto the ground and he returned the kiss. They walked in the building, hand in hand.

The hostess greeted them at the doorway, "Good evening, welcome to Spring City Burger and Steak House. How many this evening?"

"Two, please," Sarah responded to the short heavyset graying woman.

"Right this way, please," she said to Sarah and Ethan as she led them to the back corner. "This should give you two lovebirds a little privacy back here," she said as she winked at them before she walked away.

Sarah scooted into the booth first, and he quickly sat down right next to her. Sarah turned to face him. "I can't believe you're here! I thought I wasn't going to get to see you until tomorrow!"

"I just couldn't wait. I had to see you as soon as I possibly could. The boys decided not to come over tonight, and Emily is with her grandparents tonight. Grace decided she wanted to go out of town with another random guy for the week, so it was just me for the night. Might as well enjoy the night with the woman I love, so I decided to come meet you here and surprise you. From the look on your face, I would say I was successful in achieving that goal. What do you want to do when we get done with dinner? Early night in or you feel like going out and enjoying the night?"

"Oh, I hadn't thought that far ahead. I really figured I would just go back to the apartment and would crash. Would you care to join me?"

"I thought you'd never ask, Sarah! How about we just skip dinner and go back there now?" he asked as he winked at her as he pulled her lips to his.

They finished their dinner and walked out to the parking lot. Ethan held her door open for her, and then once she was settled inside the car, he gently closed it behind her. He walked to his car, got in, and then followed her back to the apartment building's garage. They walked in the lobby, where Greg greeted them. "Welcome back, Ms.

Sarah. Hope you enjoyed your time out. Is there anything I can get for you or do for you before you head upstairs for the night?"

"Thank you, Greg. This is my friend, Ethan," she said as she introduced the two men to each other. Ethan reached over and shook Greg's hand as she introduced them. Sarah saw Greg look Ethan up and down and then smiled.

"Enjoy your evening tonight, Ms. Sarah, Ethan!" He motioned her to come a little closer and then whispered, "Don't forget, the pool upstairs is all yours. No one will interrupt you two if you decide to go for a swim!" He winked at her as she stood back up. She smiled and walked toward the elevator; Ethan quickly caught up to her.

"What was that all about?" he asked.

"Oh, nothing. You'll find out later," she teased him as they disappeared into the elevator. She used her key fab, and the elevator quickly ascended to her apartment.

"Holy shit, Sarah, you weren't kidding when you said this place is amazing!"

She gave Ethan the grand tour, leaving the bedroom for last. As she turned the door handle and pushed the door to the master room open, she felt Ethan effortlessly pick her up. He carried her over the threshold of the door and moved her quickly over to the bed. As he sat beside her, he reached over and pulled him closer to her. He kissed her gently at first and then more passionately. She tugged at his shirt until he was no longer wearing it. She smiled as he sat there. "Aw, that's much better!"

"You think so, do you?"

"Yep! However, I think you are still overly dressed! Stand up and let's see if we can't rid you of these pesky clothes!"

"Yes, ma'am! Your wish is my desire," he replied as he complied with her request. She made quick work of his belt buckle and the button to his jeans. Within a matter of seconds, he was standing there in front of her in his birthday suit while she sat there staring at him. "Now, you are way overdressed for this occasion. Here, let me help you with that."

He laid her back on the bed and straddled her. They rocked in perfect rhythm.

He lay beside her on his side, out of breath, smiling at her. "What are you smiling at there, handsome?"

"Nothing! Just thinking about how happy you make me," he replied back.

"You make me feel amazing. I have never felt so alive before, that is, until I met you!"

He smiled at her and kissed her forehead. "Wanna go christen that fantastic-looking tub in the bathroom?"

"Well, we can either christen the tub or we can christen the pool!"

"Pool? What are you talking about? I didn't see a pool!"

"Well, to be fair, we didn't make it past the bedroom for me to show you the pool!" She laughed as she got up. "So, which do you want to try out first?"

"Let's go to the tub first. We have the next couple months to make it to the pool!"

They finished out their night cuddled together enjoying the jets of the tub before making their way back to the bed. "Thank you for surprising me tonight at the restaurant. I thought I was going to have to spend the first night here alone in this giant place."

"Chipmunk, I couldn't wait to welcome you back to Spring City!"

The next morning they woke up and finished unpacking her car. They took everything up to the apartment and situated it. After the car was cleaned out, they went to get groceries. Once the groceries were put away, Ethan left to go pick up Emily from her grandparent's house.

Rather than sit at home alone, Sarah left to go check out the call center. She quickly and easily found her way to the center; it was about a half mile away from the apartment.

She walked in and talked to the head of HR. They went on a tour of the center before he showed her a packet of information about the employees. She appreciated this ability to get to know a little bit about each individual and their history before meeting them the following day.

She left the call center and went back to the apartment. Greg was back on duty at the front desk. "Good afternoon, Ms. Sarah. I hope you had a good first night in the apartment!"

"I did, thank you, Greg."

"Will I be seeing more of Ethan?" he asked as she started toward the elevator.

"I sure hope so, Greg."

"If you want, I can get a key fab for him so that he can come and go as he pleases without you always having to come down and get him when he arrives."

"That would be fantastic! I really appreciate that offer."

"I'll have that for you by the time you get off work tomorrow, Ms. Sarah. Oh, that reminds me, Mark will be here in a little bit for you to cover the lease agreement with him. I will buzz your apartment when he arrives."

"Thank you, Greg! I've only lived here one night and already I wonder how I survived without your generosity!"

She made it back upstairs and settled in with Squirrel Bait and Pretty Baby, while Crackers sat at her feet. They crawled right up into her lap and purred while she scratched their chins and ears. She fell asleep and lost track of time. She woke up when Greg buzzed her intercom, letting her know that Mark was down in the lobby waiting to meet her. She gathered herself and went down to meet the property manager.

"Hello, Sarah, I'm so sorry that I couldn't meet you last night to give you the tour. I hope that Greg did a nice job showing you around."

"He did a fantastic job showing me around, thank you!"

"Good to hear. I will make this as quick and painless as possible. I just need a couple of signatures from you. The rent will be paid by Ocean Sun Bank, so you don't have to worry about that while you are here. They are also paying for all your utilities. The only thing you are required to take care of is cable and internet, if you elect to add these services while you are here with us. Normally, we don't allow pets, but we made an exception for you because Ocean Sun asked us to. It helps that the area vice president is my brother, haha. Please let me know if you have any questions or concerns. I'm just a phone call away."

She finished signing the paperwork with Mark and then went back upstairs to her suite. When she got back upstairs, she got a text from Ethan.

Ethan

12:45 p.m.

Hey, Sarah, you want to go running tonight?

Sarah

12:46 p.m.

What time & where?

Ethan

12:47 p.m.

The boys want to run w/ you.

16:00 work for you?

Sarah

12:48 p.m.

That's fine! You sure they can keep up?

Ethan

12:49 p.m.

Nope, that's why they want to run w/ you! They both want to join the spring cross-country team & know they need to build their endurance in order to do well. I told them you are the best person to work w/ them!

Sarah

12:51 p.m.

How far you want to run w/ them today?

Ethan

12:52 p.m.

Let's do the old PT course, work for you?

Sarah

12:53 p.m.

Sounds good!

Ethan

12:54 p.m.

Guess I should get back to work... See you in a bit.

Ethan

12:55 p.m.

<3 you!

Sarah

12:56 p.m.

See you in a bit... <3 you more!

Sarah set her alarm for three thirty and then put her phone down and reclined back on the couch. All three of her girls curled up down her stomach and legs while she napped. She fell asleep fantasizing about a life with Ethan would be like.

The rooster alarm went off before Sarah was ready for it to. She did not realize just how tired she was and how soundly she had slept. She got up and dressed in her running gear—a pair of black biking shorts under a pair of black running shorts and a red racer-back tank top. She applied some sunscreen to her arms, shoulders, chest, legs, and face. She took the sunscreen with her so that Ethan could apply to her back where she could not reach herself. She drove to the recruiting office to wait for the boys.

As she parked, Ethan pulled in right next to her. The boys scrambled out of Ethan's truck, all laughing. Eli got out first and came over, giving Sarah a giant hug. "Hi, Ms. Sarah. Thank you for running with us today."

"Hey, kiddo! I'm happy to run with you. I prefer running with others. You think you can handle a three-mile trip today?"

"I'll keep up, but I don't know about Manny though, he's a lot slower than I am!" Eli smiled.

"I'm not slower than you! You're the slowpoke!" Manny squeaked.

"Well, today isn't a race. Today is about form and breathing. We will start out with warming our muscles up, and then we will jog for about a mile before we run all out for a mile and then jog the last mile. We will finish with stretching. Sound good?"

Both boys unanimously agreed, "Sounds good!"

Sarah walked the boys through warm-ups. They responded to her directions very well and followed everything she asked them to do without any complaints. They started warming up their chest and arm muscles and then moved on to their backs and core muscles. They finally warmed up their largest muscles: hamstrings, quads, and calf muscles. Once they were finished, she and Ethan took the lead in their jog, jogging side by side, with the boys close behind.

Sarah turned around and faced the boys, continuing to jog at the pace she originally set. "Now, I need you to focus on your form. You will need to run in whatever way is most comfortable to you. However, most runners prefer to run either on the balls of their feet, pushing off and landing only on the balls of their feet, or they run heel to toe. You will find that your father runs heel to toe, where I run on the balls of my feet. Use the time while we're jogging to pick what's most comfortable for you.

"Once you have your style down, then I need you to find your stride. Do you take longer strides or shorter strides? Your father takes medium strides, while I have to take longer strides to keep up with most people I run with. Sometimes when I'm tired, I find that I start taking shorter strides.

"Once you've found your stride, then we're going to focus on breathing. You want to make sure you are always breathing, otherwise, you won't get enough oxygen into your muscles and they will fatigue. I recommend inhaling in a cadence, six to eight counts in and then the same number of counts back out during the exhale. For me, I count to eight during both inhale and exhale, but not everyone can do that. Find what is best for you. Questions?"

She laughed; she saw that both boys were processing everything she said to them. She could see the determined looks on their faces. They experimented with their strides and breathing. Eli seemed to be more comfortable with running heel to toe with longer strides, like his father, where Manny seemed to be settling into running on the balls of his feet with the shorter strides. They both concentrated on their breathing, and she could see as they determined the cadence to breath to.

They finished their first mile. Before she turned back around to pick up the pace, she asked, "Ready?"

"Uh?" they replied in unison.

"You'll do fine. Just know that we don't slow down for anyone… You either keep up or get left in the dirt. Don't give up no matter what, just keep going. It's only for one mile."

She then set her stopwatch and set her running pace at a seven-and-a-half-mile-an-hour pace, figuring the boys should be able to keep up with that pace fairly easily. Ethan smiled and matched his pace to hers. She looked over her shoulders every so often to make sure the boys were still there with them. Eli was about fifteen steps behind her. She was pleasantly surprised to see Manny only about six steps behind them, matching her pace fairly easily.

They reached the end of their second mile; Sarah turned the group around. "Time to return back the way we came.

Eli stopped dead in his tracks. He frowned before he gasped, "I thought we were only doing three miles today, Sarah! Not four! I don't think I can do it."

"Guess what, if I didn't think you could do four miles, we would have turned around a little bit ago, but I know you can physically do it. You didn't fall behind the rest of us. How badly do you want to join the cross-country team and be successful?"

"Badly," he said as he gasped for air.

"Okay, well, to be successful, you will have to push past what your brain tells you. You will find your brain telling you that you can't do it, that you are tired. Once you get to that point, you need to push harder. Once you get there, then you will prove to yourself that you should never quit. Are you a quitter?"

"No, ma'am!"

"Glad to hear that! Now, let's go. Next mile I want you guys out front. Your father and I will be right behind you. We are going to do sprints, running as fast as we can for short distances. We will then jog for a certain distance and then we will sprint again. We'll do that for the entire mile, alternating between jogging and sprinting. I'll let you know when we're in each phase."

They sprinted about half the next mile and jogged the other half. The boys did very well. Sarah slowed them down to a slow jog for half of the fourth mile and then to a walk for the last half of that mile. When they got back to the recruiting office, they stretched out all their tired and aching muscles.

"You are going to be extremely sore tomorrow when you wake up. To help with the muscle soreness, I need you to go home and eat a high-protein meal tonight with no processed carbs. I want you to eat a couple of bananas as well. Keep stretching the rest of the night, until you go to bed. The more you stretch your muscles, the less lactic acid will build up in your muscles and you will find your recovery time much faster. Got it?"

In unison, the boys replied, "Yes, ma'am!"

"Thank you for running with us today, Ms. Sarah," Manny told her. "I had fun and really enjoyed the variance in what we did today. At school, we just run, which isn't any fun."

"I'm glad you enjoyed the run. I am happy to run with you guys any time you want. I start working tomorrow, so I may not always be able to run with you guys right after school like we did tonight, but I promise I will come out with you whenever you ask. If you are good with it, we can always run first thing in the morning before school as well."

While the boys piled back into Ethan's truck, Ethan pulled Sarah in for a quick kiss. "Thank you for running with the boys. This means the world to them."

"They are good guys. I am happy to help in any way I can. If we go out tomorrow night, we'll take them for a light jog, maybe two miles, but not much more than that."

"Sounds like a plan. What are you doing tonight?" Ethan asked her.

"Going home and taking a shower, then I'll probably grill out some beef shish kebabs for dinner and lunch. What about you? What are your plans?"

"Gotta drop the boys off with their mother and then I was hoping that it would be possible to swing by your place for a bit, if that's okay with you."

"Sounds good to me. We can grill out together."

"Oh, I think we can do more than just that, if you catch my drift," he said as he winked at her. "Think you can hold off on taking that shower until I get there?"

"I'll see what I can do. No promises!" She winked back at him and then walked toward her driver's door to get in and go home.

When Sarah got into the lobby, she stopped by the desk. "Hi, Greg, how're you doing?"

"I'm good. How are you, Sarah?"

"I'm good, thanks. Ethan will be here in a little bit. Can you buzz me when he gets here?"

"I'd be happy to, kiddo."

As she turned toward the elevator, Greg stopped her. "Hey, Sarah, I almost forgot to give this to you. Here is the key fab for Ethan to come up and visit you whenever he wants to. Do you want to take it with you or do you want me to just give it to him when he gets here?"

"Oh, thanks, Greg. I'll take it and give it to him when he gets here." He gave her the key fab, and she walked to the elevator. She turned and waved at him before the elevator doors shut.

Twenty minutes later, Greg buzzed her apartment. "Ms. Sarah, Ethan is here for you."

"Thank you, Greg. I'll be right down."

The doors to the elevator opened, and Ethan stepped right inside. "I see you waited for me to take your shower. I can't wait to get in that steamy shower with you!"

"Oh, yeah, what are you going to do once we're in the shower together?" she asked with a devious smile on her face.

"Let me just show you!" He raised his eyebrows at her and smiled. He picked her up, and she wrapped her legs around his waist and her arms around his neck. He kissed her passionately. When he pulled back to catch his breath, she heard him say, "God, I don't know what I would do without you in my life. You are amazing,

Sarah!" When the elevator doors opened, he walked to the shower where he bent over and started the water, all the while still holding on to her. Once the water was the right temperature, he walked the two of them into the huge walk-in shower.

"Did you seriously just bring us in here in our clothes?" Sarah laughed as she reached back in for another kiss.

"Maybe! Is that a problem?" He laughed into her kiss.

"Well, kind of. It's hard to get clean with my clothes still on."

"Well, let me help you solve that problem." He smiled as he took off her tank top and sports bra, leaving her breasts fully exposed to him. He took advantage of this newly exposed skin and started sucking on her nipples.

She reached down and put her hand down inside his shorts, running her hand along the shaft of his penis. He caught his breath and moaned, "Oh boy, that felt amazing."

He pinned her to the shower wall and made love to her.

They grilled their shish kebabs and ate dinner. When they finished eating, Sarah pulled out the key fab. "Hey, Greg, got me a second key fab so that you can come and go as you please. Would you like this?"

"Woman, you better give that to me!"

"And what if I don't?"

"Oh, don't make me beg." He smiled.

Ethan helped Sarah clean up the kitchen and the grill area. Once the kitchen was cleaned, he turned and said, "Guess I should go now. You have a big day ahead of you tomorrow, meeting your leadership team and getting the center ready for trainees to come in Monday morning." He reached down and kissed her. "God, Sarah, I'm the luckiest man in the world. I love you!" He turned and walked to the elevator and left.

Chapter 7

2015–2016

The Attack

The next few months went by quickly. Sarah found her routine. Every morning she got up at four thirty and lifted her weights for an hour before her shower and breakfast. She cleaned up the kitchen and then she left for the center by six thirty. She started her mornings out by looking through the days' training material and the agents' test results from the previous day. Her leadership team came in every morning by seven thirty to cover the plan for each day. Once everyone arrived, she greeted her teams when they arrived at eight o'clock.

The first teams out of training started out strong with their customer experiences. Sarah was excited and proud of how well her team did. Lisa called to congratulate Sarah on how well the site was doing so quickly out of training. Peter called in early June to offer Sarah the permanent director position, which she accepted.

After work, she ran home and got into her running gear and then jogged down to the old recruiting office to meet Ethan and the boys for their daily run.

Sarah woke up Friday, July 10, and started her morning just like every other morning. She lifted weights and showered before heading to the office. She looked forward to her run that night with the boys; they were training for their first race at the end of July. She left work two hours early and grabbed her running gear before going to the recruiting office:

"Hi, Sarah! You think you can keep up with me today?" Eli smiled and asked as she greeted them on the sidewalk.

"Oh, is someone feeling his Wheaties today?" She smiled and joked back with him.

"Maybe!" He laughed.

"What's the pace for today's run?"

Manny piped up and said, "I think we should take it kind of slow today. How does a nine-minute pace sound?"

"Don't be a turtle, Manny, be the rabbit," Eli said to his little brother.

"How about we change the run up a bit? Rather than running a full ten miles, what if we do six but add in different stops and challenges along the way? You game for that?" she asked as she turned to Eli.

"What all do you have in mind?" he asked.

"Well, what if we jog the first mile, run the second mile as fast as we can, then the third and fourth miles we can stop and do pull-ups, crunches, push-ups, burpees, and jumping jacks every quarter mile, then the fifth mile back to as fast as we can finished by the sixth mile of jogging and cooling down? Sound challenging enough to you?"

"Sounds good to me! Let's go already!" Eli piped up.

Sarah could see that Manny was not all that excited about today's run, but he was going to be a good sport and not complain. Ethan stood there smiling, looking between the two boys and Sarah.

"Well, is everybody warmed up? Muscles all stretched out?" she asked them. After she got all three responses, she started the pace for the jog at about a nine-minute pace. She jogged backward for the first quarter mile so she could make sure everyone was keeping up and saw Manny smiling when he realized she was taking the first mile at the pace he requested. They finished their run in about two and a half hours. When they got back to the cars, she could see that the boys were both exhausted. She turned to Ethan and said, "I think they are going to sleep well tonight. They shouldn't be any problem for Sherry tonight, haha."

"You've got that right. Sherry should be thanking her lucky stars and you. If you hadn't run the energy out of Eli, I fear he would have done nothing but caused her grief tonight."

"I enjoyed tonight's run as much as they did. You coming over tonight?"

"Let me get the boys home and confirm that Grace isn't coming home. Emily is with her grandparents for the night. If Grace isn't coming home, then I'll definitely be over so we can go out to Zippy's. How does that sound?"

"Sounds good to me. I'll be waiting for your call or text."

They got in their cars; Ethan took the boys to their mother's before he swung by his place. Sarah went back to her apartment. As she walked in the door, she saw Greg was clearly upset about something. Rather than walking by and just saying hello like she normally did, she stopped by the desk and said, "Hey, Greg, what's going on? You seem upset. Anything I can do to help you?"

"Oh my god, Sarah, I'm so glad I was here to catch you! You can't go upstairs yet!"

"Wait, why? What's going on, Greg?"

"Well, Mark was here earlier covering for me so that I could go to an appointment. While he was watching the lobby, he let some guy in your apartment because he said he was your husband. I knew I had to warn you since I know that Ethan stops by from time to time and I didn't want there to be any issues."

"Wait a second, go back. Did you say some guy claiming to be my husband is upstairs? Did Mark give you his name, by chance?"

"Yes, he told Mark that his name is Alex and that you two have been married for the last five years," he told her. "Are you really married, Sarah?"

"It's complicated, Greg. Technically and legally speaking, I am still married to Alex, but I am currently in the process of divorce proceedings. For some reason though, he started dragging his feet, complicating things with the court. I am ready for this to be over so I can move on with my life. I could tell you stories for days and days, but for now, I guess I need to go find out what is going on with my soon-to-be ex-husband."

"Well, it sounds like you've got your hands full. Good luck."

"Thanks, I'm going to need it. Do you mind if I use your office for just a minute while I call Ethan to let him know what's going on?"

"Go right ahead!"

He led her into a small office, just big enough to fit a small wooden desk and chair inside. He closed the door behind him as he left the office so that she could enjoy some privacy. She immediately dialed Ethan's number. It rang three times before he picked up, "Hey, just can't get enough of me, can you?" He laughed as he answered her call.

"You busted me." She laughed back at him.

"What's wrong, Sarah? I hear the stress in your voice."

"Oh, apparently, Alex decided to show up today and somehow convinced the property manager to let him into my apartment. I just wanted you to know so that you don't come over until I know what this is all about. I just have no idea why he would be here, and I'm beyond pissed to find out that he basically broke into my place."

"Don't stress, chipmunk. It'll be okay. Keep me posted once you know more about why he's here in town. Let me know if I need to come over and beat his ass for you!"

She could not help but laugh at his last comment. "Thanks for being so understanding. I'll keep you posted."

She ended her call, left the office, and walked to the elevator. "Thanks, for letting me borrow your office and for thinking of me before letting me walk into a shit storm, Greg."

"It's my pleasure. Good luck, Sarah. I'm down here if you need me."

Sarah got in the elevator and took a deep breath as she went up to her floor. When the elevator door opened, she saw Alex waiting right inside the apartment. She did not even get out of the elevator before he started in on her, "Bitch, where have you been? What took you so fucking long to get here? I know you left the center at three thirty, and it is now six! Who have you been out sleeping with?"

Sarah tried to walk past and ignore him, but Alex got in her face. "I know you heard me, now answer me!"

She sighed and tried to walk around him. "Oh, hell no, I know you didn't just sigh at me. Where the fuck do you think you're going?"

"I did sigh at you, I'm glad your eyes and ears aren't broken! How the fuck did you get up in here?"

"That doesn't matter. What matters is that you are a married woman who is cheating on her husband. Now, who were you out fucking for the last two and a half hours?"

"Maybe I should take it back that your eyes aren't broken. They clearly must be if you think a woman sweats this much from having sex with someone. I don't know why you truly care what the fuck I do as you asked for the divorce. I gave you what you said you wanted and now you're not happy."

"Where the fuck were you?" he screamed at her.

"I don't have to account my whereabouts to you any longer as we're in the process of divorce, but to get you to quit fucking screaming at me, if you must know, I went for a run. I just got back and need to go shower. Now, move out of my way so I can do that, please."

"There's no way you were out running for that long. Now, tell me where the fuck you really were and who you were with," he said as he got back up in Sarah's face.

"You need to find your way back out of my face before I call the cops on you. This is breaking and entering as your name is nowhere on the lease agreement. Now, why the fuck are you here?" she asked him, the impatience starting to come through her voice.

"You wouldn't call the cops on me. I would just tell them that we are married, and they wouldn't do anything to me."

"Get on with whatever it is you wanted to fucking say so that you can leave."

"Who were you out fucking that took you two and a half hours to return to the apartment after you left work?"

"Again, it is like I said, I wasn't out fucking anyone. I went out for a six-mile run with Ethan and his boys. Now, why the fuck are you here harassing me and making my life miserable?"

"I know you were fucking Ethan. I want you to invite him to dinner so we can hash out the fact that he's fucking a married woman."

"Oh, glorious, isn't that the pot calling the kettle black? I know for a fact that Grace, who is still married to Ethan, comes to meet you in Fair Falcon so that you can bang her. You lie to Bethany about where you are and what you're doing, just like you did with me.

"What's the matter, did these two women finally figure out what a despicable person you are and they both kicked you to the curb, so you now think you can come back into my life? I have news for you, that's not happening. As far as I'm concerned, we're divorced. It's only a matter of a couple more weeks and then we will be officially divorced, and I won't be forced to be around you ever again."

"You'll be lost without me. You're nothing without me. You're just a fat-ass loser who will never amount to anything. No one will ever love you. You are damaged goods, Sarah. You are beyond love from anyone."

"If you say so. I would like to say that I seem to be doing just fine on my own right now without you. I am counting down the days for you to be out of my life for good! Now, get the fuck out of here."

"I'm not going anywhere until we meet Ethan for dinner and I can give him a piece of my mind. I know the two of you are sleeping together."

"Even if we are, what does it truly matter to you? You just can't stand to see me happy, can you?"

Sarah stormed away from Alex and went into her bedroom. She locked the door behind her and called Ethan.

He answered on the second ring. "Hey, chipmunk, what's up?"

"Can you meet us at Zippy's to get this asshole to shut the fuck up and leave?"

"Sure. Meet you there in thirty minutes."

"See you then."

She took her shower and got ready for dinner. She came back in the living room wearing a sundress with her hair pulled up in a messy bun. As she walked into the room, she felt Alex's eyes on her, but she chose to ignore this.

"Get your ass up, let's go," she said as she got all the way to where Alex was still sitting.

"Is Ethan meeting us?"

"Yes, we're meeting him in about fifteen minutes at Zippy's."

Alex got up, and they walked into the elevator together. When they got down to the lobby, she saw that Greg was worried about her from the look on his face. "Good night, Greg, I'm going out to dinner and will be back in a little while. If I don't catch you before the end of your shift, have a great night and give your wife a big hug for me. Please thank her again for the banana bread. It was delicious while it lasted."

"Have a good night, Sarah. See you tomorrow! I'll let her know."

Sarah followed Alex to his rental, a Nissan Pathfinder. She got into the passenger side and looked out the window. They rode to the restaurant in complete silence, but she could feel his eyes on her from time to time. They walked inside the restaurant and immediately found Ethan just inside the door talking to the hostess. She seated the three of them and grabbed their drink orders. The server came and took their meal orders. Once he left, Ethan turned to Alex and asked, "Why did you insist on the three of us going to dinner together? For someone who demanded this meeting, you sure have been awfully quiet."

"I know you've been fucking my wife. I know that you fucked her today which is what took her so long to get back to the apartment after she got off work," Alex said.

"*First of all*, not that it's *any* of your business, Alex, but Sarah and I were out running today with my boys. If you want proof, all you need to do is look at my boy's InstaChat pages and you'll see the running course and the different challenges we did throughout the run. *Secondly*, you asked for a divorce, which means in a couple of weeks, once the judge signs off on it, you'll no longer be married to Sarah, so what she does is her own business. *Thirdly*, you don't have any room to talk about what Sarah and I do or don't do. I know that you fly my wife out to Fair Falcon. I'm not fucking stupid, I just don't care what she does any more. If she's happy with an asshat like you, then who am I to stand in her way of happiness?"

"Did you just call me an asshat?"

"Oh, good, your hearing does work." Ethan laughed.

Sarah watched Alex go bright red. She then noticed his hands clenched in his lap and the vein in his forehead started popping as he replied back, "Do you want to fight? I'll fight your ass right now. Ain't no one going to call me an asshat and get away with it! Let's go."

"Sit the fuck down. Stop acting like a fucking circus clown, Alex. You sure can dish it but can't take your own medicine, can you? Big bad bully can't stand when someone treats him the way he treats others?" Ethan taunted him.

"I want you to tell me everything, every time you've had sex, what the sex was like. I want the details and I want them now."

Sarah could feel herself getting very angry, but before she could reply, Ethan piped up and said, "We made an agreement way back that first weekend we started our swinging that we would never ask each other for details about what happened in our getaways. I am not about to break that because you all of a sudden can't handle whatever is going on in that pea-sized brain of yours."

"You *will* tell me the details I want to hear. You aren't telling me that you love Sarah, are you? She isn't worth loving. She's the most worthless laziest person I've ever come across in my life. No one can ever love her."

Ethan lowered his voice and said, "What does it matter to you? You clearly don't love her, and you obviously never did. I don't know what she ever saw in you to decide to go through with a wedding and a marriage."

"She was lucky to have me, she still is. Are you saying you love a married woman?"

"Yes, as a matter of fact, I am saying that I am in love with Sarah, your soon-to-be ex-wife."

Alex continued to carry on, demanding that Sarah and Ethan talk to him about their sex life. He also continued to put her down and make her feel worthless. "You know that she is used property at this point, not that she was ever in mint condition to begin with. She was damaged property when I got her, having been raped by the star quarterback in high school. She is a lousy lay, all she does is just lie there and expects me to do all the heavy lifting. She wonders why I cheated on her all these years, well, she shouldn't."

An embarrassed Sarah got up, put her napkin on the table, and started walking toward the door. She could no longer stand the conversation. She didn't want to cry in front of Alex and encourage his behavior. Ethan grabbed her arm as she walked past him to the door, but she shook him off.

She looked at him with tears in her eyes. "Please let me go, I just need to go get some air. I'll be fine, I just can't be in here anymore."

"Are you sure?"

"Yes, I am just going to walk back to the apartment." She turned to Alex at that point and said, "Do not come back to my apartment. If you show up there, I will call the cops and I will have you arrested for breaking and entering. You are not welcome here, just leave, leave me alone."

She turned back to the door and left. She was so upset when she left the restaurant that she sobbed huge tears. The more upset she got, the more the tears flowed. The more tears that flowed, the more upset she got with herself.

Sarah, you need to pull yourself together. You are a grown-ass woman and should not be letting this child get to you like this anymore. He made it clear that he doesn't love you, no point in pining over this broken relationship, especially when you have a man who does love you.

As soon as Sarah left the restaurant, Alex turned on Ethan and said, "See what you did here. You ruined our marriage and made her upset. What do you have to say for yourself right now?"

"Are you fucking kidding me right now, asshat? You cheated on your wife from the very beginning of your relationship. She just loved you too much to want to give up and face reality. You beat her down mentally and emotionally so much that she nearly killed herself trying to make you love her. She thought if she got to 'the right size' that you would want her again. You're such an arrogant asshat."

319

"You act like you're the only one who cares about Sarah. If I didn't know any better, I would say you think you're in love with my wife."

"I do love Sarah. I love her more than you will ever love anyone, other than yourself. Even in this short period of time, I found that Sarah completes me. I build her up, make her feel better about herself and her life. What do you do to build her up? All you know how to do is tear people down. You're the most arrogant, selfish person I've ever met, Alex. You need to just let Sarah alone and finish the divorce. You're only delaying it because you know she's the happiest she's ever been and you can't stand it."

"How dare you talk to me that way. You wanna take this outside and finish it?"

"Oh my god, Alex, you're such a child. No, I'm done talking to you. I'm going to go find Sarah now. If you ever loved your wife, now is the time to go search for her and make sure she's safe."

Ethan got up from the table and walked out the door, Alex followed closely behind him. Alex shoved Ethan when they got outside, hoping that Ethan would turn around and they could fight this out. Ethan continued walking toward his car. He got in and started driving in the direction of Sarah's apartment to try to find her. Alex also got into his car and drove the opposite direction in search of his wife.

In her distracted state, Sarah didn't realize she turned the wrong way; she headed in the opposite direction of her apartment. As she continued to walk away from the restaurant, Sarah heard a noise behind her that brought her back to reality. When she came back to the present moment, she realized she was headed in the wrong direction from the apartment.

Oh, shit, where am I? How did you manage to get lost, Sarah? What was that noise?

She looked over her shoulder to see what the noise was and to find out where it came from. When she faced front again, she saw multiple young men, ages sixteen to twenty-one coming out of the shadows of the back of the parking lot she was walking through. She continued to walk but picked up her pace a little bit, hoping the men would notice the change in her speed and would turn around and leave her alone.

Everything happened so quickly after that: Sarah saw three younger men coming up on her quickly from the front, one on each of her sides and could hear what sounded like two or three more behind her. She felt her hands grabbed at her sides and pulled very roughly behind her back. Sarah smelled alcohol on the young man in front of her as he started laughing maliciously in her face. She thought he looked to be about twenty-one or twenty-two. He was tall, about six feet, three inches, with short hair. She could see that he was muscular through his tight shirt and thought that if he were not currently in her face laughing as though he was going to hurt her that he might be kind of cute. She struggled to get her arms free but soon gave up because she realized the more she struggled, the harder they pulled her arms. The one in her face continued laughing and started taunting her, "Where do you think you're going? You look like you want to have some fun tonight with each and every one of us."

"Let me go and I'll show you fun," she retorted back to him with a grimace on her face, as she tried to lurch forward at him.

"Oh, we've got a lively one here, boys. This ought to be real fun tonight," the guy in her face said to the others who were still holding her, all laughing at her. The men holding her forced her to walk to the corner of the warehouse's parking lot closest to the street to get the best lighting. She noticed they had an SUV there and two of the men had raced ahead to open the back-lift gate. She saw a young man, around six feet with short hair and a scared look on his face. She thought he looked to be around eighteen or nineteen, holding a video recorder to his face.

As they got to the back of the SUV, all but the young man who had taunted her let go of her. He pushed his body right up against hers, forcing her closer to the back of the SUV. She reached up and hit him hard in the face with a left hook, which sent him reeling backward about six steps. She tried to take the opportunity to run, but his friends quickly stopped her before she got very far. She heard the kid holding the camera ask, "Chase, are you all right?"

"What the fuck, dude? Why would you say my name? Are you a fucking moron, Charlie?"

"Sorry, it just sort of slipped out. It won't happen again."

"You're damn right it won't, moron. If you give out anyone else's name, I'll kill you!"

"I swear it won't happen again," the young man whimpered.

The young man named Chase turned on the other young men there with him and said, "I told you this was going to be a fun night, didn't I? Now, do you think you can help a brother out here and hold this crazy bitch down? I get to have my fun with her, and then you all can take your turn with her as well."

Sarah was turned to face the interior of the SUV and was forced to bend over it in an awkward position with her hands now being held down by two guys sitting in the back of the SUV. She felt Chase's hands on the inside of her thighs making their way up to her panties. "I know you want this, bitch. I'll be the best you've ever had. Think you can handle me?" she heard the young man taunt from behind her as he ripped her panties and pulled her dress up to her lower back, fully exposing her lower body. She heard his zipper as he unzipped and unbuttoned his blue jeans. She heard them fall to the ground with a thud. She knew that he was going to rape her and thought about calling out but decided not to because she did not want to encourage him to be any more brutal than he already was. She felt him enter her from behind and started thrusting inside of her. She heard him whooping as he continued to rape her and felt him stop long enough to say the cameraman, Charlie, "Now, make sure you get this from multiple angles. I want to be able to see everything. I don't want to just see my ass only. Now, get over here. You dicks up there, you got a good view, can you see how this is done, boys?"

Sarah felt the grip on her hands slightly loosen. She waited until just the right moment when they were all distracted to make her move. She took her right foot and slammed it down on Chase's right foot, she then quickly turned her body around to face him and felt his penis slip out from between her legs and quickly slammed the palm of her left hand up into Chase's nose before taking her right knee and slamming it right into his groin. As Chase immediately dropped to his knees, holding his groin and his nose in his hands, she took off running in the direction she had come from. She made it about halfway through the parking lot when two of the young men caught up with her and shoved her to the ground. They picked her up and took her back over to the car again.

She saw the anger and pain in Chase's eyes before she felt his right fist connect with her jaw. "I think the bitch broke my dick! How is that even possible? You guys better tear her up the way she tore me up. I think I need to go to the hospital." He pointed to one of the other younger guys and said, "Hey, dipshit, you're going to drive me to the ER. Go get your car, now."

Sarah was pushed into the back of the SUV and pulled into the back just far enough so that her legs dangled over the edge. She felt the next animal crawl on top of her. She heard him say to himself and his friends, "Oh, yeah, this bitch is nice and wet, all because I made her that way. Ain't none of you as good as me. She's going to be begging to have me back inside her by the end of the night."

Her hands were held above her head very tightly, and she could not move at all. One of the guys told her, "You try that shit again and I'll shoot you. You got that, bitch?" He held the nine-millimeter Glock in her face, so she could see he was serious.

She nodded, showing she understood. She studied each of their faces, memorizing every detail so that she could recount it back to authorities later. While she studied the young man holding her right arm down, she heard tires come to a screeching halt and a door slam. She heard a familiar voice, "Get the fuck off her, now!" It was Alex, the last person she thought she wanted to see ever again, but she sure was she glad to hear his voice at this very moment.

She felt Alex yank the guy who was currently on top of her off her, and then she heard him punch the guy in the face. As he went down, the guys holding her arms down tried to scramble out of the back to go to his aid, which allowed Sarah to get up.

"This guy's a pig! *Kill him!*" she heard Chase's voice ring out over the rest of the noise.

Soon everyone was at the back of the SUV. Sarah felt herself kicking the kid closest to her in the groin and then doing a round-house to kick him in the face with her left leg. She moved on to the next guy who came at her and this time came up with a right hook, followed by a left cross and then finished him out with a right roundhouse.

Alex worked his way through the group of young men who rushed over to fight him, then she heard it—*bang. Bang.* The gun fired twice, and she heard Alex groan. He stumbled back about three steps, but then he got back up and started to fight with two men. *Bang. Bang. Bang.* The gun discharged three more times in Alex's direction. As Alex went down, she felt a sudden burning in her right shoulder, then again in her rib cage. She went down and hit the pavement. She soon felt bones crushing as she looked up and saw two men, Chase and another man, kicking and stomping on her leg and pelvis. She felt a steel-toed boot in her right rib cage and knew they were shattered immediately. She gasped in short breaths for air to enter her lungs but could not catch her breath. She felt herself starting to lose consciousness.

She heard the last three men laughing and then heard them running off in the distance. "Charlie, did you catch all that on tape? That was awesome, wasn't it? We sure showed them what happens to anyone who messes with us, didn't we?"

She dragged herself by her arms over to Alex, who was about fifty feet away from where she originally fell on the ground. She wanted to pass out from the pain, but knew she needed to check on him; she still could not believe all that happened and the fact that he tried to stop her attackers. She checked his pulse first and put her hand over his mouth to check for breathing. He was still alive, but just barely. She saw that he had already lost a lot of blood and knew if she didn't get help, they would both probably die right there, where no one would find them until morning.

She was relieved to find that her phone was still in the right pocket of her sundress. She called emergency services and told them what happened. She tried to stay conscious but briefly lost con-sciousness. When she came to again, she checked back in on Alex.

He looked at her and said, "Sarah, I know that you probably don't believe me, but I have always loved you. I realized how close I was to losing you when you were in the hospital, which is why I've been dragging my feet on the divorce. I know that Ethan loves you, he told me tonight after you left the restaurant. I saw the way you looked at him and now realize that you are in love with him. I want you to be happy, know that you have my blessing to be happy. I don't want you to ever hold back in your relationship with him because we weren't able to resolve our problems. You deserve to be happy, and he is the man to help you with that. I love you, Sarah, I always will."

She heard herself reply, "I love you too, Alex. I always will, but you can't leave me. Not now. Don't go!" She held his face in her hands as he breathed his last breath. She felt tears streaming down her face.

She felt herself losing blood and knew that she would not be able to hold on much longer. She found Alex's phone and dialed her mother's phone number because emergency services had a location lock on her phone. Violet answered the phone, "What the fuck do you want, you pig?"

Sarah felt her breathing shallowing, and it was harder to catch her breath. Her voice was raspy when she answered, "Mom, it's me. I wanted you to know that Alex and I were both shot. I am certain Alex is gone, and I can feel my life fading. I want you and Daddy to know that I love you both. I need you to call my friend Ethan and tell him that I love him and I am thankful that God brought him into my life. His number is 555-480-4152. Please do not rush to the hospital tonight. I want you and Daddy to get some rest before you drive up in the morning. I don't want you getting into an accident because you're tired."

"What do you mean? Sarah!"

"Mommy, I love you, and I always will." Sarah heard the ambulance and the police sirens in the distance. She dropped the phone, and everything went black.

"Hello! Hello! Sarah! Answer me, Sarah!" Violet screamed in the phone. When the paramedics and police arrived, the head police officer on scene heard Violet's voice and picked the phone up off the ground. "Hello! Sarah! Oh my god, Sarah! Answer me!"

"Ma'am, my name is Lieutenant Eric Goldberg. I just arrived at the scene. Who is this?"

"My name is Violet, I'm Sarah's mother. What is going on? Where is Sarah? Is she okay?"

"Violet, Sarah is still breathing but is in critical condition. The paramedics and one of my deputies already left and are taking her to Spring City General Hospital."

"What about Alex, Sarah's husband? How is he?" Violet asked.

"I hate to have to tell you this, but it looks as though he did not make it, ma'am. Once the coroner arrives, we will take him back for an autopsy."

"What, what happened?"

"Ma'am, we are still working out the details, but it looks as though both Alex and Sarah were shot multiple times. It doesn't look good for Sarah. She lost a lot of blood. We will continue to investigate this case for you and will keep you apprised of the situation. I will also keep a deputy posted outside her hospital room until we apprehend the person or persons responsible for this egregious attack."

Violet hung up with Lieutenant Goldberg and called the number Sarah gave her for Ethan. "Hello?" Ethan asked when he answered the phone.

"Is this Ethan?" Violet cautiously asked the male voice on the other end of the line.

"Yes, who is this?"

"Ethan, my name is Violet. Apparently, you know my daughter, and from the sounds of it, you know her very well."

"Your daughter is who again?"

"My daughter's name is Sarah."

"Oh, yes, I know Sarah. What's wrong? Where's Sarah?"

"Sarah called me tonight to inform me that she and Alex were attacked. She was bleeding a lot from her injuries. She wanted me to call you and let you know that she loves you. Are you having an affair with my daughter?" Violet asked.

"Sarah and Alex—what? What happened to them? I just had dinner with them both less than an hour ago."

"Focus, Ethan. They were both attacked and shot. Alex is dead, and Sarah was taken to the Spring City General Hospital, where the first responders and police don't know if she will survive the attack. She lost a lot of blood. Her father and I will leave in the morning to come down from Mountain City. It'll take us about ten hours to get there, so we won't be there until late tomorrow afternoon/early evening. Now, I asked you once already and you managed to ignore my question—were you and Sarah having an affair?"

"Yes, ma'am, we were, not that this is really any concern right now. I will head to the hospital now and wait for her to get out of surgery. Do you have a place to stay when you get here?"

"It is a concern because if my daughter dies, she will go to hell for having an affair. She has remained faithful all these years to Alex, what makes you so special that she would go and have an affair with you?"

"It's a long story, and when Sarah pulls through, you can ask her that story at some point. Right now, I will focus on getting to the hospital and just being there for her. I will keep you informed of what is going on. Do I need to call her grandparents? I know that they live in town here somewhere."

"No, I will call them in the morning. They turn off all their ringers at night, so they won't answer until they wake up in the morning."

Ethan hung up with Violet and rushed over to the hospital. He had so many thoughts running through his mind:

This is all my fault. I should never have let Alex get to her like that. I should have stopped her from walking out of the restaurant. How did this happen? Where did it happen? What exactly happened? What monster could attack such a beautiful woman? How long after the restaurant did this happen? Why did this have to happen to Sarah? Is she going to pull through? What would I do if something had happened to her? I can't even imagine what I would do without her... She has changed my life in ways that I can't even believe! I should have been there with her. I cannot believe that I allowed her to leave the restaurant by herself. I should have gotten up at that time and walked out with her.

He got to the receptionist's desk and asked for Sarah's room. The friendly receptionist asked if he was family and then called Violet to ensure that it was okay to give him information about Sarah's condition. After confirming this information, she led him to the surgical waiting lounge where he impatiently waited to hear about her surgery and her prognosis. As he walked past the surgical wing into the lounge, he saw two police officers standing post just outside the doors leading into the operating rooms. He was thankful to see these men standing guard for her protection.

Hospital—First Day

Sarah woke up in the ambulance and started to panic. "Where am I? Where is Alex? What is going on?" she asked. She felt the immediate stabbing pain throughout her entire body as she tried to sit up. She tried to rip out her IVs. "Get these things off me!"

The paramedics rushed to keep her from ripping out her IVs. As suddenly as she woke, she suddenly passed out again from the pain coursing through her body. The ambulance got her to Spring City General's Emergency Room where Dr. Wylie and the emergency room doctors were all waiting for her arrival. The paramedics explained her vitals and what happened in the back of the ambulance. As they finished, Sarah sat up again. "*Where is Alex? Alex, Alex! Where are you?*" She ripped out her IVs successfully before passing back out from the pain.

Dr. Wylie looked at the head of the ER department, Dr. Tasha Smith, and said, "You need to sedate her right now to keep her from doing this again." Dr. Smith looked at her head nurse, Carrie Brown, and nodded her approval when Carrie gave her a questioning look at Dr. Wylie's request.

The transport team wheeled her up to X-Ray, where she underwent a full body scan. Sarah had seven of twelve ribs on her right side broken. Her pelvis, femur, patella, tibia, and fibula were all broken in multiple locations. After getting the extent of the damage, the surgeons determined that Sarah needed pins and screws in her pelvis and her leg to help the bones grow back together. They took her to surgery and started the eight-hour procedure to help Sarah's leg heal correctly, wondering if her leg was going to heal enough for her to ever walk again.

After Sarah waited in the surgical recovery room for a couple of hours, she was moved into an intensive care unit bed where she was put under close evaluation by doctors and nurses. Ethan was allowed to join her in the ICU room where he sat by her side. He watched helplessly as she woke from her sedation; Sarah panicked, not knowing where she was or understanding what was happening to her. She ripped out her IVs and attempted to throw her legs over the bed to get up to leave. "Where is my husband? Where is Alex? Oh, God, Alex is dead, isn't he? I have to save him. I have to save him the way he saved me," she kept saying over and over while pulling out her IVs and attempting to climb out of the bed.

Ethan reached over and hit the nurse call button. He tried to calm her down, but she was not currently herself. She was still groggy from the sedatives, and she was extremely upset. The nurses came in and gave her an injection to calm her down so they could get the IVs back in. Sarah fell back into unconsciousness. While she slept, Ethan stepped out of the room to make a couple of phone calls and to run down to the cafeteria for coffee. About twenty minutes after Ethan left the room, Sarah woke up from the sedation medication. She fought the IVs again, screaming for someone to find Alex.

The head ICU nurse, Selina, grabbed another sedative and injected it into Sarah's IV, which caused Sarah to immediately calm down. She called Dr. Rachel Martinez into the room to fill her in on Sarah's inability to remain calm. "Dr. Martinez, what can we do to help calm her? Every time she wakes up, she rips her IVs out and tries to get out of bed."

Sarah sat up and tore her IV out again for the third time that night. "See what I mean, Dr. Martinez? If we let her continue, she is going to really hurt herself."

"I see what you are talking about. Let's try a different sedative. I also want to have Sarah's wrists and her left leg tied to the bed to prevent her from being able to rip her IVs out."

"Are you sure that is going to be enough?" Selina asked Dr. Rachel.

"No, to be honest, I don't know if it'll be enough, but we're going to try this for now and see if we can get her to calm down. Now, where did that very attractive young man go who was sitting in here with her earlier? I want to have a conversation with him to let him know what we're doing."

"I think he stepped out to get some coffee. Do you want me to call him?"

"No, just call me when he gets back up here, please, Selina."

"Okay."

Selina turned back to a sedated Sarah and wiped the sweat off her brow. Dr. Wylie walked in and asked, "How's she doing, Selina?" He noticed the restraints and asked, "Is she still ripping out those IVs?"

"Yes, Dr. Wylie. She hasn't come to peace yet with what happened. Once she does, I think she will settle down and will stop pulling those out."

"Looks like she's in good hands. Keep me posted if anything changes, please."

"Will do, sir."

As Dr. Wylie left the room, Ethan walked back in. He immediately noticed the restraints and went over to her bedside. "Nurse, why is Sarah being restrained? Isn't that just cruel?"

"Ethan, it is Ethan, right?" she asked and watched him nod. "We placed the restraints to help keep Sarah safe. Every time she wakes up, she pulls out her IVs. This can be very dangerous for her and can cause infection. We want to limit the amount of damage she does to her body so we felt that restraining her was the best way to keep her safe."

"Is it normal for a patient to continually pull out her IVs?" Ethan asked Selina.

"Every patient is different, Ethan."

She picked up the tape and bandages lying around the room and then left. Ethan looked at Sarah and felt helpless. He wanted so badly to snap his fingers and make all this go away for her. He ran the back of his left hand across her forehead and tucked a loose strand of her hair back behind her right ear. He laid his head down beside her ribs and did something he had not done in quite some time—he prayed.

"Holy Father, I come before you as a humble servant. I ask that you send your Son, Jesus Christ, to be with this beautiful spirit, Sarah, taking her pain and suffering from her. Please heal her body so that she can continue to do your work. I pray these things in your name, Amen."

While Sarah lay in the bed, sedated, she saw Alex standing in the doorway. He came closer to her and said, "Sarah, I wanted you to know that in my own way, I loved you. I will always love you, but you need to let go and move on with your life."

She replied, "What do you mean that I need to let go and move on?"

"Sarah, I have been called home. When you wake, I will not be there. I am walking my own journey now, and you must continue on your journey."

"I-I don't understand," she said.

"Sarah, I am coming to you from the other side. I can tell you that it is beautiful—everything you ever hear about. I cannot stay with you much longer, but I needed you to know that I did love you and I always will. But I also want you to know that I see how much you love Ethan."

"W-who said that? What makes you think that you know how I feel when I'm not one hundred percent certain myself," she interrupted him.

"Sarah, I saw it in your eyes at dinner tonight, the way you looked at him and he looked at you. You may not truly understand your feelings and all that is happening, but someday you will. Sarah, I just want you to know that I only want your happiness. I know that many years ago we promised that if anything ever happened to the other partner, we would never remarry, but I want you to know that I want your happiness. If marrying Ethan will make you happy down the road, I want to know that I am releasing you from that promise we made all those years ago."

"How can you say you want my happiness now when all you did was make my life miserable, especially over the last two to three years?"

"Sarah, I made mistakes. I am truly sorry. Someday you will understand. I have to go now, but please remember what I said… I want your happiness, you deserve to be happy. I loved you, Sarah, and I always will. I will be watching over you and will always be here for you. Goodbye, Sarah," he said as he disappeared from her side.

Ethan could see the struggle in her face as she conversed with Alex. He watched her eyes bounce back and forth behind closed eyelids as she talked to her late husband. He hit the nurse call button, and Selina joined him in the room. "Is this normal? Is she okay? Do I need to be worried about her?" he asked as soon as she walked in the room.

"Ethan, I'm not certain what is going on right now, but whatever it is, she seems to be fine. It isn't affecting her vitals, so I'm not worried."

"Would it be okay for me to release her hand and carefully slip up onto the bed behind her so that I can hold her close as she goes through this?"

"Well, normally, I would say not because of the extent of her injuries, but I have seen how she responds to your touch whenever you touch her. You have a calming effect on her. It is worth a shot to see if that helps calm her as she comes out of the sedative this time."

Selina removed the restraint from Sarah's right arm and slowly, carefully lifted her so that he could get into position under her. He gently wrapped his arms around her chest, wrapping her right arm under his right arm. Sarah stirred slightly at the movement but seemed to relax after a moment. Ethan kissed the top of her head and rubbed her hand with his thumb. After ten minutes he dozed off but immediately woke when he felt Sarah slightly move. "Sarah, I'm here with you. It's Ethan," he calmly said as she continued to stir. "You are going to be just fine. I just need you to stay relaxed and calm."

"E-E-Ethan?" she whispered.

"Yes, I'm here, chipmunk!"

"Ethan?" She tilted her head back slightly to try to focus on his face.

"I'm here with you. You gave me quite the scare. Your parents will be here by the end of the day. They asked me to sit with you until they got here. How are you feeling?"

"I am glad you are here." She smiled into his handsome face.

"I'm glad you're here as well, chipmunk." He gently squeezed her hand, and she squeezed his hand in response. She looked back up at him as he reached down and kissed the top of her forehead again.

"Ethan, I'm scared. I hurt everywhere. W-what happened? W-where am I?"

"I will tell you everything that I know, as long as you promise not to pull out your IVs again."

"O-okay," she whispered.

He gently crawled out from underneath her weight and moved to the right side of the bed. He took her hand in both of his and told her what he knew about the events of the night, based on what she had told her mother, Violet, and what the police officers told him when they came to check on her.

"We met for dinner tonight at Zippy's after Alex showed up in your apartment. Alex caused a scene, and when you couldn't handle it any further, you got up and left the restaurant. From what I can piece together, it looks like you walked in the opposite direction of your apartment and got to a vacant lot where there was a group of at young men, waiting to ambush you. They physically attacked and sexually assaulted you.

"After you left the restaurant, Alex and I split up to look for you. Alex found you under attack, and he rushed to your aid. He was shot at least six times, and before he went down, he was able to disarm one of your attackers and shot back. Alex bled out before the ambulance arrived on the scene.

While you were on the ground bleeding out from your own gunshot wounds, you were attacked by at least one individual. All three bones in your upper and lower right leg were busted in multiple places, your pelvis was also broken. You have seven broken ribs as well as two through and through gunshot wounds and one gunshot wound where the doctor had to remove the bullet. You are going to have bruises all up and down your body, including your face where you were kicked for a while. You are lucky that whoever did all this did not break your jaw. You pulled out your IVs multiple times last night, and you tried to jump off the bed to go find Alex. The police are still processing the scene and will keep us posted on anything they find."

She sat there and soaked it all in. She tried to sit up to look at the damage to her body but quickly laid back down when the pain coursed through her body. She turned her head away from him and cried. He reached over and wiped the tears from her face. She looked back over at him. He reached down and kissed her gently on her wet cheek. "Chipmunk, I can't imagine what must be going through your head at this moment or how you are feeling, but I want you to know that I am here for you, always and forever."

She weakly smiled up at him, grateful in that moment to have him by her side. "H-have you told anyone about this? D-do my grandparents know?"

"Your parents know because you called your mother before you passed out. I asked your mother when she called me if I needed to call your grandparents, but she told me that she would do it in the morning when they got on the road to come down here. I'll be honest with you, I don't know if your mother called them yet or not. I can go call your mother if you would like to let her know that you are currently awake and check on that at the same time. Would you like me to do that?"

"Y-yes, please," she said as she slightly nodded.

"Do you promise to be good and leave your IVs alone?" he asked as he stood up to find his phone.

She nodded. He walked across the room and located his phone. He dialed the same number that had called him about twelve hours earlier and put the call on speaker phone so that Sarah could hear the conversation. Violet answered the phone, "Hello?"

"Hi, Violet, this is Ethan. I am calling to let you know that Sarah is finally awake and coherent. She asked about you and her father. She wanted to make sure you are okay."

"We're fine. We've just loaded the car and will be down in about eleven to twelve hours with all the rest stops we need to make because we're old. Please tell her to stop trying to pull out her IVs and to behave herself."

"I can do that, ma'am. Sarah also asked me if her grandparents know yet what happened last night."

"You can tell her, no, they do not know yet. I will call them later in the day. I will let you know once they are aware of the situation. Now, I must run. See you in a few hours."

After he hung up the phone, he looked at Sarah. She was struggling to stay awake. "Hey, chipmunk, I'm going to run home and shower. I will swing by the apartment and feed the girls. I don't want them to starve. Do you want me to tell Greg what happened so he knows not to expect you in the apartment for a while? Do I also need to call Peter and let him know what happened?"

"O-okay. I'll see you in a little bit," she quietly replied back to him as her eyelids grew heavier.

He walked over to her bed and kissed her forehead. "I will hold off on telling Greg anything until you're ready for him to know. I'll be back in a couple of hours." Ethan left, and Sarah fell back to sleep. She woke up when Selina came back in the room and started checking her vitals.

Ethan came back after his shower. He brought Sarah's favorite stuffed animal, Eeyore, to help her feel better. He laid it carefully on her chest and rested her free arm on top of it. She slightly stirred when he did this but calmed right back down and went back to sleep. Ethan sat at her bedside until she woke back up. "W-what's going on? Where am I?" she asked, confused and alarmed when she could not move her body.

"Chippy, it's okay. I'm here with you. You're in the hospital after you were brutally attacked."

"W-why can't I move?" Sarah tried pulling her left arm up but met resistance from the restraint. She tried moving her left leg and got the same resistance. She started to panic, getting extremely agitated in her confusion.

"Sarah, I need you to calm down. I'm here with you and will explain everything. I need you to stop pulling on your arm and leg." Ethan sat there beside her and calmly explained everything that happened the night before to Sarah again. She sat there in silence and then started crying. "Sarah, what are you thinking? What are you feeling right now?"

"I don't know what to think or feel right now. All I feel is pain. I just want to sleep and maybe I'll wake up and this will all have been a nightmare."

"As much as I would like for this to be a nightmare, Chipmunk, I have to tell you that it isn't. Your reality will be recovering from this attack."

"I don't want to think about that right now. I'm going to go back to sleep now and pray that when I wake up this was all someone's idea of a very nasty joke." She turned her head away from him, moved Eeyore up next to her face, and fell asleep again.

While she lay there, Selina came back in the room. Ethan talked to her while she checked Sarah's vitals. Dr. Martinez walked in to check on Sarah, so Ethan asked, "Is it normal for someone to have memory loss after a tragedy like this? How long will it last? How long will it be before she fully heals?"

"Ethan, I wish I could answer all those questions with specific time frames, but I can't. Honestly, it is all up to the individual how long it will take for him/her to recover. I can tell you that the memory loss is normal. She will gain her memory back, some patients get their memories back all at the same time, some patients never get any of their memories back and other patients will only get pieces back. Everyone is different. It all depends on how much damage was done to Sarah's temporal lobe during the attack."

Once Selina had everything she needed from Sarah, both she and Dr. Martinez left the room. Selina looked at Dr. Martinez and said, "This girl is one lucky girl to have a man like that waiting by her side."

"Why do you say that, Selina?" Dr. Martinez asked.

"Look at him. He is very easy on the eyes!" she said with a wink and a smile.

"Leave it to you, Selina, to notice his charming good looks, haha." Dr. Martinez laughed.

Selina smiled again and then said, "He has barely left her side since she came out of surgery. He truly cares about her, you can see it in the way he touches her and looks at her."

Violet called Ethan when she and Matthew stopped for lunch to let him know where they were at in their journey and when they should be expected to arrive. Violet also advised Ethan that she had called Sarah's grandparents to let them know what happened to Sarah. Just as he hung up with Violet, there was a quiet tap at the doorway. Ethan looked up to see an elderly couple standing there holding flowers and balloons. He greeted them and then he introduced himself to them.

Tanner walked around to the opposite side of the bed, sat down, and immediately grabbed Sarah's left hand. "Why is she tied to the bed like an animal?" he asked when he saw the restraint on her wrist and ankle.

"She kept pulling her IVs out every time she woke up. The doctor felt this was the best way to keep her from hurting herself."

"Oh, I see. I guess that makes sense. It just seems so barbaric."

Sarah woke up at hearing Pops' raspy voice. She looked around and focused on the scene. "P-Pops, is that you?"

"Hey, kiddo, it's me. Grams is here with me. Your mother called us a few minutes ago, and we rushed here as quickly as we could."

"I'm scared, Pops."

"What has you scared, little one?"

"Pops, I don't want to die. I thought I was ready to go, but I now know that I'm not. Please don't let me die, Pops." Sarah started crying. Tanner reached down and wiped her tears away from her cheek.

"Little one, what makes you think you're going to die?"

"I felt like I died. At some point, I saw Alex. He told me that he had died. I don't wanna die, Pops! I'm scared."

"Little one, you are going to die, just not today. You have a purpose in this life. God isn't ready to take you home just yet."

"How can you be sure, Pops?"

"If it was your time to go, he would have taken you last night, little one." He calmed her down by just talking to her. Her grandparents stayed about an hour or so and then they left. Sarah slept until her parents arrived about four hours later.

Ethan met her parents in the hallway and introduced himself to them. "Hi, I'm Ethan, Sarah's friend."

"You look familiar. Where do I know you from?" Violet asked him.

"We did meet once before, a few months ago when Sarah was hospitalized after collapsing while we were out running."

"Oh, that's right. Now I remember. Were you sleeping with my daughter at that point?"

Ethan tried to avoid answering this question, so he tried to distract Violet by saying, "Sarah is currently asleep, but she has been waking up about every two hours or so for a little bit before going back to sleep. She is badly bruised from where she was kicked and beaten. I also want you to know that Dr. Martinez elected to have Sarah placed in restraints. She is fine with us removing one of the arm restraints while we are in the room with her, but as soon as we leave, she wants the restraint put back on in order to keep Sarah from pulling her IVs out or trying to get out of bed."

"I see what you did there, son, don't think I didn't catch you trying to ignore my question. I will get to the bottom of all this before I leave to go north again. For now, though, let's go in the room and see if my daughter is awake. Have her grandparents been by to see her yet?"

"Yes, ma'am, they stopped by for about an hour right after you told me you stopped for lunch."

Violet wept when she entered the room and saw Sarah in the bed with bruises all over the exposed parts of her body. She immediately saw that Sarah's right leg was in a cast and propped up slightly to help reduce the amount of swelling. Her father, Matt, took the chair closest to the window so that he could look outside rather than focusing on his daughter lying there in the bed. For the first time in a very long time, he felt completely helpless. He knew that he could not easily fix his daughter's pain.

Sarah woke up and listened as her mother chatted about the drive and about Brennen. Violet talked about how Brenda was due to pop any day now with their second grandbaby. When she fell back asleep, Ethan turned to Violet and Matt and said, "Sarah offered to let you guys stay in her apartment, if you want to stay there."

"We're going to stay at Pops and Grams' place. Thanks for the offer though." They turned and left the room.

Ethan climbed up next to Sarah on the bed and lay on his side, carefully draping his arm over her. Her rhythmic breathing lulled him into a much-needed sleep. He did not hear the nurse come in around midnight or again at four to check on Sarah. He woke up around six thirty the next morning feeling a little bit sore but also rested. He had not realized just how tired he was until he woke up, realizing he had not slept since the day before last. He woke to see Sarah staring down at him, a big smile across her face.

"What are you smiling for?" he asked her.

"Oh, nothing. You get any sleep?"

"I did actually. I didn't hurt you, did I?"

"No, I'm fine. You look like you could use a nice hot shower and some breakfast. Why don't you go home and take some time for you. I'm sure my parents will be by here in a bit to keep me company."

"I'll swing by your place and take care of the girls. I'm sure they will be very hungry since I forgot to go feed them last night. I promise I won't be long," he said as he reached down to kiss her.

"Take as long as you need. It's not like I'm going anywhere any time soon." She laughed. "Ooh, that hurts, probably should make a mental note of not making me laugh anymore."

He smiled, reached down, and kissed her again and then left the room. He ran home and took a nice hot shower. When he finished shaving, he got dressed and left the house. He immediately drove over to Sarah's place. "Good morning, Greg," he said as he headed toward the elevator.

"Good morning, Ethan. Sarah's not up there, if you're looking for her. The night guy said that she didn't come home last night. I sure hope everything is okay."

"Thanks for the heads up, but she told me she wouldn't be back for a few days and asked me to swing by and take care of the girls while she is out."

"Oh, makes sense. Please let me know if there is anything I can do to be of assistance," Greg replied.

"Will do!" Ethan walked to the elevator and used the key fab to get to Sarah's suite. Pretty Baby and Squirrel Bait pounced as soon as the door opened, nearly tripping Ethan. "Meow, meow, meow, meow," they both sang to him as he walked inside and reached down to scruff their ears. They led him to the kitchen where Crackers waited for them to join her. He got their food bowls ready and provided them with fresh water. Before he put their bowls down, he got their laser pointer out and played with them. Once they were tired and panting, he put their food bowls down. They quickly downed their food while he cleaned their litter boxes. He sat down on the couch and gave each of the girls a belly rub before he left to go back to the hospital.

Ethan stopped at the local bakery and got both Sarah and him vanilla-frosted custard-filled long johns. He also grabbed her a bottle of orange juice to chase the donut down with. He got back to the hospital and parked his car. When he got just outside Sarah's room, he was stopped by a young tall dark-haired sun-kissed muscular police officer. "Who are you, and where do you think you're going?"

"My name is Ethan. I'm here to visit Sarah Jackson-Clark. I was here earlier but left to go take a shower. You are?"

"My name is Officer Tom Hardy. I need to see some identification, and I need to confirm that it is okay to let you in. Wait here."

Ethan waited until Officer Hardy came back in the hallway and verified his photo ID. Once the verification was made and the donut bag searched, Officer Hardy stepped aside and let Ethan enter the room. Ethan was surprised to see the tiny room held so many people. When he walked into the room, he saw Sarah's parents and her Grandparents in the corner and saw another police officer on the opposite side of the room. This officer looked to be in his mid to late forties. He was well-groomed with blond hair and blue eyes. He looked as though he kept himself in shape, although not as muscular as Officer Hardy. He turned when Ethan entered the room and offered Ethan his hand. "Hi, Ethan, it's nice to meet you. My name is Lieutenant Eric Goldberg. I was just about to fill Sarah and her family in on what we know so far in the case." He turned to Sarah. "Would you like Ethan to stay in the room, or do you want him to leave while I tell you what's going on with your case?"

"Please let him stay," she whispered. She motioned for Ethan to come sit with her. He put everything down on the tray at the foot of the bed and then came and sat in the chair next to her bed. He took her hand in his and gently squeezed it. Sarah's family all sat down in chairs that had been brought in and her dad held her other hand.

Once everyone was settled, Lieutenant Goldberg started, "Sarah, what do you remember about Friday night?"

"I don't remember much of anything. The only thing I know is what Ethan told me this morning."

"Well, Sarah, there was a large group of young men who attacked you two nights ago in the Bargain Barn's distribution center's parking lot. We found fingerprints all over the car they raped you in and were able to identify six of the young men. When questioned, they all flipped on each other trying to get a deal with the prosecutor. We know that there were about fifteen members to the group, ages ranged from sixteen to twenty-one. The ringleader just turned eighteen, and his group of friends wanted to help him celebrate by raping the first woman they found.

The youngest one of the group was there to record the whole thing. We have him in custody, but we didn't get to him before the ringleader, his brother, uploaded the attack on InstaChat. Sarah, I'm sorry, we are doing everything we can to get this taken off the internet, but we have to wait for a warrant to come through in order to force InstaChat to remove the material. In the meantime, I want you to prepare yourself for the fact that this has gone viral and that this video already has over ten million hits on it. The news media got their hands on it as well, so you will probably see your attack on the news as well."

Sarah cried when she found out that her attack was out on social media for the whole world to see. As she cried, she briefly remembered hearing a conversation between the camera man and the guy who attacked her. "The camera man's name was C-Charlie, I think. Is that who you have in custody?" she asked Lieutenant Goldberg.

"Yes, that's who we have in custody."

"The guy who attacked me, I believe his name was C-Chase, or something like that."

"Yes, Chase. He is the only one from the group that we do not currently have in custody. We have officers out trying to locate him now. He told his friends that he was going to murder you for embarrassing him in front of his friends the way that you did. He has not been apprehended, so until he is, we will be posting two officers outside your door day and night. Sarah, I don't want you to worry. We are going to catch this monster and lock him up for good.

"I have some pictures. Do you think you can identify Chase just so we know beyond a shadow of a doubt that we have the right person when we do find him?

"Yes, I still see his face in my nightmares. I can smell his breath and his cologne. I just want this to all be over, Lieutenant."

"We should be able to close out this case fairly quickly. We will keep you posted as the case progresses. For now, I'm going to leave Officer Hardy and Officer Metcalf posted outside your door. They will be replaced in twelve hours by two new officers and will rotate shifts every twelve hours until Chase is apprehended. We have the full weight of the Spring City Police Department [SCPD] out looking for him. For now, I must leave you so that I can get back to the office to continue the manhunt. Take care and feel free to call me day or night if you have any questions or concerns."

"Thank you, Lieutenant."

Lieutenant Goldberg left the room and stopped to give directions to the two officers posted outside the door. They sat down and kept watch over Sarah's room.

Selina came in and administered new pain medications into Sarah's IV, which caused her to fall asleep. Once she was asleep, Sarah's parents and Grandparents decided to leave Ethan there in the room with her. They left for lunch and told Ethan they would be back sometime around three.

After they left, Ethan turned on the television to catch up on world events. Every local station showed edited versions of the video. Ethan stopped to watch the news on CBS. The announcer, Baldwin Blake, a very handsome man with blond hair and green eyes was, on talking about the attack:

"We do not have much detail at this time, but local authorities are asking for help with locating this man, Chase Matthews, wanted for questioning in the brutal attack of a young woman. The attack appears to have happened the night before last, Friday night, around eight in the Bargain Barn Distribution Center's parking lot. If you know any more details about this attack, please call local authorities at 555-205-1865.

Ethan flipped the channel, and a similar story was being aired by announcer Patricia Perkins on a national news broadcast:

"We caution you when watching this video as it is extremely graphic in nature. Local authorities are asking for help with finding local teenager, Chase Matthews. Matthews is wanted for questioning in the rape of this young woman, Sarah Jackson-Clark, and the murder of her husband, Alex Clark. Matthews, along with a group of fourteen other young men, brutally attacked and raped Sarah Clark in the Bargain Barn Distribution Center's parking lot. All but Matthews have been arrested and are awaiting their bail hearings. If you know this man or know his location, please call Spring City authorities at 555-205-1865."

While the Patricia spoke, the graphic video of Sarah and Alex's attempt to save themselves played in the background. Disgusted, Ethan turned the television off. He looked over to see Sarah, tears streaming down her face at the sight of the video. "Oh, Sarah, I'm sorry. I didn't know you were awake. Are you okay?"

"I'll be fine," she sniffled. "I guess I should probably put something out on my InstaChat page. Will you help me with that?

Ethan pulled out Sarah's cell phone and helped her log in to her InstaChat page. She dictated what she wanted him to say, and he typed it out for her. As soon as the post went up, Sarah received messages from all her family members, friends, and acquaintances wishing her a speedy recovery and asking if they could help in any way. With Ethan's help, she thanked each person personally when they left her a message.

Sarah's parents came back to the room around three like they said they would. An hour later, they heard a knock at the door. "Hi, Sarah, it's me, Lieutenant Goldberg. I'm here with some good news and some bad news."

"We could definitely use some of that good news at this point, Lieutenant," Violet replied. "Come on in and sit down."

He walked in and sat down. "Chase Matthews's father saw the footage and immediately brought his son in to us for questioning."

"W-what's the bad news, sir?" Sarah asked, grabbing Ethan's hand for reassurance and comfort.

"Well, the bad news is that Chase's father is Tom Matthews."

"Why is that bad news? Who is Tom Matthews?" Violet asked.

Before Lieutenant Goldberg could answer, Ethan replied, "Chipmunk, Tom Matthews is the owner of the Spring City Football Team. He is five feet eleven inches, with sandy blond hair and brown eyes. He keeps a well-manicured mustache. You've most likely seen him on television talking about all the good he does for the community."

"I still don't understand why that is important," she cut him off.

"Little one, it means he has the money to get his son the best lawyer in the country to get him off from this charge. This kid will get a slap on the wrist and will be out before we can all say boo," Matthew said.

Violet looked at her husband and then back to Lieutenant Goldberg, "Please, say that isn't so. Please tell me that he will do hard time for this."

"Well, I wish that I could tell you that he will spend the rest of his life in jail, but I can't. Your husband is correct, with the right lawyer, Chase will probably get off with just a slap on the wrist. I wanted you to hear this from me, but Charlie, the camera operator, is Chase's younger brother.

"We are working closely with the district attorney's office to not let this happen. We have all the evidence, and we have fourteen young men pointing fingers at Chase. Just know that this will be a long drawn-out process, but we are here by your side through the entire thing. Please let me know if there is anything I can do."

Once Lieutenant Goldberg was out of the room, Violet started throwing chairs around the room. Officer Hardy entered the room to check on the family. "Everything okay in here?" he asked.

"We're fine. My wife is just processing the news that the Lieutenant gave us just now," Ethan replied.

"Okay, know that we won't let anything happen to Sarah. We will do everything we can to ensure her safety."

Violet sat down in a chair next to the window, put her hands in her lap, and started sobbing into her hands. Sarah looked at her father and said, "Dad, do you mind taking her home? I think she may need to take one of her anxiety pills and rest."

Matthew reached down and kissed Sarah's forehead. "Little one, I think you are wise beyond your years. I love you! We will see you tomorrow."

One of the shift nurses entered the room and checked Sarah's IVs and gave her another round of pain medication through the IV just as her parents turned to leave the room. Sarah watched as her parents left; her father held her mother tightly and her mother leaned into him for support. She thought about the support she needed and was thankful that Ethan was there to help take her mind off all her fears as well as all the emotional and physical pain she was experiencing. As if on cue, Ethan joined her side again. He reached out and grabbed her hand with his right hand, gently stroking the top of her hand; with his left hand, he reached up and gently stroked her cheek. He carefully tucked a piece of her hair that came out of her ponytail with her father's hug back behind her ear. He reached down and kissed her forehead. She looked up at him and tried to smile.

Ethan saw right through the fake smile. "Hey, chippy, penny for your thoughts."

"Just a penny?" she smiled.

"What can I say, I'm a cheapskate." He laughed. "But in all seriousness, what's on your mind right now?"

She let out a long slow breath. She contemplated what to say and how to say it. She was grateful for all Ethan had done to help her so far, and she did not want to be alone with her thoughts, but she was not quite sure she was ready to tell him her fears and concerns because she did not want to burden him or scare him off. "I'm fine. I really am. I just really don't know how to process everything, but I'll be fine."

"Just know that I am here for you, whenever you are ready to talk," he said before he reached back down and kissed her forehead again. They sat there in silence until they dozed off.

Sarah fell asleep shortly after her parents left. She did not want to; she wanted to stay awake and talk more with Ethan, but the medications she received were too much for her, and she drifted to sleep. While she slept, she dreamed—it was all coming back to her in a flood of memories. She remembered everything that happened. She felt all the events of the night all over again. Sarah wanted desperately to wake up to end this nightmare and find herself whole and in her own bed, but she just could not wake up. She replayed this attack over and over in her mind until she felt a gentle hand reach down and hold her. She knew that she was safe now; it was okay for her to wake up.

Ethan woke with a start when he heard Sarah crying out in agony. He watched as she tried to toss and turn and the pain that this caused as it spread across her face. He saw her breathing as it labored. He noticed that she was still asleep and watched as her eyes danced behind closed eyelids in REM sleep. It broke his heart that he could not make things better for her. He reached out to calm her and cupped her face in his hands. He started talking softly to her. Her breathing slowed, and she relaxed.

"Whoa there, Sarah, you are okay. I'm here with you. No one is going to hurt you. It's okay." She heard Ethan's quiet voice trying to calm her.

She woke up and felt the tears streaming down her face. She looked away. She did not want Ethan to see her crying. He reached over and wiped her tears from her cheeks. "I am here with you. You are going to be okay."

"T-thank you for being here with me. It really means the world to me."

"There's nowhere else I'd rather be right now than here with you." He smiled at her.

"What day is it?"

"Sunday, why?"

"You have to leave. You have to go get the boys! Oh my god, I missed my run with them yesterday." Ethan saw the frustration in her face at the thought of missing her run with the boys.

"Whoa, it's okay. Sherry knows what is going on and agreed to keep the boys this weekend. I tried to tell them what they needed to know without going into much detail about the attack, although with it all over the news, I'm sure they know more now than I wanted them to. But they can't wait for you to be up and in running shape again."

"Me too! I feel like I've been in this bed forever, and it's only been a couple of days. It's going to take me forever to get back into shape to run with the boys."

"You up for trying something?"

"What?" she asked skeptically.

"What if we try to keep you exercising while in bed? What do you think?"

"Well, um, I hate to bring up the elephant in the room, but my leg is kind of hanging in the air right now with all the bones in it broken. How in the world am I supposed to exercise when my arms and my leg are shackled to the bed? I don't think Dr. Martinez would approve of a workout regimen, do you?"

"Well, let's get creative then. What if we try to visualize the workout? I can bring the laptop in and we can work out to the trainers' instructions. It's worth a shot, isn't it?"

"I guess it can't hurt to try it. Maybe then it'll keep my mind occupied on anything other than the attack and from feeling sorry for myself."

"I'm going to go feed the girls and bring the laptop back, so we can start tomorrow. I'll be back here in about an hour. You want me to grab anything else on my way back?"

"The food in this place is disgusting. No salt and no flavor whatsoever. How about a burger from Spring City Burger and Steak House? Think you can swing that?"

"I'll see what I can do," he said as he headed to the door.

She felt herself dozing off. She tried to stay awake; she did not want to dream anymore about the events that happened just two nights prior. She could not keep her eyes open no matter how hard she willed it. She was right back there in the middle of the attack. She cried out for help, but no one answered her calls. All she heard was more laughter from her attackers. She woke up in a cold sweat. She looked up and saw Officer Hardy standing over her with a look of concern on his face.

"What's going on?" she asked, confused and disoriented.

"You were screaming like you were being attacked, so I came to check on you. Are you okay, ma'am?" he asked, concerned.

"I-I'm fine. Just a bad dream."

"Are you sure, ma'am?"

"I'm sure! I'll be fine."

Ethan returned a short time later. Before he entered the room, Officer Hardy stopped him and told him what happened while he was gone. He thanked them for the information and joined Sarah in the room.

Sarah only ate about a quarter of the burger before giving it to him to finish or throw away; she was no longer hungry after visualizing the attack a second time that day. "Guess I just wasn't that hungry," she said when Ethan looked at her, concerned.

They chatted a little while longer, and then Sarah fell back to sleep. While she was asleep, Dr. Martinez came in to check on her. "How's our patient doing?" Ethan asked her.

"Well, all things considered, she's doing well. I still want to keep her in restraints whenever no one is in the room with her and when she's sleeping because I don't want her to hurt herself. I've noticed that her heartrate jumps quite a bit when she's sleeping sometimes, and Selina told me that she's still thrashing about during her sleep. Have you witnessed this?"

"Actually, yes, I have. It has me concerned. I asked her about it before, and she just tells me that she's having nightmares. I want to help her, but I just don't know how to."

"Have you tried talking to her about the attack?"

"I told her what we know happened, but she never wants to open up and talk about it. I think she may be too ashamed or scared to talk about it—almost like if she talks about it, then it is real, and she doesn't want to face that truth. Does that make sense?"

"It does. I'm going to place a call to my good friend, Dr. Tracy Jackson, to see if she can come talk to Sarah and help her through all this."

Dr. Jackson

"Hello? Rachel, is that you?" Tracy asked as she answered the phone.

"Hello, Tracy, long time no talk to. How have you been?"

"Good, to what do I owe the pleasure?"

"Can't a friend just call another friend without a hidden agenda?" Rachel laughed.

"Most friends, yes, but with you, not so much." Tracy giggled. "What's going on, how can I help you?"

"According to medical records, it looks like you are treating one of my current patients. I need your expertise and help in how to handle her situation."

"Who is the patient so I can confirm or deny if I am currently working with this person?"

"The patient's name is Sarah Jackson-Clark. Ring any bells?"

"It does. What's going on? What can I help with?" Tracy asked.

"Have you watched the news lately?" Rachel asked seriously.

"Not really. Been busy with my patients and trying to publish a book. Why? Do I need to?" she asked.

"When is the last time you spoke to her?"

"Thursday morning when she called me for her morning session. What happened to Sarah that you're calling me?"

"Well, Sarah walked into the wrong part of town while trying to get back to her apartment here in Spring City Thursday night. While she was walking, she was attacked by a group of men who raped her, killed her husband, and then tried to kill her. She is here in Spring City General's ICU under my care. She won't talk about the incident with anyone, but if I were to guess, she's having nightmares about the attack and the events of that night. She keeps thrashing around in her sleep, and if she isn't restrained, she tries to take out her IVs and get out of the bed. Can you help me? I know that I should be reaching out to the staff here at the hospital, but I know she built a trust with you and I don't want to set her backward on her road to recovery by bringing in the wrong person."

"I will clear my schedule so that I can come visit her for the next couple days to try to help her accept what happened so she can move forward."

"Thank you, Tracy. I owe you big time for this. Maybe while you're in town, I can take you out to dinner."

"That would be nice. You can make it up to me by letting me crash at your place. We'll get together once I get there and make plans. Sound good?"

"You've got yourself a deal on crashing at my place and making plans once you're here. Drive safe. See you tomorrow!"

They hung up the phone, and Tracy immediately threw some clothes in her bag so that she could wake up early and drive to Spring City. She got to a good stopping point in her work and then went to bed so that she was fully rested before the long drive she had ahead of her.

Sarah lay awake in the hospital bed thinking, *I cannot believe how Ethan has stuck by my side. He has been here every possible minute. I hate that he is missing quality time with his boys and Emily to be here with me. I don't deserve this devotion! Ethan is such a great man. I am such a lucky person to have such a devoted man in my life. I love that he just sits with me when he knows I need quiet and when I need a distraction. He just knows how to help me stay relaxed and calm.*

She dozed off after her pain medications were administered, and when she woke up, she saw her therapist, Dr. Tracy, sitting beside her. "W-what's happening? Am I dreaming right now?" she groggily asked. "Where's Ethan? How did you get here?"

"Nice to see you too, sleeping beauty," Dr. Tracy teased before answering her series of questions. "What's happening is that I'm here to help you process this attack. You are not dreaming right now, I am here with you. Want me to pinch you so you know for sure?" she asked as she winked and smiled.

"No, I feel enough pain as it is. I don't need a pinch as well."

"As for your other questions, I got here by car, not bus, not plane, by car. Ethan has graciously offered to step out of the room so we can chat. He just wants you to be able to talk to someone about nightmares and to process the recent events. He knows that it is important for you to talk rather than bottling up your feelings. Ready to do that?"

"What if I'm not?" Sarah asked indignantly.

"Well, we're going to sit here until you start talking. I know it feels like not talking about it will make it less real, but Sarah, it is real. Your injuries are your constant reminder of just how real this attack was."

"I-it should never have happened. I'm so stupid for letting it happen. I just can't help beating myself up that if I hadn't been so stupid, maybe Alex would still be here annoying the shit out of me and I wouldn't be here in this bed. I don't want to remember. I just want it to all disappear and go away. I want to curl up in a little ball and just disappear, but I can't do that. I don't want to talk about it." Sarah started getting agitated and started pulling on her wrist restraints.

"Sarah, I understand—" Dr. Tracy started to say before Sarah interrupted her.

"*No, no, you don't!*" Sarah yelled. "*Have you ever been attacked and gang raped?*" She stopped yelling long enough to watch Dr. Tracy's head shake back and forth to state she had not. "*I didn't think so, so don't tell me you understand, because you don't. No one can truly understand.*" She started sobbing and turned away from Dr. Tracy.

"Sarah, it is okay to be upset and scared."

"*I-I'm not upset or scared. I'm* pissed," she yelled.

"Who are you pissed at, Sarah?"

"*I told you, I don't want to talk about it!*" She turned her head, and tears ran down her cheeks.

Dr. Tracy stopped pushing for a couple minutes until Sarah calmed down. "Sarah, you said you are pissed. Who are you pissed at?"

"Why do you care? Why are you here?"

"I care about your well-being, Sarah. I'm here for you."

"*I didn't ask you to come. You should go back to Fair Falcon and leave me alone. I don't want to talk about this.*"

"Okay, you know what, I'm going to give you some time alone. Get some rest, and I'll be back here in a couple of hours."

"Don't bother. I won't want to talk then either," Sarah said before turning her head away again.

Tracy left the room. She found Rachel in the employee lounge, having a hardboiled egg and drinking a glass of water. "Sounds like you've got your work cut out for you, Trace," Rachel said.

"You aint lying, Rach. I don't know if I'm going to be able to help Sarah like I did before."

"If anyone can, you can, Trace. You're the best, which is why I called you in here."

"Thanks for the vote of confidence. I need all that I can get because she's going to be a tough egg to crack."

While alone, Sarah dreamed of the attack. She saw the boys' faces so crisp and clear that she felt like she was right back there in that parking lot again. Everything was so real that when Chase started raping her, she threw up. She felt every emotion she felt the night of the attack. She could smell his breath and his cologne. She tried to get away—she stomped on his foot and broke his nose, but no matter how hard she tried, she could not get her hands and feet unbound so she could run away.

Sarah woke up drenched in sweat and covered in vomit. Selina came in to check on her and immediately went out to get help. The nursing staff carefully moved Sarah off her current bed onto a new bed they wheeled into the room so that they could take the other bed out and clean it up. Selina helped Sarah out of her current gown and gave her a sponge bath to clean her up before putting her in a new gown. Sarah smiled when she saw this gown because it was nothing like a typical hospital gown. This one had different cat pictures all over it.

Tracy walked back in the room after Sarah was cleaned up. "Hi, Sarah, ready to talk?"

Sarah scowled. "Nothing's changed. I don't want to talk about it."

"Sarah, you need to release it. Otherwise, it's going to consume you. I hear you aren't eating. If you don't start eating, they are going to put a feeding tube in."

"I will refuse the feeding tube."

"Sarah, they aren't going to give you a choice. They can claim that you aren't of a sound mind and can get it put in whether you consent or not. Do you really want that?"

"No."

"Sarah, I watched you while you thrashed about in the bed. Dr. Rachel is right, until you face what happened, you won't be able to be released from the restraints because you're going to hurt yourself. What did you dream about?"

Sarah sat there and started crying. "It's okay to be pissed, Sarah. It's okay to be angry, scared, worried. It is okay for you to feel this way. I am here to help walk you through these feelings so that we can get you healthy again."

She sat there for a few minutes before saying, "It's all my fault."

"What's your fault, Sarah?"

"Everything, it's all my fault. I wish God had taken me instead of Alex. This world would be better off without me."

"Sarah, God has a plan for you, which is why he didn't take you home yet. This world would not be a better place without you, it's a better place because of you."

"You're just saying that because you're my therapist and you have to."

"Sarah, there are people who love you, who would be truly devastated if you were no longer here with us."

"I-I don't believe you."

"Sarah, tell me why you believe this was your fault."

"Why does it matter to you? Why do you keep trying to push me to talk about it?"

"I know that you will feel better once you do and maybe you can stop having all the nightmares and can start healing, but you have to talk about it and let me in first. I promise, it will help you in the long run."

"I don't know how much of it I can truly remember, so I don't think it's going to help me."

"Let's talk through what you do remember and just see how that goes. Why is it your fault?"

"If I hadn't let Alex bully me into going to dinner with him and Ethan, this wouldn't have happened. He would still be alive, his baby wouldn't be growing up without her father, and I wouldn't be in here."

"Tell me more about what happened. How did Alex bully you into dinner with Ethan? What happened at dinner?"

"I remember going on my run after work, and when I got home, Alex was in my apartment waiting for me. He told me I was a whore and asked who I was sleeping with. He didn't believe that I had been out running with Ethan and the boys. He said he wouldn't leave until we ate dinner with Ethan."

"What happened next?"

"I asked Ethan if he would be willing to meet us for dinner, which he agreed to. Alex and I left the apartment and met Ethan at the restaurant. Alex started getting nasty with both Ethan and me, he wanted to know what happened between the two of us. He just wouldn't stop, and it really upset me, so I left the restaurant." Sarah stopped and looked up at the ceiling.

"Okay, what happened next?"

"This is where I don't know. I can't remember any of the details when I'm awake, but when I'm asleep, I feel like I remember every single detail. I've seen the video that circulated for a while online before it finally got removed, and I've heard what the news reported as well as what Ethan told me, but I don't remember it. I don't want to remember it, okay?"

"Okay, not today. Sarah, you will eventually remember everything, and you will need to talk about it to keep your mind healthy."

"Thank you for not pushing me. I don't want to remember. I want to get back to my life as soon as I can."

"Sarah, I understand that you want your life to be normal, but you need to understand that things will never be the same. Know that I am here for you when you need to talk."

"Thanks. I know," Sarah replied.

Tracy left the room, and Sarah was by herself. She wanted desperately to get up out of this bed and for almost everything to be back to the way it was before. She wanted to be at work with her teams and out on her run with Ethan and the boys. She wanted to just be able to walk through the park and smell the flowers. She decided in that moment that she was going to do everything she possibly could to get out of the hospital as quickly as possible and not spend forever in therapy learning to walk again because of muscle atrophy.

Sarah hit her nurse call button, and Selina came in. "What's up, Sarah?"

"Is Dr. Martinez available?"

"Yeah, let me go grab her for you," Selina said as she walked out of the room.

A few minutes later, Dr. Martinez walked in. "Hey, Sarah, how are you feeling?"

"I just want to get out of here to be honest, Doc. I have a serious question for you though."

"I can understand wanting to get out of here. What's your question?"

"I want to start visualizing workouts to see if I can keep my muscles in shape. Do you think that it will actually work? Is it safe to do this?"

"Well, I don't think it will hurt you, as long as you aren't actually trying to lift weights or get out of bed. Now, I have a question for you, Sarah."

"What's that?"

"What would you say to my documenting your journey?"

"Um, why would you want to do that?"

"Well, if it works, I could publish an article for the medical journals."

"I don't know, what if it doesn't work?"

"I understand your hesitation, but by publishing your potential transformation in the medical journals, I can get grants that would bring in funding for us to be able to continue providing help to patients. Plus, wouldn't it be cool to be successful and then have therapists use this with other patients in the future to help them heal faster?"

"What will all this entail? What are you going to do to document the journey? Can you publish without using my name or pictures of my face?"

"We'll take measurements and photos every three days. The photos will be kept locked up until I'm ready to publish. Your name will be kept confidential so no one will know who you are."

"Okay. I want you to be able to keep helping patients who don't have insurance. Can we start today?"

"Yes, ma'am. Let me grab Selina, and we'll get your current measurements."

Dr. Martinez walked out the door and grabbed Selina. They came back in the room with a soft tape measure and a digital camera. They carefully moved Sarah around as they got her starting measurements. After five minutes, they left her alone in the room.

When Ethan came back later that afternoon, Sarah asked him to put one of her workout videos on so that she could visualize the workout like she and Ethan previously discussed. She closed her eyes and really focused on the workout. When the workout ended, Sarah opened her eyes to see Ethan staring at her. She was dripping in sweat and was fatigued. Selina came in and gave her a quick sponge bath and helped her change gowns.

She woke up the following morning, and the muscles in her chest and triceps were on fire, just like she had physically lifted the weights and had not done so in a couple months. This pain was something that Sarah did not mind; it meant that the visualization technique must have worked out better than she expected.

Within a couple of weeks, Sarah was moved out of ICU into her own suite upstairs on the fifth floor of the hospital. Ethan continued to play the workout videos every day, and Sarah went back to work as if she were using the equipment in the gym. Within a month of fueling her body the right way and visualizing her routines, Dr. Martinez and other doctors noticed her muscles changing. Sarah's shoulders, back, arms and abs showed significant definition.

Sarah asked Ethan to run with the boys. He took his phone with him, and she gave directions on pace and activities. Eli and Manny loved this; even though she was not there with them physically, she was still there with them, setting the tone and pace of every run. Sarah's leg muscles became stronger and more defined from the running visualization exercises.

The staff was amazed to see this transformation when Sarah was still completely bedridden and not allowed to use actual weights. Dr. Martinez stayed very close to Sarah's case; she checked in regularly. Impressed by Sarah's transformation, Dr. Martinez came in and asked, "Hey, Sarah, you're looking healthy. How're you feeling?"

"Better."

Visitors

The next month or so was a complete blur. Sarah's parents came to visit her every other weekend. She enjoyed her daily visits from Pops and Grams. She looked forward to her workouts with Ethan,

Eli, and Manny. Her body continued to change, and she got stronger every day.

Lieutenant Goldberg and the district attorney, Abbigail O'Conner, kept her updated on the case against the men who attacked her.

"Hey, Sarah, I have some good news and some bad news."

"Oh boy. I guess let's start with the good news first."

"Well, thirteen of your attackers pled guilty to aggravated assault and manslaughter," Abbigail said.

"I guess that's a good thing then. What about Chase and Charlie?"

"Here's the bad news, Sarah. Tom Matthews posted bail for his two boys, Chase and Charlie. I will continue posting officers outside of your room twenty-four hours a day," Lieutenant Goldberg spoke up.

"How is that possible?" Sarah asked.

"Mr. Matthews is a very wealthy man, Sarah," he told her. "I know this is a lot for you. More bad news is that I will need you to testify against the Matthews's boys. But I do have some more news for you: I had four other women come to my office to let me know that they would also testify against the boys."

Monday, August 13, after their running session, Ethan brought Sarah a wedge salad with a few bacon bits, tomatoes, onions, and ranch salad dressing as well as a four-ounce top sirloin cooked to perfection for dinner so that she did not have to eat the hospital food. While they sat there eating and chatting about the day's events, Ethan turned the television on in her room to catch the nightly news cast, catching the tail end of the celebrity gossip news.

"You've all seen video of the young woman, Sarah Jackson-Clark, who fought off her attackers with her husband, Alex Clark, by her side. She has been hospitalized for the last month, not able to get up out of the bed due to all the broken bones suffered in the attack. However, you will see in these shocking photographs that she isn't allowing this bed rest to stop her from reaching her goals. Sarah has been using visualization techniques to help her build muscle, and as you can see, she looks healthier and more fit now than she did before she was hospitalized. Our source told us that she works out for two hours a day, visualizing running and weightlifting routines."

They flipped between channels, and every news station was showing a quick segment on her. "What is this crap?" Sarah asked Ethan, looking completely confused. "How did they get those pictures?"

She cried at the thought of being back in the media's eye—all she wanted was to not think about the attack anymore. She could hear a commotion out in the hallway. Ethan poked his head out to find reporters outside in the hallway trying to get in to interview her. Officers Hardy and Metcalf controlled the crowd, advising them that they could not enter the room. "Ooh, who is that tall, dark, and handsome fellow sticking his head out of Sarah's room?" Sarah heard one of the reporters ask loudly.

Just then the president of the hospital, Dr. Liam Wilson, came into Sarah's room. "Ms. Clark, we are so terribly sorry that your privacy has been invaded. We will do everything we can to stop this. We will find out who leaked this story to the press and will have this person terminated immediately. We will also have you moved to a more secure wing of the hospital once the press has been escorted out of the building and we are sure there are no stragglers. Again, I am terribly sorry for this."

"This is definitely not how I saw my night going."

Sarah was moved to her new room in the middle of the night. She tried to sleep once she was settled into the new suite but found it impossible to do so. Every time she closed her eyes, she flashed back to the attack. The nurse came in around three in the morning to check Sarah's vitals. Sarah told her that she could not sleep and was desperate to do so, so the nurse asked the doctor if it was okay to give Sarah something to help her sleep.

Sarah went about the rest of her week with her daily visits from her grandparents and Ethan. Every day she visualized her workout and continued to focus on getting her body stronger.

After her workouts and sponge bath on Friday, Ethan came by her room with fresh flowers and her favorite dinner from Zippy's. They enjoyed their dinner together, and after they ate, Ethan sat on the bed beside her. He reached down and gently kissed her. The touch sent shock waves through her body. She reached back up and drew him back down to her for another more passionate kiss.

They were so consumed by the kiss and each other that neither of them heard the knock at the door or the creak when it opened. They both jumped a little when they heard a low wolf whistle from one of the three men who stood just inside the doorway. Ethan quickly jumped down off the bed to face the intruders. He looked them up and down, sizing them up.

"Ryan, would you look at that? She definitely knows how to kiss a man," Sarah heard one of the men say to the tallest man of the group.

The tallest man stepped forward and held his hand out to Sarah. "Hi, Sarah, my name is Ryan Robinson. This here is Joshua Lewis," he said as he pointed to the man at his left side. "And this is Scott Adams," he said as he pointed to the man at his right side. "Do you know who we are, Sarah?"

Sarah stopped and stared at each one in turn, taking in that three of Hollywood's leading men were standing in her hospital doorway. She started with the man who introduced himself first, Ryan. He was tall, like Ethan, standing a foot taller than she did at six feet, five inches. He had chestnut brown hair that was kept short along with honey-brown eyes. He was muscular and had a great physique. She then turned to look at Josh Lewis, who had short wavy blond hair and blue eyes. He stood just shy of six feet tall at five feet, eleven inches. He was dreamy to look at. The last man, Scott, stood at six feet, three inches. He was built like a brick house, muscles popping out of muscles. Scott was bald with chocolate-brown colored eyes.

She turned to Ethan and said, "I think you need to pinch me to make sure I'm not dreaming."

Ryan laughed a little. "You aren't dreaming, Sarah. We are real, and we are here in your room with you right now. We came to talk to you about something. We were hoping for some privacy. Young man, do you mind stepping out of the room while we talk to Sarah?" he asked as he turned and faced Ethan.

"I don't know what the three of you want, but whatever it is, you can say it in front of Ethan. I trust him with my life."

"All right then, do you mind if we sit down and chat for a bit?" Ryan asked her.

"Sure. What did you have on your mind? What are three of the hottest Hollywood actors doing in my hospital room, and how did you get past my security team out front?" she asked.

"Haha, did you hear that, Ryan? She thinks we're hot!" Josh turned to Ryan briefly before turning back to Sarah. "Well, that last question is for us to know and you to never find out," Josh teased as he pulled up a chair and sat facing Sarah and Ethan, who was now carefully sitting beside her on the bed.

"Sarah, we saw the video of you and your husband fighting your attackers. You were amazing out there. What kind of professional training have you had in hand-to-hand combat?" Scott asked her.

"My father taught me hand-to-hand combat growing up. He treated me just like one of his Marines. Once in the situation, that training came back. I knew that if I didn't fight, I was going to die, and I wasn't ready to die yet," she replied, looking Scott in the eyes.

"Wow, now I'm even more amazed," Josh said. "You are Wonder Woman in real life!"

"Clearly, I'm not Wonder Woman, or I wouldn't have ended up here with half my body broken and bullets that had to be removed. Wonder Woman was able to avoid the bullets!" She cracked a smile and laughed as she responded to Josh.

"A woman after my own heart, joking about the incident and the outcome." He laughed.

"Sarah, back to the reason we came," Ryan interrupted the joking between her and Josh. "We saw the video and how you responded. Like everyone else in the country, we also saw the pictures leaked to the press about how your body is responding to visualizing your workouts and runs. You are a true badass, Sarah."

"I am no such thing," she interrupted. "I'm just a regular woman who was placed in a horrible situation."

"Sarah, you are very humble, but you are a badass. How many people do you know who would have fought their attackers the way you did? How many people would try to stay active while stuck in a hospital bed, and of those who did try, how many would be as successful at it as you have been?" Ryan asked.

"We are here because we would like to ask you to be our lead female actress in our upcoming movie about the life of a female Marine Corps intelligence officer. You will have a love interest with both myself and Josh in the movie. There will be some fight scenes and some love scenes. What do you say? You up for the challenge?" he asked her.

Sarah hesitated before speaking, "Um, I don't know if you noticed, Mr. Robinson, but I am currently hanging out in bed all day long, and I have no idea how long I'll be here."

"Oh my god, Sarah. I was told you have a sense of humor, but you are killing me right now." Josh laughed.

"Sarah, we know that you are still healing. We are all three in agreement that we want you as our lead in this movie. We want you so badly that we are going to hold off on starting production until you are fully healed and released by the doctor to come and join us. What do you say?" Scott asked her.

"I'm not an actress. I've never acted a day in my life, at least not on stage, in front of a whole bunch of people. I don't know if I would be the right person for the job. I can't remember lines. I mean, shit, I can't remember what I had for dinner an hour ago, how the hell do you expect me to remember my lines and everything else?"

"We can help teach you the business and get you ready for at least the speaking parts while you heal. We will have professional acting coaches come in and work with you, and then once you're healed, we can start filming and will work on all the choreography at that time," Ryan advised.

"That's a lot to consider. Can I take some time and let you know?"

"How about this—how about we give you the weekend to think it over and then we will be back on Monday to discuss this in more detail. Sounds like a plan?" Ryan inquired.

"Damn, you are persistent." Sarah smiled.

"You're damn right we are. We know you will be the perfect addition to the team. We need you, Sarah. The movie won't be the same without you," Josh retorted.

"Come back on Monday and I'll have an answer for you then. I want you to know that I am truly flattered that you think I would be a good fit to the team."

The three men left the room, waving at Sarah and Ethan. "Have a great night you two. We'll let you get back to your hot and heavy make-out session and will see you Monday, Sarah."

Ethan turned on the bed to face Sarah. "OMG, Sarah, I can't believe that three of Hollywood's top actors were just in this room talking to you about joining their movie as the lead actress. What is currently going through your mind right now?"

"I don't even know how to process this. If you weren't in the room with me, I would be thinking this was all a dream."

"Are you going to take them up on this once-in-a-lifetime offer?"

"I really don't know. I feel like I've been in the spotlight enough to last five lifetimes. I don't know if I want to have that spotlight on me any more than it already has been, do you know what I'm saying?"

"Well, think about it, pray about it. It's getting late, so I'm going to leave you for the night. I'll be back tomorrow night. The boys and I have our 10k run tomorrow afternoon."

"Oh, Ethan, I can't believe I forgot that is tomorrow. Please make sure you call me before the race starts so that I can wish you all good luck and speed for the race!"

"Will do. Good night, Sarah. I love you," he said as he reached down and gave her a quick kiss.

"Good night, I love you too."

Second Attack

Ethan called the next afternoon before the race and did a quick video call with Sarah and the boys. She noticed they were all wearing gray tank tops and black shorts. The tank tops had her picture on the back: *Running for Sarah*.

"Hi, boys!"

"Hi, Sarah," she heard in unison.

"Boys, I wanted to tell you to kick butt today! You guys got this! I'll be running with you in spirit! You better call me after you finish the race!"

Just as Sarah nodded off for her nap, she received a video call from Manny, so she answered. "Hey, Manny, how'd you do?"

"Sarah, you won't believe it, but I came in third overall!" Manny said, bouncing the camera around with him.

"Way to go, buddy! I'm so proud of you! What was your final time?"

"I had about a six minute and a half minute pace the entire race. I finished the race in about forty minutes and twenty seconds."

"*Wow, that's amazing, Manny! Your hard work has really paid off.* How did your brother and your father do?"

"Well, Eli was about a minute behind me, and Dad was just right behind him. They both placed in the top fifteen runners."

"That's awesome! I'm so proud of you."

"I can't believe I beat Eli and Dad. I remembered what you said, 'Make sure you do not overexert yourself at the beginning of the race. Wait until the last mile to make your move, and then when everyone else is tired, you will be able to pass them because you still have gas in the tank.'"

"Sounds like that's exactly what you did! Congratulations, Manny. We'll have to celebrate once I'm back on my feet and out of the hospital."

"I can't wait, Sarah! Hey, Dad wants to talk to you a minute."

"Manny, I'm proud of you! Put your dad on," Sarah replied as he handed the phone to Ethan. She saw his dopey smile.

"Third overall? That's something for him to be proud of." She smiled at Ethan through the camera on her phone.

"I'm proud of him. He worked super hard for that third-place medal. Hey, I am going to take the boys home so we can shower and then take them to the steak house to get a celebratory steak. Do you want me to bring you anything once I've dropped the boys back off at Sherry's place?"

"Nah, I think I'm good tonight. Just enjoy your time with the boys, and I'll see you when I see you," she smiled.

They hung up, and she fell right to sleep with a smile on her face as she pictured Manny pulling off his third-place finish in his first race of the season. These thoughts were quickly replaced with her nightmare. She tried to wake up and get out of the attack, but she just could not force herself to wake up. She started thrashing about in the bed; she nearly fell off the side. The nurses came in and held her down until she woke up.

She quickly calmed down once she was awake. Sarah was thankful for the distraction from the thoughts in her mind when Ethan walked through the door. She watched all the video footage from the boys' racing cameras to see how they raced. She beamed with pride when she saw Manny catch up, pace. and then pass his brother with about a half mile left to go.

After watching the race footage, Sarah and Ethan talked about the visitors from the day before. "So, chipmunk, you had a big day yesterday. What are your thoughts about the question that Ryan, Josh. and Scott posed?"

She looked away for a few seconds before looking up at him. "I… I really don't know, Ethan. I've never acted before. I don't know what would make them think I could be the lead in their movie."

"That's not true, Sarah. You acted as though you were happy every day with Alex when in fact you were miserable. I would say you are a very talented actress. Your family bought your story."

"But I don't think they really did. Grams knew all along that I wasn't happy with Alex, but she went along with the act to make me happy. I don't think I can do something like this."

"Chippy, you can do anything you put your mind to. Look at you right now, you're lying in a hospital bed with almost half the bones in your body broken and yet you look like you never went through this ordeal. You visualized yourself being successful with getting your body back into shape. You can visualize yourself as the lead actress in this movie alongside three of the hottest men in Hollywood."

"You really think so?"

"Baby, I know so. The worst thing that could happen is that you try and you don't enjoy it. No one is saying that you have to stay in Hollywood and keep making movies. Although, I'm pretty sure that once you have a record-breaking box office hit, it'll be in your bones and you'll want to keep making movies. Every director in Hollywood will want you in his or her movies after this."

"You're just saying that to make me feel better!" She smiled.

"Is it working?" He smiled playfully. "In all seriousness though, I know you can do this. I have faith in you. You need to have faith in yourself!"

Sunday went by way too quickly for Sarah's liking. She was nervous the entire day, trying to visualize how the conversation was going to go with Ryan, Josh, and Scott.

What do I want to do? How am I going to face these three hunks tomorrow? What am I going to say to them? How can I possibly say yes? Why am I terrified of this opportunity? I know I'm not good enough! I shouldn't be given this opportunity—I don't deserve it!

Sarah could not sleep that night. She kept waking up thinking about the conversation.

She was thankful when Dr. Martinez and Dr. Baker, the head of the rehabilitation unit, came in to check her. Transport came into the room and took Sarah to radiology, where the radiologist took a full body and bone scan to see how her body was healing.

Sarah fell asleep in the scanner and did not know she was back in the room until she was startled awake. She felt as though she was being watched. She heard familiar voices, as she opened her eyes. "She doesn't look so scary now, does she, Charlie? This bitch needs to pay for breaking my nose and bruising my junk. Because of this bitch, I had to have surgery, and the doctors still don't know if I'll be able to have sex right in the future."

She tried to get out of bed but was still restrained from the scanner. She tried to scream for help but felt a gag placed in her mouth, which prevented her from doing so. Sarah felt completely helpless.

She could not fight in her current condition, and she could not flee to safety. All she could do was lie there helplessly as she listened to the heated conversation between Chase and his brother Charlie.

So many thoughts raced through her brain:

How did these two boys get into my room completely unnoticed? How did they find me? How in the world did they know which room I am in? God, I am scared. Please be with me! What exactly is Chase talking about... What is he going to do to me now? I wonder how long it will be before someone on the medical staff comes in and sees what is happening?

"Chase, we shouldn't be here. *We need to go, now.*" She heard the panic in Charlie's voice.

"Shut up, you're such a fucking pansy. Just watch and hit Record on that stupid video camera of yours. I'm going to fuck this bitch up and you're going to record it. If you don't, I'll kill you, little brother!"

"I just want to leave. I don't want to go to jail, Chase."

"Do you want to die instead?"

"No, of course not!"

"If you don't hit Record, I'll kill you right here!"

"I'm recording, I just don't want to go to jail."

"Just shut the fuck up and record. I want to be able to watch her reaction to being completely helpless as I fuck her up and rebreak every bone in her body. This bitch will pay for what she did to me, and there isn't anything she can do to stop me this time. No one is going to come to her rescue. I made sure of that."

"How did you do that?" Charlie asked.

"Don't you mind that right now, just know that we won't get caught anytime soon." Chase laughed maliciously.

She felt Chase get up onto the bed with her. As he got up, he took her right leg out of its sling and put it down on the bed. He proceeded to stomp on it with his left foot and then his right foot. She felt the bone snap, and she screamed out in pain against the gag. He then stomped down on her pelvis. She passed out from the pain.

Sarah's heartrate soared at the new wave of pain, and her monitor started sounding an alarm. She had no idea how long she had passed for out, but when she came to again, she was relieved to see that Chase and Charlie were in handcuffs being hauled out of her room by Lieutenant Goldberg and Officer Hardy.

Sarah started crying. She became angry. She felt betrayed but did not know who betrayed her. She wanted answers. "How did they get in here? How did they know where I was?" she asked Lieutenant Goldberg.

"Sarah, we don't have those answers for you at this time. We are going to do everything we can to get Charlie to break and tell us everything. In the meantime, we are going to post an officer inside and outside your room at all times so that this can never happen again. Those two violated the conditions of their bail arrangement, so they will be locked up until they go to trial."

As soon as Lieutenant Goldberg left the room, Sarah was wheeled back up to the radiology department for new scans. Dr. Adam Baker, an older short man with salt-and-pepper hair, came in and delivered the bad news. Chase managed to break her leg and pelvis again, which meant that she needed to go back in for surgery to repair the fractures and put more pins and screws in to hold her leg and pelvic bones in place during the healing process.

Sarah lay in the bed waiting for the transport team to take her back up to the surgical prep room. She found herself praying for death: "God, please just bring me home! I am not strong enough to pull through this. I am lost, and I feel so alone. I want to die, please just let me die! Please, God, just bring me home."

As she lay there, the anesthesia kicked in and put her to sleep. She saw Alex in the far corner of the room. She tried to reach out to him, but he was too far away for her to grasp. "W-what are you doing here? Am I dead?" she asked him.

"No, Sarah, you aren't dead. I am here to tell you that you will be okay. I know it doesn't seem like it right now, but you will pull out of this and be okay. You need to pull on the strength of your faith in God. He put strong people such as your grandparents, parents, and

Ethan in your life for a reason. They will help you get through this, but you have to let them be your anchors in the storm to help you come out of this stronger than ever before. Sarah, I know I didn't tell you this enough when I was alive, but you are the strongest woman I know. You will be okay. I will always love you. I have to go now, but I wanted you to know that you are going to be just fine."

"D-don't leave me, Alex. I need you."

She blinked, and Alex was gone; she was alone again. She felt the pain of the pins being placed into her leg, but she was paralyzed; she could not move at all. She panicked. She felt a pain in her chest she had never felt before, like a sumo wrestler sitting on her chest. She could not breathe. "Page Dr. Wiley stat," she heard someone across the room yell; it sounded so distant and far away. She felt a sharp pain and then felt the burn of liquid rushing through her arm into the rest of her body. She passed out again.

When Sarah woke up, she was back in her room with her hands secured to the bedframe again and her right leg slightly elevated. She saw Officer Hardy standing next to the closed door, her grandparents were in the corner of the room, closest to the window. She focused on Ethan. He was right by her side, holding her hand, watching her sleep. As she stirred, he said, "Oh my god, Sarah, you gave us quite the scare."

"W-what do you mean?" she asked him. "W-what happened?"

Ethan teared up; he couldn't bring himself to tell her what happened this time. He sat there and just looked at her with tears in his eyes. Pain coursed through her body; pain she had not felt in over a month. That's when she remembered pieces of what happened— what felt like days was only a matter of a few hours. She closed her eyes; she did not want to feel anything.

When she woke again, she was alone in the room with Officer Hardy standing guard at the door. She focused on him, realizing she had not ever really paid much attention to this man. He was slightly shorter than Ethan, standing at approximately six feet and two inches. She figured he weighed about two hundred pounds. He had a fair complexion with dirty blond hair and blue eyes. The sleeves of his uniform were tight against his chest, biceps, and triceps. She quickly looked away when she realized he caught her staring at him.

"Ms. Clark, Ethan wanted you to know that he ran out to grab something to eat but that he would be back shortly. He left about ten minutes ago. Your grandparents also left when you fell asleep."

"O-oh, okay. Thank you for the information," she politely said before she tried to reach for the TV remote on the side of her bed.

"Here, let me help you with that, Ms. Clark," Officer Hardy said when he saw her struggling to turn on the TV. "What channel can I flip the TV on for you?"

"Uh, you have to swear not to laugh." She hesitated. "But can you turn it to my favorite reality show, *The House Is Always Watching*? I believe it should be on now."

She saw him chuckle as he replied, "It's my favorite show as well."

He flipped the channel to the network where *The House Is Always Watching* should have been on, but instead of mindless noise and drama to take her mind off her concerns, she got a glimpse of the breaking news.

The news anchors appeared to be just outside the hospital. She asked Officer Hardy to turn up the volume, only to discover that the breaking news story was about her. She cringed and tried to turn away. She did not want to be reminded of what happened today. She turned back to the television when she heard the handsome lead news anchor, Harry Granger, in the studio talking with his coanchor, out live on the scene of the breaking news. "Can you repeat that news again, Tae?" he asked the man out in front of the hospital.

"Well, Harry, as you can see behind me, there has been a big break in the Sarah Jackson-Clark case. The Spring City Police Department apprehended two of Sarah's attackers just moments ago."

The cameraman focused in to show two young men being led out of the hospital in handcuffs by Lieutenant Goldberg. Seeing those faces again made her physically ill. She immediately threw up on herself. Officer Hardy pushed the call button for the nurses to help get Sarah cleaned up.

"Oh, my God, Harry, that is great news for Sarah. I'm sure viewers were definitely excited to see that breaking news," Amelia said as she turned to face Harry in the studio.

"I'm so sorry, Officer Hardy!"

"Don't be, Mrs. Clark."

"Sarah, please call me Sarah."

"Okay, don't be embarrassed, Sarah. You've been through a lot."

She felt numb inside. "C-can you please turn this off?" she asked Officer Hardy.

"Sure, Sarah. Is there any other channel you would like to watch instead?" he asked her as he picked up the remote.

"N-no, thank you. I-I just want the TV off right now. Thank you."

As Officer Hardy turned his back to her to turn the TV off, she felt giant tears slide down both sides of her nose as she wept silently. Just then, Ethan walked in the room with a dozen yellow and orange roses. She looked up and wondered what she had done to deserve such a wonderful man who stuck by her side. He reached down and kissed her forehead. "Hey, chipmunk, I brought these for you."

"They are beautiful, thank you," she replied. "Me, not so much. Sorry you had to come in and see me like this!"

"Chipmunk, this is not your fault."

Selina walked in with Sarah's head nurse. The ladies cleaned Sarah up and then left her there with Ethan and Officer Hardy. "Thank you, ladies!" Sarah told them as they left her room.

Ethan spent the rest of the night holding Sarah while she read to him out of the newest biography she was reading about Queen Elizabeth, Queen of England and Ireland from November 1558 until March 1603. Once she fell asleep, he kissed her forehead and quietly slipped out of her room.

Wednesday morning Ethan came to visit Sarah and spent his day off with her in her room. They chatted about Ethan's run with the boys the night before, and Sarah beamed as she heard that Manny was consistently overtaking Eli, on their runs. Even though she did not have to, Selina came in and administered all of Sarah's medications, which caused her to nod off. When she woke from her nap, she heard Officer Hardy stand up and put his hand on the butt of his gun as he unbuttoned it in his holster for a quick draw, if needed.

She heard him ask, "Hold up, who authorized you to come in this room?"

She was shocked to see Ryan, Josh, and Scott standing in the doorway.

"It's okay, Officer Hardy, these three are welcome to come in the room and visit," she told him.

"Are you sure, Sarah?" he asked before relaxing, refastening his weapon and allowing the three men into the room.

"Positive."

The three Hollywood hunks walked into the room and sat down on both sides of the bed. "W-what are you three doing back here?" Sarah asked, looking at each of the men.

"We told you we were going to be back to get your answer about the movie. Here we are, Wonder Woman," Ryan replied.

"Well, about that," she started.

"What about that?" Josh asked, smiling at her. "Does this mean that you're onboard with joining us in the movie?"

"Weeeelllll, I don't know if you've watched the news over the last couple of days, but, I have had a minor setback in my healing and recovery. Instead of being ready to go home in a couple of weeks to finish my healing and recovery at home, I now get to stay here even longer, lucky me!"

"What do you mean you have to stay here longer?" Scott asked.

"Did you see the news?" Ethan interjected.

"No, we haven't seen the news. What happened? I know we were advised we couldn't come visit her Monday morning when we stopped by, but we never heard why," Scott replied.

"Sarah's attackers came back in Monday morning and attacked her. They broke her leg and pelvis again, lengthening out her recovery time. During surgery to set the broken bones, Sarah had a minor heart attack because her heart just couldn't keep up with the trauma to her body."

"Oh my god, Sarah, we had no clue," Ryan said. "We can leave, if you'd like us to."

"You don't have to leave. Let's talk about the movie. Are you truly willing to postpone the movie another six to twelve months, at a minimum, for me to completely heal from these attacks?" she inquired.

They looked around at each other and turned back to her. Ryan looked Sarah in the eye and said, "Yes, we are willing to postpone the movie until you are completely healed and are cleared to shoot with us."

"You guys didn't even talk about it. How do you know that I'm the right person for this role?" she asked, looking at each of them individually.

"Sarah, I have a gut feeling, and I learned long ago to trust my gut because it's always right," Scott said to her.

"I just don't want to let you guys down. I'm going to have a lot on my plate over the next few months. Along with now being stuck in the hospital longer than I planned, I will also have to possibly testify in court. I just don't know if this is the right thing to do."

"If the attack hadn't happened two days ago and you were headed out the door to go home next week, what would your answer have been?" Josh asked her.

"It would have been yes," she replied.

"Well, okay then, there is nothing further to discuss. As far as I'm concerned, this is a done deal. I will put you in touch with an amazing agent who will help you navigate all the legalities of everything, and then we will get an acting coach to help you with your lines until you are healed," Ryan said with a smile on his face. "Welcome to the team!"

Going Home

Sarah's time in recovery sped by. She had so much to focus on that helped take her mind off everything. Ethan continued to visit her every day after he left base, Sally and Lisa came to visit from Fair Falcon for a long weekend, her grandparents came by every three days, and her parents came down twice a month to help her pass the time until the trials began. Sarah continued to work with Dr. Tracy Jackson over the phone to process her thoughts and feelings every week.

Once Sarah healed enough, she spent three to five hours a day in with her physical therapist; she continued to strengthen the muscles around the bones to keep them strong. Ethan and the boys continued to run with Sarah every night after Ethan got off work. She spent anywhere from two to three hours a day with the acting coach via the video conferencing program built into InstaChat, when her coach could not be there in person.

On Wednesday, October 3, Dr. Baker came in Sarah's room. "Good morning, Sarah. How are you feeling this morning?"

"No offense, Dr. Baker, but I'm really tired of being here. I am ready to go home and see my fur babies. I'm sure by now they've forgotten who I am," she responded with a sullen look on her face.

"I'm sure they will be happy to have you home again full time. I know they have missed you as much as you've missed them."

"I hope you're right."

"Well, Sarah, you're going to find that out for yourself fairly soon. I will be releasing you from hospital care Friday morning. You will be able to go home and finish your recovery there."

She looked up and studied his face. "A-are you serious?" she asked hesitantly.

"I am dead serious, Sarah. You have done remarkably well considering the trauma you endured. You will need to continue with your physical therapy as well as with seeing your therapist, Dr. Jackson. You still have a long road ahead of you." He smiled at her and then turned and walked out the door.

Sarah couldn't wait to share the news with Ethan and her family. She sent Ethan a text message:

Sarah

9:15 a.m.

Wanna hear some good news?

Ethan

9:20 a.m.

I could use some good news right now. Please share!

Sarah

9:22 a.m.

I'm getting sprung from this place Friday morning!

Ethan

9:25 a.m.

WHAT?!!!!! That's AWESOME! I can't wait to celebrate tonight when I get done w/ my run w/ the boys. What do you want me to bring for dinner?

Sarah

9:27 a.m.

IDK, 'prize me!

Ethan

9:30 a.m.

Chipmunk, I'm so excited! I can't wait to see you tonight! Are you good w/ my telling the boys?

Sarah

9:32 a.m.

If you want to tell them, I'm good w/ that!

Ethan

9:35 a.m.

I'll see what their moods are later before I decide what to do. You completely made my day! Can't wait to see you later! <3 you!

Sarah

9:37 a.m.

<3 you more! See you soon!

When Sarah hit Send on her last message to Ethan, she pulled up the dial pad on her phone and called her mother, Violet, and her grandma Hailey on conference call.

"Hello? What's the emergency, Sarah? You know I'm at work and can't really talk right now, right?" Violet asked when she answered the phone.

"Hey, chipmunk!" she heard Grams say when she answered the call.

"No emergency, Mom, I just wanted to let you know that I get to be sprung from the hospital Friday morning. I thought you might enjoy hearing that news."

"Well, isn't that great news, kiddo?" she heard her grandma ask before she heard her mother say, "That's good news, Sarah! I have to get back to work."

She heard the beeping in her ear indicating that her mother ended her part of the conference call. She immediately felt dejected. Tears started to well up in her eyes when she heard her grandma's voice, "Chipmunk, that is such amazing news. I am so happy for you. Pops and I will be by later today to celebrate your hard work and recovery. Do you want anything special to celebrate, honey?"

"Naw, I'm good. Just visiting with you and Pops will be enough. I love you, Grams. I should probably let you go so you can get back to whatever you and Pops were doing before I called."

"Chipmunk, nothing is more important in this moment than hearing this news. Know that Pops and I are happy for you. This has been a long hard road for you and you came out ahead. Love you too, chippy. We will see you shortly."

Sarah called Lieutenant Goldberg, "Spring City Police Department, Officer David speaking, how may I help you, sir or ma'am?"

"May I speak with Lieutenant Goldberg, please?"

"One moment please," she heard before she heard hold music.

"Lieutenant Goldberg speaking, how may I help you, ma'am?"

"Hi, Lieutenant Goldberg, this is Sarah Jackson."

"Oh, hey, Sarah. What can I do for you?"

"I just found out that I'm being sprung sometime Friday morning."

"Officer Hardy told me the good news. I'm happy for you, Sarah. We're going to keep a guard with you even once you leave the hospital."

Wednesday and Thursday flew by, and before Sarah knew it, it was time for her to finally go back to her apartment. She was scared that her boss, Peter Castle, would tell her she needed to vacate the apartment because she wasn't actively assisting the call center, but he told her not to worry about her apartment or her job while she was in the hospital recovering. He wanted her to focus solely on getting better so that she could come back stronger than ever to help the team.

Ethan and her grandparents arrived at eight. They were as excited as she was to finally see her back into her own apartment. Dr. Baker entered the room about fifteen minutes later with all of Sarah's discharge paperwork and instructions. To ensure Sarah's protection, Dr. Baker arranged for a therapist to come to Sarah's apartment every morning, starting the following Monday morning.

Ethan pulled into the apartment complex's parking lot. "You ready to get home and sleep in your own bed?"

"More than you will ever know!" She smiled at him.

He got out of the driver's side and grabbed her crutches from the backseat of his 2012 black Ford Edge. He brought them around to her side of the car and opened the door for her. He helped her out of the front seat and steadied her on her crutches. Once steadied on her crutches, the two of them walked into the lobby.

"Oh my god, Sarah, you look amazing. We are so glad to have you back in the building!" Greg exclaimed as he got up from behind his desk to greet her. "Can I give you a hug?"

"Sure," she replied.

He briefly embraced her in a quick hug and then released her. "Oh, by the way, there was an officer trying to get into your apartment. When I told him I didn't care who he said he was, he stormed out of here."

"Did he give you his name or show you his shield?"

"No, he didn't, which I thought was odd."

"What was that, sir?" Sarah heard a familiar voice behind her. She turned to see Lieutenant Goldberg and Officer Hardy walking in the door about five minutes behind her.

"Who are you?" Greg asked him, standing a little straighter and putting Sarah behind him.

"I am Lieutenant Goldberg, the lead detective working Sarah's case and the head of her security detail. This is Officer Hardy. He was stationed in Sarah's room and knows her very well. Who are you?" he asked as he pulled his shield out to show Greg.

"Sarah, do you know this man?" Greg asked her without turning around to face her.

"Yes, Greg, he is legit," she replied.

"Okay, well in that case, my name is Greg Jones. I am the doorman for this apartment building and have been for over fifteen years."

Lt. Goldberg stepped forward, extending his right hand to Greg. Greg took it and gave it a firm shake before releasing it again. "Now, Greg, do you mind repeating what you told Sarah as I was walking in? If you can, please try to give me as much detail as you possibly can about the man you saw—what he was wearing, hair and eye color, build, height, weight, and whatever else you remember about him."

"Well, Lieutenant, the man who came in here was about six feet tall, bald with brown eyes. He had a sort of hatchet face—long, thin, and unpleasant. His nose and chin were both pointed, and his eyes were slanted toward his nose. His complexion was colorless, making him look kind of evil. He was muscular in the chest and probably weighed around two hundred and fifty pounds, give or take. It looked like he only worked out his chest and arms and never put down the donuts. He wore a uniform similar to yours, except his had a different type of patch on both of his arms. His was more rectangular versus your patches that look like shields. I didn't get a close look at what the patches said, but I just had a strange feeling about him. I've never seen him in the building before."

"That's a really good description of him. Do you think if I put you with a sketch artist you could help the artist sketch the man?"

"I can do you one better, Lieutenant. I took the liberty of printing out his face from the surveillance footage. He didn't realize that we have cameras all over this lobby, and he didn't try to hide or conceal his face."

"Good man, Greg. Thank you for all these details," Lieutenant Goldberg said as he gave Greg a pat on the back.

Lieutenant Goldberg pulled Officer Hardy off to the side of the lobby where they had a brief discussion. When they finished, he turned back to Sarah and Ethan. "Ethan, can I speak with you over here for a minute in private?"

"Sure," Ethan replied before turning to Sarah. "Be right back."

The two men walked back to the corner of the lobby where Officer Hardy was still standing. "Are you by any chance planning on staying here tonight?" he asked Ethan.

"I planned on it. Is that okay?" he asked the lieutenant.

"Do you know how to shoot a gun?"

"I would hope so… Every Marine is a rifleman first, plus I'm an MP."

"Do you have a weapon on you by chance?"

"I have a concealed carry license when I'm off duty. However, I did not carry today. I didn't think I was going to need it."

"Do you know if Sarah owns a handgun?" Lieutenant Goldberg interrupted.

"I know that she used to own a Glock nine-millimeter. I don't know if she still has it. Do you mind telling me what is going on and why you are asking all these questions?" Ethan asked, concern spreading across his face. "Has Sarah's location been compromised?"

"I'm not going to lie. It appears as though it may have been. I am going to station Officer Hardy and two other undercover officers downstairs in the lobby, and I want you to be prepared in the event this man returns."

"What are we going to tell Sarah? She was so excited to return home," Ethan asked.

"We are just going to tell her that we are continuing to take all precautions when it comes to her safety. If we feel like we need to, we will relocate her and the cats to another apartment, where only I and four other officers will know her location."

"Are you trying to say I wouldn't be allowed to visit Sarah? What about her physical therapist?"

"We will take this all one step at a time. Hopefully, we won't have to resort to this, but if we do, you will not be allowed to see Sarah. We will get her an untraceable phone and would expect you to do the same if you wanted to be in communication with her. Sarah's safety comes first, and I cannot risk someone finding her again."

Ethan hung his head for a moment, taking everything in for a moment. Once he composed himself, he turned back to look at Sarah, who was in the middle of the lobby talking with Greg. "I suppose we should get back to Sarah and get her upstairs."

"Before you go upstairs, I will have my officers search her apartment to ensure that everything is safe."

About ten minutes later, the two officers returned to the lobby and walked straight toward the lieutenant. "All clear, boss."

"Sarah, thank you for your patience. You are now free to go upstairs to rest. Ethan will stay with you through the weekend. When he leaves for work on Monday morning, I will have an officer stationed upstairs just off the elevator with you."

"If you think that is necessary. I just want to get upstairs and hug my babies before I crash for a nap."

Lieutenant Goldberg accompanied Sarah and Ethan up the elevator. He watched as Sarah grabbed her Glock out of the safe and gave it to Ethan. Once he felt comfortable, he went back down the elevator. Sarah went into the bedroom and immediately fell asleep, completely unaware of any of the plots on her life.

Hired Hit

Sarah woke up when Ethan got out of the bed on Monday morning. "Do you have to go? Can't you just play hooky and stay home with me all day?" she begged him as he got dressed and got ready for work.

He leaned over and gave her forehead a quick kiss. "I wish I could, chipmunk, but I have to go run a simulation training today."

"Okay, fine then, just run off and leave me here all alone," she playfully pouted at him.

"Oh, Sarah, don't do that. It is hard enough leaving you without that little pouty lip action you have going on!" He smiled at her.

Before he left, he turned to her and, with a very stern and serious look, said to her, "Sarah, I know you hate having your Glock out, but I need you to carry it with you everywhere you go. I know you aren't leaving the apartment, but I need you to have it glued to you at all times. I don't care if you are in the kitchen making lunch, in the bathroom doing your business, or here in the bedroom taking a nap... I want it with you at all times."

"Where is this coming from?" she asked him, shocked at the seriousness in his voice.

"Sarah, please just do this for me, no arguments?"

"Okay, I promise."

Ethan handed her the handgun and the holster from his nightstand. He then bent down to give her a kiss before he headed to the elevator.

Sarah got up and put her feet over the edge of the bed. She convinced herself to get up and put some weight on her legs, even though just sitting up sent a sharp pain through her lower body. She stumbled into the bathroom, about a hundred feet from her bed, without her crutches and then made her way back to the bed. She lay back down and closed her eyes for what felt like only five minutes but ended up being an hour.

When she woke up, she decided to satisfy her grumbling stomach with a couple of scrambled eggs and two slices of white toast. She used one crutch to stabilize her as she walked over to the couch. She sat down and immediately turned on the television for white noise while Pretty Baby and Squirrel Bait curled up on either side of her lap as she ate her breakfast. She cleaned her plate and the pan she used to cook the eggs in before heading back into the living room to watch television before therapy.

Sarah zoned out while watching television and did not originally hear the elevator door ding. She felt Pretty Baby tense up and heard her start growling and hissing. Squirrel Bait and Crackers joined her hissing. Sarah felt a lump in her stomach as she turned around toward the elevator, looked up, and saw a strange man standing just outside of the elevator brandishing a handgun pointed in her direction. Her heart sank as she thought this was how she was going to go out of this world, alone and disheveled.

"Who are you, and what do you want?" she managed to squeak out of her throat.

"It doesn't matter who I am, you just need to know that Tom Matthews paid to have you shut up permanently, once and for all. I will be the last person you see before you push up daisies," he mocked.

"Are you in the business of shooting a woman? Does that make you a man?" she mocked back to this stranger. In that moment, Sarah remembered that she had her Glock hanging around her shoulders, hidden. She turned back toward the television and gently slid it out of the holster, keeping her movements small enough to remain hidden and not alert this stranger to what she was doing.

Once her Glock was firmly in her hands, she turned back around and in one fluid motion raised the gun and pointed it at the stranger standing in her doorway. She pulled the trigger before he even knew what was happening. She fired the weapon five times, aiming right in the man's chest. She placed all five shots successfully. The man dropped to the floor, and the gun he held fell out of his hands on to the floor.

She stood up shakily, so she grabbed her crutch and slowly made her way over to where he lay on the floor. She used her crutch to push the gun away from his limp hand. Once she was convinced he was completely immobilized, she walked back over to the couch where she grabbed her phone and called Lieutenant Goldberg.

"Hi, Sarah, what can I do for you today?" he answered her as he picked up on the fourth ring.

"Well, Lieutenant, we have a slight problem," she answered, her voice shaking as the adrenaline started wearing off.

"What do you mean by a slight problem?" he asked her, concern in his voice.

"Well, sir, I have a man lying on my floor bleeding out, if he isn't already dead."

"Wait, what?"

"I was sitting on the couch, waiting for my therapist to arrive. I must have fallen asleep again after breakfast. I heard and saw my cats go tense and start growling and hissing. When I turned around, there was a strange man in a police uniform standing just off the elevator entrance brandishing a weapon in my direction. He advised me that Tom Matthews had paid him to shut me up permanently. I turned back around, faced the television, and unholstered my Glock. When I turned back around, I placed five rounds in a tight pattern in his chest. He immediately dropped, and he is now lying there ever since."

"Oh my god, Sarah, I am on my way. I will dispatch paramedics, and we will be there in less than five minutes. Are you okay? Were you hurt?"

"I'm fine. I just want this nightmare to be over. I'll be waiting."

Sarah heard the sirens coming down the block. She waited patiently for Lieutenant Goldberg to make his way up the elevator. As the doors opened, he immediately saw the scene: bald man with brown eyes; long, thin hatchet face; and colorless complexion lying completely still in a pool of blood. He noticed the police uniform with the rectangular patches on both shoulders. He knew this was the man from the surveillance video that Greg had given to him Friday.

As he pulled Sarah into the bedroom to get her away from all the police and emergency personnel, she heard one of the paramedics say, "This guy is dead. We need to call the medical examiner. This could take a while to clear because I know he's backed up with two other bodies before this one."

"Yeah, well, I know I shouldn't be saying this, but damn, do you see how tight that grouping is? I wouldn't ever want to get on this lady's bad side. She can clearly handle her own," she heard another paramedic say.

Lieutenant Goldberg startled her when he asked, "Sarah, are you okay? I know what you just went through can be very traumatic. How about you sit down on the bed," he said as he motioned to the bed from the doorway.

"I-I just don't understand why this family won't leave me alone," she said as the tears slipped down her face. She felt her knees give out and felt the lieutenant grab her before she fell to the floor. He helped her over to the bed and then helped her get up and lie down.

"Sarah, this man is a very powerful man in town. He thinks that if he gets rid of the star witness and victim to what his boys did that they will get off without penalty. He is used to getting his own way, and he doesn't care who he hurts to get his way. You are a thorn in this man's side, and he wants to get rid of you no matter what. He's already been able to get two of two of the other witnesses to recant and decide they are not going to testify."

"H-how does he keep managing to find me?"

"Sarah, I think I've found the leak. It looks as though there is a dirty cop on your task force that keeps giving him the intel on where you can be located."

"How do you know this? D-do you know who it is?"

"The man who came up here today is a former officer in our precinct. His name is Christopher Richardson. Richardson was fired for misconduct on the job, taking bribes and many other things. He partnered with another young officer, Brian Hall, before he was fired from the force. I know that Officer Hall was terrified of his partner and refused to tell the Internal Affairs Bureau what he witnessed Officer Richardson do, which made conviction so hard.

"When I look back at the logs of who was watching over your room the day that the Matthews boys attacked you in the hospital, it was Officer Hall who stood watch over your room. He was by himself for a couple of hours while we did a switching of the guard for your second officer. Officer Hall was on duty this morning downstairs in the lobby.

"It appears he took advantage of the short window of time he was alone. He is currently in custody and is waiting to be questioned by one of the IAB detectives for his part in all this."

"I-is that supposed to make me feel better? How do I know that Tom Matthews doesn't have more cops on his payroll ready to come after me?" she asked.

"Sarah, I have my best detectives on this case. They all worked with your brother, Harrison. They will lay down their lives to keep you safe...for Harrison. They are looking into ways to tie Tom Matthews to Officers Richardson and Hall. Once we have that, we will be able to arrest him as well for soliciting a murder for hire.

"His boys face trial next month. He is desperate, but he will not get away with any of this. I will personally see to this man being taken down and broken. In the meantime, we need to move you to a new location, one where no one knows your location, not even Ethan."

"I don't want to go. I want to stay here. I just got home. I don't want to go anywhere else."

"Sarah, I obviously cannot protect you here. I need you some place where I can better control the situation. You will have a total of six officers guarding you in rotation. These will be men and women that I know I can trust and have been fully vetted."

"Are you sure there isn't any other way? I really don't want to go!" She tried to push back the tears that threatened to unleash themselves onto her cheekbones.

"I am positive. We can reevaluate the threat once the Matthews boys are charged and sentenced. I heard that your lawyer filed a civil suit against Tom Matthews. We will keep you safe during that trial as well."

Lieutenant Goldberg helped Sarah pack up necessary items and the cats before helping her down the elevator to a car that was waiting to take her to an undisclosed location. He called Officer Hardy in to escort them to the hotel room.

Chase and Charlie Matthews' Trial

A week after the intrusion in her home, Sarah woke up early to get ready for the first day in court. After she got out of the shower, she felt sick to her stomach. She knew she could not kneel down on the floor to throw up in the toilet in her current condition, so she picked up the trash can and threw up in it. She rinsed her mouth with water, then brushed her teeth, and rinsed again with mouth wash. Once her stomach settled down a little, she got dressed in a dark-gray pantsuit with a light-pink button up shirt.

When she finished getting ready, Officer Hardy escorted her down the back of the hotel through the employee elevator to the parking garage. She got into an unmarked darkly tinted car to avoid possible detection in the event there was another contract out on her life. She got in the backseat of the black Dodge charger next to Officer Hardy.

She could not believe that the day had finally come for Chase and Charlie to be tried in court. District Attorney O'Conner kept Sarah up to speed on the cases of each of the other young men involved in her attack. Five of the young men pled guilty to the lesser charges of involuntary manslaughter for agreeing to testify against Chase Matthews for his involvement in planning the attack. These five pled guilty and received twenty-five years in jail, with possibility of parole after ten years. The remaining eight men were charged with Alex's murder and aggravated assault against Sarah, landing them twenty-five years to life in jail. With thirteen of the men already through their trials, Sarah could not help but wonder what the jury would come back with for Chase and Charlie Matthews.

District Attorney Abbigail O'Conner also advised Sarah that Mr. Matthews would be charged with soliciting her murder. The district attorney's office was going to go for the maximum punishment, life without the possibility of parole, in his case. Officer Hall agreed to testify against Mr. Matthews in open court and the district attorney got Mr. Matthews's accountant to testify that he was threatened to make the funds available to both Officer Hall and Christopher Richardson for the contracted hit on Sarah.

All Sarah knew was that she wanted this nightmare to be over so she did not have to wake up in cold sweats thinking about the close calls with her own death over the last three months or so. She discerned that she wanted Chase to get the strictest punishment of the two boys. She recognized based on the way Charlie cowered when Chase yelled at him that he was afraid of what Chase might do to him if he did not comply with his brother's demands. She also remembered both occasions where Charlie protested against the attacks before being bullied and threatened by his older brother.

Twenty minutes after leaving the hotel, the Dodge charger pulled up to the back entrance of the courthouse. Officer Hardy and Lieutenant Goldberg escorted Sarah in through the back hallway to the courtroom. Sarah sat right behind DA O'Conner with both Officer Hardy and Lieutenant Goldberg on either side of her. She looked back and saw Ethan, her grandparents and her parents all take their places in the seats directly behind her. Ethan squeezed her shoulder and gave her a quick kiss on the back of the head. "Hey, chippy, I've missed you!" he whispered in her ear as he sat; having Ethan was there to support her helped calm her down a little bit.

Court was set to start at nine o'clock sharp. She was not at all surprised when the boys were brought in to sit at the defendants' table at just how sharply dressed they both were. They both had fresh haircuts and were clean shaved. Charlie was in a charcoal-gray suit with a white button-up shirt. and a royal-blue tie. Sarah noticed that his head and shoulders were slightly slumped; he looked as though he was truly ashamed of his behavior and wanted to crawl in a hole. Chase, on the other hand, came into the courtroom in a dark-blue suit, with a white shirt and a matching blue tie to his suit. He walked in with an air about him that made Sarah uncomfortable. He was not fazed by the situation, and she found herself wondering how many times this young man had been in a courtroom before this.

Right behind the boys, Tom Matthews sat with a blank look on his face. Sarah noticed that he had on a matching charcoal-gray suit with a white button-up shirt, and a dark-blue tie to the suit Charlie wore.

There was a woman sitting beside Mr. Matthews whom Sarah had never seen before. She sat stoically in her seat, looking straight ahead and not interacting with anyone beside her. She looked to be approximately five feet, two inches with short black hair, cut in a pixie style haircut. She did not turn around, so Sarah could not get a better look at this mystery woman. She was left to assume that this mystery woman was the boys' mother or stepmother. She also wore a charcoal colored suit with a light-purple camisole under the jacket.

At nine, the bailiff announced Judge Sophia Turner's arrival to the court room.

"All rise for the Honorable Judge Turner." Everyone rose in their seats as she made her way to the bench. She looked to be in her early forties, her auburn hair drawn up into a tight bun at the back of her head. As she sat down, he told the crowd to sit. The bailiff escorted the jury from the hallway to the jury box. Once everyone was seated, Judge Turner instructed the jury on what to expect and then turned to ask DA O'Conner to start with her opening statement.

Abbigail got up and faced the jury. Sarah was drawn to her dark-blue pantsuit with the crisp white camisole she wore under the blazer. She had never noticed that DA O'Conner was quite tall for a woman, standing at five feet. eight inches without any heels on; today. she stood about five feet. ten inches with her two-inch chunky heels. She wore her long blond hair in a snug bun.

Abbigail opened the proceedings with a very strong opening statement. She laid out the case against the two men, gave the jury a glimpse into the evidence she had and what they could expect from her throughout the course of the trial. When she finished, she sat down and gave Sarah a quick glance and a small smile.

The top-notch defense attorney Robert Downs got up and gave his opening statement. Sarah had an uneasy feeling when she was first introduced to him during her deposition. She knew that he was used to getting his wealthier clients out of whatever pickle they got themselves into and that he would be a tough opponent for Abbigail. He tried multiple times to get Sarah on her own, away from DA O'Conner, but Sarah refused to go with him. She did not want to hear anything he had to say to her and did not want to give him an opportunity to try to intimidate her against her testimony.

Downs wore a black suit with a white shirt and a gray tie. His jet-black hair was cut short, and he was clean shaven. He had a grin on his face that Sarah wanted to get up and wipe right off for him.

After opening statements, Judge Turner called for a brief recess before starting in with Abbigail's witnesses. Lieutenant Goldberg escorted Sarah through the crowded hallway of cameras and reporters out into a private conference room where Ethan, her parents, and grandparents were all allowed to come in and visit with her. She let out a big sigh of relief when she entered the room, not realizing until then just how tense she really was. Ethan came over and placed a comforting hand on her shoulder.

When court broke for lunch, Sarah asked Officer Hardy and Lieutenant Goldberg to escort her back to her room. She did not return to the trial until the following morning when it was time for her to give her account of what happened. She could not go through sitting there watching the trial unfold and hearing Mr. Downs rip apart all of DA O'Conner's witnesses in person. She stayed in the hotel room and listened to the first day's activities via television broadcasting.

It was time for Sarah to return to the courtroom to give her account of the tragic events from that day that changed her life forever. Sarah did not sleep much that night before her court appearance. She tossed and turned, reliving the nightmare repeatedly in her head. She woke up with tears streaming down her cheeks, the desire to throw up overwhelming. Her three cats tried to cuddle with her, tried to comfort her, not understanding why she was so upset.

As she got out of bed, she grabbed the trashcan right next to her bed and threw up. Sarah grabbed her crutches and went into the bathroom to get ready for her day in court. She sat in the chair left for her and brushed her hair, pulling it into a French braid, and then brushed her teeth. She worked her way into her suite's closet, where she decided on a navy-blue skirt and jacket with a white camisole and a navy-blue scarf. She put in a pair of small gold studs in her ears. To complete the look, Sarah grabbed her glasses and put them on.

She made her way out to the living room. Officer Hardy was already standing guard just inside the suite's door. "Sarah, you look very nice," he said.

"Thank you, Officer Hardy."

She sat down and turned the television on, trying to pass the time until Lieutenant Goldberg arrived to escort her to the courthouse. When the TV came on, it was turned to the local news. The broadcasters were talking about the trial.

"Sarah Jackson-Clark is the prosecution's main witness—how do you think she is going to hold up on the stand today, Anita?" Andrew asked his coanchor.

"This is going to be extremely difficult for Sarah. How do you face your attackers in court and rehash the events that happened that horrific night?" she replied back to him.

Sarah turned off the television. She did not want to hear anyone else trying to get into her head and express that they even remotely felt they understood how she was feeling. She did not even know how she felt. The closer it came to her testifying, the more torn she was.

I want to see the boys punished for what they did. However, I hope that the jury is more lenient on Charlie. This is way too hard. Alex should still be here. If I hadn't gotten distracted that night, I would have walked the right way toward the apartment rather than walking in the wrong direction. I should have been the one to die, not Alex. Why can't I just die, then everyone else's life would be easier. What if I just stopped eating and wasted away?

Sarah was lost inside her own thoughts. She jumped when she heard Lieutenant Goldberg's voice in the room. For a second time, he asked her, "How are you this morning, Sarah?"

She looked at him and sighed. "That good, huh?" He smiled at her. She tried to smile back at him, but the best she could do was a pained smile.

She stood up and grabbed her crutches and a second pantsuit. The three of them walked to the elevator and out to the car. She tried to clear her mind and think of happier times on the drive to the courthouse. She tried to imagine her life with Ethan and the boys, but no matter what, she kept coming back to the events that night.

Tears streaked down her face again. She felt guilty—what if she had not let Alex push her into going to dinner that night?

What if I had not gotten mad at Alex and left the restaurant and tried to walk back to my apartment? What would have been the outcome

if I had not fought back and had just let the boys have their way with me?
You don't deserve to live. You are a bad person, Sarah. You are selfish. You
should have let Christopher Richardson kill you… You shouldn't have
killed him. You don't deserve Ethan or the boys and Emily.

Lieutenant Goldberg handed her a tissue to wipe her face. They pulled up in the courthouse's parking lot. Officer Hardy opened the door and helped her out of the car. They escorted her to the bathroom, clearing it before she went in. Sarah stood there looking at herself in the mirror for a minute before finally turning on the water to rinse her face.

When she got into the courtroom, she sat behind DA O'Conner with the two officers beside her. Ethan came in and sat behind her. She turned around and gave him a weak smile when she smelled his cologne. He reached down and gave her a quick peck on the cheek. "Hey, chippy, you look like hell."

"Is that really how you greet the one you love, whom you haven't seen in ages?" she asked him, a slight smile crossing her face.

At exactly nine, Judge Turner entered the courtroom. She instructed the jury to enter and take their seats. She then turned to DA O'Conner and advised Abbigail to call her witness to the stand.

Abbigail slowly turned and faced Sarah. Sarah stood, Officer Hardy helping to steady her until she had her crutches in place. She made her way to the witness stand where Bailiff Colleen Hernandez swore her in. Once sworn in, DA O'Conner asked Sarah to recount the events of the night.

Sarah made the mistake of looking over at the defendants' table. She noticed that Charlie had tears streaming down his face. Chase, however, sat there with a smug grin on his face. She looked behind the boys to where Mr. Matthews sat and saw the same smug grin across his face. The mystery woman was there, next to Tom Matthews. From this angle, Sarah was able to see that this was the boys' real mother. Charlie looked more like her, where Chase looked more like their father.

Sarah was brought back when Abbigail asked her again to recount the events of the night in question. Sarah took a deep breath before starting. She looked at Abbigail, who gave her a reassuring smile and nod, letting her know that it was going to be okay.

"Sarah, please start from the beginning and tell us what happened that night," Abbigail said.

Sarah started narrating the events of that night:

"I got off work that afternoon at three o'clock. I ran home and got into my running gear. I met Ethan and his boys at the Marine Corps Recruiting Office for our daily run. We ran six miles that afternoon. I got home around five forty-five. When I got back to my apartment building, my soon-to-be ex-husband, Alex, was waiting in my apartment. He demanded that Ethan meet us for dinner, so I called Ethan and set up dinner plans to meet at Zippy's.

"When we got to the restaurant, Alex started a fight with Ethan and me. When I couldn't handle Alex's degrading comments any longer, I got up and left the restaurant. I was upset and apparently got turned around after I left the restaurant. I turned the wrong way down the street. I got lost in my thoughts when I heard a noise.

"By the time I realized what was happening, it was too late to turn around and go back the way I had come. I was surrounded. My hands were pulled behind my back as Chase got in my face, laughing maliciously. His breath and clothing stank heavily of alcohol. I remember trying to pull my arms free, but the more I tried to free myself, the harder they held me. They pushed me toward the back of an SUV.

"Once we got to the back of the vehicle, everyone but Chase let me go. He pushed his body up right next to mine, taunting me. I reached up and hit him in the face. I tried to run away at this point, but some of the other guys caught me before I could get very far.

"At that time, I heard Charlie call Chase by his name when Charlie asked if Chase was okay, which made Chase very mad. He told Charlie to shut his mouth and record everything. I was forced back to the back of the SUV, only this time, Chase bent me over the back. My hands were held down tightly."

Sarah stopped and took a deep breath. She looked at Abbigail then looked over to Ethan. She did not want to continue. She was afraid of what Ethan would think of her when he knew the details of what happened that night. Ethan reassuringly smiled at her and made her feel better.

"Do you need to take a break, Sarah?"

Sarah shook her head and continued, "I felt Chase's hands slide up under my dress as he continued to taunt me, telling me that he was going to be the best lay I've ever had. I smelled the alcohol on his breath and clothing as he taunted me."

Recounting the smell caused Sarah to smell Chase all over again. She started to gag; she stopped and took a breath, trying not to throw up. The feeling was so strong that she could not resist it any longer. She leaned forward and threw up over the railing of the witness chair.

Judge Turner stood up and excused the jury before sending everyone out of the courtroom. Officers Gordon and Morgan moved to the witness stand to help Sarah get up and escorted her to the bathroom. Violet was allowed in to help Sarah clean up.

Once she was cleaned up and changed into her new suit, she was escorted back into the courtroom. Abbigail asked, "Sarah, I know this isn't easy to recount. Are you good to finish?" Sarah nodded and then continued with where she left off:

"He then unzipped his pants. I heard his pants hit the ground behind me. I then felt him enter me. Chase turned to Charlie and told him to make sure that he got this all on video, from multiple angles.

"I felt the grip on my hands loosen, so I took advantage of this slack. I slammed my foot down onto Chase's foot. I turned around, slammed my hand into Chase's nose, and then slammed my knee into his groin. I was terrified for my life after I hit Chase again.

"I then heard Alex yelling at the group as he pulled up into the parking lot. We tried to fight the group, but we were both shot. As I went down, I looked up and saw Chase and another boy over me, kicking me. The next thing I know is that I was waking up in the hospital."

Sarah stopped at this point in her testimony and waited for Abbigail's next question. Abbigail was not able to ask her next question because Judge Turner called for recess.

When they came back from recess, Abbigail stood and asked Sarah, "Sarah, you've given us a lot of information that was painful to recount already. I know this hasn't been easy, but I need you to recount the events of the second attack."

"I spent months in the hospital recovering, and I was just about to be sent home when I woke up one morning to familiar voices. Chase and Charlie managed to influence one of the officers to let them into my hospital room. Chase got up on the bed and slammed his foot down into my pelvis. The pain caused me to black out. When I woke up, every bone in my lower body was rebroken."

Sarah heard gasps from those in the back of the courtroom as she narrated the events. After Sarah finished telling the jury about the second attack in the hospital, Judge Turner dismissed the jury for the night.

Sarah was disappointed. She did not want to have to come back to face the Matthews's attorney but did not have a choice. Before leaving the courthouse, Sarah was able to speak to Ethan privately for a few minutes while Officer Hardy stood guard.

"Hi, chippy," he greeted her with a quick kiss on the cheek.

She smiled nervously and kissed him on his cheek.

"How are you feeling, chipmunk?" he asked her, looking at her with concern on his face.

"Well, I know that the worst is yet to come, but I can't help but wonder how much you hate me right now," she replied as she turned away from him, tears in her eyes.

"What are you talking about, Sarah? How could I ever hate you?"

"Well, I just told a courtroom full of strangers and reporters that we were having an affair. I can't imagine that will go over very well with the jury. I am sure you hate me now," she said.

"Oh, Sarah, I could never hate you. You had to tell the back story of why you were so distracted that night. Sarah, I love you, and your telling this story does not change that fact."

Tears started rolling down her cheeks. Ethan reached up and wiped them away before reaching down to kiss her. "I love you too," she said.

Sarah was escorted back to her hotel room for the night. Court was going to get a bit of a late start the next day due to conflict in Judge Turner's schedule. Sarah was relieved that she did not have to get up early for court, but she wanted to just to be done with Mr. Downs's cross examination.

She tried to eat her dinner but did not have an appetite. She sent the room service tray back untouched. She tried to sleep but could not do that either. She found herself uneasy and wanted to be comforted. She longed for Ethan's touch, to hear his voice telling her everything was going to be okay and that she was worrying for nothing.

Her brain would not shut off. She kept playing the day's events over and over in her mind:

Did I say the right things? How did the jury react to my account? Did I say too much? Did I not give enough detail? Should I have started crying on the stand? How could Chase sit there and smile through my entire testimony? Is Chase a psychopath? Did he enjoy listening to every detail, replaying that horrible night in his head, enjoying overpowering me and my fighting back? How is Charlie holding up? How does Mr. Matthews feel knowing that his son will most likely end up on death row? How is Mr. Downs going to attack me tomorrow? Why can't this just be over?

Sarah woke in a cold sweat as that night replayed back in her nightmares. She did not sleep well, and her body was feeling the fatigue. She tried to sit up but felt a wave of dizziness and nausea wash over her like a tidal wave. She laid her head back down on her pillows. Sarah lay like that for another hour before attempting to sit back up again. This time she was able to sit up without the dizziness.

She went about her morning routine and got ready for the grueling day she had ahead of her. She put on a light-gray skirt and jacket over a pastel-blue button-up shirt. She went out into the sitting area of the room to wait for her ride to court.

The day's events started at one, after lunch. Sarah was asked to take the witness stand again, and this time she faced Mr. Downs's questions. She figured he would attack her on a personal level, try to make her look bad, but it still shocked her when he attacked her and tried to make it look like everything was her fault.

"Is it your testimony that you were distracted and not paying attention to where you were walking, Ms. Clark?"

"I was upset about how the night's conversation unfolded at the restaurant. I could not stop playing the events over in my mind. I did not realize at first that I took a wrong turn and ended up going the opposite direction from my apartment. I had no idea that I was going to be ambushed by a bunch of horny teenage boys or that it was a crime for me to walk in the wrong direction of my apartment. Are you trying to say that this is my fault? I somehow led these boys on?"

"Ms. Clark, please only answer my questions and do not give me additional commentary," Mr. Downs scolded her. "How long before your encounter with the boys was your last sexual encounter with your husband, Alex?"

"I don't see how this is relevant," she answered him.

"Please answer the question, Ms. Clark.

"We were in the process of getting divorced. Why does this matter?"

"I asked you how long ago your last sexual encounter with your husband was. Now, answer my question before I ask to have you treated as a hostile witness."

"It had been years close to two years."

"How long before the attack did you have sex with your boyfriend, Mr. Miller?"

"Again, why is this relevant?" Sarah looked over at Abbigail.

"Mrs. Clark, answer the question," Judge Turner said as she looked over at Sarah.

"It had been about a week, not that it is really any of your business," she resentfully replied.

"How were you dressed that night, Ms. Clark?"

"What does that have to do with the price of tea in China?" She felt herself getting very angry and knew she needed to calm down. "I was wearing a long sundress. I would say that I was dressed appropriately and not dressed provocatively, if that's what you're trying to get at."

"You said yesterday that you physically attacked my client, not once but twice, is that correct?"

"The first time I attacked him, he was getting ready to rape me and was laughing about it, and the second time he was actually in the process of raping me. If it were your daughter being raped, would you want her to just lay there and take being raped, or would you want her to fight back?"

"You feel you were justified in attacking my client? Did you know that you broke his nose? You also caused enough damage to his genitals that he had to have one of his testicles removed, did you know that?" he asked her.

"I figured I broke his nose when he started gushing blood everywhere, and I will be honest with you, I don't really care what kind of damage I did or that he had to have a testicle removed. He raped me, encouraged his friends to rape me as well, and forced his brother to record everything. Before I passed out and was taken to the hospital, I remember seeing his face as he kicked me over and over and over again while I was on the ground bleeding out from my gunshot wounds. I heard him laughing when he figured out that Alex had died, saying 'Serves him right for getting involved in things that didn't concern him.' Chase is an evil young man."

His questioning finally ended. She was frustrated by his line of questioning but even more frustrated at the fact she let him get to her and she showed it on the stand; she played right into his hand. She was afraid this would cause her to look bad with the jury. Sarah was relieved when Lieutenant Goldberg came to get her and escort her back to her room.

Sarah did not leave her room for the remainder of the trial. Trying to clear her mind and not think about things, she asked Lieutenant Goldberg to bring her books from her favorite authors, Steve Alten and Orson Scott Card, to reread.

Sarah got word from DA O'Conner late Tuesday afternoon that they were finishing up with closing arguments and that the jury would start deliberating after that. "Due to the length of the trial, Sarah, I wouldn't be surprised if we have to wait a day or two before we get a verdict. I would recommend that you do your best to continue distracting yourself from thinking about it. Justice will be served!"

Sarah was just about to finish her fourth book in the *Meg* series when Lieutenant Goldberg entered her room. "Sarah, you need to get dressed for court. Jury is back with a decision."

"I thought Abbigail said it would take them a couple of days to deliberate. This can't be good news," she said as she got up from the couch to get ready.

"Sarah, don't let yourself read too much into the quick verdict," Lieutenant Goldberg replied.

Once everyone was in the courtroom, Judge Turner called the jury in and asked the foreman, "Mister Foreperson, have you reached a unanimous verdict in the case of *Spring City vs. Charlie Matthews?*"

A tall elderly man with gray in his beard and his hair stood up in response to Judge Turner's question. "Yes, we have, Your Honor. In the case of *Spring City vs. Charlie Matthews*, we, the jury, find Charlie Matthews on the count of fourth degree rape guilty. On the count of third-degree assault, we find the defendant guilty. On the count of involuntary manslaughter, we find the defendant Charlie Matthews guilty."

Sarah heard gasps from those behind her while she breathed a sigh of relief when the verdict came back for Charlie. She knew deep down inside that Charlie had not wanted anything bad to happen; he was terrified of his older brother, and so it was easier to go along with the actions that night than to stand up to Chase.

Sarah's anticipation and anxiety were so thick that it could be cut with a knife as she waited to hear what the jury decided in Chase

Matthew's case. She jumped slightly when Ethan reached out and put his hand on her shoulder, giving her a reassuring squeeze that he was there with her.

Judge Turner turned to the foreperson and asked, "Mister Foreperson, have you reached a unanimous verdict in the case of *Spring City vs. Chase Matthews?*"

"Yes, we have, Your Honor. In the case of *Spring City vs. Chase Matthews*, we, the jury, find Chase Matthews on the count of first-degree rape guilty. On the count of third-degree assault, we find the defendant guilty. On the count of first-degree murder, we the jury find Chase Matthews guilty.

As soon as the verdict was read, Sarah felt the tears rush down her face. She could not believe that this was case was finally over. She was so excited for the verdict that she momentarily forgot that she had to go before the jury in the case against Tom Matthews for her attempted murder and still had the civil case against Tom Matthews.

Sarah was escorted out of the courtroom into a private room where she was able to spend time with Ethan and her family. Once she was out of the cameras, she melted into her chair. Ethan sat down in front of her and held her face in his hands. She could see his smile through the tears. She could not believe that her nightmare was now over, and she could breathe a sigh of relief.

"Hey, chipmunk, that was a good outcome, huh?"

"Indeed! I just wish it was completely over."

"It will be soon enough, chipmunk!" He reached out and kissed her.

Chapter 8

2017

Moviemaking

The year following the Matthews's trial went by quickly. Sarah rented an apartment on the West Coast to start filming with Ryan, Josh, and Scott; she attended the sentencing hearing for both Charlie and Chase. She was called to testify against Tom Matthews in his conspiracy to commit murder case and then the civil case against the Matthews for all the medical bills she incurred after the attacks, and she was cleared by her doctors and therapists to start running again.

Before the end of the criminal case for Charlie and Chase, Sarah's attorney Stacey Downs encouraged her to file a claim in civil court to get Tom Matthews's estate to pay for her medical bills and the cost of burying Alex. She was reluctant to go back into court because she was worried that the jury would not award her anything to pay for the medical bills because she had Alex's inheritance from his grandparents' passing to fall back on. She was shocked when the jury came back and awarded her five hundred million dollars.

Sarah was excited to start filming and putting her new acting skills to the test. She took this opportunity very seriously. She worked hard with her trainers to make sure she had the stamina for the different scenes. When she was not filming, working out with her trainers, or running, she felt like she was stuffing her face full of proteins and carbs.

Her first day on set, Sarah could not believe all the big-name stars walking around. The man cast to play Sarah's father and the Marine Corps base commander, Brigadier General Hunter Smith, was none other than Bradley Davis. As soon as he spotted her, Brad walked over and introduced himself to her. "Hi, I'm Brad. It's nice to meet you, Sarah. I can't wait to work with you."

Sarah stared at him for a minute, taking him in. She thought he looked more handsome in person than on the big screen. He was an older man, who had black hair streaked with silver throughout. He kept his hair fashioned in a high and tight, having retired from the Marine Corps as a master sergeant.

"Hello?" she heard him say as she stood there staring.

"I'm so sorry. I still can't believe this is all my new reality," she replied when she came back to reality.

Ethan came out to meet her the first weekend she was on set. After filming her scenes with Brad, Sarah and Ethan went out for a night on the town. They started with dinner at the local dive bar, which sat on the corner of two busy streets intersecting together. As they walked down the stairs into the bar itself, Sarah was greeted with the smell of stale beer and fried foods as Ethan opened the door for her. The inside looked like it was about to cave in and had furniture that had holes and tears in it. The bar had ten bar stools, full of patrons. She could not believe that this dumpy-looking place was completely full with only one table left in the back corner of the bar. They enjoyed their meal and the company around them.

After dinner, they walked down the bustling street to the street carnival, taking in all the different smells in the air—a mixture of the different types of foods served in the little mom-and-pop restaurants, the smell of stale beer, and the different food trucks lined up down the street selling their own version of street tacos. When they made it to the carnival, Sarah immediately challenged Ethan to a shooting contest to see who could knock over the most tin cans at the shooting gallery.

"Step right up, step right up, and choose your weapon," the red-haired pimply-faced teenage boy said when he saw the two of them headed toward him.

"Which stuffed animal do you want as a prize when I beat your ass?" she teased him.

"Who said you're going to win? Girls can't shoot, I'm a shoo-in to win this contest," he teased back.

Sarah took the first shot and knocked down her first tin can with her air rifle. "That was just a lucky shot." Ethan winked at her as he picked up and fired his own air rifle, knocking over a can.

"Oh, is that what you think?" Sarah asked him as she picked up her rifle and aimed it at the next tin can and the next and the one after that. When she finished, she had knocked down all ten of the tin cans. Ethan was still shooting, so she decided to reach over and whispered in his ear, "Don't miss," taunting him by grabbing his left butt cheek in her hand. This distraction caused him to miss his last shot as he turned to face her.

"Dammit, woman!" he teased as he put his little air rifle down on its stand. "I guess I'll take that gigantic pink unicorn and I'll walk around town with it all night. Thank you for winning it for me, chippy," he said as he smiled down at her.

"Wanna get frisky atop the Ferris wheel?" She winked and smiled at him.

"Oh, you know it!" he exclaimed as he took her hand and led her toward the far end of the carnival where the Ferris wheel stood.

The next night, they went over to Ryan's mansion to eat dinner with Ryan and his wife, super model Ashlyn Andrews; Josh and his girlfriend, actress Amy Ambroe; Bradley and his wife, Anni; and Scott and his partner, famous fitness trainer Craig Walker.

As they pulled up, Sarah could not help but look in wonder. The house looked like a modern-day castle. Six thick round towers scattered in a very strategic pattern looked as though they were built for defense and were connected by big chunky walls made of gray stone. A sizeable gate with huge metal doors stood the end of the property at the street. A hand dug moat surrounded the house, with a regular bridge that led from the street to the house's multicar garage.

They pulled up to the end of the drawbridge; Ethan pushed the button for the intercom, "Who goes there?" rang out from the speaker.

"The Prince of Thieves," Ethan replied.

"Enter" rang out before the drawbridge was lowered.

Ethan pulled the car up in the driveway outside the garage. Once they walked up to the massive wooden doors, Sarah rang the pull cord for the doorbell. She heard the doorbell chimes sound their arrival. When the massive door opened, Ryan greeted Sarah and Ethan. "Welcome to my humble abode," he said as he opened the door, welcoming them inside the foyer. The foyer opened into a giant split and winding staircase that led up to the second floor of the house. To her left, Sarah saw a beautiful library full of books and antiques. To her right, she noticed a beautiful formal dining room already set with candles and formal place settings.

Ryan led them into the family room and introduced them to everyone else. Once introductions were over, Ryan said, "Dinner will be served here in a few minutes. I just need to put the finishing touches on everything. Please feel free to pour yourselves a drink and get comfortable."

"Ryan, you have this huge mansion, don't you have staff to cook your meals for you? What are you trying to do, poison us all?" Josh teased Ryan when they walked into the formal dining room.

Ryan walked back to the kitchen. He invited everyone to join him in the dining room once everything was set. Sarah walked in and looked at the feast covering the table: two turkeys set on both ends of the table, a carved ham in the center of the table, mashed potatoes, sweet potatoes, green bean casserole, cranberry sauce, and rolls.

"Gotta love Thanksgiving in the middle of the summer," Scott said. "Thank you for making such a beautiful-looking dinner, Ryan."

"Thank you for the invite," Sarah and Ethan said in unison.

As the group dug into their food, silence filled the dining room. It was not until the pumpkin, apple, caramel apple, and pecan pies were brought out that conversation started back up in the room.

Once dinner was over, Sarah helped Ashlyn clean up the dishes and the kitchen. "Are you excited to be filming your first film?" Ashlyn asked Sarah.

"I am so nervous and excited. I don't feel worthy of this opportunity. I am terrified that I am going to be a flop and ruin the movie for everyone."

"From what I hear, you're doing amazing on set. It is rare for me to hear Ryan speak so highly of one of his new amateur coworkers. He said that if you want to continue pursuing acting that you have a good career ahead of you. You have a good head on your shoulders, you follow instructions and always keep a positive outlook, no matter what."

"That's good to hear. Thank you for telling me because it helps put my mind at ease that I am not a complete flop," Sarah said, a slight smile crossing the corner of her lips.

Filming continued, and Ethan worked out with his command where he could visit her every other weekend. They planned for the boys to accompany him for a weeklong visit over their spring break. Sarah was not certain who was more excited when they broke the news to the boys, her or Eli and Manny. She knew they were excited to see the ocean and learn to surf. She was excited to have her running partners there to run with her.

Friday night, Sarah drove to the airport to pick up Ethan and the boys. She could not believe how much stuff two boys thought they needed for a weeklong trip to the ocean; they each brought a large oversized suitcase that was stuffed so full that the zippers nearly busted at the seams.

They spent all day Saturday at the beach. The boys got up early and went down to the water. Sarah and Ethan enjoyed catching up while watching them hit on a group of girls enjoying time at the beach.

"This could be interesting," Sarah commented when she saw both boys hitting on the same girl, who appeared to be right in between the two boys in age around fourteen. She was tall and kind of lanky for her age with curly red hair and freckles. She had perfectly symmetrical dimples whenever she smiled.

"Don't you know it. I guess it's all harmless, as long as they don't end up fighting each other over her." He laughed.

"Ah, she seems pretty content to just flirt with both of them for right now."

The boys surfaced for lunch. "We're hungry, can we find somewhere to eat?" Manny asked.

"Sure, what are you in the mood for?" Sarah asked. "Looks like we have some different vendor carts along the beach, or we could go into one of the restaurants and eat a little bit nicer meal."

The boys talked among themselves for a minute, and then Eli came back and said, "We vote to go in and sit down to eat lunch."

The four of them walked down the beach to a local restaurant and went in. They enjoyed lunch and went back to the room for naps before going out to dinner and a show later that night. The four of them enjoyed their weekend together, shopping, eating, exploring, and playing in the water.

Monday morning rolled around, and Sarah had to go back to the set for filming. She dreaded this week's scenes: this was the week she had to film the two different sex scenes between her character and Josh's character and then her and Ryan's character. She kept thinking to herself that there were probably hundreds of thousands of women across the different age groups who would gladly trade places with her, her included back in the day, but as the days came closer to filming these scenes, she found herself nervous and scared.

Filming was set to start with her and Ryan's intimate scene Wednesday morning and Josh's intimate scene the following day. As filming ended on Tuesday afternoon, Ryan called Ethan.

"Hello?" he asked as he answered the phone.

"Hey, Ethan, it's Ryan. We're down here at the studio, and we're not exactly sure what is going on with Sarah, but we need you to come calm her down. She is just sitting in her dressing room rocking herself back and forth. She won't talk to anyone."

"Hey, Ryan, the boys and I will be right down. Sarah started having bad anxiety attacks again after being attacked. What she needs is her running shoes and the ability to just run and not think about things. She will be fine. I'll bring her running gear to her, so we can go run."

"Hey, don't you have the boys with you?" Ryan asked Ethan.

"Sure do."

"Hey, why don't you bring the boys down to the studio with you and I'll take them with me for the night. I'm sure my boys would love the company."

"I'm sure they would love that. Are you sure though? They are a couple of rambunctious teenage boys," Ethan joked.

"Pretty sure they'll fit right in with my boys. I can find something for us to do for a few hours. You can pick them up at the studio in the morning."

Ethan and the boys arrived on set about twenty minutes later with Sarah's gear. Josh, Ryan, and Scott escorted the boys around the set and showed them around, introducing them to all the cast and crew. The boys enjoyed every minute of this; they snapped pictures with some of their favorite stars. When they were done, the boys hopped in the backseat of Ryan's red Mercedes-Benz GLC 4-Matic E350.

Ethan immediately entered Sarah's dressing room and found her still rocking back and forth, looking straight through the wall. He gently laid his arm on her shoulder and said, "Hey, chipmunk, everything is going to be okay. I have your shoes and your gear. Why don't you get changed and we'll go for as long of a run as you need to clear your mind?"

She looked up at him and kind of jumped back as though seeing him for the first time. "W-what about the boys? Where are they? We can't just leave them at the hotel while we go run!"

"The boys are taken care of. They already left to go hang out with Ryan's family for the night. All you need to worry about is running and clearing your mind."

She gave him a weak smile and then changed into her running gear—a red racerback sports bra with black running shorts. She pulled her hair back into a braid to keep it from getting tangled during the run. Once dressed, they set off. At first, she started sprinting as fast as she could, only when Ethan asked if they could slow the pace down did she slow down. She realized this was going to be at least a ten-mile run, and she could not keep that pace up.

When they arrived back to her dressing room two hours later, the rest of the set was cleared out and no one else was around. They quickly entered so that she could grab her clothes from earlier. They walked the six blocks from the set back to the hotel.

"So, chipmunk, what's going on?" he asked, grabbing her hand in his and giving it a quick squeeze.

"I know I messed up. I'm a complete failure! No one is going to want to ever work with me again! They all hate me and wish they never asked me to be a part of this movie!" she exclaimed, on the brink of tears.

"Hey, hey!" Ethan grabbed her and pulled her close to him. He gently grabbed her chin and tilted it up so that she was looking him directly in the eyes. "They feel no such way! What has you so scared, Chippy?"

"You're going to laugh at me, so I would rather not say anything."

"You know me better than that, Sarah. Now, out with it."

She melted against his sweaty chest. She looked down at the ground and said, "I'm terrified of the scenes I am shooting the next two days. I thought I could do it, but now that the time has arrived, I don't think I can."

"What scenes, Sarah?"

"I just don't know if I can do the intimate scenes with Josh and Ryan where everyone is watching while I film these scenes. It brings back too many feelings and memories I never wanted to think of again."

"On top of it, I've only ever had consensual sex with three people in my entire life, and within the course of two days, I will increase that to five. Yes, I understand that there will not be the same as when I make love to you. I still don't know if I can stand there completely naked for the entire world to see and criticize my body and all its flaws."

"Sarah," he said softly as he gently pulled her chin back up to gaze into his eyes. "You are absolutely gorgeous, and you should never worry about what others have to say about you or the way you look. You are perfect in every way imaginable because of your beautiful spirit. That is what makes you who you are, not the way you look.

Would it be better or worse if I were there with you the next two days as your morale support?"

"But the boys!" she started to interject before he cut her off.

"The boys will be fine. I will find something safe for them to do to keep them occupied while I am with you on set."

"But I just couldn't do that. They came out here to spend time with you, exploring and going on new adventures."

"Honestly, Sarah, I think I may be cramping their style a little bit," he laughed, causing her to slightly smile.

"I'll tell you what, let's go get cleaned up and grab dinner, then we can run things by Ryan when we go pick the boys up for the night. How's that sound?" he asked her.

"Okay."

They finished walking back to the hotel. Sarah undressed and went into the shower. Ethan joined her in the shower and nuzzled her neck. He continued kissing her down her shoulder blade around her collarbone across her chest as he slowly turned her around to face him, and then back over to the other side of her neck before finally settling on her lips. He softly pinned her up against the far wall of the shower and lifted her up, so she could wrap her legs around his waist and her arms around his neck. He rocked with her until he was overtaken with the pleasure of releasing inside her. "God, I love you," he whispered in her ear before he pulled out and put her back down so they could finish their shower. She smiled up at him and then turned back around to finish their shower.

The next morning was her intimate scene with Ryan. Sarah ran back over the script. Some of the scenes she had already acted out with Bradley Davis, others she had already acted out with Ryan.

> Sarah's character, Jane Rose (took her mother's last name to avoid comments about her command being given to her because of who her father was), had gone away to officer candidate school after graduating college because that was what her father, Brigadier General Travis Campbell, wanted her to do, and she never went

against her father's wishes. She was dating Justin McCoy, her high school and college sweetheart when she left for her ten weeks of training. Justin asked for and received the general's permission to propose to Sarah, if he agreed to her joining the Marine Corps officer's candidate program. Justin proposed to Jane before she left for OCS.

Jane fought her way through OCS to please her father, knowing that when she finished, her fiancé would be waiting for her and they would start planning their wedding. She broke her leg on the final run of the physical fitness test for the training but still managed to beat out all the other candidates in their run, running three miles in sixteen minutes and thirty-two seconds. Even with a broken leg, Jane managed to run another lap to help encourage her fellow candidates to finish training out strong.

Jane came out of the infirmary on crutches but was still allowed to graduate with the option to accept or decline commission. Jane did not see her family before the ceremony began and only after accepting her commission as a second lieu-tenant did she see her mother and father in the crowd. She went over to find out where Justin is, only to find out that he wrote her a note to dump her because he got another classmate of theirs pregnant.

Jane came home to heal before going back for her training at the basic school and then on to the school for her specialty. Her father pushed her to join Intelligence, so she excelled and got accepted as a part of the Intelligence team. Her first duty station was out of the country, in England, with Scott's character, Second Lieutenant Nathan Small, and Josh's character, Captain Daniel Wise. She did not meet Daniel until later in the plot; however, she and Nathan became very good friends as they went through OCS, TBS, and Intelligence training together before being stationed together. Nathan wanted to move their friendship to the next level; however, Jane had not fully given up on the possibility of rekindling things with Justin.

After two years abroad, General Campbell pulled strings to get Jane transferred back to Virginia. Jane said her goodbyes to her team and transferred home. When she got home, she found out that her father let Justin move into the spare bedroom, situated across the hall from her old bedroom, but he was not there when she first arrived. Her parents took her to celebrate the Independence Day parade and activities just off base in town. She ran into Justin, who was out with his new girlfriend, which crushes Jane. She turned to walk away and act like she never saw them when Justin called out to her, forcing her to interact with the two who ruined her engagement and future.

The two of them argue, which caused Jane to leave the park and go back home, where she stayed the rest of the night. The next day, her parents let her know that they were traveling abroad for a month and would not be home, leaving her stuck in the same house as her cheating boyfriend, whom she still secretly wanted to work things out with.

A couple days before she was scheduled to meet with her new commanding officer, Jane came back from her morning run to take her shower. When she got back into her room, she locked the door and headed to the shower. When she finished, she wraps herself up in her towel and started drying her hair. While lost in her own thoughts, she realized that Justin let himself into her room and was standing there staring at her as he relieved himself in her toilet.

She tried to cover herself up, feeling uncomfortable with his staring at her. He told her that he forgot how beautiful she was as she told him to get out of the bathroom. He walked up behind her and kissed her neck and jawline until he spun her around to kiss her on the lips, all the while telling her how beautiful she was. She got wrapped up in all this and ended up in her bed making love to him like she did before.

After they finished, they lay there wrapped in each other's arms, and they started talking about how much they missed each other. He said he was a fool to leave her, but that he can't come back to her either because he was about to have a baby with his girlfriend. Jane told him to leave the room, and then she called her new commanding officer and asked to be transferred back to her old command. She left without talking to her parents or Justin and went back to England.

Once back in England, Jane discovered that she was pregnant with Justin's baby. With this news, her command then assigned her to go out on an undercover operation with Captain Wise, posing as his pregnant wife. While out on assignment, they were captured, tortured, and forced to make love in front of their captives, who do not believe the two were in love. As she spent more time with Daniel, she found that she did truly fall in love with him after having to rely on him to survive. They escaped their captives, killing every last man in the compound, and returned to England, where they got married. Daniel adopted the baby as his own, and then nine months after Lora Lei was born, they welcomed their own son, Anthony, into their lives.

After rereading the scenes, Sarah slipped into character and mentally prepared herself to start filming the shower scene with Ryan. Ryan found Sarah before she left for wardrobe and pulled her aside for a moment.

"Hey, are you okay?"

"Yeah, why?"

"I know this can't be easy for you, but I want you to know that you will be amazing, like you have been so far."

"I hope you're right. I just need this to go right so we don't have to keep reshooting."

"Can I give you a piece of advice to help you feel better about the scene?"

"Please!"

"Don't picture me as me… Picture me as Ethan. How do you feel when you make love to Ethan? Imagine everything in this scene is Ethan touching you, kissing you, making love to you, and it will be so much easier for you to get into role."

She smiled at him, and he finished by saying, "Oh, yeah, and just know that while you're imagining me being Ethan that hundreds of thousands of women will watch this scene and wish they were in your shoes, making love to me," before walking away to his own dressing room.

"Only you!" she yelled after him as he walked away. This made her laugh, and she went to get ready.

The scene with Ryan went very smoothly; Sarah took Ryan's advice and pictured Ryan as Ethan. Ryan wore Ethan's cologne for the scene, which helped Sarah picture her lover. She found Ryan's hands were silky smooth compared to Ethan's rugged hands. His touch was light. They made it through the scene in less than ten takes.

Josh was as thoughtful the following day; he also wore the same cologne as Ethan to help Sarah make it through their scene. It was harder to get through because there were more people watching, and they were right up in the scene. Sarah tried to concentrate but lost her focus more easily. After ten takes, they broke for lunch; the director gave her a break to refocus.

Josh followed her off the set and grabbed her arm in his hand, "Hey, I know I'm not as good-looking as Ryan, but I promise if you'll let me in, I'll be better than him! What do you need for me to help you through this?"

"It isn't you, it's me, but I promise I'll get it right when we come back from break!"

After a thirty-minute break, they went back to the set. Sarah nailed the scene in the second take. Sarah felt good about the outcome.

The Proposal

The film wrapped up, and Sarah was invited to audition for another role, this time costarring with Oliver Petersen. With a little guidance and support, she was selected to be the lead female, Christy Andrews. She was excited to be filming along such a Hollywood giant.

Once editing was done on her first movie, she and her three Chipketeers, Josh, Ryan, and Scott were invited to many different talk shows and radio stations to promote the movie. They spent three months on the road, traveling all over the world. She could not believe all the rave reviews people gave her performance in the teaser trailers. People were genuinely excited to go watch her performance.

Before going on the road, Sarah made arrangements for her family to meet her in Spring City to watch the University of Spring City Broncos play the Mountain City University Cougars for their season opening football game. She could not wait to watch the Broncos beat the Cougars. In reading all the preseason statistics, sportscasters across the country were raving about the talent pool in the Broncos lineup.

She bought tickets for her parents, grandparents, her brother's little family, and for Ethan and the kids. They were all excited, and this was going to be the first time since the first day of the trial that they were all in the same spot together. Sarah was super excited and could not wait.

She got into town late Thursday evening and immediately went to Grams and Pops' place to get settled in for the weekend's activities. She quietly snuck into the already dark house and headed past the kitchen, through the dining room and down the open staircase that sat in the middle of the entryway. She looked into the empty dark living room and saw the silhouette of the furniture occupying the room. She made her way down the stairs to the basement bedrooms. Grams left a hall light on to help her see her way to her room.

She opened the door to her room, turned on the light, and looked in to find the bed made up with a handsewn quilt that Grams made with her mother before she passed. The beautiful oak furniture lining the room was all hand built by her great-grandfather after the Great Depression. The headboard was simple yet elegant. The dresser and chest of drawers stood along the closest wall.

Sarah slipped into the large walk-in closet and hung up her clothes to prevent wrinkling. When she came back out, she let out a brief scream when she realized she was not alone in the room. Grams heard her sneak in and came down to make sure she was able to settle in.

"Ahh! Oh my goodness, Grams, I didn't realize you were down here. Did I wake you?"

"Sorry, I didn't mean to startle you, chipmunk," Grams replied. "No, I was still awake watching the clock for your arrival. I heard the door open and the deadbolts turn into place when you came in. I just wanted to make sure you have everything you need. Do you want a nightcap before you go to bed? I know where Pops keeps his hidden stash," she said as she winked at Sarah.

"Nah, wouldn't want Pops to have his secret revealed." Sarah laughed. "After traveling all day, I think I'm ready to just get some shut-eye, if that is all right. Can we catch up in the morning?"

Grams walked toward Sarah, hands out, and gently placed both hands on either side of her face. She gently kissed Sarah on the forehead before saying, "You bet your sweet ass we're going to catch up in the morning." Before Sarah could reply, Grams turned and left the room, leaving her standing there in amusement at her grandma's behavior. She was seventy-two, and she still acted like she was twenty-two. That was one of the many things she loved and admired about her grandmother.

She woke the next morning and went upstairs to find her grandparents both sitting at the kitchen table drinking their hot tea and eating homemade donuts. Sarah immediately grabbed a tea bag and made herself a cup of Earl Grey before joining them at the table. They sat there all morning, laughing and joking. When it came time for lunch, Sarah helped Grams make lunch for the three of them.

As the day wore on, more of the family arrived for the long weekend. Sarah received a text message from Ethan.

Ethan

4:00 p.m.

Hey, Chippy, I got some bad news for you! :'(

Sarah

4:01 p.m.

What sort of bad news? You better not be canceling on me! You'll make me pout. :'(

Ethan

4:02 p.m.

I hate to say it, but I can't come home for the weekend. My TAD got extended 2 more weeks.

Sarah

4:03 p.m.

What about the kids? They will be devastated that you aren't here to watch the game w/ them!

Ethan

4:04 p.m.

Don't you think I already know that??!! I told them 1st. The boys got off the phone & Emily started crying :'(I don't have a choice, Chippy!

Sarah

4:05 p.m.

This stinks! You sure you can't tell the CO that you need to come home?

Ethan

4:06 p.m.

I will watch the game w/ you from the hotel room here in 29 Palms. We can text when there is a good play & whatnot.

Sarah

4:07 p.m.

It won't be the same w/o you here! :'(

You better plan to make things up to me the next time you are home! **wink wink**

Ethan

4:08 p.m.

Oh, you know I will!

Sarah put her phone down, disappointed with the news she just received. She finished out the day with dinner and dessert with the family. Brennan convinced Sarah to play a game of memory with him before he went to take his bath and went to bed. She forgot how much fun this game was and how challenging it really was especially when playing with a smart six-year-old who had a great mind for the game. She went to bed shortly after her nephew in anticipation for the upcoming events: breakfast, game, and then a barbecue dinner with the family. Little did she know what Ethan had in store for her.

Sarah's bladder woke her up earlier than usual that Saturday morning. When she got up to use the restroom, she noticed that the alarm clock read it was only four in the morning. She shook her head and crawled back into bed with her girls, who made the trip with her. They instantly curled back up around her, cocooning her into the bed. She did not wake again until she smelled cooking bacon wafting down the stairs from the kitchen up above her.

She stumbled upstairs and grabbed a tea bag and the water kettle and poured herself a cup of hot tea. She sat down at the table with her mom and grandparents.

"Someone has a serious case of bedhead going on," she heard from the baritone voice entering the kitchen.

"Look who's talking, dweeb!" she replied back to her brother as he reached her and playfully tussled her hair.

"Where's Dad?" she asked as they ate breakfast.

"Oh, don't worry about him. He got up early to run an errand," her mother replied nonchalantly.

They ate breakfast, and Sarah helped Grams clean up the kitchen. Once the kitchen was cleaned up, she went downstairs to get ready for the day. She put on her Broncos gear. As she dressed, she found herself saddened by the fact that Ethan would not be there to watch the game with her and wear the matching shirt she bought for him to wear.

She sauntered her way back up to the living room to see what everyone was watching on the big screen. She did not want to watch the old Western movie that currently filled the screen, so she decided to go outside and enjoy the beautiful morning.

When she got outside, she saw her father exiting the backseat of a town car. She gave him an inquisitive look, but he walked past her and did not say a word. She continued walking down the driveway to the edge of the road. She then walked alongside the roadway about a tenth of a mile to the edge of her grandparents' property line. She turned back around and walked back the way she came. As she walked back to the driveway, she saw a black BMW M6 convertible Gran Turismo pull into the drive and head up to the house.

Her curiosity piqued, she picked up the pace to see who in the family was sporting such a nice brand-new car. She did a double take when she got to the house and saw her father in the driveway talking to Ryan and Scott like they were chummy pals and have known each other a whole lifetime.

"Hey, Sarah, why didn't you tell us that your costars were joining us today for the football game?" her father asked her.

"W-what are you talking about?" she asked as she turned to look at Ryan and Scott.

"Yep, we found out through the grape vine that Ethan couldn't join you today, so we wanted to make today memorable without him for you," Ryan replied.

"You guys are supposed to be spending time with your families this weekend before we go out on the road again on Monday before the red carpet movie premier later this week!" she exclaimed, looking at them. "What would ever possess you to want to hang out with my family over yours?" she asked.

"We just did. We're here, nothing you can do about it except shut up and get in the car. We're going for a ride before the game starts," Ryan told her, a big smile on his face.

"You better just get in with them, Sarah. Enjoy the ride in that b-e-a-u-t-i-f-u-l looking car!" her father said to her as Ryan and Scott ushered her to the front passenger door of the car.

"What in the world are you two chuckleheads doing here?" she asked them again before Scott opened the door. "What exactly are you two up to?" She eyeballed them both suspiciously.

"Never you mind that, just get in. Let's just enjoy a beautiful morning with great company," Scott said.

Scott opened the door for her to slide in. Sarah noticed the interior was dark charcoal-gray color leather. She stood for a minute taking it all in until Ryan brought her back to reality. "Are you just going to stand there staring all day, or are you going to get your ass in the car?"

She got in the passenger seat while Ryan crawled into the driver's seat and Scott joined them in the backseat. "I would have sat back there so that you could have more room up here," she looked back and told Scott.

"I got plenty of room, don't you worry about me, Sarah!" she heard him reply.

Ryan drove around the circle drive and back down the driveway to the street. They drove, and Ryan asked Sarah to give him directions to drive by places that were important to her. "We want to get to know the real Sarah Jackson-Clark," Scott said as they drove around.

After about an hour of driving, Ryan pulled over in an abandoned parking lot at the old community college building on the opposite side of town. They all hopped out of the car and looked over the city. "Turn around and face the car," he said.

"W-why? What are you two up to?" she asked as she saw Scott come alongside her and hand Ryan something that she could not see. Sarah started feeling anxious.

"Do you trust us?" they asked her in unison, devious smiles lining their faces.

"Something tells me that I probably shouldn't right now."

"We need to blindfold you now. Once you're blindfolded, we need you to change your shirt with the shirt we're about to give you. We're also going to put noise-canceling headphones over your ears. We will then drive around for a while, and when we stop, we will pull you out of the car and will carry you wherever we go so you won't have to worry about tripping and falling. Ready to play this game with us?" Ryan asked her as he slipped the blindfold around her eyes and tied it around the back of her head. He then handed her a T-shirt for her to put on. "No cheating! You can't remove the blindfold or the headphones until we tell you to!"

"How am I supposed to change shirts in the dark, and how do I know you aren't looking?"

"Remember that we've seen you naked!" Ryan laughed.

"Hey, not fair! Do I get a say in this?" she asked.

"Nope, just trust us."

"I don't want to miss the start of the football game, so whatever adventure you have us going on better get me to the stadium on time!"

"Everything is gonna be all right," she heard as she slipped back into the passenger seat before putting the cordless Bose noise-canceling headphones over her ears.

They drove around for what seemed like two or three hours turning left and then turning right, then turning right before turning left again. Sarah thought she could keep up with all the turns but quickly lost track of where they were with the blindfold and the headphones on. She felt herself dozing off before they stopped for good. Ryan helped her out of the car. As promised, she felt Ryan pick her up and put her on Scott's back, making her feel like a child on her father's back doing piggyback rides around the zoo.

They walked for what seemed like a mile, up some stairs and down a hallway that felt familiar before finally stopping. Scott gently let her back down on the ground, and the two gentlemen guided her to sit in a padded folding chair. She sat there for a couple of minutes before her headphones were removed.

Sarah was not aware of this, but Ryan had circled back around during the drive to park just outside the Spring City Bronco's football stadium, which was across the street from the recruiting office. During one of the stops along the drive, they picked up a new passenger, one that Sarah was not aware had joined them, costar Josh Lewis.

Before removing the headphones, Sarah heard Ryan's voice in her ears, "Sarah, we're going to remove the headphones now, but please don't say anything until we tell you what to do. Also, please do not remove your blindfold quite yet. We will advise you when you can remove that. Nod if you understand."

Sarah gave a quick nod with her head. She sat still as the headphones were removed from her ears. She waited for what seemed like five minutes before she heard Ryan say to her, "Sarah, we're in some place important to your history. We wanted to learn a little bit more about you, so we brought you someplace special. We are now going to play a game where we ask you questions and you answer them truthfully. Please make sure you keep your answers G-rated. Ready?"

"I-I guess so." Her voice squeaked a little bit, not having been used in a couple hours. "Can I get a sip of water before we play your game?"

Ryan handed her a water bottle and let her know it was already open so she would not have to open it and so she would not spill it on herself. Ryan started with the first question: "Sarah, tell me how you and Ethan first met."

"What?" she asked. "Why do you want to know that?"

"I just do."

"We first met when he called me to set up an appointment to come into the recruiting office to talk about joining the Marine Corps' officer candidate program after I had filled out some information online stating that I was interested in learning more about what the Marines had to offer me if I joined. I then met with him, and his commanding officer, in the recruiting office three days after he called."

Sarah heard Scott's voice for the next question. "What was your first impression of Ethan when you walked in and saw him for the first time?"

"Really? What is this?" she asked.

"It's a form of twenty questions. Please answer my last question. What was your first impression of Ethan when you walked in and saw him for the first time?"

"I thought he was cute and filled out his civvies very well."

"Who is cuter, Ethan or me?" she heard a familiar voice ask her.

"Josh, is that you? When did you get here?"

"Never you mind about that, I want to know who is cuter? Ethan or me?"

"I hate to disappoint you, Josh, but I'm going to go with Ethan being the cuter of the two of you!" she said with a smile on her face.

"Who is cuter, me or Ryan?" he asked, then got cut off by Ryan, "Josh, you're asking questions out of turn."

"Answer, I need to know!" Josh said. She could hear the laughter in his voice. "Ryan, you're just afraid she's going to say I am cuter than you are and it'll hurt your ego."

"If I had to pick, I would say Ryan." She smirked as she answered.

"Oh, ouch! I know what you say when it's just the two of us," Josh teased her.

"Okay, on to the next question, when did you first know that you were in love with Ethan?"

"Oh, that's tough to answer. I would have to say I thought I loved Ethan when we first started hanging out on one of my trips home to Star City from Fair Falcon, but I knew I was in love with him when he came and spent time with me every day I was in the hospital."

"Awe, how sweet. We all want to know, Sarah, is Ethan a good kisser?" she heard Scott ask.

"Haha, I'll never tell. One does not kiss and tell, that's rude and you guys should know better." She smirked as she answered.

"Who is the better kisser? Ethan or me?" Josh asked her.

"What I will say is that Ryan is a better kisser than you, Josh," she laughed.

She felt a gentle touch on the top of her hands by hands that felt familiar; the electricity of the touch coursed through her body, and she shivered. But she knew it could not be Ethan; he told her he was not going to be able to join her for the game and dinner that night because of work. She felt her heart skip a beat in anticipation of it being Ethan's voice she would hear next. Her pulse quickened.

"You came into my life seven years ago, and I was a fool to not snatch you up then. I waited three years before taking my chance to really get to know you and have you become a bigger part of my life. Every day for the last two years, you found a way to make me fall further in love with you. I did not think I could ever feel the way I feel about you. I thought after my second marriage started to fail that I must be defective, but you made me see past those insecurities and made me see what I was missing in my life. You have been a great influence in the lives of my children, and they love you more than you will ever know. Sarah, I say all of this to ask, Will you do me the honor of being your husband, challenging me to be a better man every day for the rest of my life?'"

"Pinch me, this can't be happening right now. Are you for real? Am I really hearing you correctly?" she asked in complete shock.

"You heard me correctly! Chipmunk, I want you to be my wife."

"*Yes, yes, I will happily marry you!*" she exclaimed, trying to stand to hug him but slightly faltering before sitting back down. She felt the two-karat yellow diamond ring slide onto her left ring finger.

She felt herself lifted from her seat and Ethan's embrace as he spun her around in a circle.

"Can I take off this blindfold now, please?"

Ethan gently removed the blindfold from around her eyes. She kissed him passionately once she could see his face. She heard clapping and cheering from a distance, then she heard the band play the national anthem. As she looked around the room, she saw she was back in the recruiting office.

Sarah, Ethan, and the three Chipketeers, Ryan, Scott, and Josh, all accompanied Sarah to their private booth where the rest of both families were waiting for them. She was bombarded with hugs when they first got to their booth.

She was still in shock. "How did you accomplish all this?" She turned and asked Ethan.

"It was like magic," he laughed and told her. "You don't need to worry about how I orchestrated all this, just know that this isn't the end of the surprises for the day." He smiled and grabbed her into another hug as he kissed her.

"What did I do to deserve someone as thoughtful as you?" she asked him.

They watched the Broncos come out and lead the first half of the game. She was impressed with how solid both the offense and defensive lines were playing. The Bronco offense made every catch and breaking through the Cougars' defensive lines without any turnovers. The Bronco defensive line caused the very young Cougar offensive line to make mistakes, two of which the Broncos took advantage of and resulted in touchdowns. By the time both teams went into their respective locker rooms to analyze the first half, the Broncos led 35-3.

Ethan had another trick up his sleeve, which he revealed at half-time. He worked with their favorite baker, Rocco Alfonsi, to have enough cake made for the entire stadium to enjoy a piece of cake to help them celebrate the proposal. Sarah was completely shocked when she heard the announcement made as the band made its way to the field for the halftime show. Rocco came to their box and gifted Sarah with her very own champagne cake.

During the start of the fourth quarter, Sarah started feeling anxious and overwhelmed. She struggled to keep her emotions in check:

I shouldn't be here watching this game. This is something that Alex and I used to do. I don't know how I ever thought this would be a good idea to watch our favorite team in their season opener. I shouldn't be here without Alex. This was our tradition, I shouldn't be starting this tradition with Ethan.

How can I take pictures with the teams? There should be other people they want to take pictures with, not me. I'm no one special.

I still can't believe that Ethan orchestrated this whole thing. How did he pull it off? There's no way that I'm good enough to be his wife!

Ethan saw the emotional roller coaster happening in Sarah's mind flash across her face. He walked over to her in the corner of the booth and leaned in close enough that only she could hear him, "Sarah, it is okay for you to enjoy this day. I know that you have a lot of mixed emotions right now, and that is okay."

"I-I just don't know if I can handle all of this right now."

"You are strong. You deserve to be happy. Let yourself be happy!" he whispered to her.

"How? Why do I deserve to be happy when Alex is no longer here? Why do I deserve a man like you who knows how to help put me at ease when I am anxious and overwhelmed? How do I face all these people after the game who want an autograph or a picture with me? I'm a nobody. I don't deserve all of this!" She started shaking as she spoke.

Ethan reached out and pulled her into a hug. She sank into his chest; he felt her relax substantially. They stood in the corner for about five minutes until the Bronco's third string pulled in another touchdown, bringing the score to 63-17.

Hunter and Brenda left at the start of the fourth quarter to take baby Hazel and Brennan home for naps. Emily also needed a nap so they agreed to take her with them back to Grams and Pops' place.

The game ended, and the family left the box; they headed home. Sarah was surprised when her mother asked Eli and Manny if they wanted to ride back to the house with her and Matthew. Sarah and Ethan were left alone in the box.

"What I could do with you right now if we weren't in such a public place!" He smiled as he grabbed playfully at her butt and squeezed it.

"Really? What exactly would you do right now?" she teased him, nibbling at his earlobe then licking her lips.

"Oh my god, Sarah, what wouldn't I do to you right now if I could!"

She sensed the sexual tension building in the room. She wanted him more now than she ever had in the past, and she knew she could not have him quite yet.

The tension was interrupted when the Bronco's team manager knocked and came in the box with them. "Am I interrupting something?" she asked, smiling deviously after looking at both Ethan and Sarah's body language. Sarah noticed that Christina was shorter than her by about two inches. She had blond hair, freckles and was very fit.

"What can we do for you?" Ethan asked her.

"Well, both teams left the field and are ready to get some photos with Sarah, Ryan, Josh, and Scott. Do you know where the other three are so we can get started?"

"They left to go mingle with some of the fans. We'll go with you to find them."

They left the box and found the three Hollywood stars at the base of the stadium stairs taking photos with some of the fans still left in the stadium.

"Who are we going to meet with first?" Sarah asked the Broncos' team manager, Christina.

"The Cougars need to head out of town as soon as you are done with pictures, so you will join their team first."

They stepped into the opposing team's locker room. Sarah could not help but notice the bright yellow all over the walls and the lockers themselves. She had never seen that before, so she asked, "What's up with all the yellow in here?"

"That's a secret that not everyone is privy to," Christina replied.

They moved back out onto the field and snapped their pictures with the whole Cougar team and then the offensive and defensive lines in turn. Once they were done, the team grabbed their bags and got on the bus to head home.

The Broncos all came out in matching shirts, the same shirt Sarah, Ethan, Ryan, Josh, and Scott were all wearing for the game. Each of the shirts had the player's jersey number and last name on the back, along with the Broncos logo on the front. Sarah's jersey had the number 1 on the back with the name D'Artagnan. She noticed that each of her Chipketeers also had their own shirts with Athos, Porthos, and Aramis on the back. Ethan's shirt had Panda and the number 1 on the back. She looked over at Ethan. "How did you manage to get the entire team to wear a shirt that isn't available for purchase?"

"Never you mind that, just enjoy wearing your matching shirt with the team!" He laughed at her.

They took serious pictures with the whole team and then with the offensive and defensive lines as well as the special teams. Once the serious pictures were all captured, they started in with the fun pictures. Sarah was shocked at just how much fun the team wanted to have after the game. They all had musketeer hats to put on for some of the fun pictures. Once the pictures were over, Ethan had one more surprise for her: he brought her running clothes to help her process everything and help her settle her nerves.

"Hey, chipmunk, I know you were anxious earlier and you seem to be doing better, but I wanted to make sure you had your escape before I add more to your list of surprises tonight. How far would you like to run?"

"How far were you thinking?"

"We can either run three miles back to my parents' place, four miles back to Pops and Grams' place, or we can run eight miles back to our place. The kids are all over at Pops and Grams' place with your family, so I want you to keep that in mind. My parents are also going to be over there for a little bit."

"If we run back to our place, we have the entire place to ourselves and don't have to worry about visitors, right?" She winked.

"I guess we'll have to run the distance and find out, won't we? How fast you want to run?"

"We haven't done a fartlek lately, what do you say, you up for that for eight miles?"

"No way to find out other than to get started."

They changed in the locker room and gave their clothes to Ryan to keep for them. They switched up between jogging, running, and sprinting for six of the eight miles. They took a mile at the beginning and the end to use for warm-up and cooldown. They made the run in an hour and a half.

When they got to their place, Sarah flopped down on the kitchen floor and started stretching. Ethan stopped and watched her stretch. "Damn, is there anything you do that doesn't make you look sexy?"

"I wasn't aware that stretching could be sexy," she teased. "Time to get this stench off. You coming?"

She got up and walked to the shower. She undressed and started the water. She hopped in the shower. After a couple of minutes standing in the warm water, she felt a slight breeze when Ethan opened the shower door and joined her. He slid right up behind her and took her breath away when he reached around her waist and pulled her in close to him. He started nibbling on her earlobe before kissing the right side of her neck and then worked his way down her shoulder blade. She melted into his touch. She turned to face him and met his lips with her own.

Their kissing became passionate. He could not keep his hands off her, and before long, he had her pinned up against the shower wall. She wrapped her legs around his waist as he picked her up. He slid right inside her.

"God, this feels amazing! You are amazing!" he exclaimed as he reached orgasm.

When they finished their shower, they dried off. Sarah walked toward the bedroom. He caught up to her, picked her up, and turned her around to face him. She giggled like a little schoolgirl and then quickly started kissing him. He walked her back to the edge of the bed. He gently laid her down with her legs hanging off the edge of the bed.

He gently scooted her to the middle of the bed and then climbed on top of her. He rocked into her. When he finished, he flipped over and pulled her on top of him. She fell asleep wrapped up on his chest, feeling completely at peace in his arms, head on his chest.

Ethan woke up before her and quietly eased his way out from under her without waking her. He grabbed her next surprise out of its hiding place and pulled it out of the garment bag.

She woke about five minutes later. She got up from the bed and immediately noticed the sleek halter-topped black sequined dress hanging from the hanger on the wall. "Where did this come from?"

"Does it matter?"

"I guess not, but it sure is beautiful!"

"Only the best for my beautiful chipmunk. Are you ready to put that on and see how it looks?"

"I don't know, depends on what is up next. I would rather wear my blue jeans and a T-shirt. Can I do that?" She winked at him.

"Nope, you sure can't. I can't wait to see how that dress accentuates your curves."

"Mind telling me where we're going?"

"I do mind. Just get that sexy little ass in that dress and let's get going."

He could not keep his eyes off her as she put her hair up into a tight English braid and got dressed. "What are you looking at?"

"I just can't help but stare. I need you to pinch me!" He smiled.

She cleared the five feet between the two of them, reached out, and pinched his arm.

"Ouch! What was that for?" he squealed as he pulled his arm away from her grip.

"You told me to pinch you, what did you expect me to do?" She laughed as she reached up to kiss him on the cheek.

"I shouldn't have expected any less from you." He kissed her. "I still can't believe all this is real! You really said you want to be my wife! Can we go to the top of the mountains so I can shout from the top just how much I love you and how lucky I am?"

"I can't believe it's real either. How did you manage to get this all put together? I am just in awe. Here I was, sad because I didn't think we'd get to enjoy the game together and all along you had this planned. How did you get Josh to keep a secret for so long? You know he can't keep secrets? What did you bribe him with?"

"I'll never tell!" He laughed. "That's between Josh and me. Now, get that little ass of yours dressed. We gotta get going for your next surprise."

"Holy guacamole, Batman! I can't believe you're not going to tell me," She faked crying with him before turning to smile at him.

She got dressed and turned around to face him. She was immediately drawn to his dress attire. He dressed in a black tuxedo with tails. She found his eyes plastered on her with a goofy-looking smile on his face. "What are you smiling at?"

"I-I...you look amazing. I knew you would, but God, that dress fits you like a glove."

"You clean up pretty good yourself," she said as she raised her eyebrows and wolf-whistled at him.

She took his arm and walked with him to the car. "How did you know we would end up back here to leave the car here?"

"I know you, probably better than you know yourself!" He laughed. "Do you trust me?"

"You know I do, but why are you asking me that question?" she asked him skeptically.

"Well, because I'm going to need you to put this blindfold back on and trust me. I don't want to ruin this next surprise."

Sarah got in the car and then allowed Ethan to tie the blindfold around her eyes. He walked around the car and got into the driver's seat. They drove back toward town, but she could not tell where they were with all the turns he took before stopping and turning off the car.

"I take it we're here?" she asked. "Where are we?"

"You'll find out before too long."

Ethan got out of the car and walked over to her door. He opened it and gently guided her out of the car. He wrapped his arm around her waist and guided her to a doorway. Sarah became suspicious when they walked in because it was too quiet. As she stood there listening for some clue as to where she was, she felt the blindfold removed from her eyes. She slowly opened her eyes and could not believe what she saw:

She was in her absolutely favorite restaurant, the Pepper Palace—a very romantic and intimate steak house with a forty-foot mahogany-topped bar at the back of the restaurant, stocked with top shelf liquor and expensive bottles of wine. The entire restaurant's lighting was subtle, creating the romantic atmosphere that couples enjoyed; children were not allowed in the restaurant. The restaurant required a dress code where women were required to be in formal dresses and men required to wear tails. The tables were covered in white tablecloths with candles in the middle of the table to help set the mood. The music played lightly with Frank Sinatra's voice wafting through the air.

Sarah noticed that some of the tables and chairs off to the side of the restaurant were replaced with a wooden dance floor. As they entered the restaurant, she quickly realized that there was not a line of people waiting for their tables to open up; instead, she saw a group of people near the bar area, all eyes on her. Ethan guided her to the back of the restaurant, where she immediately saw her parents, grandparents, brother, and Ethan's parents. She also saw faces staring at her that she recognized and quite a few that she knew who they were but had never formally met.

"What is going on here?" she whispered to Ethan.

"I don't know what you are talking about." He smiled as he led her further into the restaurant.

Before she got all the way to the back of the restaurant, Josh came out of the bar, followed by everyone else.

"Congratulations… Here's the happy couple now!"

He reached out and embraced Sarah in a big hug. "It's not too late to come home with me." He laughed in her ear.

"What about Amy? She'd be a little pissed, don't you think?"

"Amy, Amy who?" he teased. "Have you seen everyone who is here to celebrate with you?"

"Where did they all come from?" she asked Josh.

"They all flew in this afternoon to celebrate with you, Ethan, Ryan, Scott, and me. The party came to you, rather than you having to go to LA."

"How did we get this particular location? This is their busiest night of the week. They don't shut down for *any* reason."

"They were offered a deal they couldn't refuse!" Josh joked.

"What is that supposed to mean?"

"Don't worry about all that. Just focus on having fun, enjoying a good dinner, and getting out of there and socializing with some of the biggest names in Hollywood. You just never know what all that could lead to."

Sarah and Ethan greeted their guests. They made the rounds and enjoyed talking to everyone there. As Sarah walked through the crowd, she realized just how lucky she was to have such a wonderful man in her life. He knew that by asking Josh, Ryan, and Scott to get involved in making her weekend special that it meant he would not get to spend a lot of alone time with her, and she could not believe that he was so willing to share her with the best of Hollywood.

After everyone finished their individual dinners, Jen walked over to Ethan and Sarah's table. "Damn, girl, you clean up pretty damn well!" Sarah wolf-whistled to Jen when she got there.

"Back 'atcha, girlie! Hey, come with me a second," she whispered in Sarah's ear.

"Where are we going?"

"Quit asking questions and get off your ass, just come with me, now!"

As Sarah got up, Ethan leaned in and gave her a quick kiss, smiling at her. "What are you smiling at?" she playfully asked him.

"You better hurry up and go with Jen and then get that sexy ass of yours back over here as soon as possible."

Sarah followed Jen out to the parking lot. "Just what in the hell are we doing out here? Are you Sarah-napping me? Or did you bring me out here to tell me you bought me a new car?" She laughed, playfully punching Jen in the arm.

"Look in the back there, Sarah," Jen replied as she opened the driver's side passenger door.

Sarah looked in and saw a black garment bag from Spring City Bridal Boutique. She looked at the garment bag and then turned around and looked at Jen. "Where did this come from?"

"I thought it was pretty obvious where it was from, dodo head! Are you really that dense? If you are, how were you able to make two movies?" She laughed.

"Oh my god, just shut up already!" she teased back.

"Just grab the bag and go in the bathroom to change already, would you?"

Jen pulled the bag out of the backseat and handed it to Sarah before shutting the door and locking the car. The two friends turned and walked back into the restaurant and immediately into the restroom where Jen locked the two of them inside to ensure no one walked in on them.

Sarah slowly unzipped the bag to reveal a rose-red-and-black 1920s-style beaded sequined deco fringe flapper Gatsby dress. She was drawn to the slight V neck, sleeveless, knee-length design. Hanging off the hanger was an ornate silver headband with leaf and pearl accent. In the bottom of the bag was a pair of black leather dancing shoes with t-straps, with two-and-a-half-inch chunky heels.

She quickly made her way out of her black dress and got into the flapper dress. She turned around, "Hey, since you're still in here, zip me up."

Sarah finished getting ready with Jen's assistance. "Ooh, la la!" Jen whistled as she saw Sarah spin around in the flapper dress. "I know at least one person who is going to have a good night tonight!"

They opened up the door and walked out of the restroom. Sarah noticed that the restaurant was empty. The only person left in the restaurant, outside of the staff, was Ethan. She tried not to laugh when she saw what he was wearing: a pair of khaki plus four pants; a pair of black tall argyle socks; a brown, light-brown, and white checkered sweater vest with a white button-up dress shirt; light brown newsboy cap, and two-tone brown-and-white lace-up Oxfords golf shoes. He stood there leaning against a steel-shafted driver.

"Where did everyone go?" she asked, acting as though she did not want to laugh at the outfit Ethan was currently sporting.

"Damn, that dress is even more stunning than the last one. I didn't think that was possible."

"Well, I don't know what to think about that outfit! I am very torn right now: part of me wants to laugh because someone six feet, four inches tall should not be wearing plus four pants and argyle socks, but the other part of me just wants to rip those pants off you right now. What to do, what to do?"

"Well, I am flattered that you want to laugh at me and more flattered that you want to strip these off me, but that's going to have to wait. I need you to walk with me."

"Where are we going now?"

"Don't worry about that! Just continue trusting me. You had a great time at dinner, right?"

"Yeah, I would have to say that dinner was fun."

They got in the car and drove to the opposite side of town. Ethan pulled up to the backside of the Spring City Resort and Golf Club. Sarah looked up at the building in awe, never having stepped inside the building. It looked like an old European-style castle: four towers laid out around the main building, all attached to the main building by breezeways. The resort was centered on seven hundred acres with two different eighteen-hole golf courses on the property for guests to enjoy. The hotel had four huge banquet halls. Every room in the hotel had a walk-in shower as well as a Jacuzzi tub.

As soon as Ethan pulled up to the back of the building, they were greeted by hotel staff. One young man came around to her side of the car and helped her out while the other young man took the keys from Ethan, giving him a valet ticket to hold on to.

Ethan held his arm out for her to grab, and she did. The man who helped her out of the car escorted them inside the building. He took them to the banquet hall in the north wing of the hotel. The hallway leading to the ballroom was dark. Just outside the main entrance was a manufactured hallway with a door. The door had a peephole in it. Ethan knocked three times on the door, where a man dressed in 1920s attire opened the peephole. "Password?"

"Bees' knees."

The door opened wide for Ethan and Sarah to enter. The ballroom was set to look like an old-fashioned speakeasy. The lights were dimmed in the room as Sarah walked in, but she recognized many of the faces in the room from the faces that joined them for dinner.

Sarah laughed as she noticed some of the guests on the dance floor doing the turkey trot. Ethan guided her to the middle of the dance floor to join in the festivities.

They enjoyed a night of dancing, laughing, and drinking before heading out of the ballroom to their hotel room. When they went upstairs, Sarah could not believe what she was seeing: the door opened into a two-room suite. The first room had a couch, two recliners, a desk and office chair, and a seventy-inch television. The second room led into the master suite: a king-size bed lined in white bamboo sheets with a white bedspread, two dressers, and a hundred-inch television. The bedroom opened into a two-room bathroom that was the same size as the master bedroom. Inside the bathroom was a six-foot-by-six-foot walk-in glass shower with a seat at the back of the shower, along with a six-foot-by-six-foot Jacuzzi tub and a long counter with dual sinks. The second room of the bathroom housed the intelligent toilet that had a nightlight in the bowl, and the seat was heated. The toilet was completely hands-free.

Sarah stripped out of her dress, giving Ethan a strip tease. When she finished undressing, they headed toward the Jacuzzi tub. She could not wait to feel the jets swirl the water around her tired and achy muscles. As she leaned over to turn the water on, she felt Ethan slide right up behind her. He grabbed her waist and gently turned her around to face him. She jumped up in his arms and wrapped her legs around his waist. He stepped into the tub while holding her in his arms. He gently placed her in his lap as he sat down on the tub's seat.

"Thank you for this magical day! I don't know how you pulled this off, panda. You are one amazing human being, and I love you with *every* fiber of my being. I *cannot* wait to be your wife. *I love you, Ethan Miller!*"

"*I love you more!* I'm over the moon in love with you, chippy, and can't wait to spend the rest of my life with you!"

The Marine Corps Ball

After the movie premier, Sarah and Ethan went back to Spring City. They bought a house together about five miles off base. Sarah fell in love with the house as soon as she walked in. The house had two floors—each floor was five thousand square feet. The house had seven bedrooms, seven and a half bathrooms, and a four-car garage. The upstairs housed the master bedroom suite, a half bath, a formal family room, a breakfast room, the kitchen, a formal dining room, a library, and the billiard room. The downstairs held the remaining six bedrooms, a fitness room, and a game room.

The exterior walls were made of brick, with columns on the front porch. There was a covered wraparound porch around the entire house and both floors, along with an outdoor kitchen grill. The kitchen had all Whirlpool appliances: state-of-the-art dishwasher, two stainless steel 24.5-cubic-foot four-door French door refrigerators, with granite countertops. The kitchen had two six-burner stainless steel stoves with dual ovens.

Once they purchased the house, they brought the family over to see the place. "Oh my god, Sarah, this place is gorgeous," Grams said. "Are you sure you're going to be able to live here?"

"We wanted something fairly modest, but we needed enough space for the kids to have their own bedrooms when they are with us and a place for guests to stay as well."

Once the house purchase finalized, Sarah worked with her realtor to find space where she could open a couple of different shops for military families. She knew the Marine Corps Ball was coming up very quickly and knew that some of the Marines and their families did not have the money to buy formal dresses to attend their unit balls. Sarah wanted every family to have the opportunity to go to enjoy the yearly Marine tradition.

Sarah worked with high-end fashion designers to get many different types and sizes of dresses in the shop for the wives to come in and borrow whenever they needed clothing for formal functions. She worked with all the unit wives to get the word out, and they started making appointments to get the wives fitted for their dresses.

Along with the dress shop, Sarah opened a photography store for the families to have a place to get free family photos. She hired the top photographers in the area to staff her photography studio. Within a month of opening, Sarah had to bring ten more photographers into the store to keep up with the demand. Families enjoyed the ability to come in and get their photos done for free.

Sarah received a phone call at the beginning of the year from Ethan's commanding officer, Colonel Jeremy McGrath. "Hello?"

"May I speak with Sarah Jackson-Clark, please?" the deep bass voice on the other side of the line asked.

"This is she. How may I help you?"

"Hi, Sarah, this is Colonel Jeremy McGrath. I am reaching out to see if you would be willing or able to help the unit's birthday ball planning committee plan the birthday ball."

"I would be honored, sir."

Before moving to Hollywood, Sarah met with the planning committee early in the year to start making plans. She met the committee at the Spring City Burger & Steak House. She walked in the door and was guided back to the table where the ten men were already sitting. They stood as she arrived. "Good afternoon," they said in unison.

"Hello, gentlemen," she said as she shook their hands. They all sat and got started.

"I want to start out by saying that I am truly honored to be here giving my input to your birthday celebrations," she said when she sat down.

"Well, we are excited to have you here as well, Ms. Clark," Sergeant Chen said to her.

She started out, "What is your budget, and have you thought of the venue where you want to have the celebrations this year?"

"We haven't really thought about the venue yet because we're still trying to get the funds to cover the food and cake."

"Would it be a problem if I picked up the cost of the venue, the cake, and the music?"

She walked out of the meeting and called her favorite cake designer, Rocco Alfonsi. "Hey, Sarah! How's life?"

"Hey, Rocco! Life is good. I was just invited to help plan a Marine Corps birthday ball celebration for Ethan's unit."

"Ah, that's exciting! Do you have an idea what you want to do as far as the cake goes?"

"I am hoping that you will surprise me on this! You always do such a fantastic job that I don't want to stunt your creativity. The ceremony cake needs to be elegant, but anything else you do is totally up to you."

"Oh, you gotta love the creative license with no limitations! I'm so excited and can't wait to show you what we come up with. What's the budget?"

"I'm footing the bill, so I want to keep it under ten thousand dollars. I need enough cake or whatever to feed a thousand people or so."

"Sounds good. When do I need to have it there?"

"I need everything ready to go by Saturday, November 7, please."

Her next call was to the Spring City Resort and Golf Club. She made an appointment to talk about her booking needs. She set up the appointment with the banquet and catering manager, Tamara. Sarah arrived a bit early for her meeting and was directed downstairs to Tamara's office. As she made her introductions, she could not help but be drawn to Tamara's beauty. She stood about five feet, two inches tall; if Sarah had to guess, Tamara weighed around 120 pounds. She had strawberry blond hair and had piercing blue eyes.

"Hello, Sarah."

"Hello, Tamara."

"Please sit. Can I get you anything, water or a soda?"

"No, thanks. I'm good right now."

"So, Sarah, please tell me what your needs are for your special event."

"We need about five hundred rooms reserved in a block of rooms, and we will probably need three banquet rooms to make it easy for us to do what we need to do and to give you time to maneuver around us."

"What all are you planning for the night's activities?"

"Well, we need to have a cocktail hour in one banquet room. We will then move everyone in to the second hall so that we can have the ceremony. The ceremony lasts about an hour, after which we will need to move back to the first room to eat dinner. After dinner, we want to have a place for everyone to let loose and have a good time. We will most likely be bringing in a couple of musicians to perform live. I also need a room set aside for stylists to come in and do hair and makeup before the ceremony. We'll need that room from about ten in the morning until about five."

"Three banquet halls it is then. What do you want to do about meals?"

"Would you be willing to allow us to cater in from the Pepper Palace, or do we need to work specifically with your catering department?"

"We do not allow outside catering. We have world-class chefs employed here, so you need not worry that the food won't be up to snuff. Are you looking to do a plated dinner or buffet?"

"Plated dinner, please."

"Let's go upstairs and do a quick taste test of some of the items we have available to select from. We have a good variety of options—we have beef, chicken, lamb, seafood, vegetarian, and vegan meals available. Do you already know what you would want as meal options?"

Sarah followed Tamara to the elevator upstairs to meet the head chef, a man who stood five feet ten inches and had sandy-blond hair with hazel eyes. Tamara introduced them, "Sarah, this is Gene, our head chef. Gene, this is Sarah."

"Hi, Sarah," he said.

"Hello, Gene," she replied.

"I have a few different items for you to try today. I hope you brought your appetite with you." He laughed.

He brought out a small cut of prime rib, along with chicken cordon bleu. She was blown away by how juicy the beef was and how moist the chicken stayed.

After she finished eating the two options presented to her, she worked with Tamara to make the accommodations for the celebrations. She put down the security deposit to reserve the venue.

Sarah spent every day she was home after her movie debut in the dress and photography shops she had opened just off the base. She loved seeing the smiles on everyone's faces when they were able to walk away with beautiful family portraits and their children. She got excited watching women's faces light up when they found the perfect dress for their formal events.

As the days grew closer to the birthday ball, Sarah called the local salons to get stylists to volunteer to come to the hotel to help the wives get their hair and makeup done up for the celebrations. She wanted everyone to have a chance to feel beautiful without having to pay a penny to do so.

That morning she spent all morning coordinating with the stylists in order to make sure that every woman was able to get ready for the ceremony. She stayed so busy that she missed lunch. She had fun taking pictures for the wives as they got ready.

Sarah was so wrapped up in making sure the other women of the unit were taken care of that she had not stopped to get her own hair and makeup done yet. "Hey, Sarah, are you going to get your hair and makeup done? You know the festivities start here in a couple of hours," her friend, Amanda McGrath, said to her.

Sarah stopped what she was doing and turned to face her friend. Amanda was Colonel McGrath's wife. Sarah and Amanda were introduced at a wife's club meeting for the unit. Sarah was immediately drawn to Amanda, a woman who stood the same height as Sarah. Amanda had jet-black hair that went all the way down to her lower back when she wore it down. Amanda had just finished with the stylist and now wore her hair in an elegant updo.

"Um, what was that, Amanda?"

"Are you going to stop helping everyone else get ready and go get yourself ready?"

"Oh, I guess I probably should do that, shouldn't I?" Sarah laughed.

Sarah walked into the banquet room and sat down in an open chair. She loved the feeling when a stylist played with her hair, so the time she sat in the chair was very relaxing to Sarah. She had her hair put up into a knotted braid with loose curls. The young makeup artist helped her to put on just enough makeup to help accentuate her features.

Once she was finished with her hair and makeup, she went back upstairs to her room to get into her dress. The night of the ball was finally here. She was about to see all her hard work and planning come together. She could not wait to celebrate with her very own special first sergeant. She had a dress special made for her big night: a halter dress with gradient coloring from black to scarlet; it was a backless A-line chiffon dress with sequins, crystal beads, and rhinestones at the top.

Ethan waited for Sarah in their hotel room. He let out a low whistle when she walked out to meet him. *"Damn!"*

"You clean up really well yourself!" she said as she looked him up and down. He stood there in his long-sleeved midnight-blue form-fitted jacket with standing collar and white web belt around his waist. His sky-blue trousers had a scarlet stripe down the outside of each leg. He held his white barracks cover tucked under his right arm, his hands covered in his white gloves. His chest was full of all the medals he earned throughout his service. "That uniform suits you, panda!"

They took the elevator down to the banquet rooms and walked into the cocktail hour. Sarah was impressed by how beautiful the event space was decorated. She saw that there were a bunch of high-top tables lining the floor of the room. There were four portable bars placed around the room. Marines and their significant others started to enter the room. Sarah and Ethan walked around and chatted with multiple couples until the start of the birthday ball ceremony.

After the hour-long ceremony, they went back across the hall to the first room. The high-top tables were replaced with round tables and chairs. Ethan led them to their table where they enjoyed their plated prime rib dinners.

After dinner, they moved back across the hallway to enjoy the music and dancing. Sarah had a big surprise for Ethan's unit that only his CO and planning committee knew about. She used her newfound connections to bring in two of the biggest names in the entertainment industry to play live for the night. She was able to get Eddie McIntyre and Cassandra Edwards to help the unit celebrate their 242nd birthday.

Ethan took Sarah's hand and guided her onto the dance floor. She rested her head on his shoulder as they swayed to the music. She looked up into his eyes. "Happy Birthday, Marine!"

Chapter 9

2018

The Wedding

The next nine months passed by very quickly. Sarah and Ethan started planning for this day the day after Ethan's proposal.

Sarah could not sleep that night. Her mind raced with all the things she still had to do before the ceremony. She got up and put on her light-purple terrycloth robe and made herself a cup of Earl Grey tea before sitting down at the kitchen island. She still could not believe this day was really here. When her marriage to Alex started failing, she vowed she would never marry again if things ever ended between the two of them.

She sat there so long she got lost in her thoughts about her past that she did not hear Ethan come downstairs and say, "Earth to Sarah!"

She jumped when he reached down and kissed her neck. "Oh my god!" she shouted out.

"Haha, did you really not hear me come up behind you?"

"No! Are you trying to give your blushing bride a heart attack the day you're supposed to walk down the aisle and say, 'I do?'"

"No, absolutely not! I called out to you before I kissed you… Where were you off to? Not getting cold feet, are you?"

"Really, you think I would get cold feet? I can't wait to walk down the aisle and pledge to love you for the rest of my life in front of our closest family and friends."

"Okay, good, glad to hear that. Where were you?"

"What do you mean?"

"You know what I mean... You were off in some other world when I came down. You never let me sneak up on you, even when I try to be stealthy."

"Oh, you know... I was just daydreaming about what life will be like after today."

"Chipmunk, I've seen your daydreaming face, and I've seen your reminiscing face. You were reminiscing about something, something that had you distracted."

"Ah, just thinking back to everything that led up to this very moment. Wondering how I got to be the luckiest woman in the world that a man like you chose me to be his wife, to spend the rest of our lives together. I'm no one special."

Ethan reached out and cupped her chin in his hand, gently turning it up to face him. "You know I hate when you talk like that, Sarah. I love you and need you to know that you are special! You always have been and always will be. We were meant to be together!"

She smiled gently and then reached up and pulled his head down toward her face. She extended her face up to meet him halfway in order to kiss him. "You always know what to say to pick me back up!"

He gently pulled her up out of the kitchen chair and wrapped his arms around her waist. She immediately looked up to him, anticipating the kiss that was coming. She faintly licked her lips, inviting him to kiss her more passionately. He obliged her request. As the kissing became more and more passionate, he pulled Sarah up to allow her to wrap her legs around his waist and her arms around his neck. As soon as she could hold herself in place, he reached down and untied her terrycloth robe, pulling it off her shoulders, exposing her chest to him. He tilted his head to grab her right breast in his mouth, alternating between tracing her nipple with his tongue and gently pulling on it with his teeth.

As she enjoyed the wave of pleasure washing over her, she felt the wall press up against her back. She reached down and fondled him in her hand. He pushed her back a little harder and slid her back down his waist a little bit. She felt herself dripping in anticipation. Ethan felt it too and obliged her by rocking himself into her. They rocked back and forth in perfect fluid motion. She cried out in ecstasy as Ethan came inside of her.

As he finished, he put her down and quickly kissed her as she started to say, "Oh, you're awfully sure that I won't get cold feet and leave you standing alone at the altar!"

"You wouldn't!" he exclaimed.

"No, you're right! I would miss this too much!" she said as she grabbed his balls and jiggled them around a little bit before releasing them.

"Hey, you keep that up and you'll be pinned back up against that wall again!" he threatened her with a smile on his face.

"Oh, is that a threat or a promise?"

"Why don't you keep it up and find out?"

"Ooh, don't tempt me!" she said as she reached out and grabbed his peck playfully in her mouth and nipped him before taking off running up the stairs. "Catch me if you can!"

He gave her a five-step head start before running after her. He caught her at the top of the stairs and grabbed her up in his arms, swinging her around in a giant circle in the ten-foot open landing. "Caught you, whatcha gonna do now?"

She played like she wanted to wiggle out of his arms so that he would pull her in tighter to him. She got what she wanted. As she pulled away from him, he drew her in tighter to his body. She felt him poke her from behind. "Wow, watch where you're pointing that weapon, First Sergeant!"

"Oh, I'll point my weapon wherever I want to, ma'am! Whatcha gonna do about it?"

"I could do this all day, cowboy! *But* we've got to get ready for the wedding."

The rest of the day's events went by so quickly, and before Sarah knew it, the time to get into her dress arrived. She looked at herself in the mirror:

Her makeup, done by her makeup artist, perfectly accentuated her facial features without making her look like a china doll. Her hairdresser fixed her hair into a sweeping low bun, pulled off to her left side a little bit. Her best friend, Jen; her friend, Zoey; soon to be stepdaughter, Emily; and Jen's girls JoyJoy, Julia, and Jamie all got their hair and makeup done to match Sarah. Jen, Zoey, and the younger girls stepped into their scarlet-colored dresses. Jen and Zoey both wore a one shoulder A-line dress while the girls wore a high neck A-line scarlet dress.

Once dressed, Jen walked over to where Sarah's dress hung on the back of the door, and Emily left the room to go find her brothers. Jen's girls went to be with their father, and Zoey left to go help finish setting up the gift table. As Jen slowly unzipped the garment bag, she asked, "Who would have ever imagined that my pushing you two together the first time I ever met Ethan would end up here, with the two of you getting married?" She paused for a moment and then turned back to Sarah with a giant smile on her face as she said, "Oh, yeah, that was me, wasn't it? I don't really want to say 'I told you so,' BUUUUUUUUUUT I told you so! Don't you just hate when I'm always right?"

"Oooh, why don't you shut your mouth when you're talking to me?" Sarah teased back.

Jen walked toward Sarah and embraced her in a hug. "No way! You need to hear the truth! I knew before you did that you two were meant for each other. You just had to take a leap of faith and trust me! In all seriousness though, I am excited to see you so happy again. Over the last couple of years, I've really watched you come out of your shell and open up. I didn't realize just how closed off you were to everyone when you were with Alex until I saw you with Ethan. This man, the man you are about to marry, is *definitely* worth all the waiting and suffering you endured in your marriage with Alex.

"Your first love, the fairy tale love was with Isaac Dole, your first boyfriend.

"Alex was your second love, the hard love…the love that hurts. All lies, pain, and manipulation.

"Ethan is the love you never saw coming. Just remember that while you expect everything to go wrong… It won't! Ethan is your soul mate. I can see when I look into his eyes how much Ethan loves you and I know that I never have to worry about your well-being again! I love you, Sarah! Thank you for letting me be such a big part of this moment!"

"Jen, you're such a brat! You're going to make me cry and then Brianna is going to have to redo my makeup, and I promise you she won't be very happy about that!"

After the hug, Jen walked back over and carefully pulled the dress out of the bag, still hanging from the hanger. As Sarah looked at the dress hanging there on the back of the door, she was overcome with a wave of emotions and with so many different thoughts swirling through her mind.

So nervous—what if I'm not the woman Ethan truly wants to marry, and he isn't waiting for me at the alter? What if I fall flat on my face in front of all my family and friends? What will happen if I mess up saying my vows because I am so nervous? That dress is way too pretty for me. There is no way that I can make that dress look good.

"Earth to Sarah!" She snapped out of her own head when she heard Ethan's voice on the other side of the door.

"W-what are you doing here? Aren't you and the boys supposed to be getting ready?"

"Everyone is just waiting on you!"

"Well, why don't you and the kids go start to take your photos with your side of the family, and I'll be out here in a few minutes to take my photos with everyone but you."

"Sounds good! Sarah, I want you to calm all those thoughts and fears currently racing around in your head. I'm not going to leave you at the altar, you're not going to fall flat on your face, no one will know if you make a mistake on your vows except for you...aaaaand, chipmunk, that dress will come alive once you're inside of it! It was made for you."

"H-how did you know what I was thinking?"

"Seriously? I know how your mind works at this point! That's what I love about you. Now, hurry your ass up and get into that dress. We need to get all the pictures of everything except the ones of us so that we can focus on the pictures with us together after the ceremony! I'll be waiting for you at the far end of the aisle. I can tell you right now that your father can't get you down that aisle fast enough! I am so excited that after today, you will be Mrs. Sarah Jackson-Miller!

She put her head against the door jam and said, "That sure has a nice ring to it, doesn't it? I can't wait to be yours and for you to be mine! I love you, Ethan Miller!"

She heard him turn and walk away from the door, calling to the boys and Emily as he walked down the hallway. She turned back to Jen, "Okay, help me get into this dress, *woman!*"

Jen pulled her dress out and held it up a little bit. Sarah stopped and took it in. This was the dress she had custom designed by the best wedding dress designer in the industry, Randy Collins. He created a one-of-a-kind custom dress for Sarah's ceremony, which Sarah had not seen before this very moment. The dress was an off-white color with scarlet roses embroidered into the silk material. The neckline was designed as a halter top. Randy intended the dress to accentuate Sarah's natural curves so he put her into a trumpet silhouette. It had a train that extended out from the back of the dress about three feet.

As she slipped into the dress, she felt like she was in a completely different world. This dress fit her like a glove; she could not have asked for anything more perfect. "Holy shit, Batman!"

"Holy shit, Batman, what, Jen?"

"You clean up pretty fancy, if I do say so myself!"

"You clean up pretty fancy yourself!" Sarah laughed as she reached out to give Jen a quick hug.

Just then, Violet and Grams walked into Sarah's dressing room. Grams rushed over and embraced Sarah in a tight hug. "Chipmunk, you have always been the most beautiful girl in the world, but today, that glow you are wearing makes you a hundred times prettier! I am so happy to see you glowing again."

When Grams released Sarah, Violet reached out to give Sarah a hug. "You really do look stunning, chipmunk. Are you nervous?"

"No, I'm actually super excited!"

Violet turned and left the room while Grams stayed behind. "I remember the day I walked down the aisle to your Pops. It was the best day of my life, followed closely by the birth of my children and then my grandchildren. I want you to always remember that Pops and I are so proud of you, Sarah. You are such a beautiful soul."

Jen walked out of the dressing room before Sarah to ensure Ethan was nowhere to be seen. When she was sure that Ethan was back in his dressing room, Sarah came out of the room to take her part of the pictures with everyone before the ceremony.

The photographer, David Berenthal, ushered Sarah outside. He took Sarah to the antique bridge overlooking the waterfall to get some photos of her in the dress standing there looking into the distance. After getting photos of Sarah by herself, David got Jen and Zoey to join Sarah. She then brought the rest of the bridal party and both Ethan and Sarah's families out to join Sarah in the photos.

They took the better part of an hour capturing the before photos. When picture taking finished, Sarah went back to her dressing room to relax for a few minutes before the ceremony started.

Matthew came in to join Sarah. "Chipmunk, you look absolutely stunning!"

"Thanks, Daddy!"

"Are you ready to walk down the aisle to the man of your dreams?"

"Daddy, do you think that I am making a mistake?"

"What? Why would you ever think that?"

"Well, it's hard to imagine being so happy after I was miserable for so long. This will be my second marriage and Ethan's third marriage."

"You have a man who makes you happy and you make him happy. He is not Alex. You are not his first two wives. You two found each other when you least expected to do so. You need to let yourself be happy! Let Ethan help you stay happy!"

"Thanks, Daddy! You always know what to say to help me feel better!"

Sarah leaned into him and gave him a hug as he gave her a quick kiss on her forehead. Matthew put his arm out for Sarah to wrap her arm around his.

"Ready, chipmunk?"

"Let's do this already!"

Matthew led her out of her dressing room and walked through the church lobby, stopping just out of sight of the doorway. Sarah heard "Trumpet Voluntary" playing over the speakers in the sanctuary as Ethan walked Violet and Blaire, his mother, down the aisle to their seats. Eli and Manny stood there waiting with Jen and Zoey for their turn to walk down the aisle after Ethan got situated. Once Jen and Eli and Zoey and Manny made it to their places JoyJoy, Julia, and Jamie followed with the scarlet aisle runner before Emily and Brennan moved down the aisle. Emily dropped her little scarlet-and-white rose petals as Brennan held a little sign that said Here Comes the Bride. As soon as they reached the end of the aisle, Sarah and Matthew moved into place at the backside of the large oak doors leading into the sanctuary.

As the doors opened, Sarah heard "Canon in D" through the speakers. She looked down the sixty-five-foot aisle toward the stage where Ethan was standing. She looked to both sides of the main aisle and saw that the 350 seats were all full. The rows were all decorated simply with rose bundles filled with scarlet-and-white roses. She saw two columns on each side of the altar wrapped with greenery and roses. She was happy with how the church turned out, simple yet very elegant. Matthew patted her arm with his right hand and leaned over to her. "You ready?"

She leaned back into him and gave him a kiss on the cheek. "Let's go. Ethan's waiting, and it's rude to keep him waiting too long." She laughed.

They walked to the end of the aisle where Ethan waited. Matthew shook Ethan's hand and kissed Sarah on the cheek before sitting next to Violet in the front row. Ethan reached out and grabbed Sarah's hands in his, giving her a gentle squeeze. They turned back to Pastor Daren to start the ceremony.

Everything felt like a dream. Sarah felt giddy as Pastor Daren asked, "Do you, Sarah Jackson, take Ethan Miller to be your lawfully wedded husband, to share your life openly, standing with him in sickness and in health, in joy and in sorrow, in hardship and in ease, to cherish and love forever more?"

"I do!"

The rest of the ceremony flew by. Sarah gave Ethan his simple, elegant eighteen-karat white gold wedding band with a designed wave in the band when it came time to exchange rings. He gave her back her two-karat yellow diamond set in eighteen-karat white gold entwined with two new matching bands entwined with one-karat yellow diamonds per band. She looked down in complete shock and awe when he put the ring on her left ring finger. The changes he made to the band were absolutely beautiful.

After the ring exchange, Pastor Daren prayed a blessing over the marriage before saying, "Sarah and Ethan, through their words today, have joined together in holy wedlock. Because they have exchanged their vows before God and these witnesses, have pledged their commitment each to the other, and have declared the same by joining hands and by exchanging rings, I now pronounce that you are husband and wife.

"Those whom God hath joined together, let no one put asunder.

"You may now kiss the bride!"

Ethan and Sarah reached toward each other. Ethan gently wrapped his arms around her waist, pulling her into him. He then reached in and kissed her, pecking her on the lips twice before reaching in and kissing her more passionately.

When they parted, Pastor Daren asked them to turn and face the crowd, "Ladies and gentlemen, it is now my pleasure to present for the first time, Mr. and Mrs. Ethan and Sarah Miller."

The crowd started cheering, and Ethan grabbed Sarah's hand in his and gave it a quick kiss as they waited for "Ode to Joy" to play over the speakers. As the music started, they walked back up the aisle to the giant oak doorway to the rest of their life together.

About the Author

Amber Paul grew up in Central Iowa and graduated with her BA in US history from Missouri State University in Springfield, Missouri.

She and her husband, James, and their cats have called nine states home since they married in June 2000. Amber enjoys watching TV, movies, traveling, seeking out waterfalls and other interesting things in nature, and spending time with her family and friends.

CPSIA information can be obtained
at www.ICGtesting.com
Printed in the USA
LVHW041552110621
689976LV00002B/46